Praise for D:

'A riveting, thoughtful fantasy tha[...]
Kay and Brandon Sanderson, set in a richly [...]
where battle-hardened heroes confront their most dangerous
enemy: the truth about the nature of their heroism and what
the magic they rely upon costs the world around them. Full
of nuanced, loveable characters whose complex relationships
with each other and with themselves make *The Burning Land* a
compulsively readable adventure not to be missed!'
Sebastien de Castell on *The Burning Land*

'Classic fantasy fiction. It captures the feel of *The Fellowship of
the Ring* and that is no bad thing . . . I would recommend this
novel wholeheartedly . . . great characterisation, a sense of true
companionship, world building, battles, and twists'
SFBook Reviews on *The Burning Land*

'Hair has created a brilliant group of contrasting characters . . .
kept me interested right up to the final page'
Witchy Reading on *The Burning Land*

'Filled with action and adventure yet was also rich in
characterisation and contained a spectacular created world'
Muse Books on *Sorcerer's Edge*

'The world [Hair] has built grows out of the pages, and I am left
feeling as I was at the end of book one – anticipating the next
instalment and eager to see what else will be revealed'
The Quaint Book Nook on *World's Edge*

'Plenty of action, treason, intrigues and some gore . . .
Highly recommended'
Annarellix on *World's Edge*

'A page-turning adventure filled with excitement and intriguing characters. For those loving an epic fantasy with plenty of sword-fights, gun-play, bare-fisted combat and battles between sorcerers, this book's for you'
Amazing Stories on *Map's Edge*

'A fast-paced, entertaining read, set within a world that I want to explore more of'
Beneath A Thousand Skies on *Map's Edge*

'There's a lot of cool stuff, ancient civilisations, magic, a heist, personal loss, love, and humour. I enjoyed this so much'
Al-Alhambra Book Reviews on *Map's Edge*

'I thoroughly enjoyed this magic- and quest-filled fantasy. I love the way David Hair writes . . . and the world he has created is a very solid one that holds the story perfectly'
Dawn's Book Reviews on *Map's Edge*

'Hair is a talented storyteller and *Map's Edge* a satisfying and fun read, entertaining and rewarding that will sate the appetite of any fantasy lover looking for an epic adventure'
The Tattooed Book Geek on *Map's Edge*

'Easy to read with lots of substance, well-realised ideas, action and themes'
SF Crowsnest on *Map's Edge*

'Hair is adept at building characters as well as worlds'.
Kirkus Reviews **on** *Mage's Blood*

'Promises to recall epic fantasy's finest'
Tor.com on *Mage's Blood*

THE BURNING
LAND

David Hair, an award-winning writer of fantasy, has been inspired by his travels around the globe. He was born in New Zealand and has spent time in Britain, Europe and India (which inspired The Moontide and Sunsurge Quartets and The Return of Ravana series). After some years in Bangkok, Thailand, he and his wife returned to Wellington, New Zealand, where they are now settled (for the time being). His epic fantasy sagas include The Moontide Quartet, The Sunsurge Quartet, The Tethered Citadel trilogy and the YA saga The Return of Ravana, as well as his new fantasy adventure series, The Talmont Trilogy, starting with *The Burning Land*.

THE BURNING
LAND

TALMONT BOOK 1

DAVID HAIR

Arcadia

First published in Great Britain in 2024
This paperback edition first published in Great Britain in 2024 by

Arcadia
an imprint of
Quercus Editions Ltd
Carmelite House
50 Victoria Embankment
London EC4Y 0DZ

An Hachette UK company

A CIP catalogue record for this book is available
from the British Library

PB ISBN 978 1 52942 287 0
EBOOK ISBN 978 1 52942 288 7

This book is a work of fiction. Names, characters,
businesses, organizations, places and events are
either the product of the author's imagination
or used fictitiously. Any resemblance to
actual persons, living or dead, events or
locales is entirely coincidental.

1

Typeset by CC Book Production
Printed and bound in Great Britain by Clays Ltd, Elcograf S.p.A

Papers used by Arcadia are from well-managed forests and other responsible sources.

This book is dedicated to those who strive to make Planet Earth, the only one we've got, a better place for all. Profits and power mean little compared to the shared wellbeing and survival of everyone and everything aboard this rock spinning in space. Down with authoritarian tyrants, ignorant superstitions and greed-head profiteers; up with humane science, democratic freedoms and the easily ridiculed concept of love for all.

TABLE OF CONTENTS

Part One:
LOSS AND BLAME

Part Two:
HUNTERS AND HUNTED

Part Three:
ON THE THRESHOLD

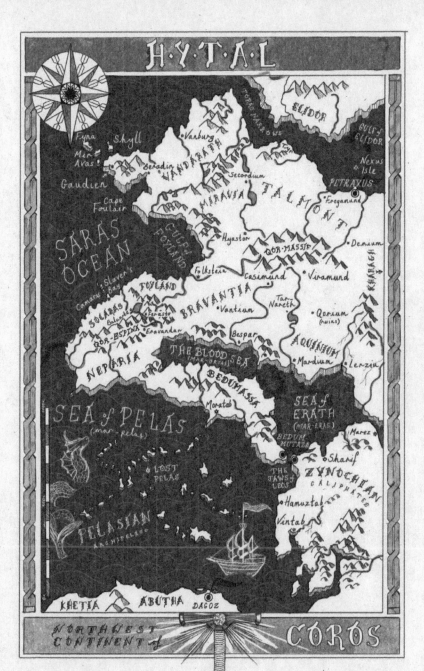

Talmont: A History

The caliph asked me today why history matters. It was no idle question. The past is gone, he argued, and only the present and the future matter. Why devote time and energy on documenting things that no longer matter?

What he was really asking me, his history tutor, was, 'What are you for?'

Make no mistake, my entire future was at stake.

I began by reminding him that every decision is rooted in our own experiences, not just as a person, but as a collective. We know our enemies by their treacheries and warmongering. We trust our friends due to their known fidelity. While the past does not predict future actions, it is a guide, a consideration in every new decision. As individuals, we learn from life. So too does a body of people learn.

The caliph's question was driven by new demands from the Hierophant, our overlord, that appear to favour his homeland, Talmont, over the rest of the Triple Empire. 'Is this offer as treacherous as it seems?' our young ruler wished to know.

'Only in the era of the Sanctor Wardens could Talmont be trusted,' I replied.

'Who were the Sanctor Wardens?' the caliph asked.

I reminded my lord of this ancient group of sorcerer-knights from barbarous Hytal, who came to the aid of the King of Talmont at the height of the siege of Petraxus, in the tenth century. The famous Charge of the Wardens broke the invading armies of Kharagh, saving the city and ultimately the north. By the eleventh century they had become the power behind Talmont, known for their integrity and fidelity.

However, during the rise of the first Hierophant and Triple Emperor, Jovan

1

Lux, it is said that they fell into evil, and were superseded by the Order of the Vestments of Elysia Divina – the 'Vestal knights'. Rumours of conflict between the rival sorcerer-knights persist, but the Vestal knights claim the Wardens, recognising their own decline, disbanded voluntarily.

And this is where history is needed, for the old tales of the Sanctor Wardens speak of honour and justice, their nobility and virtue, though more recent Talmoni historians have labelled them degenerate and corrupt. Yet those recent histories also claim the Vestal knights to be the pinnacle of chivalry, while we their enemies know them as the iron fist of Talmont.

Which is true? Only by piecing together the fragments of evidence remaining, can we learn. But those pieces are constantly changing, some proving untrustworthy even as new clues are unearthed, until it feels as if trying to understand our past is as impossible as mapping clouds, or waves in the sea.

'Then truth is merely what we believe,' the caliph commented.

'Certainly the most powerful tale is not always the true one, but the one that is believed,' I responded. 'However, false stories are like the flesh of a rotting corpse. In the end, only the bones of truth will remain.'

Preface to *Talmont: A History*
by Inchalus Sekum
Scribe to the Caliph of Mutaza, 1467

The Hierophant

One Faith, Many Peoples

Before the coming of Jovan Lux, our world was racked by war. But Jovan's Edict brought all of Coros to the Light, uniting the three warring empires of Talmont, Zynoch and Abutha. The newly created Triple Empire is a union of the elites that transcends race, creed and colour, in which peace and prosperity reign: a true golden age. And now the throne of Jovan passes to a new heir, Eindil III. Long may he reign.

PATRIARCH VYNE, AT THE CORONATION OF EINDIL III, 1454

Jovan replaced race wars with class wars, elevating the elites through the oppression of the common people. By uniting Abuthan gold, Zynochian produce and Talmoni sorcery, he bonded a ruthless elite that transcends national boundaries. His court does indeed throng with people of all races – unified by one goal: self-enrichment, at the cost of the exploited masses.

NILIS EVANDRIEL, RENEGADE SCHOLAR, 1469

Petraxus, Talmont
Summer 1472

Eindil Pandramion III, the Hierophant, God-Emperor of Talmont, Triple-Emperor of Coros, sat on the Throne of Pearl, wondering whether he was strong enough for the time he'd been born into. Today, the Sunburst Crown was a crushing weight, bowing his head and bending his back. All the lives in his care, all the wealth and history, were chains dragging him under the flood of dire news.

3

Coros is burning . . . our world is dying.

Fires were spreading in huge swathes from the northwest, sending smoke and ash across the hinterland. Even here in mighty Petraxus, heart of the empire, it tainted every breath. All over Hytal, crops were failing, while desperate refugees fleeing the growing dustbowls to the south were choking the roads and descending upon overwhelmed, frightened cities like swarms of ravenous insects. And among them the corrupted vyr moved unseen, sparking rebellion and lighting ever more fires.

That this long-prophesised ending should come during Eindil's reign haunted him day and night, despite knowing this was all the will of his divine ancestor, Akka Himself. *My burden is to do what must now be done and preserve all that is good in Coros.*

With that in mind, he steeled himself to face the latest news from the western isles, where this current crisis had begun. 'Send in the courser,' he told the stentor, Robias.

At the herald's signal, a muffled hammer struck the gong to his right. The booming note reverberated through the many-pillared hall, lined with the polished bronze statues of his forebears. At the far end, giant doors opened a crack. The bar of pallid light which penetrated was briefly broken by a silhouette, which vanished as the doors closed again. For a full minute, Eindil tracked the courser's progress only by the clip of her boots on the marble as she made her way in darkness, past eyes and blades she never saw, until she emerged into light at the base of the dais, just ten paces away. She knelt and pressed her forehead to the floor.

Robias signalled and a guard ghosted from the shadows, lifted her chin and placed a blade to her throat. 'You are in the presence of the divine,' Robias said. 'Swear that no word of falsehood shall pass your lips.'

'I . . . I so swear,' the courser replied, her clear, youthful voice tremulous, her coppery desert skin gleaming with sweat. She was a Zynochian, an embodiment of Eindil's empire, which covered all of the known world, from Hytal in the frigid north to equatorial Zynochia and the jungles of Abutha, a rainbow realm in which the old dividing lines of race and religion had been erased by loyalty to his throne and Akka the Father.

But those precious gains will be lost if I can't win through this crisis.

The guardsman carved the ritual line across the courser's throat, just breaking the skin. For all her youth, her throat was covered in such scars, most old and white, a few still scabbed. When he withdrew, the courser sat back on her heels, head bowed and hands clasped. Her face was wind-chaffed, her ebony hair matted and her green uniform damp with perspiration, but she looked composed, a veteran of such ordeals.

Around her, cloaked and masked courtiers emerged from the shadows, moving about her like dancers. This was the Night Court, where counsellors spoke with the protection of anonymity, to encourage frankness and the airing of hard truths.

'Great One, my tidings are two days old,' she said. 'I come from Avas, via sail and steed.'

Avas was the third in a chain of isles at the western tip of Hytal, one thousand five hundred kylos away. Fyna, the first, was already abandoned; its neighbour Mir was also under attack.

'Why did you take so long to reach us?' Stentor Robias asked. 'It is surely for this reason the empire maintains the portali gates? You could have been here in mere hours . . .'

'The gate on Avas Isle was lost, the day before I left,' the courser explained. 'I had to sail to the mainland and use one in Port Gaudien.'

The loss of a portali was grim news. 'Speak on,' Eindil said.

'Avas burns, Great One. The vyr have lit fresh fires that are sweeping across the island. All the shards on Avas have been destroyed and the populace has fled to Long Bay, on the east coast of the island. Governor Durand begs leave to evacuate them all.'

'What say the Vestal knights stationed there?' Eindil asked, struggling to sound regal in the face of such dire tidings. 'Surely they fight on?'

'The Vestal knights do, with all their strength,' the courser replied, 'but the vyr strike where the knights are not. Their corruption is everywhere.'

'Who leads the knights on Avas?'

'Siera Romara Challys, of the Falcon Century. They're the last of the Order still protecting the island. Two other centuries were redeployed to Mir a week ago, to ensure we hold at least one island of the group.'

Eindil frowned. 'Challys? Remind me?' The name sounded a little familiar.

'She is a veteran of ten years, from a noble house in Miravia, Great One,' a masked female courtier advised. 'Daughter of the Lord of Desantium. She is regarded as sound.'

'But women are unsuited to command,' a male courtier in a goat mask countered. For all the Vestal knights were the vanguard for equality, such views persisted.

Eindil raised a hand for silence. 'I should not have to remind *anyone* that our beloved Vazi Virago, our Exemplar, is a woman,' he said firmly. He leaned forward, looking at the courser. 'Tell me more of this Romara Challys.'

'She is a credit to her Order, an experienced fighter from a noble Miravian House,' she responded. 'When I parted from her, she was holding the retreat to Long Bay, having repelled several vyr raids while protecting the refugees.'

'But why are they not driving forth the foe?' Goat-mask sniffed. 'Timid retreats win nothing!'

Eindil had grown impatient with the man's whining. They all knew the shape-changing vyr had been causing havoc for generations now. 'Driving forth the foe' was impossible when you couldn't find the evil degenerates hiding among the innocents.

'Where is my Exemplar?' he asked, unable to turn his mind from the woman regarded as the greatest knight of the Age. 'Where is Vazi Virago? Does she travel to save the island?'

'The Exemplar is in Neparia,' the stentor reminded him. 'She will return soon.'

I knew that, Eindil chastised himself, but her absence from court gnawed at him. 'Does this Romara Challys concur with Governor Durand's request to abandon the Isle?'

The courser bowed her head. 'She concurs. Avas is lost, but the people can still be saved.'

Eindil considered, then nodded to Robias, permitting him to make the sign of mercy to the guards waiting behind the courser. They'd heard no lie in her words, so she'd be permitted to leave the Night Court alive.

'The Pearl Throne thanks you, Courser,' Robias said. 'You will be taken to the probationary cells until your words are proven.'

The courser would be pampered, but there would be bars on her windows and doors until her story was corroborated; only then would she be freed. Lies were the most dangerous of all evils and must always be nipped in the bud.

She kissed the first step of the dais, where Jovan Lux's footprint was preserved in the stone, rose gracefully and backed into the hands of the waiting house-servants, who led her away.

The silence was punctuated by the whispers of his masked courtiers as they waited for Eindil to allow them to speak aloud.

'Withdraw,' Eindil told Robias. 'I would seek the unrecorded advice of my counsellors.'

Once the herald had taken the scribes and gone, the Night Courtiers closed in. There were a few dozen tonight, masked and glittering darkly.

Eindil cleared his throat, then addressed the faceless gathering. 'I commanded that none should give ground before the fires,' he reminded them. 'Am I to renege upon my stated will?'

The masked courtiers murmured, then a Zynochian woman spoke. 'Let the people see your compassion. Akka is a just god. Elysia is Mercy personified. Allow the evacuation.'

'But they have failed to defend their own lands. They have failed us.'

'It was a task beyond them,' said a man with a deep Abuthan voice. 'This ending is fated.'

Eindil hated to think that his reign was predestined to fail. 'Regardless, Akka expects us all to do what is right, and I have declared that there will be no retreat.'

'Which we, the Night Court, counselled against,' another woman said coolly.

'But the Day Court said—'

'The Day Court are venal, self-serving weaklings,' a lion-masked male growled.

'They are the voice of commerce, the makers of the shoes we walk in,' Eindil stated.

'But we are the voices of true knowledge,' a woman replied. 'Hearken to those others, consider their requests, but do not accede to their demands without consulting us. They may be the shoes we walk in, but our eyes are on the horizon, not upon our feet.'

The Day Court administered the day-to-day running of the empire, but the Night Court, who concerned themselves with strategic matters, carried the greater weight.

'Your point is made and understood,' Eindil told her. 'But I am not deaf to other voices.'

'Crowns are heavy, Great One,' another masked adviser said soothingly. 'But we can guide you through these treacherous days and into the light which lies beyond. The Day Court is the voice of common men, but you are one of us, in the end.'

Faced with that truth, the decision was made. 'Then I will order the evacuation. But what of Governor Durand and Romara Challys, who have been unable to discharge my will?'

More murmuring and hissings, and then another hooded woman spoke, a Bedumassan, by her accent. 'Either they have failed you, betrayed you or been given a task beyond them. That is the factual situation. But emotionally, your people expect to see blame apportioned. Choose a scapegoat and conduct a trial. Be seen to be just, and strong.'

'Which one? Governor Durand?'

'The Vestal knight,' the lion-masked counsellor replied. 'She's a veteran, nearing the end of her usefulness. She's expendable.'

Eindil decided they were right: governors tended to have powerful connections, so punishing Durand would be divisive and potentially risky. But a veteran of the Vestals could be sacrificed.

'Thank you for your guidance,' he said. 'Hold a trial. Let justice be served upon her.'

'Thank you for hearkening, Great One,' the masked courtiers replied, then with a swishing of robes, they dispersed into the darkness, leaving Eindil sitting alone in a pool of light in the vast hall. A moment later, the Watcher's Bell tolled on the mainland, the twenty-two chimes telling him that it was two hours until midnight and he must return to the Sacred Palace, where that night's chosen wife awaited. After that, there'd be the ritual cleansing and, finally, rest, before facing the next day's battles.

He gestured, and Stentor Robias reappeared from the shadows. 'Stentor, I return to the palace,' Eindil told him. 'Oh, and lower the banner of Avas on Imperium Square.'

I have lost part of my realm . . . this Romara Challys must pay for that.

Part One
LOSS AND BLAME

A Wall of Fire

The Blessed of Akka

It is known that Akka the Father, and Elysia his Handmaiden, dispense fortune to those they favour. Thus may you know the righteous: by their riches and largesse. The wealthy and powerful are the blessed of Akka, and to serve them is to serve the Father.

LANCEL, THIRTEENTH GUARDIAN, 1312

Long Bay, Avas Isle
Summer 1472

The sky was a dull, throbbing red, smoke clogged the nostrils, heat basted skin and the wind howled with demon voices, clawing at the eight thousand remaining refugees huddled on the beach of Long Bay. They sang hymns imploring divine rescue, but it was the wooden ships standing off the coast which would save them, and Romara Challys's soldiers who protected them.

We should have been long gone by now, Romara thought grimly.

A courser had arrived finally, a full week after the first one left, giving permission to depart, but it had taken another week for the evacuation fleet to arrive and even then, there were too few ships moving far too slowly for the refugees of Avas trapped between the fires and the waves.

Somehow, no one blamed the man responsible for the delays: His Serene Majesty Eindil Pandramion III, Hierophant of Talmont. It was everyone else's fault.

But we'll catch the blame, Romara worried. Her Vestal century had been the last to evacuate; those left till the end always got the worst of these situations.

Her morose thoughts were interrupted by the arrival of a grey-robed Akkanite pater, Vostius, a tonsured priest with a serious mien. He had to look up to Romara, who stood almost six foot – but he had a lordly presence that added invisible inches and left her feeling the shorter.

'Greetings, Siera Romara,' Vostius boomed. 'This is a blessed day.'

'It will be, if we all get off in one piece,' Romara agreed.

He surveyed the windswept beach and the smoke-wreathed marshland inland. 'Is there any sign of the vyr?' the pater asked anxiously.

'Nothing so far. My magia, Elindhu, will sense them if they come, but they must know we're leaving. There's no rational reason for them to launch an assault.' She pulled a rueful face. 'Not that they're famed for their rationality.'

'True enough,' Vostius sighed. 'Are your knights at full strength?'

'With the shards destroyed, our *glyma* is depleted,' Romara admitted, patting the elobyne orb on the pommel of her sword. Without the shards the Church had planted every twenty kylos or so, the only way to refill the orbs and renew their weapons was an orison; the communal ritual would draw energy from the congregation itself. 'But we'll manage,' she assured him.

'I will call an orison,' Vostius declared. 'The people will show their devotion.'

It was a generous offer, but orisons took quite a toll on the participants. 'They've already lost all they have, and they're exhausted,' Romara protested. 'To also give prayer is too much – some may not survive.'

'They have more to give. Let them show you their love of Akka.'

He sounded disturbingly fanatical. Romara scanned the nearest people, seeing exhaustion, defeat and loss. *They've got nothing else to give*, she thought. *They'll need what little strength they have left for the journey to safety.*

But Vostius didn't answer to her, and a priest's reputation rested on the efficacy and frequency of his orisons. He was probably trying to make a name for himself – and to ensure no one could blame him for this débâcle.

'Very well, I'll gather my knights,' she conceded.

While Vostius prepared, Romara called in her pentacle, the elobyne-bearing men and women who led her century: loyal and idealistic Jadyn Kaen, her seneschal; Ghaneen Suul, a headstrong, macho Zynochi; world-weary Obanji Vost, the Abuthan veteran, and the birdlike mage, Elindhu Morspeth. They'd been here on Avas for nine months now, and given their considerable all.

It hasn't been enough.

As the Falcon pentacle assembled, Vostius went to his wrought-bronze Orison Bell hanging inside a tripod of oak and hammered on it. Heads turned as the doleful noise sounded down the beach, tired faces lifting at the familiar sacred sound. 'Kalefa, kalefa ap orison!' – *we are called, we are called to prayer* – he shouted, and the cry was quickly echoed by his acolytes.

Romara was humbled to see hope kindled on the exhausted faces, and sure enough, in minutes hundreds of refugees had gathered and were watching reverently as Vostius' acolytes laid on the ground the sacred Weave, a web of elobyne crystals woven in a geometric pattern into silk.

The islanders, villagers and farmers alike had been ripped from their homes by the vyr onslaught; they'd carried their last possessions on their backs for days, only to be stranded here for almost two weeks. Romara marvelled that they had anything left to give. But they willingly grasped the strands of the Weave with white-knuckled desperation. Children knelt with them, wide-eyed and fervent, and those who couldn't reach the ropes clasped the shoulders of those in front so all could share their devotion.

Romara led her pentacle through the gathering, the refugees reverently brushing her white tabard with their fingers as she passed. She knelt in the middle, pulled forth her wavy-bladed Order flamberge and planted the tip in the sand, the softly glowing elobyne pommel eliciting cries of awe and adoration. Jadyn Kaen presented his blade next, his homely face as ever humble. She met his eyes, a fleeting glance of mutual devotion forged through ten years of shared service and friendship.

Our time will come, Farm Boy, she thought wistfully, although she couldn't imagine life outside the Order. But they were both approaching thirty, so that day would soon arrive. *We'll take the land and pension package, retire and finally be free to love.*

Ghaneen Suul was next to kneel, brandishing his sword ostentatiously, while the black-skinned Abuthan, Obanji Vost, was characteristically restrained. Their small, waddling mage, Elindhu Morspeth, lifted her crystal-tipped staff to the heavens, her long-nosed face peering from beneath a tower of grey braids.

My brothers and sisters, Romara reflected proudly. *They fought with all their strength for Avas and they don't deserve the blame for this – but no doubt it'll be heaped upon us.*

She shook the thought off: it was unworthy, in this moment of sanctity. Instead she focused on the ritual, gripping her weapon just under the cross-piece.

'Behold this blade,' she recited. 'It is a *flamberge* – the flame-blade of Talmont – forged from Miravian steel by the master-smiths of Hyastar and entrusted to me by the Hierophant himself. Through the grace of Akka, I am a Knight of the Vestments of Elysia Divina, a servant of all. Ar-byan.'

'Ar-byan!' her comrades responded. *By God's Will.*

She raised the pommel towards Heaven, letting the crystal orb catch the sunlight. 'Behold the Orb, pure elobyne from Nexus, the sacred isle, gifted to humanity by Jovan Lux. Through its holy power, I am more than a woman: I am a Knight of the Vestments of Elysia Divina, a servant of all. Ar-byan.'

'Ar-byan!'

'I renew my pledge to wield this gift for Akka, for Elysia, for Talmont. May I serve faithfully, and do honour to those who have gone before me. I am a Knight of the Vestments of Elysia Divina, a servant of all. Ar-byan.'

'*Ar-byan!*' the congregated refugees shouted. From the expressions on their exhausted, grief-stricken faces, they were pinning all their hopes and prayers on her pentacle – on her. It was a burden, but one she was proud to bear.

When she stood, Jadyn, Ghaneen, Obanji and Elindhu rose with her and together, they lifted their weapons to heaven, shouting, 'Lux Eternal!'

'Elysia be wit' ye, Vestals,' a fisherman cried hoarsely. 'Bless ye!' His call was echoed on all sides.

'Akka be with us all,' Vostius shouted, sweeping his stern gaze over the sweaty, soot-streaked islanders. 'Orison eli volso.' *The orison has begun.* 'Let us pray!'

The veneration began. Even Romara, who'd participated in this ritual so many times, felt her skin prickle in anticipation and wonder, because this ritual was unique to the Vestal Order.

In past creeds, prayers were just wishes, sent into the sky in superstitious hope, the way pagans still prayed today. But for worshippers of Akka and Elysia, the King and Queen of Heaven, the orison made prayer real and tangible, binding them to the thrones of Heaven, and to their protectors.

Vostius led the chanting, exhorting the faithful to give their hearts as he invoked Akka, calling His divine gaze to this place. Their ragged voices grew stronger as the familiar words took root. Then came the emotion, initiated by the younger women, so often the most passionate of any congregation. Girlish faces became flushed and fervent as an ecstatic anguish overtook them, their bodies beginning to shake as they raised their faces to heaven and shrieked in rapture, *'AKKA! HEAR US! ELYSIA, I LOVE YOU! SAVE US!'*

As the congregation roared, the air inside the circle throbbed. United by their faith, rich and poor, elders and children, and especially the youth, with all their fire and desire, competed in fervour, storming heaven, eyes skywards and hands clasped to the Weave.

This is Talmont, Romara thought, *where the love of Akka gives us the power to prevail.*

The crystals in the Weave began to glow, a pale light that began at the edges, illuminating the ropes that extended into the massed refugees, then flowing inwards, gaining intensity. The children all squealed in wonder, while the adults, exhausted from the effort, roared in triumph.

The light became a blaze that flowed from crystal to crystal, converging on the centre, where Romara and her pentacle waited, holding ready their flamberges. It coalesced suddenly – and a bolt of pure energy flowed into their elobyne crystals. Feeling the jolt like a physical blow, they all bowed their heads in thanks, while the congregation roared in victory, an enraptured call that encompassed exultation, relief and utter exhaustion.

Girls and boys alike were fainting, and even adults were swaying, dazed, as the wave of tiredness that inevitably followed a successful orison swept over the crowd. The orison gave, but it also took, especially from the weak and sickly. Some even chose to die that way, giving the last of themselves to Akka – after all, it guaranteed a place in Paradise.

The weapons of Romara's pentacle tingled with new energy. Such a small orison could do only so much, but everyone had been lifted by it: prayers had been heard and the bonds of community renewed. Vostius made the final blessing sign, his work done, his reputation cemented.

Now I must play my part, Romara thought, as she faced the crowd, her long scarlet locks catching the wind as she held her flamberge aloft, hilt high. 'In the name of Akka and Elysia, I thank you all,' she shouted hoarsely, kindling light in the crystal to show that the prayers had been effective. 'The glyma is with us. Ar-byan, Ar-byan.'

Ghaneen Suul, ever the dramatist, flourished his own sword dramatically, crying, 'I pledge to keep you safe. Ar-byan!' He was their youngest and considered himself their best blade.

The refugees cheered him rapturously.

Obanji, who actually was their best blade, shared a laconic glance with Elindhu, while Romara smiled wryly at Ghaneen's antics.

'Falcons, go forth!' she ordered, and they began extricating themselves – which was not so easy when people wanted to kiss the hems of their tabards and otherwise venerate them as avatars of the gods – but eventually they managed to break away. They strode down the beach to rejoin the Falcon century stationed at the southern end.

The lonely, desolate stretch of shingle and sand known as Long Bay faced the mainland to the east, a stony strip between the brackish swamp and the hungry waves, now choked with fearful refugees. Smoke clogged the air, reducing visibility to a few hundred paces. Black-and-white quartered tabards marked out Romara's Falcon century of Vestal guards, holding a perimeter along the fire-ditches. They all turned anxiously as Romara and her pentacle approached: they'd be the last to be evacuated, and only then if there was room on the ships for them. So Romara couldn't answer their questioning looks. Like them, she could only hope they'd get off this cursed island today.

'Four hours, the governor estimates,' she called aloud, lighting up her pommel-orb to show that she and her pentacle had energy left. 'Do your duty, Falcons.'

'Falcons Eternal!' they roared back. But most threw resentful glances along the shore at the ranks of blue-clad imperial soldiers already lining up to embark.

Over the next few hours, as each boat rowed in and collected another load of evacuees – and the governor's men – to load into the ships at anchor beyond the breakers, those still waiting became increasingly desperate, until the governor's soldiers formed a cordon to keep control, lest the boats be swamped.

We mightn't get off today after all, Romara worried. She doubted the vyr would attack now, but if they were stranded overnight, an assault was far more likely.

'I miss the days when all I had to think about was keeping my blade sharp and my tabard clean,' she muttered. 'I'm sick of having to worry about everyone else.'

'No, you aren't,' Jadyn grinned. 'You love bossing us around.' The others chuckled wryly.

'Well, that's true,' she admitted. 'Come on, you lot, let's get up to the headland and see what's to be seen.'

She led her pentacle up a windswept bluff that offered views north over Long Bay, westwards along the southern coast, a rugged wall of broken stone, and into the interior, where the burned-out marshland lying between the hills and valleys told a tale of destruction and defeat.

The four knights sat, breaking out water bottles and whet-stones, and set to sharpening the rippled edges of their swords as they discussed their situation. But Elindhu planted her staff and gazed about, her eyes gleaming glyma-blue. 'No vyr-sign,' she reported. 'All quiet.'

'Did the Boars get back to Gaudien safely?' Obanji wondered aloud, his voice a deep basso.

'Who cares?' Ghaneen grunted. 'Pricks.' He gave Romara a sour look. 'You should have pressed harder for us to be taken off before them. We'll be blamed for this loss simply by dint of being the last ones here.'

He was probably right, but done was done, and in any case, it hadn't been up to her. 'It was the grandmaster's decision to evacuate the Boars first,' Romara reminded them.

'You should have befriended him,' Ghaneen told her. 'The Boar's commander drank with him all the time – that's how things get done.'

Aye, Romara thought glumly, *but that's not how it should be.*

'Any losses overnight?' she asked Jadyn; her second-in-command always knew these things.

'No deaths,' Jadyn replied. 'Corporal Geraint broke his hand trying to right a cart and Metcham got bitten by a kiss-adder – it got into his bedroll. Got him right on the butt,' he clarified, adding, 'He'll be fine, though.'

'Did the physicians suck the venom out?' Obanji chuckled.

Ghaneen winced. 'Jag that! I'd've let him croak.'

'That's 'cause you're a heartless bastard,' Romara quipped, though she wasn't joking. 'How many are we down? Twenty-seven, yes?'

Jadyn nodded. 'That's right, dead or wounded. Morale is holding, but we all want to get off.'

If her century had been at full strength, Obanji, Ghaneen and Jadyn would each be commanding a fighting cohort of thirty men. As well, she should have a centurion, a banner-man, a logisticalus, directed by Elindhu, and ten non-combatants to look after engineering, medicine and baggage. As it was the losses were fairly evenly spread, and everyone was overworked.

'It's the islanders I feel for.' Obanji was watching the refugees milling below. 'They've lost everything – their homes, their livelihoods, every place that has meaning to them. I know what that's like.'

'It's like this on Fyna and Mir too,' Ghaneen pointed out. 'And the refugee camps these poor fools are headed for will be plague-ridden cesspits too.'

'I grew up in such a camp, in Aquinium,' Obanji mused. 'They're no place to bring a family. People should live in dignity.'

'I agree, but does Petraxus care?' Elindhu asked, rhetorically. She might be the least martial of them, this short woman with a pot belly and a pile of grey hair, but she was wisest in arcane lore, and for all she was the most vulnerable, she was often the most opinionated.

'You lot get back to your cohorts,' Romara said, not wanting to hear any more criticism of the hierarchy. It wasn't that she agreed with everything their superiors did, but you had to trust the chain of command. 'Make sure they're all briefed about the evacuation. We may yet come under attack. Elindhu, remain with me; I need your mage-eyes.'

The knights donned their Falcon-helms, the silver tarnished by the salt and smoke that was also turning their white tabards an unsightly grey.

'Have a care,' Romara warned. 'The vyr may not be finished with us yet.'

While her knights returned to their cohorts, Romara took Elindhu up to the pinnacle of the hill, from where they could gaze inland upon the marsh, a dried-up stretch of scorched reeds and cracked mud dotted with charred tree-stumps. Fire had raged through here some weeks back, during a sharp, sustained battle. Now ash covered the ground and charred bodies lay unburied, fought over by squabbling gulls and crows.

'We don't criticise our superiors,' Romara reminded her. 'They know more and see more than us. We must trust in them.'

'I'm sorry, I couldn't resist. We've been abandoned out here – one island after another falls and still Petraxus does nothing.'

'See, you're doing it again,' Romara said. 'And I don't disagree, but we must keep such thoughts inside.' She changed the subject abruptly. 'Do you sense any vyr near?'

'You'll be first to know,' Elindhu replied, but she raised her staff and closed her eyes, opening herself to the world around her. Unlike the knights, who were honed for war but severely limited in non-battle magic, her mind was sensitive enough to detect the unseen.

'Someone's coming,' she said, pointing westwards, along the southern coast.

A few moments later, a young man appeared, stripped to the waist, jogging towards them. 'I thought everyone left on Avas was either with the vyr, or on that beach,' Romara muttered. 'What's to the west of us?'

'Cherenton,' Elindhu answered. 'The governor's soldiers cleared it weeks ago.'

'So where's this lad come from? He's comely – if an unusual mix,' she added, as he drew closer and they got a better look at him. His skin was darker than the pallid native islanders, but his facial structure was Abuthan, from far south across the Sea of Pelas.

'A southern sailor's by-blow, maybe?' Elindhu suggested.

Romara went to meet the newcomer, hand on hilt despite the apparent lack of threat – a vyr looked ordinary, right up until the moment they changed and tried to rip you apart. 'Halt!' she called, when he was twenty paces away. 'Declare yourself.'

The young man took her in with what appeared to be surprise. She presumed it was for her gender. She had the aristocratic, aquiline features of the Miravian highborn, while her cascade of scarlet hair spoke of Foylish blood. She'd been called beautiful when younger, but knighthood had aged her, stealing her youth and freshness and leaving her hardened and haunted.

He dropped to one knee, blurting, 'Elysia akemia! Please, help us, Great Lady!'

The youth looked seventeen at most, but he was strongly built,

22

his rippling chest and belly muscles and broad shoulders the equal of any young knight she'd seen.

'Tasty,' Elindhu commented, under her breath.

Romara gave her a hard look – Vestal knights and mages were sworn to chastity, for very necessary reasons. 'What's your name?' she asked warily; he might look like a boy, but he could still be a vyr.

'Soren var'Dael of Cherenton.' He looked awestruck, no guile or malice on his handsome face. 'Please, Lady, my father broke his knee and we don't have the strength to get him here.'

'You look like you could carry a wagon on your shoulders, lad,' Elindhu remarked.

He blushed and shook his head. 'My pa's a big man, an' there's Ma an' my sister to manage. Others too, and they're all old or childers. We need your help, Lady. *Please.*'

Is this a trap? she wondered, but Elindhu was ahead of her.

'I feel no lie in him,' she murmured.

Reassured, Romara asked, 'Where did you leave them?'

'Pa fell at a cove about two kylos back,' the young man answered. 'No way we can get him up. An' there's fires burning inland of the cove . . .' His voice cracked. 'I thought I saw vyr shadowing us. Please, we need help.'

Romara sagged, thinking of the hard climb back along the coast, the risks of being caught in the open by the vyr, or cut off by a rush of flames. Then she straightened. *We're here to serve.*

'Of course we'll help. How many people?'

'There's more'n two dozen, Sier,' Soren answered. 'We've been hiding out in the wilds since the vyr raided. We were too scared to come out when the soldiers came. Pa an' I are the only fighting-age men.'

'He's telling the truth,' Elindhu muttered again, 'or what he believes to be true.'

'We'll need to send at least a cohort to recover these people,' Romara calculated.

'At least,' Elindhu agreed. 'And if there's vyr shadowing them, we may need more.'

'Aye, I know. But we're also needed here.' Romara looked towards Jadyn's cohort, now just a few hundred paces away. 'We'll bring Jadyn's thirty, and leave the rest here to protect evacuees. But I want my entire pentacle with me.' Then she said to the boy, 'Bravely done, lad. We'll see your people to safety.'

Arranging the rescue party took more time than she liked. The governor and his household staff were fussing over a mountain of baggage, so she'd hoped Durand would just acquiesce unquestioningly to her message, but instead he rode up the hill to see her in person.

'Ho, Siera Romara,' the governor boomed as he arrived, trailed by an armoured man with a hawkish face and a mane of grey hair. The governor wore his chain of office, but the other man had no insignia.

Ambrose Durand was a portly man, with the kind of ageless visage his first name evoked. He clasped her hand amiably, then gestured at the mess on the beach. 'I'm required by protocol to bring off all tax records and ceremonial accoutrements,' he complained. 'If it prevents anyone from getting off, they're going in the sea.'

'Just so long as there's enough room for my lads,' Romara responded. 'Do you know when that will be?'

'Well, the vagaries of seamanship aren't my expertise, but I'm told my men will embark within two hours, and your men in three.' He dropped his voice. 'If the vyr attack the beach, we're in deep trouble.'

Romara shared his fear. Her Falcons were the only Vestal century left here, and only her pentacle could face a draegar or vorlok – the knights and mages of the vyr – with hope. 'We've seen no sign of them,' she reassured the governor. 'But a runner's come with word of more refugees, from Cherenton. They've seen vyr and beg help. If we don't go, they'll likely die.'

Durand looked worried. 'It reeks of a trap. What do you think, Corbus?'

Romara started, realising that the other man was the Archon, Corbus Ritter, the head of her Order. She dropped to one knee, stammering, 'Milord – I'm sorry, we've not met and—'

'Enough of that,' the Archon interrupted. 'I'm here incognito – can't have you bowing and scraping all over me.'

She stood again, conscious of her men watching. 'It's an honour to meet you, Milord.'

The Archon was in his fifties and despite having retired from active service, he looked formidably fit. He still carried a flamberge, the elobyne crystal replaced with a ceremonial gold pommel. Transitioning from a glyma-wielding warrior to a bureaucrat wasn't easy, but Corbus Ritter had risen quickly through the ranks and had led the Order for almost a decade now.

'The honour's mine, Siera Romara,' the Archon replied. 'I arrived today, to ensure that none of our people are left behind. You've done well here. Everyone is singing your praises.'

'Thank you, Milord,' Romara replied gratefully. *Maybe I won't be blamed for this, after all.*

'Now, what of this runner's plea?' the Archon asked. 'Do you sense a trap?'

'It's a common vyr ploy, sir. The Wolf century lost three knights in just such an ambush, last month. But I believe this time it's genuine.'

The biggest frustration fighting the vyr was that there was nothing about them to betray what they were. They were ordinary people, living normal lives – until a vorlok tempted them into joining their coven, turning once-peaceful villagers and farmers into bestial berserkers. It wasn't impossible that some were encamped on the beach, even now.

The Archon considered, then turned to Durand. 'Governor, what do you think?'

'If they attack the beach, we'll need the Falcons here,' he worried.

'My magia, Elindhu, is adamant there are no vyr nearby,' Romara replied. 'We'll be an hour at the most, Milord. The vyr prey on the vulnerable – they're far more likely to attack these stragglers than assail your soldiers.'

She waited anxiously while the two men considered. Many people would have no sympathy for these stragglers, but Durand was a decent man, and Ritter had a good reputation.

'Our whole purpose is to protect the citizens of the empire,' the

Archon said, at last. 'I'm in favour. We have enough fighting men on this beach to hold if the vyr do attack.'

Durand pulled a face, but agreed. 'Very well. But don't be too long, Siera Romara.' He turned to go, then paused and said, 'By the time you return, I may well have embarked. If that's so, I thank you for your service here. You've done sterling work.'

'As have you, Milord,' she replied honestly. They'd worked together closely these past months and she liked him. But Avas was a disaster from which their careers might never recover. *Petraxus will want people to blame, and he and I are the prime candidates.* So this felt a lot like a last goodbye. 'Bene fortuna atou,' she told him formally.

'Best of luck to you too, Siera Romara. Elysia be merciful, for this isn't our fault.'

As he walked away, Romara looked uncertainly at the Archon. 'Is that what you'll tell the Day Court, Milord?' she asked. 'Every century of the Order who fought here these past few months has given their all, but it's been like fighting shadows. We needed more support.'

'From whom?' Sier Corbus asked sharply, as if sensing criticism.

'From the empire. From Petraxus,' Romara replied, struggling to remain calm. 'We fought hard, but every time we gained a respite, another century was withdrawn.'

'Avas isn't the only place the vyr are gaining ground,' Corbus replied. 'There are rebellions and wildfires in every province of every kingdom. The Order is finite, so once it was clear Avas was lost, we were only ever fighting a rearguard action to buy time for the full evacuation.'

'But couldn't the Hierophant have sent more regular army—?'

'There's no one to send. The Kharagh are restless, Pelasian and Khetian pirates are sinking ships on the trade routes and raiding ports. Foyland threatens Bravantia, and the list goes on. We're fighting too many battles.' He drew himself up to his full height. 'But I tell you this: I am Archon of the Vestal Order and my creed has always been of unity. From the lowliest man-at-arms to the heroic knights and mages who wield the sacred glyma, we are one. Have faith, Siera Romara. The Order looks after its own.'

He offered his right hand and when she took it, he clasped his left over hers. 'I promise you, Siera, you will emerge from this secure – and indeed, enhanced. I promise you that.'

It was such a relief to hear and witness her Archon's support that Romara had to swallow a lump in her throat. 'Thank you, Milord,' she said thickly. 'It is an honour to serve.'

'We serve together,' Corbus replied, still holding her hand. 'There's another thing, Siera . . . a personal matter. Word came to Gaudien as I left. I'm sorry, but your brother Reshar died, five days ago now. His heart gave out. He'll have been buried yesterday.'

Romara closed her eyes and took a moment to breathe. 'It's not a surprise, in truth, Milord,' she replied. 'He's been ill a long time. My parents kept trying to pull strings to have my service in the Order cancelled.'

Corbus gave her a wry smile. 'I know. Their requests reached my desk, but unless a knight wishes to be discharged, it can't be forced upon them.'

'This knight doesn't wish it,' Romara told him. 'I loved my brother, but once I realised that the Order was my home, I've never wanted to leave.' She bowed her head. 'But he's died without issue, so now I'll have no choice.'

'You're the sole heir to House Challys once your parents pass on,' the Archon confirmed. 'That's a considerable legacy – not just managing the estates, but the political responsibilities. Even I can't protect you from those.'

She groaned, remembering the horrible, stiffly formal life she'd been born into, her rapacious father and brittle mother, and poor sickly Reshar, who'd been forced to try and take all that responsibility on his frail shoulders.

'I used to be one of those dreadful hollyhocks, primping about in lace and learning dance steps and etiquette,' she confessed. 'I was a dreadful creature. When I gained the Gift, I cried. But the Order's been the making of me.'

'That will stand you in good stead when you do take your place in high society, Siera Romara,' Corbus replied. 'The Order needs friends in the nobility, and your time with us couldn't have gone on for ever. But I'm sorry to be the bearer of this bad news.' He looked at her waiting men. 'Now, go and save those refugees. I must depart, but I will see you in Gaudien. Akka be with you, Lady Challys.'

Lady Challys ... She swallowed. *That's a title I've been running away from for a decade.*

But for now, thankfully, duty still called. She faced the Archon, they thumped their right fists into their chest in salute, then marched in opposite directions.

'Was that the *Archon*?' Jadyn asked, striding up.

'I can't possibly say.' Romara winked.

She knew she should tell Jadyn about her brother, but now wasn't the time. *Even though once I'm Lady Challys, I'll be wanting him as my Lord.* She'd tell him later, once she'd had a chance to take it in. 'Falcons, on your feet! Pentacle and Cohort One!'

Jadyn mustered his cohort and they were preparing to leave when she heard someone shouting, 'Siera! Siera!' Soren var'Dael came running up. 'Let me show you the way!'

She'd completely forgotten that the boy would want to get back to his loved ones. 'Of course, my apologies, Please, come.'

The youth fell into step with Obanji, looking at the big man with awe. 'Are you from my homeland?' he asked eagerly. 'How can you be a knight?'

'The Order recruits among all the faithful,' Obanji rumbled. 'We're all Akkanites here, lad, living under Jovan's Edict.' Then he asked Soren something in Mbixi that the young man clearly didn't understand. 'What's your name?' he clarified in Talmoni.

'Soren,' the boy responded. 'Sorry, I only know a little Mbixi.' He puffed out his chest. 'But I'm the best swordsman on Avas.'

Ghaneen Suul snorted. 'Based on what?'

'I won the Junior Shield at the last Aventus Night tourney.'

'Juniors,' Ghaneen snorted. 'Where's yer sword?'

'My family only have one; Pa's got it,' the boy mumbled, then looked up. 'I'm gonna be a Vestal knight, too.'

Ghaneen laughed, but Obanji asked, 'Have you been tested for the Gift, lad?'

'Aye ... I failed ... but it's not too late.'

Ghaneen went to say something, but Romara laid a warning hand on his shoulder and interjected, 'Aye, it's not too late, but rare for glyma to come as late as – what, nineteen?'

'I'm only sixteen, and still growing,' Soren replied firmly.

Sixteen? Well, the Gift could indeed develop in him.

But she had more immediate matters on her mind, including the nagging fear that this was a vyr ruse. That sharpened her nerves, as she led her Falcons west over the towering cliffs, skirting the burned-out hillsides inland, which still offered plenty of cover.

Why do the vyr burn the land they hope to rule? Romara wondered. *It doesn't make sense.*

As they travelled, the cloying smoke grew thicker and everyone wrapped scarfs around their faces, protecting noses and mouths, though they couldn't do anything about stinging eyes. As the risk of ambush grew, Romara sent Obanji ahead to scout.

'It's going to be a relief to get off this rock,' she muttered to Jadyn.

'Aye, but I keep asking myself if we could've done more,' he replied.

'Always. But only with complete foreknowledge, and not even Elindhu has that.'

The Falcons had been in the isles for almost two years, helping evacuate Fyna, then moving to Avas when the vyr-lit fires broke out here. They'd been giving ground constantly ever since. The ecology of the archipelago had been collapsing for decades, locals said, blaming the empire and in particular, the elobyne shards the Empire had planted, but the scholars in Petraxus said the crop failures were part of global change, a predictable and regular turning of the Ages. Lies and half-truths abounded on all sides; all she could do was trust her superiors and fight on.

'Nothing we've done was ever enough,' Jadyn sighed, for once letting his mask of stoic optimism slip. Only with Romara did he express such doubts, and she countenanced them only from him.

With Ghaneen, she had to be firm, and even with Obanji and Elindhu she maintained the official line. But Jadyn was different.

One day we'll walk away from this together, as husband and wife.

'Let's find these last refugees, get them to safety, then we'll be off home,' he said. 'I'm thinking about Vanberg beer and Bravantian wine, and food that isn't peppered in ash.'

'I'd be happy to just wash the soot from my hair,' Romara replied longingly.

The journey along the coast was hard work, but they could see the central highlands of Avas: a majestic sight, made foreboding by the great grey clouds streaming overhead. Maybe in winter, once the fires were burned out and the rains had fed the soil, life might return. But right now, the villages and towns were just charred shells, the famous vineyards vanished. It was conceivable that Avas would never be properly resettled.

Soon after, Romara led her men down a precipitous path, to be greeted by twenty-odd Avas folk, almost all aged or children, except for Soren's family. His father, Dael var'Dael, was a tall, craggy Avas man with a sour face and domineering manner. His tiny wife was as dark as Obanji; she was clutching the hand of a daughter of about twelve who shared Soren's colouring. The father greeted Soren with a bark of impatience, which might, Romara thought, go some way to explaining why both wife and daughter looked browbeaten.

'Took yer jagging time, din' ye?' he snarled. He had a sword strapped across his back, the only armed man among the refugees, despite looking like he was barely able to walk. 'Too damned lazy, yer whelp.'

Romara had to push away her instant dislike towards the man. *Perhaps the pain of his injury clouds his gentler urges*, she thought charitably.

Elindhu examined the man's knee, and once it was strapped up, Jadyn assigned four of his men to help carry him, while others were tasked with helping the refugees. They passed out water, then helped them all back up to the clifftops, where Romara permitted a rest by a patch of dry broom, contorted by the sea winds into twisted shapes. Worryingly, it was unburnt; fire would rip through it like a cavalry charge.

'I don't like it here,' Elindhu told her. 'Best we get moving.'

Romara gave the command and the men got wearily to their feet. As they began to move off, she called Soren and asked, 'Where did you see the vyr trailing you?'

'I saw someone in the ash fields half a kylos west of the cove,' Soren said fearfully. 'A man with antlers.'

That's not good. Vyr didn't shape-change unless a vorlok was near, but she kept her face calm. 'Stay close to your family, lad. All will be well.' Then she went down the column, calling, 'Stay alert, Falcons. Let's pick it up.'

The soldiers lifted the dozen or so children onto their shoulders and began to hurry, chivvying the old folk, helping them where they could. From time to time, Romara thought she glimpsed movement in the brush, but nothing more threatening than a hare emerged, and after an anxious half-hour the headland marking the south end of Long Bay was in sight.

Then Elindhu gasped and turned her way. 'Ach, Romara, I'm sensing vyr!'

Romara scanned the scrub on the landward side of the cliffs. 'You sure?'

'Am I ever wrong?' the magia said sharply, before winking. 'Rhetorical question.'

Romara snorted, then called, 'Falcons, form up! Face inland!'

'Wish we'd brought the whole century,' she heard Ghaneen grumble.

So do I, she thought, *but wishes don't catch fishes.*

Jadyn took up her commands. 'Refugees to the rear – Falcons, form a line: prepare to fight!'

The Falcons might be tired, but they reacted with discipline and alacrity. A few herded the refugees back to the cliff's edge, while the rest deployed with seasoned efficiency. Romara shot out orders: 'Obanji, Ghaneen, Jadyn, anchor the front line. Elindhu, damp down this wind!'

Elindhu snorted disgustedly. 'I'll do what I can. They're almost upon us.' She touched her temple. 'There's a silent roar and it's getting louder.'

Romara could now see movement on the brushy slope below. The air was getting hotter, the inland fires rolling towards them like a breaking wave. Orange flames flared up on the lower slope and she felt a quiver of fear as she saw shapes moving among the flames.

They're not waiting for us to leave. They want us all dead . . .

She hurried to the centre of the line of men huddling behind shields with their spears presented. The Vestal guard were among the finest soldiers in the empire, but if a draegar or vorlok came, it would fall on her pentacle to keep everyone alive.

Behind them, the refugees were clinging to each other in fear, knowing that if the Falcons failed, they were doomed. For a moment her eyes settled on young Soren var'Dael, who had brought them here. He looked scared but resolute as he listened to a stream of low words from his cantankerous father.

Stay safe, she silently wished the boy, then she prepared once again to face death.

In minutes the booming of the waves on the rocks below was supplanted by a new sound, that of hot winds raking the broom and washing heat over their faces, making them sweat, then evaporating the perspiration. The winds began to howl with the voices of beasts.

Romara drew her flamberge and lit the elobyne crystal in the pommel. 'Akka be in my heart,' she prayed. 'Thy power be with me.'

The clear elobyne crystal turned a cool blue, evoking the state of mind required to master the glyma, but drawing on that energy was anything but calming, for it woke a surge of edgy heat in the chest and head, accompanied by an aggressive rush of exhilaration, hunger and potency. If she rode that swirling wave, the energy would become an inner blaze – the same violent, destructive, berserk rage that the vyr wielded.

She countered it with the iron discipline of the Vestal Order, quelling those fires by seeking the centre of that inner storm – the famed Eye of Silence, the inner calm that enabled a trained glyma-knight to control the flow of energy, using it to conjure combat runes, primarily *Potentas* for strength, *Salva* for shielding, *Pulso* for force and *Flamma* for fire – the words weren't totally necessary, but they gave focus. There were many other runes, but only those four mattered in a fight. The rest were for the mages.

Her eyes sought Jadyn again, as her body shivered with pent-up energy. They were forbidden sexual love – because for glyma-wielders, the interchange of energies could kill – so the only physical expression of love they'd found was the dance of blades. Duty drove them, but it was in these moments they felt truly alive.

Come, my love, she thought, *let's become one again* . . .

As if in response, the flames began to roar towards them, the smoke streaming into the air moving over the conflagration like some kind of roaring, snarling beast. Then a wailing shriek pierced the flames and her skin prickled.

A moment later Elindhu called, 'There's a vorlok out there. Maybe a draegar, too.'

A vorlok and *a draegar* . . . Romara groaned inwardly. *Akka be with us.*

She glanced down the lines: Ghaneen was pacing like a panther and Obanji, who was deadly with a bow, had his arrows nocked. Elindhu was behind the line of men-at-arms, attuning herself to the more arcane but less martial aspects of the glyma.

'*They're coming*,' someone shouted. Then, '*They're here!*'

A moment later, human figures came wading through the brush, misshapen and apparently immune to the flames, accompanied by snarling low-slung forms. Then a shocking number of beasts and humans erupted from the bushes, wreathed in the smoke and flames that flared and surged past them, towards the thin line of black-and-white-clad Vestal guards.

Romara unleashed *Pulso*, a burst of force into the faces of the oncoming enemy with enough force to break a man's limbs or ribs or neck. She heard startled cries and furious roaring, then howls shredded the air and the enemy were upon them . . .

For a moment, Soren had found himself looking into the eyes of the knight-commander, the redheaded woman with the aristocratic face and haunted eyes. She probably wasn't even thirty, maybe a dozen years older than him, but there was a whole world between them. She was living the life he dreamed of.

But his reality was a father who, despite being barely able to stand, wouldn't relinquish the family sword. 'It's mine,' Dael repeated. 'Carried it through the border wars and the Mar-Pelas. I'm ten times the man you'll ever be, boy.'

His father had returned to Avas from the southern wars with an Abuthan wife and for a time they'd been happy, but the collapsing ecology of Avas took its toll, stripping him first of his savings, then his empathy and finally his pride. He'd been a good soldier, a fine swordsman, but he was a terrible farmer and father.

Not that that mattered any more, for the whole world was ending. The farm was ash and Dael's family had had no choice but to join the exodus, a throng of scared people hauling along all they had left – clothing, pots, crockery, ornaments and heirlooms, even the pickles they'd made last summer. They'd slept huddled together on the ground, starving, choking on the smoke and burning up from thirst. Some never got up. Others slunk away to join the vyr. But Soren's father drove them on.

'*Get to Long Bay and we'll be evacuated,*' he kept saying, '*if the bastards will take us.*'

Dael var'Dael might have loathed the Order, but the Vestals were Soren's heroes. And his whole family were in their hands now. Fear flooded him, knowing he could die here: that his sixteen years of repressed desires and hopes could come to naught.

'The army is a man's life,' Pa always said, even though the Imperial Army had chewed him up and spat him out – but it was still the life he demanded for Soren, and he'd drilled his son like a tyrant. Soren would have run away, had it not been for his mother and sister.

'Boy,' Pa barked now, 'Stop yer moonin' an' help me up, so's I can fight.'

'Let me use it, Da—' he tried, but his father cut him off.

'Shut yer gob and help me up!'

Soren flinched, but obeyed. The moment he'd pulled his gaunt, bitter father to his feet, Dael shoved him away, drew his old longsword and faced the smoky hinterland, as if he alone could beat the vyr.

Then the flames burst over the clifftop and terrifying shapes erupted from the smoke.

'They're coming!' someone shouted. 'They're here!'

Soren balled his empty fists and prepared to face death.

Two giant shapes reared up over the heads of the other men and creatures running towards them from the flames, and in moments the Falcons were fighting for their lives.

'*Salva!*' Romara shouted, summoning a shield; the unseen barrier protected her and those behind from the blast of stones and sparks flying at them. Though it dampened the waves of heat rolling over them, they were still left gasping. Her fellow knights, strung out across the lines facing the burning brush-land, shielded the men-at-arms as best they could.

Seconds later, a flood of birds and animals smashed into their arcane and conventional barriers. Wolves and foxes and badgers, all with singed fur and a feral light in their eyes, started savaging everyone within reach, until they were skewered by spears and swords.

Then came men and women warped by the vyr into muscular, leathery-skinned savages with vicious teeth, claws and horns and the ferocity of rabid dogs, though they'd been ordinary people until the vyr-madness took them. The Falcons fought desperately, holding the line while the knights blasted fire and force – *Flamma* and *Pulso* – into the attackers' faces. Romara and Jadyn, their limbs filled with glyma-energy, wielded their blades and bodies in almost psychic union, a back-to-back dance of swirling steel and pulsing energy. They slashed through hide and bone and flesh like butter, immune to rage, for they were dancing in the Eye of Silence, fighting in a state of heightened perception. Romara's whole being was consumed by that unity, the rhythm of combat which drew them together and made her and Jadyn one. It felt like love.

At last the assault faltered, the frenzied men and women wailing in despair as they were cut down by the well-trained soldiers – until a great swirl of smoke heralded the coming of a vorlok, a vyr mage. Romara saw a clawed hand, big enough to cover a horse's skull, rip at her shielding, and a massive charred-skinned hag appeared, hunched over, yet still dwarfing her. A crude sword, as long as Romara's body, came whistling round at waist-height – Romara cartwheeled away, while Jadyn hit the dirt, letting the arc of steel flash by.

Romara regained her balance and had an instant to glance to the right, where, some sixty paces away, a draegar, the vyr equivalent of a Vestal knight, had emerged opposite Ghaneen: a giant slab of muscle eight foot tall, with the head of a flayed lion, a hideous thing to behold.

Jadyn's archers unleashed a flight of arrows, but the vorlok and draegar had all the advantages of the knights: they slapped at the air, cracking every shaft aside, then another savage gesture unleashed a wave of force, blasting the archers behind the knights off their feet.

Romara and Jadyn rekindled wards and went for the hag-like vorlok, while Ghaneen and Obanji charged the draegar. But before they could reach them, the two giants reared up and roared out a gale of fire from their mouths, enveloping the onrushing knights. In seconds, they were awash in flames, blinded and choking on the smoke, and their foes crashed into them as they reeled.

Soren and his family were directly behind one of the Vestal knights, the arrogant Zynochi, and half a dozen men-at-arms. Through the thin line of soldiers, he saw the brush igniting as a wall of warped animals and men crashed into the lines of soldiers. The line buckled as a savage fight broke out, but with the knights cutting a swathe through them, the attack began to falter – until two gigantic shapes crashed forwards. The redheaded knight-commander and her blond seneschal took on one, while the Zynochi and the Abuthan ran to face the draegar, a bipedal leonine monster, a thing of nightmares.

In Soren's imagination, he ran with them, sword ready, kindling magical energy.

'Curse ye, Akka,' his pa muttered, swinging his blade. He'd never forgiven the gods for denying him the Gift. 'Give me yer strength, damn ye!'

There's nothing behind us but cliffs and the sea, Soren thought, holding on to his frightened mother, Uti, a timid bundle of grey hair, desert-land skin and stick-thin limbs, and his nine-year-old sister Enid, who was shaking with terror. His father was halfway to the line of soldiers, leaning on his crutch and waving his sword about, his family forgotten.

I have to protect Ma and Enid, because he won't, Soren thought.

He saw the Zynochi knight reach the draegar, who was wielding a huge axe and gushing flames from its mouth, but the knight rolled to one side, then took him on with his flamberge, ducking beneath the massive axe before slashing upwards, opening the giant's belly. The draegar roared in anguish, but the wound blazed dark light and sealed in seconds.

The Abuthan was coming for the vyr champion now, but he and his handful of men were forced backwards by the belching flames, even as more hideously warped half-naked men and women appeared, shrieking hate. They hit the Falcons' shield-wall like boulders, bearing a trio of men to the ground, which allowed the attackers to swarm through the gap towards the cowering refugees.

Enid squealed, but Pa was bellowing in defiance.

'Pa—!' Soren shouted in warning, as Ma and Enid clutched at him.

The draegar smashed his massive axe into the Zynochi's shield, staggering the knight, who struck back cleverly, hacking at the giant's leg with his glowing blade, piercing the limb to the bone. Three crossbow bolts thudded into the draegar's torso, knocking him back on his heels, and Soren shouted in triumph—

—too soon.

The draegar swung again, a blinding blow that caught the knight in the midriff, cleaving him to the spine and hurling his broken body halfway to where Soren was standing. The soldiers wailed in dismay as the attacking vyr renewed their assault, breaking through as the Abuthan sought to rally them.

'Pa,' Soren shouted again, 'no—!'

But his father had lifted his relic of a blade, calling, 'For Avas! Avas eternal!' as the draegar roared and came right at him.

*

The vorlok woman's torrent of burning spittle flashed towards Romara, but she used the glyma-energy in her limbs to turn her evasive leap into another superhuman somersault, landing two-footed and ready outside the wash of flame and heat – then she charged the huge hag as the ever-dependable Jadyn came steaming in from the other side.

But even as Romara leapt towards her assailant, an arrow from out of the burning brush slammed into her side and her graceful leap became a sprawling tumble into the smouldering dirt, cracking her nose and grazing her face. The vorlok ignored her, instead smashing her insanely big sword down on Jadyn, who planted himself beneath the blow, one knee on the ground and his own blade held in a firm cross-grip.

Romara was seeing stars, her vision was blurring and blood thundered through her skull. The arrow in her side was agony, but she managed to snap it off; she could deal with it later. In a haze of pain, she focused on the fight, just as the vorlok's blade dashed Jadyn's flamberge from his hands. The impact hurled him onto his back, as the tip of the massive weapon raked the ground beside him. Then the giantess lifted her foot, talons unfurling, to slam it down on him.

'*Potentas!*' Jadyn shouted, kicking into a spinning roll that took him out from under that foot, leaving the plunging claws ripping the turf where his head had been. But the hag hadn't finished; she raked sideways and her claws caught his back, catching in his mail and ripping it open, leaving him defenceless, flailing for his lost sword, but it was out of reach.

Romara saw blood spurt from his back and shrieked, '*JADYN—!*'

In that hideous moment, she lost the Eye of Silence. Her glyma-control snapped, her vision went scarlet and her control collapsed like a falling dam – but the power that swept in was like hurling oil onto a fire. Her lungs filled to bursting and her muscles found extra strength, bearing her up and into action at a blinding rate.

The vorlok sensed her coming and tried to hack her apart in mid-air, but Romara exploded past that flailing blade, punching her own rippled blade upwards into the giant woman's mouth. The hilt jammed on yellowed teeth as lethal as a cat's, then the blade's tip burst through the top of her head and she began to collapse. Romara planted her feet and drove the blade in, her vision fixed on the glowing orb on her pommel, the centre of a spiralling swirl of forces that were ripping her apart. It went from pale icy blue to scarlet and she howled in horror and triumph.

The hag's giant skull burst apart in a burst of bloody energy and her body went limp and fell away. A moment later, a male voice rang out in utter horror and grief, wailing, '*MOTHER*—'

Mother?

Romara looked round until she found Jadyn lying on the turf, his back in bloody ribbons. But the fear on his face wasn't for himself, it was all for her.

'*Rom, hold on,*' he pleaded. '*Rom*—'

She couldn't. It was too much.

She rose and faced the flames, because the vyr were still coming, rallying to the remaining draegar a hundred paces down the line. All control gone, Romara ululated and charged them, roaring at her men to follow. The Falcons responded, rushing a ragged bunch of bestial vyr.

The mystery voice bellowed again, sounding utterly despairing, and she veered towards the sound, cutting down a fur-coated woman with a weasel-like visage, then a reptilian man holding a giant cleaver. At last, she saw the archer, standing in the fire, immune to the heat and flames. He was a bear of a man, his bearded face full of grief and fury.

He roared one last time as she bore down on him, swinging his bow at her face, but she was already hacking it in two before she slammed into him, hammering her forehead into his left temple, and he went down like a pole-axed steer. She pivoted and went to behead him while choirs of Serrafim screamed for blood . . .

. . . but somehow she realised what was happening to her and instead drove her blade into the ground, blasting every last vestige of energy into the earth, despite *craving* the glorious ecstasy of killing to go on and on. She tried to find the Eye of Silence, but her vision, now just shades of scarlet, was dimming, and she sank to her knees, her body emptying of strength.

Hold on, she told herself. *Hold on, for Jadyn . . .*

She reached for her lost control, begging for clarity, but the urge to destroy everything wouldn't leave. Again, she discharged power into the ground, again and again, then she threw her blade aside, hugged herself and just held on, trying to keep herself *here . . .*

'Commander?' someone shouted, and she realised the men were staring in dread – whether in fear for her, or of her, she couldn't say.

'Are you all right?' someone asked anxiously.

'I'm fine,' she panted, her eyes and nose seeping blood. 'It's all fine.'

They backed away, suddenly aware of the danger – everyone knew the glyma was a double–edged weapon, that no one could wield for very long.

They think I've lost it . . . I think I have . . .

She sought Jadyn's reassuring face, saw him staring. 'Farm Boy, you okay?' she croaked.

'Aye,' he replied, through gritted teeth. 'Just scratches. You?'

'Yes, yes, I'm fine,' she blurted. 'Everything's fine.'

But it wasn't, and he knew it.

All Vestal knights had a limit. The elobyne gave them a storm of energy, but only the knight's self-discipline prevented that force from becoming a murderous tempest. They all had a limit, and she'd reached hers . . . then gone beyond.

I was a heartbeat from becoming just like that vorlok.

She looked up, her vision clearing a little, and then her heart lurched as she realised that the fight was still going on the other flank, where the draegar had broken through the lines.

She went to rise and go there, but instead the world went sluggish and dark, then the sky lurched and the ground punched her in the back of the head.

Soren watched aghast as his pa staggered towards the charging draegar.

'Pa, no!' he howled, going after him as soldiers closed in, trying to close the rip in their lines, but no one could reach Dael var'Dael in time.

The lion-headed monster backhanded his father contemptuously, six-inch knuckle-horns punching into the old man's chest and hurling him away. Soren howled as his pa went down, crutch and sword flying, face bloodied and torn, but his wild eyes still flashing.

'*Fight*—' he rasped at Soren, '*fight, yer coward*—'

The draegar's foot slammed down on Pa's chest, shattering his ribcage, driving broken bones into his heart and lungs, then it turned on Soren, rearing up, fire blooming in its mouth . . .

. . . just as Soren moved instinctively, the fruit of endless years of training forced on him with demented fervour by his father. *A man must fight*, Dael's voice rasped inside his mind, *so fight!*

The blast of burning vomit seared past him as he hurled himself aside, grabbed his dead father's crutch and blocked the giant swinging axe, just below the massive head. The impact snapped the wood in half, knocking him off-balance. Behind him the refugees scattered, but his mother and sister were petrified, standing there unmoving as the draegar bore down on them.

Soren stood his ground as the draegar's axe swung again, swaying aside at the last moment, as his pa had taught him. He slightly misjudged, for the edge of the blade carved a furrow down his left arm – then he tripped on something behind him and crashed to the stony ground. Seeing a flash of steel, he scrabbled for it, snatching it up as the draegar reared above his mother and sister.

Then the Abuthan knight loosed an arrow that thudded into the giant's side, a shaft with a glowing tip that punched through hide and bone and penetrated the ribcage. The giant vyr-warrior staggered, but still reached a taloned hand towards Uti and Enid.

Ma, startled into movement, tripped – and vanished over the edge of the cliff.

Enid screamed – and fury overwhelmed Soren. His vision blazing, a haze of blood overlaid everything he saw as he charged, shrieking like an avenging angel.

The draegar's axe scythed around, but Soren hurdled it, drawing back the sword he'd grabbed to strike, only realising that it was the dropped flamberge when the orb on the pommel lit up.

For a moment, time froze. Soren had a vision of himself, standing at the pinnacle of a tower, a tiny square of stone, while a cyclone raged around him, shrieking like a horde of demons. It sucked him upwards, dragging him into the maelstrom of screaming air . . .

. . . but he clung on with all his will to the small platform of solid stone, *willed* himself to remain there with all his soul . . .

And suddenly, he was solid and secure on that tower and the sound fell away, leaving him in a place of silence . . .

. . . and then he was back in the real world, driving the incandescent sword into the shoulder of the draegar, punching it all the way through until the monster jolted, going rigid – its chest filled with flame, and as it crashed down on its back, Soren fell onto it, driving the flamberge deeper in as the flayed lion face roared at him . . .

And then it went limp and lifeless.

Soren stared at that ghastly face as it emptied, seeing a contorted, terrified face reflected in the empty eyes. Then the Abuthan stormed up, shouting in amazed horror, but Soren's hearing was receding, his sight becoming just a smear. He had a moment to wonder if he'd been wounded and hadn't noticed, before he too crashed to the ground and the world fell away.

'Elysia, have mercy,' Jadyn Kaen panted, rolling Romara over onto her side, taking in a rip in her side that had been seared closed, her undershirt soaked in blood and her battered face smeared in gore.

Unconscious, but she was still breathing, though blood was dripping from beneath her eyelids.

She lost it . . . She's lost her control . . . It was one damned fight too many . . .

He bowed his head, sick to the stomach. A Vestal who lost control was a menace to all. They'd lock her up and he'd never see her again. There'd be no retirement, no honourable discharge. The blissful future he'd always known they'd have disintegrated before his eyes.

'Sier?' Argon Roper's voice intruded. 'Seneschal Kaen! You must see to Siera Romara.'

Jadyn's mind stalled. 'I . . . she . . .'

The centurion gripped his shoulder, his rough face torn by grief and denial. 'Sier, she's fine. *She's fine.* She's just wounded, she is. Let the healer tend her.'

Their eyes met and Jadyn realised what the sergeant was offering. He'd lie about this – they all would – because they respected her, and they knew he loved her.

He bit his lip, because this was the Order and rules existed for good reasons. *If she goes mad like that again, she could kill innocent people.* But his love for her overrode all of those considerations. They'd graduated together, served together and forged a bond in every way but the one people thought mattered most. For a Vestal knight, chastity saved lives, preventing the tumult of glyma-energy passion from becoming destructive. They'd held to their vows, but their love transcended all that. It was a current that chained them together, heart to heart, soul to soul.

I can't lose her . . . We have a life together awaiting us.

'Thank you, Centurion,' he replied, regaining control. 'Let's do that.'

Roper was already waving in their chief healer. 'We'll handle it, Seneschal. You'll need to take control of the century.'

Jadyn blinked, his numbed brain catching up. *Akka on High, I'm in charge. For now.*

That thought forced him to put aside his terror for Romara and leave her to Healer Burfitt, while he started down the line, checking each wounded man in turn, men whose quartered black-and-white tabards were stained red, shaking hands and wishing them well, making his way to where the draegar had been slain. When it fell, the remaining attackers had lost their ferocity, and those who hadn't fled had been cut down.

At the sight of a body in a pure white tabard lying motionless, he broke into a run, thinking, *Dear Elysia, who have we lost?*

He pulled up short, stifling a cry as he recognised Ghaneen Suul. Grief smote him, but he forced himself to think as a commander and swept the scene with his gaze. The draegar lay nearby, a flamberge buried right up to the sword-catcher six inches from the hilt. The blade was Ghaneen's, and the pommel-orb was still glowing.

He must have died as he gave the demon-spawn its deathblow. He died a hero.

Ghaneen had never been easy company; like many young knights he was arrogant in his power and contemptuous of lessers, but they'd fought alongside each other for too long for his death not to hurt.

Jadyn turned to examine the dead draegar, which had already sloughed its dire form, becoming someone who could have been anyone's father or brother. He fought the urge to hack the body apart, the residue of his own glyma use, while wondering how an ordinary-looking man could become such a monster.

By losing control, just as Romara did; that was the chilling answer. Tears stung his eyes. *Regardless of whether we can cover it up, it's too late for her. She'll have to retire now. Our future's just been torched . . .*

Swallowing hard, he sought out Obanji, the person everyone in the Falcons went to when life knifed them in the back. The Abuthan veteran was kneeling over someone: the brown-skinned youth who'd guided them here. Beneath the boy's natural colouring he'd gone pale as a ghost, and his breathing was shallow. Obanji was holding his wrist, glyma-light in his fingertips, feeding energy gently into the boy's system.

'What are you doing?' Jadyn asked.

Obanji looked up, his expression a blend of grief and wonder, then he indicated another corpse; the boy's father, whose chest had been crushed. 'When Ghaneen fell, Soren picked up his flamberge and it came to life. It was he who killed the draegar.'

Jadyn swallowed. 'But didn't he say he'd failed the tests?'

'Aye. But the tests aren't always reliable.' The Abuthan indicated the young man's sister, a copper-skinned, big-eyed girl of maybe twelve. 'Here, lass, where's your mother?'

Her face was ashen as she gestured at the cliff's edge. 'Ma . . .'

She started sobbing uncontrollably. Elindhu joined them, her weathered face full of concern. She caught the girl's shoulders and set about calming her down.

'Her name's Enid,' she reported after a moment. 'Her mother went over . . .'

Jadyn went to the edge, and saw a body rolling in the waves below:

impossible to recover without a major effort, and his first loyalty had to be to his men.

Centurion Roper gave a full report: although the bodies strewing the clifftop were mostly dead vyr, they'd lost several of their own, mostly to the vorlok and the draegar, and many more were injured from burns and bites. Jadyn took it in, gave the necessary orders, then returned to Obanji's side. The Abuthan veteran had removed his helm and was running his fingers through his closely cropped grey curls. He was nearly forty, an extraordinarily long career for a Vestal knight, and had pretty much seen it all.

'How's the boy, Obanji?'

'He used the glyma, so under the Code, we'll have to take him in.' Obanji glanced at the girl Elindhu was comforting. 'It's her I feel for most; she's lost both parents and now her only brother will be taken away, too.'

'We'll see her to a convent on the mainland. It's all we can do.'

Jadyn headed back to where Romara was being tended. While Burfitt, the healer, worked on her, Centurion Roper was examining the female vorlok, now an ordinary-looking woman in shredded robes. She was perhaps fifty years old, with long tangled grey hair. She didn't look evil, but evil she'd been.

They couldn't remain here: the vyr might be dead or gone, but the fires they'd kindled were still burning, enveloping them in choking smoke. 'Up, Falcons,' he shouted. 'Let's get back to the beach. Move!'

Argon Roper took up the order. In moments they were all moving again, herding the refugees on towards Long Bay, carrying their dead and wounded.

He was about to follow when he saw the vyr archer Romara had struck down, lying at the edge of the smouldering brush; the man twitched.

Jagatai, that bastard's still alive.

The fire below, now a full-on inferno, was beginning to roar up the slopes. If he left the man, he'd die in agony, burned alive while the air was sucked from his lungs. But still he hesitated.

The Code forbade any form of mercy for vyr, and all communication with them was banned; not even knights or mages could question them. *But while everyone else was turning into half-beasts and monsters, this man stayed rational enough to use a bow, and when that vorlok died, he called out 'Mother' . . .*

A foolish idea struck him: if the man wasn't a vyr, but merely a human ally, then *maybe* he could be a useful prisoner. Questioning a vyr, especially a vorlok or draegar, was strictly forbidden by the Vestal Code, for they were known to be so beguiling they could corrupt even a virtuous knight. But this man might be someone they could legally interrogate.

Dear Akka, I have so many questions . . .

So he conjured *Potentas* for strength, because the man was much bigger than him, heaved him over one shoulder and set off staggering down the hill.

Centurion Roper hurried back to meet him, clearly worried Jadyn was doing something reckless in reaction to Romara's plight. 'Sier? We can't – The Code—'

'He was with the enemy, but he never changed,' Jadyn said. 'We're taking him prisoner. The lictor in Port Gaudien will want to talk to him.' He gripped the centurion's shoulder. 'I want him aboard our ship when we sail.'

Roper's face cleared. Handing him over to a lictor was fine: they virtually wrote the laws. 'I'll see to it, Sier.'

Jadyn oversaw the prisoner's bindings, before heading off in search of Romara. He found her awake but groggy, her eyes already blackening as Healer Burfitt straightened her nose. In a thick, nasal slur, she managed, 'Y'righ? I's a'bit jagged, righ' nah.'

'You stay down,' he told her. 'Burf, check her vision – concussion can kill.'

'I know me job, Sier Jadyn,' the healer grumbled.

Jadyn studied her, wondering how he'd cope with command if she couldn't go on. *She's a natural leader, while I'm just a plodder.*

Burfitt had turned his attention to the wound in her side and was digging for the arrowhead. Jadyn squatted beside her, holding her hand to help her through the pain. Her eyes, though puffed-up and discoloured, were clear of blood, at least.

'You okay?' she murmured.

'I'm fine,' Jadyn told her, only now remembering the gashes in his back, which were throbbing painfully.

'Roper says we've got a prisoner,' Burfitt noted. Clearly the healer disapproved.

Romara demanded details and Jadyn explained, 'He didn't change form, so he's not a true vyr. The Code is silent on such a thing, so I'm taking him to the lictor.'

She met his eyes. 'Fine, but no one talks to him. I mean it, Jadyn: *no one.*'

She knows I want to question him myself. After ten years of frontline fighting, he burned for some kind of explanation for this senseless rebellion. *For decades the vyr have plagued us, but we still don't really know why.*

Romara winced as Burfitt worked his tongs into her side. 'Jadyn, he called her "Mother". If he's a vorlok's son, he's possibly one himself. You know the rules.'

He did: any captured vyr must be instantly executed. No questioning, except if sanctioned by a lictor. No exceptions, no extenuating circumstances.

'But he didn't change or use magic,' Jadyn repeated. 'He's kin by blood, but not by sorcery: we all know that the Gift isn't hereditary. We could learn—'

'The Code is vague, yes: which means the lictor could choose to interpret it whichever way he likes,' Romara interrupted. 'You do *not* want to end up on the wrong side of one of those pricks.'

'How are we supposed to know what we're fighting if—?' Jadyn threw up his hands, then swallowed the rest of his tirade: the men-at-arms didn't need to see his frustration. *Know your Enemy*, the philosophers said, but the Hierophant apparently wanted them to fight blind.

Then Burfitt pulled out the arrowhead and Romara made an agonised sound through clenched teeth. 'No poison,' the healer noted, 'but we'll still need to cauterise the wound.'

'Oh goody,' she muttered caustically. 'Another scar.'

'Who's gonna see it, holy virgin?' Burfitt chuckled, with a distinct lack of reverence.

'Jag off,' Romara snorted, pulling out her dagger and handing it to Jadyn hilt-first. 'Be a darling and heat this up, Jadyn. You go and find someone else to play with, Burf.'

Burfitt gave her a wry salute, looking at Jadyn. 'Let's see your back first, Sier.'

Jadyn's mail shirt was still hanging off his back and he knew there were some deep cuts and tears, which the glyma had numbed for a bit.

'You'll need stitches, Sier,' Burfitt told him after a moment, 'but it's not urgent. I'll come back later.'

He went off, while Jadyn settled beside Romara, heating her knife with glyma-energy to sear her wound. She bore it with fortitude, biting down on a leather scabbard so as not to scream, her eyes bulging. Afterwards, she could barely speak.

'You'd think after so many wounds they wouldn't hurt any more,' she groaned, finally.

'Pain's still pain.' He smiled at her. 'How are you doing now?'

'Fine,' she said, looking away. 'I'll need thicker make-up at my next ball, but—'

'No, how *are* you?' Jadyn insisted, meeting her gaze. 'I saw ... your face ... your eyes flashed red.' He dropped his voice, and added, 'Everyone saw, Rom. *Everyone* saw.'

Romara flinched at that awful memory, the worst part being how terrifyingly wonderful it had felt to lose control. But that was the insidious part: losing control was self-destructive and corrupting, but it felt *so damned good.*

I'll be locked away in a Convalesium, drugged until I can't remember who I am.

The Order were ruthless with those who fell from grace – they had to be, because a knight who lost control was as deadly as the vyr they fought. But the Order was clever too: accumulated pensions were forfeited if you succumbed to the rage, unless you submitted to treatment, in which case you could assign the pension to someone else. The whispers about the Convalesiums were dire: they were supposed to be places of healing, but no one ever seemed to recover.

She'd never thought it would happen to her, not with Jadyn's devotion to anchor her. *But when I saw him go down like that, I exploded . . .*

'I'll give my pension to you,' she said hoarsely, seizing his hand and clasping it to her. 'All of it. My family are dreadful, they mean nothing to me, but you—'

'Hush,' he whispered, meeting her stinging eyes. 'Roper's passed the word. No one's going to say anything. They all respect you too much. We're going to get off this damned rock, and when we get to Gaudien, you'll take retirement and walk away. And so will I.'

She shifted his hand to her heart, which was thumping madly. 'You mean that, Jadyn?'

Because if you do, having to retire and become the dreaded Lady Challys will be bearable.

'I do. I love you, Romara,' he said, huskily. 'Coros can burn, so long as I have you.'

A massive lump welled up in her throat, and before she knew it, she was sobbing against his chest, unable to believe that her life was being torn apart like this.

Perhaps it's destiny; I was going to have to leave the Order anyway, now that my brother is dead. She'd hoped against hope that Reshar would father a child before he died, so she'd never have to see her family again. But if she was going to have to be Lady Challys, then only with Jadyn at her side could she endure it.

And if it pisses off my snooty family, it might even be fun, she thought grimly.

Her parents would try to force her to marry some shit-wrapped-in-silk nobleman, but she'd defy them and marry Jadyn the moment he could secure his discharge. Her Farm Boy, suddenly gentrified? It would be perfect.

That problem solved, she surrendered to the lurking oblivion.

Jadyn laid Romara down again, feeling like he was in a play and at any moment someone would tell him that he'd got his lines wrong.

He called Burfitt in again, to ensure Romara wasn't concussed after all, then went to find Obanji.

He found the Abuthan sitting with the young man, Soren var'Dael, who clearly also had southern ancestry. *The last thing we've got time for right now is to deal with an initiate*, Jadyn thought, but the Code was clear: it was required.

'Soren, I'm Jadyn. Has Obanji explained what happens now?'

We drag you away from all you know and turn you into a killing machine.

The young man looked stunned, an echo of the disbelief he'd just seen in Romara's eyes. His life was also turned upside down. He also saw loss, and anger. He knew the sort: this one would be another supernova, a star that blazed and quickly winked out.

'My sister—' the boy blurted, but Jadyn was already waving away his objection.

'She'll be looked after,' he interrupted. 'You have manifested the Gift, and under the Vestal Code you must be inducted into the Order. Obanji, will you sponsor him?'

The Abuthan looked like he wanted to refuse, but he bowed his head. 'Aye.'

'Then as acting Commander of the Falcon Century, I formally invite you to join the Order of the Vestments of Elysia Divina. I name you Soren var'Dael, Initiate. Do you accept?'

Soren looked at him. 'What do I say?'

'Yes. No isn't permitted.'

'Uh, yes, then.'

'Good lad.'

'It's only until we can get you to a Vestal bastion,' Obanji put in. 'After that, you go into the system. You'll be assigned a training bastion and get educated properly – not just in weaponry and glyma, but reading, writing, numbers. It'll be the making of you, as it was me.'

The boy wore a glassy-eyed look of disbelief, but raised no objection. His parents were dead and his sister was destined for a nunnery, so perhaps he realised that there was no alternative.

The hard truth is, this is the best outcome for him, Jadyn thought. *If he hadn't manifest like he did, he'd be dead, so would his sister, and perhaps more of the Falcons.*

'Lad,' Obanji said, 'once you graduate, you'll be paid regularly, enough to see your sister into comfort, and able to make a good marriage. And you'll never want for anything.'

Except for peace and love, Jadyn thought. *You'll never know those while you wear the tabard. And their lack will probably break you, as it breaks us all, in the end . . . even my Romara.*

2

Forbidden Questions

The Vestal Knights

The Knights of the Vestments of Elysia Divina, colloquially known as the Vestal knights, derive their arcane power – called glyma – from elobyne crystals. The glyma augments otherwise unremarkable magical potential, giving them super-human strength, speed and endurance. Only the demonic vyr, who corrupt that same power, can rival them.

THE ANNALS OF TALMONT, 1397

Coastal Vandarath
Summer 1472

Soren var'Dael slumped against the ship's rails, keeping out of the way of the sailors as they did whatever it was sailors do. His attention was on the smoke-shrouded island behind them slowly falling beneath the horizon.

Avas, my home . . . all I've ever known . . .

He would have died before admitting it, but he was utterly terrified. His mind was racked by his last sight of his parents alive, and the horrified look on his sister's face as she was torn from his arms. She was bound for a refugee camp in Beradin, but this ship was going to Gaudien. He might never see her again.

As I will never see Ma again. Fish will devour her, the current will pull her bones apart.

And he would never hear his father's voice shouting about footwork, about keeping his parry high and never over-lunging. About how he wasn't a man unless he could fight.

I'm going to be a knight now, he told that angry man's ghost. *Or die trying.*

The latter was far more likely. Everyone knew that Vestal training was lethal, that many never made it. The glyma ate your soul, if you couldn't leash your anger . . . and right now, anger was all he could feel. He'd spent all his life being spat at, punched and insulted for his mixed blood and race. He couldn't imagine that the Order would be any different.

A heavy hand fell on his shoulder and he turned to find the burly Abuthan knight. Sier Obanji Vost's lined face was framed by cropped greying curls and scars around his throat. His eyes were solemn and sad, but he had a kindly air. As the embodiment of his ambitions – an Abuthan Vestal knight – the man was already his hero.

'You all right, boy?' Obanji asked.

'Aye,' Soren lied, trying to look brave.

Obanji clearly saw through him. 'Enid will be fine. The Akkanite Sisterhood will look after her. You will see her again, you know – and you can write too, once you learn how.'

Right now, that was hard to believe. 'Why couldn't I go with her?'

'Why, do you want to be a nun?'

He couldn't help snorting in amusement. 'I could'a looked after her, found work—'

'No, you couldn't,' Obanji interrupted. 'You manifested power through that orb and killed a draegar. It's in the Code: anyone with the Gift must join the Order. You're bound for a life of glory, boy.'

The dry irony in Obanji's voice was clear, but the words spoke to Soren's inner world. Pa had been obsessed with the knights, speaking of them with equal measures of hate and envy. Soren had loathed his father, and he still couldn't grieve – all his tears had been for his ma and sister, not for that brutal, bullying shell of a man – but he couldn't deny that the killing thrust that slew the draegar had been all his father's training.

But the energy I drew on came from me, he thought anxiously. *Everyone says that the glyma can kill you.* 'I don't know if I'm worthy,' he worried.

'You don't have a choice, boy. It's a mandate, straight from the

Throne of Pearl. You have glyma, you're for the Order – or condemned as a potential vyr.' Obanji put a comforting hand on his shoulder. 'It's not a bad life, and once you've learned to control the glyma, the world will open up for you. You'll have a good ten years, maybe more, until you can't control it any more.'

Soren swallowed. 'If I live that long.'

Obanji patted his shoulder. 'I'm in my late thirties, boy, and I'm still going. Whatever you've heard, most knights retire younger than me with a healthy pension and a good life before them. Then you can reunite with your sister, find a wife and settle down. You're one of Akka's chosen, boy: Fortune has smiled on you.'

Soren forced a smile, but he didn't feel chosen or lucky. He felt doomed.

Romara was still unconscious, but according to Burfitt, it was down to exhaustion and overdrawing on her powers, not concussion. Jadyn thanked him and left her in his care, and just before dusk, went on deck. Obanji was with Soren, explaining the Order to him, and Elindhu was working with the captain and navigator on finding a helpful wind to speed their journey.

He watched the sailors at work as the dull scarlet glow of Avas fell into the sea. The dark silhouettes of the other ships in the flotilla vanished into the gloom until all that was left were their lanterns, staring at him like vorlok eyes in the night. But the three moons were rising, the eerie Skull first, then the Dragon Egg and the Eye, painting the sea in copper hues. The continent was burning and their lives were turning to ash.

Akka, Elysia, grant us your mercy, he prayed. *And forgive what I must do.*

He knew all the cautionary tales about retired Vestals failing in their new lives; many sold up and bought illegal elobyne blades, becoming mercenaries, then ended up being hunted down by their former comrades. But he would never go down that route.

Our pensions won't be enough, but I was raised on a farm. I'll make it work.

But before that happened, there was something he had to do.

The vyr rebellion had been going on for decades, but their foes – where they came from, how they recruited and why they fought at all – were still a mystery. Of late, the gaps in his knowledge were preying on Jadyn's mind. It galled him to not fully understand why their enemy fought; and if he and Romara were retiring, he'd never know – unless he asked questions now.

Damn this, I'll do it.

The decision made, he pulled rank and commandeered the ship-master's cabin, then had Argon Roper bring the captive to him. The centurion brought in the gagged prisoner, tied him to a chair and then left, giving Jadyn warning looks he chose to ignore. Once they were alone, Jadyn focused on the prisoner, who was fully awake and glaring, his gaze sullen and wretched.

His cheeks are tearstained, Jadyn noted. *Do vyr cry?*

The Code demanded that he surrender this man, unquestioned, to a lictor as soon as possible. If he did this, he'd lose this chance to understand the war that had cost them so much.

Akka, Father of Knowledge, you owe me this.

Holding onto that thought, he sat opposite the man, studying him. He was tall, built like a bull, caked in soot and streaked in blood, his left eye almost closed from Romara's blow. From his colouring, he was a northerner, but under his furs, his arms and legs and face were deeply tanned and weathered. He had surprisingly soft brown eyes, not full of madness as Jadyn had expected.

'What's your name?' he asked the prisoner.

'You killed my mother,' the man snarled.

'She was trying to kill us.'

'She was fighting for our lands.'

Glyma had a short temper, and despite his placid nature, Jadyn wasn't immune to its sting. 'She was a vorlok,' he snapped. 'You're burning your own lands, forcing tens of thousands into exile. Are you proud, you bastard?'

The big man looked round. 'Where's the lictor? You aren't one – I saw you fighting. Lictors only come out when it's safe, so they can torture the helpless.'

'There's no lictor here,' Jadyn replied. 'Just me.'

'Oh, so you're out for some sly revenge, are you?' He spat at Jadyn's feet.

'No. I just want to understand why you're burning your own land? Why would you turn yourself into a monster? Help me understand.'

'Understand? You're an imperial slaughter-whore – and you're the cause of all this, you stinking hypocrite, do you not understand that? Just send in the blasted lictor and have done.'

It took time to force his anger back down, but somehow, Jadyn managed. 'I want to understand,' he repeated.

Something in Jadyn's need must have got through, because the prisoner sagged in his bindings, his face becoming more calculating. 'My mother was Fritha. I am Gram Larch, a trapper from Bamford. I have no living kin now. You can't hurt me any more.'

'The lictor can,' Jadyn reminded him. 'But I'm not here for that.'

'Are you not? I think the only difference between you and the lictor is that you're a weakling who doesn't know how to torture a man properly.'

He's trying to goad me into killing him, Jadyn realised. *I must stay calm.* He was about to repeat his first question when the door opened and Romara, pale-skinned, black-eyed, lurched in and grabbed the wall. 'Jadyn, wha' you doin'?' she slurred.

He tried to get her to sit, but she shoved him off. 'I said, *Seneschal*, what are you doing?'

'He's not a vyr,' Jadyn answered. 'It's okay to question him—'

'The lictor won' see it like that.'

'Jag the lictor! Ten years we've fought these scum and I want to know why—'

'We all do—'

'Then leave, and let me find out.'

She folded her arms across her chest. 'I'm staying. Ask your blasted questions.'

He went to argue, but Romara was clearly in one of her Lady Challys moods, so it was futile. And in any case, she was just as curious as him, he knew.

'All right,' he sighed, turning back to Gram Larch. 'Why are you fighting?'

The prisoner glared up at them, his eyes ranging from face to face, lingering most on Romara's broken-nosed, black-eyed visage, which had a lofty kind of grace. 'That's your question? Don't you know the rules? The only question the lictors sanction is this one: *Who else do you know among the vyr?* They don't give a shit about why.'

'Why?' Jadyn asked again.

Gram frowned. 'Because we're trying to save us all.'

Romara's face hardened with contempt. 'You're saving the world by burning it?'

The trapper gave her a cold look in response. 'Jeer all you like, Vestal, but it's a fact. The End of All Things is coming, the end of us all. We're trying to prevent it.'

Jadyn was trying hard to comprehend. 'If the End is coming, surely it's your doing? You're the ones setting the wheat plantations and the pine stands alight – do you not know how deadly such fires can be?'

'We do light them,' Gram admitted. 'Jagat, we've got no choice. We must destroy the shards, before they destroy us.'

The elobyne shards planted by the Triple Empire covered the empire so the Vestal knights could replenish their powers, no matter where they were. Destroying them, weakening the knights, was always the vyr's first priority when they attacked.

'Liar. You destroyed all of Avas, not just the shards,' Romara accused. 'We have a power given by Akka the Father, while you and your mother serve the Devourer.'

'There is no Devourer—'

'The Devourer's first lie is to deny her own existence,' Romara recited back.

'There's no talking to you; you've already made up your mind.' He faced Jadyn. 'You're listening, she's just ranting. Get her out.'

'Jag off,' Romara snarled. '*I'm* the Knight-Commander here.'

Gram glared at her, then he exhaled, bringing himself back under control. 'Listen, then: ever since those damned elobyne shards were placed in our lands, our lakes and rivers started drying up; animals, birds and plants began vanishing from our forests and meadows. They're ruining our world – they must be destroyed.'

Romara gave a harsh, derisive laugh. '*That's* your truth? Jagat, man, don't you know anything? The "elobyne destroys the land" fallacy has been utterly disproved. *There's no truth in it.* We're entering a Fire Age, part of a natural cycle, not an apocalyptic crises. Our world has been going through these cycles since time began. Our scholars have explained it all.'

Gram looked up at the wooden ceiling, as if his patience were being tried past bearing. 'You're the ones peddling lies: your scholars *lie*, even though they know the truth.'

Romara looked ready to hit the man, so Jadyn laid a warning hand on her arm. 'Hear him out, then decide,' he murmured. 'Even lies can be instructive.'

She glared at him, but remained silent.

'Tell us *your* truth,' Jadyn said to the trapper.

'All right,' he growled, 'but you won't care for it. I was born on Avas. I've never left the isle in my life, not until now. My mother Fritha bore me when she was fifteen, to a trapper she eloped with. When he died, I took over, but feeding us got harder every year – springs were drying up, fields going barren. Everyone knew that it all started when an elobyne shard was planted in the valley. Folks tried to have it removed, but the imperial scholars said no. Yes, I've heard the blather about a "Fire Age", but we knew it was the shard ruining us.'

'The Hierophant ordered an imperial investigation into such claims,' Jadyn replied evenly. 'It totally disproved any connection between the planting of elobyne shards and the ecology. The only deserts in Coros are outside the empire – think on that.'

'I don't give a jagat about foreign deserts. It's my home being destroyed that concerns me.'

'There are legitimate channels for complaints,' Jadyn reminded him.

'"Channels for complaints"?' Gram scoffed. 'Are you jagging mad? Good folks are reduced to poverty for *daring* to voice their concerns – even the mayor of Cherenton got flogged for going to the governor after Lake Roishan went dry.'

'That was bad farming—'

'No, it was your jagging shards – that's what the scholar Nilis said, and I believe him.'

Jadyn's heart thumped. 'You've heard *Nilis Evandriel* speak?'

Evandriel was a renegade scholar who'd been plaguing the outer reaches of the empire for more than a dozen years, spreading lies about the Hierophant and elobyne. Despite being declared a heretic and condemned to death *in absentia*, the commoners had closed ranks about him, so he'd eluded capture thus far.

'Yes, I have,' Gram answered. 'Me and Ma both. He convinced her to join the rebellion. She knew she had the Gift, see, but she didn't want to join your people.'

'Nilis Evandriel has been discredited,' Romara broke in.

'Who told you that? Your superiors?'

'Aye!' Romara replied. 'Because Evandriel is a liar.'

Sadly, some of what he says, especially about the complaints, rings true, Jadyn had to concede. Governor Durand might have been a fair man, but he'd only recently arrived and his predecessor had been brutal. But as recently as three months ago an imperial scholar had arrived on Avas to report yet again that the shards were safe.

The vyr are trying to dismantle the shard network, the scholar had told an assembly of Avas elders. *They spread their lies among the disaffected to weaken us all, but it's they who burn the crops, not us.* Even in the face of such research, many preferred to believe the lies. *Sadly, this interrogation is only reinforcing the fact that our enemies are deluded.*

'How does burning crops and destroying farms help anyone?' Jadyn asked.

Gram flinched. 'It's unavoidable.'

Romara snorted in derision. 'Really?'

'It takes tremendous heat to crack a shard – it's something to do with the elobyne sucking in the heat until it can't take any more. Forests can grow back, farms can be rebuilt, now the shards are gone – in a few years, Avas will be resettled. Our people are prepared to martyr themselves for the greater good.'

'*Martyred?*' Romara hissed. 'How dare y—'

'How dare I? My mother died to help us be free,' Gram fired back. 'My mother, whom I loved, but who lost herself to the rage and paid the price. The *martyr's* price.'

Romara squared up to him, glowering. 'Your mother is being Devoured even now.'

Jadyn stepped between the two and put a hand on Romara's shoulder. 'He's deluded and knows no better,' he told her, willing her to stay calm. 'He'll pay for his sins. The lictor will decide his fate.'

'Good. So are we done?' She dropped her voice and added, 'Was this worth risking your career?' Then she turned and stomped out.

Was it worth it? Jadyn wondered. *It merely confirmed that our enemies are misinformed and being manipulated.* He turned back to Gram, thinking about Nilis Evandriel, the scholar who'd apparently fuelled this insurrection. *Are the old lies about elobyne truly all that's behind this? Surely there must be more?*

'Tell me about your mother,' he said abruptly.

Gram put his head in his hand a moment, visibly fighting grief, then composed himself and looked up. 'She was a gentle soul. You won't credit that, but she was. Even when her life fell apart, she did all she could for me. We lived hand to mouth until her cousin took us in. But he made us work for him and he—'

He stopped, took another breath and went on, 'He treated my mother like his personal slave and got another child on her. Then he drank himself into a grave and we all danced on it. By then I knew how to trap and hunt, and Ma worked the land. But the shard drained life from the soil, sure as a leech sucks blood, until we lost the farm. There's naught there now but ash and ruin.'

These peasants always blame their failures on others, the scholar had told the Falcon pentacle, but Jadyn kept his mouth shut about that. 'Go on.'

Gram's face became haunted. 'My sister ended up in a tavern in Cherenton, got knifed and died. Ma had realised that she had your Gift after touching a crystal in the Weave, so we took to the hills, and lived off the land.'

'She should have come forward. Akka on High, we're screaming out for new blood. Even at her age she could have found a role as a mage.'

'Are you mad?' Gram snorted. 'We *hate* you Vestals . . .'

Jadyn bit back an angry retort and instead asked, 'What happened next?'

'We were terrified, living in constant fear of being betrayed and executed by the authorities – or of Ma burning the place down. But she learned how to control the rages and involuntary eruptions of . . . weirdness.'

'She just needed training.' Jadyn sighed. 'Don't tell me, I already know you hate us. It's just a blasted waste.'

'Not in our eyes,' Gram retorted. 'We hid out until a vorlok woman found us. She took us into her coven and treated us well, but Ma changed as she learned to use her power. She grew hard, and her rage ignited at any moment, but she directed it at all things imperial.'

'In other words, she went mad and turned on her own kind,' Jadyn pointed out. 'Thousands died on Avas, and tens of thousands lost everything they had.'

'Their lives were already ruined.' Gram looked up at Jadyn, his eyes pleading. 'We aren't what you think, truly: we're not monsters – we're *angry*. We're not crazy, either – Ma was rational, right to the very end.'

'We saw what she was.'

'No, you saw her rage – the darkness.' Gram fell silent.

Jadyn decided there was nothing else to learn from this man. 'Nilis Evandriel lied to you,' he told the trapper. 'You should have trusted the empire. We get most things right.'

Gram shook his head. 'No, he told the truth and had to flee for his life. He's a prophet.'

Jadyn found himself simmering in anger at the man's obstinacy. 'You have no proof—'

'Not true. Nilis Evandriel talked about a spell called "Oculus Tempus" – he said it enables the caster to look backwards through time, not at small things, but at big things – the shape of the land, the seasons passing; as if seeing through the eyes of the gods. He said it proved the effect of the elobyne on the land.'

Oculus Tempus ... Jadyn didn't know the spell, but he wasn't a mage. 'I'll ask.'

'Be careful,' Gram warned. 'He said the lictors forbid it.'

'Perhaps, but you've still given me nothing that looks like proof.'

'You dismiss everything I've said as a lie. I have nothing else. But I warn you, say "Oculus Tempus" in the wrong company and you'll be in a world of trouble, Vestal.'

I'm a knight, not a mage or a scholar or a lictor. My duty is to obey those who know more than I, not to question them.

'I'll think about what you've said,' Jadyn answered, which was true; Gram's words would haunt him. He turned his mind to security, contrasting the hideous giantess he'd slain to the placid-looking woman she'd reverted to, wondering whether this man might conceal a similar power, even though he'd not shown it before. If Gram Larch had some facility with fire, he'd be a danger to them all on board this wooden vessel. 'Are you also a vorlok?' he asked him.

'No.'

'Then how did you survive the flames unscathed?'

'When we join a vorlok's coven, we all gain something ... but I couldn't protect Ma unless I remained calm, so I held back, relying on my bow.' He bit his lip, then sagged in his chair. 'So I suppose, yes, I am a potential vorlok, but I have never manifested that power.' He looked rueful. 'You really shouldn't be talking to me, Vestal. The lictor won't like it. You'd be better off tossing me into the sea, so I can't reveal our conversation to him.'

Jadyn grimaced, regretting his actions, but done was done. 'I'm not a murderer.'

'It's your funeral,' Gram grunted. 'The truth is, yesterday Ma finally succumbed to the madness – just like your woman did. I saw her eyes. Like you, we can hold it in abeyance a while, but eventually we break, then we're lost. It just takes less time with us than for you. I wanted to spare Ma that fate, so my last arrow was intended for her.'

Thankful he wasn't a lictor and required to adjudicate, Jadyn decided he'd heard enough. He stepped outside, put his back to the door and breathed deeply.

Romara was waiting in the narrow corridor for him, caught between denial and despair, now that her temper had abated. 'Did you hear?' Jadyn asked her.

'Aye, but I don't believe him. We're the shield against the night: it's in our oath. Our scholars have done great things – they have served all humankind. Nilis Evandriel is a heretic who's inspired a revolt so destructive it threatens our whole civilisation. I know who I believe in.'

'I know, I know . . .'

'And as for this "Oculus Tempus" – forget you ever heard those words.'

'Because they're true?'

'How would I know? I'm not a mage. There's hundreds of spells that are forbidden, and I don't know any of them. But it's not worth the risk. Why would our scholars, who live in our world too, lie about something so important? If the elobyne really was dangerous, they'd know – they'd be taking steps.'

What sort of steps? Jadyn wondered. *Transitioning us away from the use of elobyne? Or just eradicating all dissent?* 'Surely it's our duty to ask our superiors about this?'

'No, that would be suicidal,' Romara replied. 'Trust me on this.'

He nodded glumly; she was highborn and knew about court politics. Such matters always confused him, turning his black-and-white world grey. 'Of course I trust you.'

'I refuse to be believe we're in the wrong,' she told him. 'We don't burn villages and farms – we're the opposite of that man and his witch-brood. You must never forget that.'

Her certainty steadied him, but underneath, he could still hear her simmering rage, and that terrified him. He gathered her into his arms and hugged, trying to impart his love. 'Rom, just let it go,' he whispered. 'None of it matters any more. Just sleep . . .'

Just sleep with me, he almost blurted out, but he stopped himself. So soon after her breakdown, and with his own emotions in turmoil, it would be a dreadful mistake. Even if both retired tomorrow, the day they could finally consummate their lifelong love was still far in the future, when they were both purged of the glyma by time and discipline.

She understood. 'You should rest, too. You work yourself too hard. But Jadyn, that flash during the fight ... I've only got a short time left in the Order.'

He nodded numbly. 'Nothing lasts forever,' he said. 'We knew this day might come. Just hold yourself together another few days, and you'll be free of all this.'

'I know. I'll hold steady, I promise you.' She stroked his face, looking up at him wistfully. 'Tomorrow, I'll resume command and handle the briefings with the grandmaster in Port Gaudien. I'm better at that sort of shit than you, anyway.'

'That'll be a relief.' He indicated the captain's cabin. 'I'll have the prisoner removed, then you should use the cabin. Lady Challys deserves her own space.'

'Such a gentleman. You'll make someone a wonderful husband one day,' she quipped, the old semi-joke that told him they were back on familiar emotional ground, their bond intact.

One day we'll be free to love, he thought. *Let it be soon.*

3

Heretical Knowledge

The Edict

*Until Jovan Lux proclaimed his Edict of One People under One God, war
savaged us. At times we Zynochi dominated; at others the Abuthan or the
Hytali stood first. But now, under the peace of Akka, all men are equal, a true
brotherhood – and indeed sisterhood – in which only merit and dedication
to humanity matters.*

CALIPHA SEERA GUNDA, BURDOK, ZYNOCHIA, 1466

*The calipha is deluded. The only things that matter under the Edict are wealth
and power, and never have those two things been more unequally distributed.
The Edict must be broken, before it's too late for us all.*

NILIS EVANDRIEL, RENEGADE SCHOLAR, 1467

Port Gaudien, Vandarath
Summer 1472

Romara watched from the railings as a bound Gram Larch was led
down the gangplank, into the mob that had gathered when word
went round of a vyr prisoner. Rotten fruit pelted him, then a woman
took it further, hurling a bucket of piss and faeces over him.

He deserves it, she told himself. *We should never have spoken to him,
legal or not.*

It was fear fuelling her vindictive mood, she knew. She was terrified
that someone would tell the local lictor that forbidden questions had
been asked, and he'd rip apart her world – that world being Jadyn.

So long as we survive the debriefing with the local grandmaster, I can retire unscathed, she resolved. *So long as no one says anything about my …* lapse, *we're fine*.

She refused to blame Jadyn for the interview with Gram Larch, though it would never have happened had she been fully herself. But her breakdown on Avas had shaken her, and left her seeking understanding of what the vyr were.

But it only confirmed that they're deluded fools, she thought morosely.

Rather than watch the mob, she walked to the seaward side of the vessel and tried to prepare herself. *There's a power-mad lictor here in Port Gaudien*, she remembered: Yoryn Borghart had forged a reputation for implacable brutality and vaunting ambition. *If he gets wind of what we did, we're in trouble. Petraxus will be seeking someone to blame for Avas, and Governor Durand's untouchable. My head could be on the line for this.*

Not literally, she hoped, but it felt like everything was closing in on her. She'd even contemplated tossing the trapper overboard in chains, to shut him up for good. But that felt too low a deed to stoop to.

To add to her problems, Port Gaudien was in Sandreth lands: the banner hanging from the massive flagpole above the docks proclaimed that Lord Walter Sandreth himself was here. She prayed she wouldn't see any of that clan, but doubted she'd be that lucky.

'Good day, Siera Romara.' Vostius walked over to stand beside her.

Something in the priest's demeanour made her nervous. She'd already marked his ambition. 'Holy Pater,' she replied, wondering if he knew about the interrogation. 'Will you be staying long in Gaudien?'

'I'll be required to report,' Vostius replied. 'And to see to the well-being of my congregation.' He gave her an earnest look. 'I trust you will give good account of my efforts on Avas?'

'Your orisons were potent,' Romara replied honestly. 'We will give the highest praise. I trust you will do the same?'

'For Lady Challys, of course,' Vostius said. 'Her favour is prized.'

He knows about my brother, Romara realised. 'I'm not Lady anything yet,' she told him. 'I am Siera Romara of the Falcons, and my favour is not won by flattery, but praise of my century.'

Say nice things about my Falcons and I'll be nice about you.

'All from Avas praise your Falcons,' he assured her, bowing low.

After he'd departed, her pentacle gathered, as if sensing her unease. Obanji had the new boy, Soren, lurking in his shadow, and Elindhu had re-braided her towering pile of grey hair. Even Jadyn was wearing his cleanest tabard, which was somehow still rumpled.

They knew what she and Jadyn planned, of course, so this was the beginning of goodbye.

'Thank you all,' she told them. 'I'm proud to have served with every one of you.' She clasped their hands, even Soren's, then turned to Jadyn and for a moment there was just her and him.

As it will be from now on. May we grow old together.

'Well, Seneschal,' she said, 'the grandmaster awaits our report. Let's get this over with.'

Tar-Gaudi, the local Vestal bastion, had been a castle in a former age; now the brickwork was crumbling, the corridors were dank and the tapestries riddled with mould. But the throne hall in the central core was heated by a big fire-pit that warmed its core.

Striving to hide her anxiety, Romara entered the grandmaster's office with Jadyn at her heels. She felt brittle and on edge, knowing she looked a fright with her face swollen and discoloured by purplish-yellow bruising.

We're in danger here, she worried. *I should have forbidden that interrogation. We risked everything to learn nothing. If we're accused, I'll blame the glyma-rage, surrender myself and bequeath my pension to Jadyn . . .*

Together they approached the desk where the grandmaster sat and slammed their right fists into their chests, above the heart. 'Siera Romara Challys, knight-commander of the Falcons, reporting from Avas,' she announced. 'Sier Jadyn Kaen, my seneschal, accompanies me.'

There were no scribes or servants in the room, just three people, a woman and two men. Winifreda den Orlas, the elderly Grandmaster of the Western Peninsular and Isles, had fawned on Romara before they left for Avas, declaring her to be 'the image of myself in younger days'. But now she was visibly withdrawn, and looked intimidated by the two men with her.

The lictor, Yoryn Borghart, was a forbidding Talmoni with a bald pate, jaw-hugging goatee and piercing eyes. As a Vestal knight he'd been feared: a regional champion who'd tried for Exemplar, but on failing to attain that title, he had transitioned to the Justiciary and now controlled Order justice in the northwest.

But the presence of the third man reassured Romara: the tall, grizzled man with tangled grey curls she'd met on Avas was now clad in an Order tabard and a gold chain of office: Corbus Ritter, Archon of the Order of the Vestments of Elysia Divina.

We protect our own, he'd told her.

She and Jadyn touched right fists to their hearts again, and bowed. 'My lord Archon.'

Ritter returned the greeting, then Siera Winifreda said, 'We await your report, Siera Romara. What happened on Avas?'

'Avas Isle has been evacuated as the Hierophant commanded,' Romara answered. 'The drought, the fires and the loss of crops before harvest all made sustaining a presence untenable. At the height of the fighting this year we had five centuries supporting ten thousand imperial men at arms, but once the west was lost and the Heron Century were caught in the blast of an exploding shard, it was deemed that defending Avas was no longer viable and units were gradually withdrawn. My Falcons fought to the very last hour, slaying a vorlok and a draegar just an hour before disembarking. They did all they could.'

'Yet Avas is lost, on your watch,' Lictor Borghart noted coldly. 'You were the senior knight-commander, responsible for strategy and bringing the vyr to defeat.'

Romara felt sweat prickle her armpits, but replied with dignity, 'With respect, Milord, this was the culmination of a trend that started decades ago, one that successive regimes were unable to check. I wasn't placed in command until more than half our manpower had been redeployed, by which time, defeat was inevitable.'

'Not according to your predecessor's valedictory report.'

'With *utmost* respect, Lictor Borghart, we found many things in his report to be erroneous, as my own reports indicated.'

This was dangerous ground: her predecessor claimed to have 'saved' Avas by 'wiping out' the vyr on the island, and was trading on that 'success' back in Petraxus. He was now an important member of the Order's hierarchy, and had recently claimed that the vyr were only back on Avas through Romara's negligence.

Winifreda ben Orlas was clearly in no mood to support a failed underling over a successful overlord. 'Perhaps you were inadequate to your task, Siera Romara?' she suggested querulously.

'Not at all, Milady.'

'Yet you failed.'

'We got tens of thousands of people off the island,' Jadyn burst out.

'Did we ask your opinion, Sier Jadyn?' Borghart snapped.

Jadyn swallowed. 'No, Milord.'

Romara looked at Corbus Ritter, thinking, *Stand up for us, damn you. We're your people.*

The Archon said nothing.

Borghart leaned forward. 'How can five Vestal centuries fail against these feral rabble?'

'With respect, the vyr can move unseen among the populace, as they're doing all over the empire,' Romara retorted. 'I kept our forces together through ambushes, wildfires and shard explosions, and we accounted for dozens of vorloks, draegar and countless of their acolytes. And we got the people out.'

'Those who weren't corrupted to the vyr cause,' Borghart sniffed. 'Ten shards were lost in the isles – a fortune in elobyne. Do you know what those monsters use the cracked shards for? Making more vyr.'

Romara hadn't known that; she looked questioningly at Corbus Ritter, but the Archon hadn't reacted. 'That's not something that we have been informed of,' she said uncertainly.

The room fell into frigid silence. Then one of the tapestries rustled and a stately woman emerged. Her elaborate coif of grey hair was laced with gemstones, and she wore rings on every finger. Her gown of deep maroon velvet had the Sandreth crest woven into the fabric in gold thread; it glittered less than her piercing eyes.

Romara didn't feel any safer.

'Lady Elspeth,' Grandmaster Winifreda greeted her, as if she were expected and had every right to be here. Romara looked again at Corbus Ritter. This was Order business, not a matter for outsiders; by what right was the wife of a feudal lord here?

Still the Archon stayed silent.

'Siera Romara,' Lady Elspeth Sandreth purred, looking at her with predatory eyes. 'Lovely to see you again, dear. Romara and I go back a long way.' She turned to Corbus Ritter. 'She was almost my daughter, believe it or not. I think my son Elan still carries a torch for her. And now we learn that her poor brother has died. How sad.'

Her words hit Romara like a punch to the guts, bringing unwanted memories of Elan, flustering her when she needed to be resolute. She was also conscious that Jadyn was staring at her, and she wished she'd told him already about Reshar's death. She threw him a guilty glance, feeling like she'd suddenly stepped onto shifting sand.

'My brother is – was – the heir to my House,' Romara replied. 'But Father still controls the family estates, and he has many years of life left. There's no need for me to leave service immediately.'

'Provided you are of sound health and wellbeing,' Corbus Ritter put in.

Oh jagat, does he know of what happened to me on Avas? Romara wondered. Somehow, she steeled her face, and said, 'Of course, but I'm perfectly fine.'

Lady Elspeth was appraising Jadyn with cool disdain. 'You're her seneschal, yes? I'm sorry, I don't know your House?'

'I have none,' Jadyn mumbled, going red. 'My parents are ... were ... farmers.'

'The Gift does elevate many of the lower classes,' Siera Winifreda put in. 'Akka calls, and the Gifted hearken. The Order is grateful.'

'But there's so much more to life than just the decade a knight spends in the Order,' Lady Elspeth said brightly. 'Years in which the Gifted can truly make an impact in the wider community.' She faced Romara again, making her feel small and foolish, just as she had all those years ago, when she was being courted by Elan Sandreth.

'*Courted*,' she thought, colouring. *Now there's a word that can cover a multitude of sins.*

'Dear Romara must retire now and take up the reins of an important noble house,' Elspeth purred. 'I'm sure she's eager to rejoin high society, aren't you, dear?'

'I've not given retirement a thought yet; the news of Reshar's death is still fresh,' Romara managed to reply. 'I would have years of service before me, were it not for him passing.'

Lady Elspeth smiled slyly, as if she knew better.

Someone's talked, Romara realised. *They know I've lost control of the glyma . . .* Her heart began to thud as the threat of being invalided to a Convalesium loomed.

'My Elan and young Romara were quite the couple, before she was called by her Gift,' Lady Elspeth went on airily. 'The stars of their debutante year, a match made in heaven. And I've heard a rumour that at long last, she is considering hanging up her flamberge. You know, Elan is still single. It feels like fate, doesn't it?'

Elan's still unwed? Romara's gut churned. *No, I never want to see him again . . .*

'You used to look so lovely in a dress, darling,' Lady Elspeth went on, giving Romara an indulgent look. 'It will be wonderful to have you back among us.'

'This is all very *nice*,' Lictor Borghart put in, in acid tones. 'But I'm here to learn how we lost Avas. I've made a career of following my instincts, and they're telling me that something's amiss here. I must be permitted to investigate fully.'

'Siera Romara is an exemplary servant of the Order,' Corbus Ritter replied, finally standing up for his subordinates. 'I see no further need to question Siera Romara.'

The lictor gave him a hard stare, but Grandmaster Winifreda backed her superior. 'Nor I.'

Romara felt herself beginning to breathe again. This had been uncomfortable, but the Archon had been as good as his word, protecting her and her Falcons. Borghart was glowering, but he didn't press his case further.

She eyed Lady Elspeth coolly, feeling in control of her fate again. *When I retire . . . which will be too soon, damn it, I'll not be pulled back into your webs, you bitch.*

The Archon turned to Lictor Borghart. 'Do you have any further questions for Siera Romara?' he asked.

Borghart went to say something, then harrumphed and shook his head. 'None.'

'Then may we go, Milords?' Romara asked, exhaling in relief.

'You may go,' Grandmaster Winifreda said, in her dry voice. 'Thank you, Siera Romara.'

She and Jadyn bowed, thudded fists to chests again, and turned—

'Not you, Sier Jadyn,' Borghart rasped. 'We want to hear about your interrogation of the vyr, Gram Larch.'

Neither Archon Ritter or Grandmaster Winifreda batted an eyelid.

Romara's skin went clammy and the old saying echoed in her mind: *Frost Giants have two boots, and both can crush you.* Disasters came in pairs.

Jadyn spoke before she could. 'Siera Romara wasn't present. She had nothing to do with it.'

Romara tried to interject, but the archon cut her off. 'Then it doesn't concern her,' he said firmly. 'Siera Romara, you may go. Now.'

Jadyn felt something like an invisible serpent's coils close round his throat. He watched Romara waver, as the situation became clearer: the Falcons *were* being scapegoated, but their commander could escape . . . because she was highborn. He hoped he'd done enough to get her out of this sudden fix – if she contradicted him now, she would be calling him a liar and implicating herself, to no gain. Even so, Jadyn could see that she wanted to.

Get out of here, he urged silently. *Please! Better it's me who goes down than you.* She mattered. He didn't. it was that simple. Especially now that she was sole heir to House Challys.

Why didn't she tell me? he wondered. *I thought we shared everything . . .*

She swallowed, gritting her teeth – then at a sign from Corbus Ritter, she relented, and backed through the door. Two guards, knights of the Order, closed it firmly behind her.

Jadyn faced the questioners again, wondering at the horse-trading that must have gone into this moment. *They needed to blame someone and our names were at the top. But the Sandreths want to court Romara, so they intervened. So they have settled on blaming everything on me, especially as I have given them a stick with which to beat me.*

It hurt, really hurt, that the Order were prepared to throw him away like this.

They'll strip me of everything. I'll be cast out in disgrace, after ten years of service . . .

But he kept his head high, clinging to the knowledge – the certainty – that no matter what, Romara wouldn't abandon him.

'So, Sier Jadyn,' Lictor Borghart said, in a voice like a blade, 'what did the vyr tell you?'

Caution told him that he should say, 'Nothing at all.' But someone had informed on him, and to be caught lying would be worse. *And just maybe, if I reveal what I learned – what Gram Larch alleged – then something new might begin here?*

He glanced at Corbus Ritter, seeking guidance, and to his surprise the Archon gave him a small nod. *Perhaps he's here for the truth too,* he dared hope. *Put your trust in the Archon,* he told himself. *He won't abandon his own.*

He'd thought Lady Elspeth might leave, but she had settled into a chair, despite this being an Order matter. That troubled him. He'd known Elan Sandreth had courted Romara before she gained the Gift, but she had never discussed the details.

Perhaps she's here to ensure I'm condemned, so I don't come between Romara and her son?

With increasing apprehension, he began, 'Gram Larch is not a vyr. He fought alongside them, but he never visibly used magic.

73

Therefore I deemed him outside the Code's strictures on questioning the vyr. My only purpose was to learn whether he knew anything of value.'

'If someone fights alongside the vyr, they're a vyr,' Borghart snarled.

'That's not in the Code,' Corbus Ritter replied. 'Speak on, Sier Jadyn.'

Heartened, Jadyn told them what Gram had said; about the links to Nilis Evandriel and the *possibility* that elobyne had destroyed the ecology of Avas, not the vyr. 'He said there's a spell that can determine, called "Oculus Tempus"—'

But as he said those words, it felt as if the air in the room had frozen, even though the archon and the lictor barely reacted, and Lady Elspeth just tsked under her breath. Only Siera Winifreda looked perplexed, but she kept her mouth shut.

'But it could all be lies,' Jadyn added, distancing himself from Gram's tale as best he could. 'The rebels are deluded and they lie – we know that.'

'"Oculus Tempus" is forbidden, and named as such in the Code,' Borghart said.

'There are more than a thousand forbidden spells in the Code,' Jadyn protested. 'No one in the ranks knows them all.'

'But I do. And you all know not to talk to those animals!'

'But he isn't a vyr, and—'

'Witnesses had him emerging from the fire,' Borghart replied. 'It is *heresy* to converse with vyr, Sier Jadyn.'

What witnesses? Jadyn wondered. *And who told you?*

'Was anyone else with you?' Corbus Ritter asked. 'Anyone else from your pentacle?'

'No one else,' Jadyn answered. 'It was just me.'

His interrogators looked at each other thoughtfully, then Ritter said, 'What are we to do with you, Sier Jadyn? An unsanctioned interrogation is a serious offence.'

Borghart rapped the table. 'Archon, with all respect for your office, the decision is mine and mine alone. This man rescued a vyr and conversed with him. He's admitted as much. That is a matter for a lictor, not the internal discipline of the Order. *It's my jurisdiction.* The question is whether it's an error of judgement, in which case he should merely be stripped of all rank and pension and cast from the Order; or whether he consorted knowingly with heretics and should kneel at the executioner's block. My role is to adjudicate.'

'It's in my purview to grant mercy,' the archon reminded the lictor.

'That is true, but only *after* I adjudicate,' Borghart insisted. 'My instincts tell me that this man is seditious. I demand the right to question him fully.'

Jadyn flinched, under no illusion as to what 'question him fully' meant.

The room fell deathly silent, until Borghart began tapping his quill on the table, *click click click click* ... Despite occupying the central throne, Siera Winifreda was looking away, distancing herself. Lady Elspeth studied Jadyn's face with her unnervingly direct stare.

'The Order does not abandon our own,' Ritter mused. 'But no one is above the law.'

He stood, and walked out.

Jadyn felt as if he'd been slammed in the belly with a spear butt. He struggled to breath, while the remaining trio eyed him like vultures waiting for a bleeding calf to do the decent thing and expire.

'Do you know why we have laws about heresy, Sier Jadyn?' Borghart asked, after a minute of contemplation – or more likely, to just enjoy Jadyn's mute terror.

'Aye, Milord,' he answered hoarsely.

Ritter walked out on me ... He said he could *grant mercy ... But* will *he?*

'Heresy is defined as voicing words contrary to the Sacred Word of Akka, handed down by Jovan Lux,' Borghart went on, clearly relishing his power. 'It is one of the high crimes, Sier Jadyn – because only by adhering to the Sacred Word can we hope to see Elysium on the day of our death. Anything that raises doubt in the mind of the faithful will condemn them to Devouring instead. Would you have that on your soul?'

'No, Milord. I sought only to know our enemies. We've been fighting blind—'

'No!' Borghart thundered, 'we have been fighting in the holy light of Akka and Elysia! You are the one who has been blind. I hereby charge you with heresy. The rightful punishment is disgrace and death.'

Jadyn blinked furiously. 'No, I—'

'*SILENCE!*'

Fear and anger flared in equal measure, and suddenly he was thinking not in terms of explanations and arguments but in swords and lines of flight . . . He saw it clearly, in his mind, the movements, the spells and blow . . . and how it would end, so vivid he swayed, and felt the agony of his own inevitable deathblow, for his weapon had been surrendered outside. There was no way he could battle his way out of here.

He knelt and bowed his head, accepting his fate.

'There will be a hearing,' Borghart went on, his voice once more measured and precise. 'In the meantime, you are under arrest.' He paused, and added, 'Submit quietly, Sier. Resistance will not play well.'

Borghart was right. His only chance was to plead foolishness and fall back on his service record. So Jadyn remained passive as the knights returned, clamped gauntlets to his shoulders, and hauled him to his feet.

Thankfully, they led him away via the back stairs, so that Romara wouldn't see his disgrace.

Soren var'Dael had no idea what was going on, except that Sier Jadyn Kaen was in trouble. Something had happened on the ship, and now the other pentacle members were arguing in the hostelry while he'd been abandoned in the dormitory in the bastion of Tar-Gaudi, waiting for the Squire Master who was to formally induct him into the Order.

'Stay here, talk to no one,' Obanji had told him, before hurrying away.

He buried his head in his hands, feeling bereft. Enid would still be at sea, on her way to a nunnery in Beradin. Pa had been buried on Long Bay and sharks were devouring Ma. That he still lived felt like a mistake.

He looked up as a cluster of men and women in white tabards entered. They all wore a Red Lion badge. 'Hey, who're you?' one asked. 'Outsiders aren't allowed in here.' His comrades gathered round. They all looked like fully trained Vestal knights, much older than him. None looked friendly.

Soren rose and faced them. 'I'm Soren var'Dael,' he managed. 'I'm new.'

'What kind of new?' the closest man sniffed. 'Where's your colours?'

'I, uh, I've not received any—'

'That right?' the knight harrumphed, planting myself in front of Soren and jabbing a finger into his chest. 'Then how do we know you're even meant to be here, eh?'

Soren swallowed a flash of temper. 'I'm with the Falcons—'

'Ha! The Chickens, you mean! The weaklings who flew from Avas with singed feathers.'

The other Lion knights, a woman and two men, closed in. 'I knew a Chicken once,' the woman tittered. She was tall and muscular, with close-cropped brown hair. 'A dickhead named Ghaneen Suul. Remember him, Morden?'

'I do indeed, Siera Halyn,' the first knight, evidently named Morden, drawled. He looked Soren up and down, then his hand flashed in and yanked Soren's blade – Ghaneen Suul's weapon – from the bed. 'You steal this, boy?'

'I earned it,' Soren gritted. 'I manifested the Gift and slew a draegar.'

Morden's mouth twitched in amusement. 'Sure you did.'

Soren's temper blazed, but he clamped down on it. 'Put down my sword.'

'Or what?' Morden grunted, giving him an insolent smile . . .

. . . and then smashing the pommel into Soren's stomach.

The blow was like an explosion of nausea and weakness, leaving his limbs hollowing and his belly convulsing as he folded to the floor, throwing up arms to ward off further blows.

But Sier Morden just spat on him. 'Welcome to the Vestal knights, kid.' Then he dropped Suul's blade on the bunk and sauntered away, while his pentacle laughed and clapped his back.

Soren was still peeling himself off the floor when Obanji and Elindhu returned.

'You all right?' Obanji asked.

Soren swallowed the bile in his throat and mumbled, 'I'm fine. Just met some of my new comrades.' He clutched at his throbbing belly, trying to keep from vomiting.

'You get any names?' Obanji asked.

'Morden . . . and Halyn.'

'Ahh.' His expression hardened.

Elindhu sat beside him and pressed his stomach, muttering as the crystal on the end of her staff glimmered. Immediately, the pain eased. 'Not all those with the Gift are good people,' she told him, 'but most of us have learned basic decency.'

'Sure,' Soren groaned. 'What's going on? Where are Siera Romara and Sier Jadyn?'

The bird-like magus looked up at Obanji, who shook his head. 'It's none of your business, lad, and that's for the best. Jadyn's being blamed for Avas. The Falcons will likely be disbanded.'

Soren stared. 'But why? What did he do that warrants that?'

'Nothing,' Obanji growled, 'but that's irrelevant.'

'They'll break us up,' Elindhu put in, her birdlike face radiating misery. 'Disgraced centuries are bad for morale, so they're erased. They'll burn our banner and our men will be given punishment details in the worst places.'

'But that's not fair,' Soren blurted.

'Fairness is a meaningless concept.' Obanji replied stonily. 'But it doesn't affect you, lad. You'll be placed into training. If it goes well, you'll have a new century inside six months, and after two years' service as an initiate and squire, you'll be knighted. You've got your whole career ahead of you.'

'I don't want another century. You saved my life. I'm a Falcon.'

'Come tomorrow, there'll be no such thing. We just came to wish you luck,' the Abuthan said gently. 'Wait here; the Squire Master will be up shortly to take you to the Induction Room.' He offered a hand. 'Good luck, Initiate Soren var'Dael. I look forward to hearing of your deeds.'

Soren watched numbly as the man he'd begun to see as a model of the person he wanted to be walked away. He felt like a door had been slammed in his face.

Once he was alone, he thought hard. Then, before anyone else came, he scooped up Ghaneen Suul's flamberge and left the dormitory.

'Dear Akka, watch over him,' Romara pleaded. 'Dear Elysia, be merciful.'

If Akka and Elysia heard, they gave no sign, no cracks of thunder, not even a flickering of the candles. And her knees ached from the hours she'd been kneeling here on the cold chapel floor, beseeching them for mercy for Jadyn.

It had been hours before she'd finally learned why Jadyn hadn't emerged from the grandmaster's office. The heresy charge had realised her worst fears. *But why didn't the archon intervene? Corbus Ritter promised me he'd protect us!*

She'd talked to Obanji and Elindhu, so they knew what was coming, also confessing the news of her brother's death, and outlining their increasingly tenuous situation. Jadyn would be the scapegoat and the Falcons would be disbanded. She would have to retire, but she was determined to defend Jadyn, if they'd let her speak at the trial. She'd stand by him, even if he was disgraced and left with nothing.

At least we'll be together.

That his punishment might be worse, she refused to countenance. Not when the rage she'd succumbed to on Avas still burned inside her. Though if it came to that, she'd set the world alight before she let him go.

She wanted to seize Siera Winifreda and berate the gutless hag, or corner Corbus Ritter, pin him to a wall and beat out his chicken-shit liver. But instead she ranted until her voice gave out, while Obanji hung his head sadly and Elindhu wept. In the end she'd come to the bastion chapel, to plead with Akka and Elysia for the impossible.

No one survives a heresy trial. Once a lictor gets his claws into you, they refuse to be wrong.

It was hard to be rational about it, and as the night deepened she fell into exhaustion, physical and emotional, terrified for the man she loved. Her thoughts became incoherent, a blur of prayers, wishes and misery. Finally it occurred to her that what she needed to do, more than pray, was sleep, so she clambered to her feet, her knees creaking like they wouldn't have five years ago, or even three.

I'm nearly thirty. A veteran, she realised. *Not the girl I was . . .*

Gripped by forebodings, she headed for the doors, wanting to walk until she fell off the edge of the world, but she was only halfway down the aisle when the doors swung open to admit Elan Sandreth.

His face hit her like a blow from a vorlok.

'Elan,' she managed, somehow.

'Romi,' he purred, tossing his hair in that way she used to find entrancing. 'Tell me you haven't been in this dingy chapel all evening?'

He knows full well where I've been.

Elan hadn't aged well; his elfin face had filled out, as had his middle, and his long blond hair was thinner now. His eyes, once brilliant blue but now dulled, scanned her body. It made her clench inside to feel them on her, as if they were brushing her skin.

But he came right up to her as if she were still the girl she'd been, desperately in love and willing to do *anything* to please him – soon to be his fiancée, or so she'd dared hope, until the night he'd put a flake of elobyne under her tongue, promising her enhanced pleasure and incredible post-coital dreams. Unbeknownst to either, she had the Gift, and in her confused terror she had hurled statues and furniture round the room with nothing but terrified thoughts.

A glittering future as one of the exalted of Vandarath felt like it would be hers, a wondrous alliance with Elan and his unconquerable lust for *her*, when he could have had *anyone*. But there was no denying the Gift, and if neglected, it was perilous. So she'd gone to the nearest bastion and surrendered her future into the Order's care.

It had given her a life unlike all her hopes, yet fulfilling in ways her old self would never have understood: a life of service, of saving lives and slaying monsters, as heir to a sacred trust. It had even taught her responsibility and presence of mind, enough to be elevated to command a century. And it had given her Jadyn.

The foolish girl I was died years ago, along with my desire for this wastrel.

But here he was, clearly believing he still owned her soul, clasping her to him and forcing a kiss to her unmoving lips. His breath stank of wine. 'Oh, come on, Romi,' he whined playfully, stroking the side of her face. 'I've missed you. I think about you all the time, you know.'

'No, you don't,' she retorted, struggling to conceal her distaste. 'That was twelve years ago.'

'And yet you're still the one I long for. What does that tell you?'

'That you're a pig no one else wants.'

He tittered as if she'd complimented him. 'It's because I miss you, Romi,' he told her, in that wheedling voice she used to find wickedly exciting. Now it just sounded crass. 'What we had never came to a natural end. It's never been over. But now, you're going to leave the Order and we can pick up where we left off.'

He tried to kiss her again.

She planted her hands on his chest and shoved, glaring furiously. 'It *ended*. I was claimed by the Order and I'm a sworn Vestal knight,' she snapped.

He laughed. 'Oh Romi, we cavorted like rabbits. You're no virgin knight.'

That was true, tragically. But it was also *history*. 'I am now. Being a Vestal knight means more to me than rekindling an *ancient* dalliance.'

'Does it?' His lip curled. 'Yet here you are, weeping over your seneschal's plight. What have you and he been up to, eh? Or does he not count as a "dalliance"?'

'Jadyn and I have *never*—' she began, then stopped. He was owed no explanations. 'You know nothing.'

'And yet I know how to smuggle you in to visit him, while the citadel sleeps.'

It was as if the air had been sucked from the chapel. She reeled slightly, her tired brain struggling to process what he offered. A chance to see Jadyn, before he . . .

Akka and Elysia, it could be the last time I ever see him!

But Elan Sandreth was not someone she wished to put herself in debt to. Not the way he'd turned out: pampered, entitled, self-obsessed and vain. *Like I was when he and I were lovers . . .*

It was clear in hindsight that Elan had preyed on her, seduced her and used her like a whore, to get control of her family's wealth. The Gift manifesting in her had prevented what would have been a hideous marriage. And now, rumour had it, his family had made some bad investments. So she believed nothing about this show of nostalgic longing. He just wanted the Challys fortune.

I'd rather die than have anything to do with him and his poisonous family.

'I can see him without your help, Elan,' she snapped, feeling her residual fury simmering. 'And if you think I want anything at all to do with you, a dozen years after whatever it was we had, you're wrong. There's nothing between us any more, and there never will be again.'

She expected to see thwarted ambition at this emphatic rejection, but he just smirked.

'No, no, no,' he chuckled, pulling two sheets of official Order-embossed parchment from his pocket. 'Here's how it is, darling Romara. Your little "Farm Boy" – that's what you call him, isn't it? – is going to be executed.' He waved one of the parchments in her face. 'This is a copy of the warrant. It only needs Archon Ritter's approval to be enacted. He'll do it, too – unless you retire, and marry me.' He brandished the second sheet. 'This is your discharge; which he's pre-signed. Sign it, and your Farm Boy gets to live.'

She stared in contempt – and paralysing fear. 'You *bastard*.'

The Sandreths heard of Reshar's death and sought leverage. They'd have used my lapse to force me to retire, held it over my head . . . and they still might. But this is even better, from their perspective . . . Interrogating that jagging vyr gave them an even better hold over me.

Why Ritter would aid them, she had no idea, but clearly the Sandreths owned him.

82

Elan took her stunned immobility for surrender and stepped in close, placing his hands on her upper arms and nuzzling her. 'Don't look on it as coercion,' he murmured. 'Once you're out of the Order, you'll remember all the good times we had. I took your virginity, remember? You begged for it, gave me whatever I wanted.' He pulled her in and whispered in her ear, 'Remember all the sinning we enjoyed?'

She did, horribly, and it all came flooding back as the smell and touch of him flooded her senses. *Elysia, how did I ever get so desperate for this shit-smear?*

'I'd rather not,' she croaked.

Elan smiled his mother's smile, feline and predatory, and produced a ring, a heavy diamond and gold one styled like a Foylish torc. 'Will you marry me, Romara Challys?'

His smug face, and the certainty in his voice as he lorded it over her, rekindled the fires of fury inside her. She had no strength to resist as her temper cracked. She wrenched herself from his grip and slammed her right fist into his belly, then drove her left up under his jaw as he doubled over. Hours of training every week had made her body into something that some might dismiss with uncomfortable envy as 'mannish', but it served her well. Even as Elan went down, she was on him, gripping his throat and throttling him.

Inside her a beast growled, and her vision began to tinge red . . .

She let it speak. 'You said you could get me into the cells! *How?*'

'I can't tell you,' he quavered, terrified suddenly. 'Your eyes—!'

She smashed her forearm down on his throat again, while planting her knees on his arms, knowing she had to keep him pinned and unable to cry out. He'd have guards outside. Then she drew his dagger and shoved it into his face. '*How do I get into the cells?*'

Elan capitulated spinelessly, babbling directions – a back stair, a hidden door behind an old rotting tapestry, in a corridor on the north side. 'Please don't kill me—'

She reversed the dagger, smashed the hilt into his temple and he flopped into stillness. For a moment she contemplated driving it into his black heart, but somehow, despite the glyma-rage inside her breast, she pulled back from the brink. Instead, she dragged him into an alcove, bound and gagged him, then locked the chapel doors and exited through the empty vestry.

Her heart thudded in utter horror at what she was doing. *This is it . . . my fall . . .*

But she already knew she'd rather spend one day of freedom with Jadyn than a lifetime knowing they were prisoners, locked in separate cages.

4

Let Truth Be Known

The New Theology

Early pagan religions worshipped pantheons of divine beings, who were patrons of elements or harvests or war or child-begetting and the like. But Jovan Lux's revelation led him to see that life was a struggle between Virtue and Sin. This, he declared, was embodied in the forms of Akka, the Skyfather of Elidor, and Urghul, a serpent goddess of the Kharagh pantheon – The Devourer of Souls. His Edict calls for us to choose between them, and thus between Salvation or Despair.

SHAN EL BEDUM, RELIGIOUS SCHOLAR, 1465

Jovan's 'Great Revelation' was to infantilise life down to a choice between his 'Good' and everyone's else's 'Evil', all the while taxing and tithing his own worshippers into penury.

NILIS EVANDRIEL, RENEGADE SCHOLAR, 1465

Port Gaudien, Vandarath
Summer 1472

Jadyn supposed he should be praying, but it was hard to focus when his world was disintegrating. *Romara was going to leave us regardless, and she never told me.* That fact thundered round and round inside his head. At first he was angry, but it was his nature to see other's points of view – and in general, make excuses for them. That, and his love for her, enabled him to make peace with it. *She'd have told me once we walked free.*

But now, he never would.

Part of him said that he deserved this: he'd foolishly exposed himself to forbidden knowledge and recklessly endangered Romara and the others. But justice and fairness said that the information he'd just learned shouldn't be suppressed, but properly investigated. Elobyne was the pillar of the Triple Empire: if it was also destructive, that needed to be known. No wonder Nilis Evandriel found willing ears, when the Order let such claims fester.

Let Truth be known, the Book of Lux said. *Let it be our only guide.*

To which his seldom-heard cynical side replied that if Evandriel wasn't a liar at all, then the mighty knew what they were doing and didn't care.

That's madness. Surely they'd act, if it were true. They breathe the same air as us.

Unfortunately, a decade as a Vestal knight had shown him the dark side of the imperial elites. Some took the responsibilities of power seriously and tried to serve the people well, but most lived for themselves.

The vyr are burning our world – but if Gram Larch is right, we who use elobyne crystals are piling up the tinder for them. And those at the top are unaffected, so do they even care?

Somehow, he had to persuade Corbus Ritter or Yoryn Borghart that he was *serving* the empire, not betraying it – or his career would end in the disgrace of execution, an unmarked grave and the expunging of his name from the records of the Order. It would be as if he'd never existed.

All he'd dreamed of, before he even knew he had the Gift, was to be a knight. He'd grown up with the old tales of the Sanctor Wardens, who'd defended Talmont against the Kharagh Invasion. They'd had their own form of magic – the aegis – which came from the purity of their hearts. The Vestal knights were their successors, and he'd been so proud to join them.

But in the Order he'd been taught that the Sanctor Wardens had been ordinary fighting men, and there'd never been an 'aegis'. The only real magic was glyma. Having his boyhood fantasies crushed had been part of growing up.

I was a dreamer . . . my tutors taught me to live in the real world.

And soon he might be dying in it.

Lifting his head from his internal struggles, he looked around properly for the first time. His cell was dismal, a subterranean rat-hole with plastered walls crumbling from the damp, revealing the brickwork behind. There were manacle rings in the walls but they hadn't chained him. He'd been disarmed and stripped of his mail, though he'd been permitted to keep his white Falcon tabard – for now. The cot had a hard mattress and a moth-eaten blanket, and there was a piss bucket that reeked of waste and fear.

The door was heavily reinforced and the only light came from the moons, shining down through a high grilled window, though light from an oil lamp shone through the grille in the door. He could hear a constant scratching sound, and grunting noises coming from somewhere down the corridor. The voice sounded female, and he shuddered at what might be inflicted on a woman down here.

'Hey,' he called through the grille, 'Leave her alone!'

No one replied, and the grunting just redoubled. Then he heard an explosive gasp, and one of the bricks burst from the wall, falling onto his cot amidst a shower of grit and dust.

'E Cara,' a dark voice panted through the hole. 'Hola, novo chico, com'ha?'

Jadyn blinked, his tired, swirling mind unable to process. *Nepari? A Nepari woman here?* Suddenly the female sounds were more explicable, and less uncomfortable. He walked to the bed and peered through the hole, where a single eye – dark with long, thick lashes, stared back at him. 'Sorry, what?'

'Ah, tu e Talmoni!' she exclaimed. 'Heh heh, how you like own dungeon, ombro?'

'These aren't my dungeons,' Jadyn retorted, then he remembered that in fact, they were. It also reminded him that while his case was unjust, the other prisoners had been legitimately arrested. So he picked up the brick and pushed it back into the hole.

'Eh, ombro!' the woman protested. 'Was hard work.'

'Go away,' he told the wall, then he bent to brush the grout from his blanket.

The brick flew out again and almost struck his head, before breaking on the floor. 'Hey,' the Nepari woman hissed, 'am talking at you.'

'Go away,' he repeated. 'I need to sleep.'

'No, don't. I hear you, pace-pace-pace. You need talky-talk, amigo.' Then she whistled. 'E Cara, you wear *Vestal* tabard, ombro? What you do?'

He felt himself colouring. 'I've done nothing.'

She snorted. 'Si, and Aura no caught with fourteen purses.'

'You're a thief?' It figured, all Nepari were thieves, or so it was said.

Her voice lost its humour. 'Si. They cut her hands off tomorrow.'

Akka on High. Jadyn shuddered in empathy. Talmoni justice was hard, he knew that – hard but fair, people said. It wasn't something he liked to dwell on. 'I'm sorry.'

'Not sorry as Aura, ombro. Walk into sea after, am thinking . . .' She paused, as if digesting what she'd just said, then she gulped and asked, 'What about you, Vestal? Why you lock up?'

Abruptly, he realised that she was right, he did want to talk. 'Heresy.'

'Ola-la!' she breathed. 'Tu e jaga, ombro. Chop, gone. Lo siento, verite.'

'There'll be a trial,' he protested. 'There's still hope.'

She laughed bitterly. 'You think? You dumber than looking.'

He bowed his head, because she was probably right about that too.

'What name is?' she asked.

'Jadyn. Jadyn Kaen.'

'You no look like knight, Jadyn-Jadyn. Look like farmer.'

He'd always had coarse features, a propensity to freckle and flaxen hair that refused to lie flat. And he did walk like he was pulling a plough. 'It's just "Jadyn". My parents were humble people. I have no, um, breeding.'

'Every people have breeding,' she replied, her voice puzzled. 'Else, how be you here?'

'Um, I mean lineage, not um . . . forget it. What's your name?'

'Auranuschka,' she replied, her accent giving it a magical air, like a fairy name from old tales.

It was also unpronounceable. 'Aur . . . Auranoo . . .'

'Just "Aura" be fine,' she tsked. 'Talmoni have graceless tongues. No soul, no music, all business and urges. Should never come here.' Her veneer cracked and she gave a small sob. 'Will die here.'

'Why did you come to Vandarath?' Jadyn had often fantasised of living somewhere like Neparia, where there was sunshine and heat. Why leave such a place?

'Follow Sailor Boy. Stow away, lose him. Been dancer, been singer . . . been thief.' Her voice cracked. 'Wishing had never been. When hearing voice, footsteps . . . fear *lictor* is come.'

Jadyn felt his heart go cold. *What's Lictor Borghart done to her?*

He was at a loss at what to say, but just then they heard boots clipping along the corridor. Aura stifled a weak cry, while Jadyn hurriedly pushed the brick halves back into the hole, then sat on his cot, wondering who the guard was coming for.

If it's Borghart, it had better not be for her . . .

A moment later, the boots scraped to a halt outside his door. He made the Sign of Akka over his heart, praying for strength, as a key scraped in the lock, the handle turned and the door swung open. He rose to face his accusers.

But it was Romara who stood framed in the doorway, her face as white as a sheet. 'Jadyn?' she squeaked.

'Rom? What are you doing?'

'I'm . . . I'm getting you out . . .' she replied, though she looked utterly rooted to the spot.

'But . . .'

To run is an admission of guilt. I'm not a runner . . .

'I'm not sure . . .' he faltered, and Romara rocked back on her heels. Neither of them had ever knowingly broken a law before, let alone broken out of a jail. This felt utterly surreal. *Perhaps I'm dreaming . . . ?*

'Jagatai!' the Nepari blurted, from the next cell. 'You getting out? Help me!'

Aura's voice was like a slap to the face. This was real: he was a condemned man in all but name and they had only moments to act. He stumbled to the door, grabbed Rom and hugged her, then stepped into the hall. A gaoler was lying on his face by the door, and Romara was holding a loop of keys. To his surprise, there was a small portal in the back wall, behind a ragged tapestry that Romara must have pulled aside.

'How did you know about that?' he asked.

'I, um, asked a friend,' Romara blurted. 'Come! We have to go before the alarm's raised.'

'Hola! What of Aura?' the Nepari wailed. 'Unlocking door, am begging!'

'Wait,' Jadyn told Romara, taking the keys. 'If we're doing this, we're doing the whole thing.' He dashed down the corridor, not to Aura's door, but to Gram Larch's cell, where he began trying keys in the lock.

'What are you doing?' Romara asked fearfully. 'Come on!'

'We need him.' Jadyn found the right key, the lock clicked and he pushed open the door. 'Hey, you!'

'Uh?' Gram grunted, who'd clearly been sleeping, but been roused by the noise. 'What—?'

'Did you lie to us?' Jadyn demanded.

The big man lurched to his feet. 'What? No!'

'Then come with me and prove it.'

Romara grabbed his shoulder. 'Wait, we're not breaking a vyr out—'

'Hey, Virgin knights!' Aura called, louder this time. 'Am just here!'

'We need him,' Jadyn repeated, grabbing Gram's shoulder and pulling at him.

'*And me!*' Aura shrilled, her face appearing at her door-grille. '*You need me, Talmoni. I cook, clean, warm bed, no charge—*'

Romara slapped her door. 'Shut up! Who the jagat is she?'

'*Am Aura, pretty lady! I cook for you too, comb hair, warm bed—*'

'Shut up!' Romara pleaded.

The damned girl will rouse the whole bastion, Jadyn fretted. *And I can't leave her to Borghart's mercy . . .*

'Hush, I'll let you out,' he exclaimed, fumbling for the right key. 'Got it . . .'

Aura wrenched open her cell door, ran to the gaoler and stole his dagger, then headed for the hole in the wall – until Romara thrust a leg out, tripped her and sent her sprawling.

'We all go together,' Romara told her, 'or you go back in your cell.'

The Nepari woman sat up, rubbing her knees and bridling. 'Just finding way,' she muttered, eyeing up Gram. 'Who he? What specie?' When Gram growled at her, she tittered nervously, 'Ah, is bear.'

Jadyn looked in the two other cells, but they were empty. 'Right, let's go. Which way?'

Romara gulped. 'I don't know.'

'Aura is knowing,' Aura said quickly. 'Follow.'

'Really?' Jadyn asked, sharing a doubtful look with Romara.

'Si, si. Got caught breaking in. Escape easy.'

'You got caught breaking *into* a Vestal bastion? It's the most secure building in the province.'

'Now you telling! We go?'

Romara led the way back into the secret passage – Gram barely fitted through the hole – and Aura shut it behind them. Jadyn was still profoundly nervous in the vyr's presence, but hoped the man was rational enough to put aside vengeance for his mother; though rational and vyr weren't words that went together.

They ran up several flights of narrow, pitch-dark stairs to the door, where Romara held them back while she listened before leading them into a back corridor of the main keep, at least one level above ground.

Aura pointed down a long shadowy hall. 'This be way,' she whispered.

'Are you sure?' Jadyn whispered.

'Are you thief?' she retorted. 'This be way.'

She led them silently along the stone floor, pausing at a door that was slightly ajar, from where dim light emerged, illuminating little, and peeking inside, then drawing back and making a warning gesture, a stricken look on her face. When she padded onwards, they followed, but Jadyn couldn't resist peering around the door Aura had looked through. It was an office, where Yoryn Borghart was seated at a polished walnut desk, scratching away with a quill at some parchment. Signing a death warrant, perhaps. He had a faint smile on his thin lips.

The man opposite him, sipping a goblet of wine, was Pater Vostius.

So that's who told them, he thought grimly. Part of him ached to burst in and confront them, but Gram was tugging his sleeve, a finger to his bearded mouth, and the mad impulse dissipated.

They turned a corner and slipped along a corridor, past a dozen darkened doors ... until they reached another where light shone beneath. Aura, leading the way, pressed her eye to the keyhole, then stifled a snicker.

Romara gave her a disdainful look as they heard throaty chuckles and a feminine groan. Scowling, she shouldered Aura aside and knelt, then gave Jadyn a sickened look and moved aside, mouthing, '*Look.*'

Jadyn knelt stiffly, feeling uncomfortable about spying, and pressed his eye to the hole.

It was a bedroom. Oil lamps lit the scene in rose-gold, illuminating the foot of a four-poster bed on which a couple were entwined, the man on his back and the woman sitting astride his loins, grinding herself onto him, and moaning voluptuously: Corbus Ritter and Elspeth Sandreth were clearly renewing their alliance.

This is not the Order we joined, he told himself, sickened. *This is not what we are.*

Aura led them to another room, a luxuriously appointed office with padded furniture and a well-polished writing desk, the walls hung with tapestries and paintings, and the shelves holding treasures from foreign lands, including the heads of an Abuthan lion and a Zynochian jackal. The Nepari woman went to the desk and pocketed a purse and various other valuables, then made four daggers disappear about her person, ignoring Romara's disgust and Gram's amusement.

Then she opened a cupboard and Jadyn saw his own flamberge, still in his trusty shoulder-harness and scabbard, hanging from a hook. He grabbed it, almost shaking with relief. Romara helped strap it on, then hugged him, knowing what it meant.

'See, thieving not all bad,' Aura whispered. '*Now* we go.'

She opened the balcony door and led them through. The outside air was cold, but the moons were shining brightly, making the sea-mist in the bay glow. Gram sniffed the air warily, then pointed out guardsmen, just forty paces away across an empty space. Below them was a narrow courtyard between the outer walls and the inner bailey – and an old sortie gate. The balcony was joined to the outer wall by a narrow bridge; they crept along the top bent double to avoid making silhouettes of themselves, and reached a narrow stone spiral stair descending to the ground level and the gate.

Aura's deft fingers had it opened in seconds and she led them down an alley into a cobbled street that ran down towards the harbour. They could hear the sounds of revelry, a nightly occurrence, from the docklands, half a kylo away through the maze of alleys.

Jadyn turned to Romara, who looked like a Foylish ghost, a redwitch of fable. 'What have we done?' he whispered. 'The Order is our life.'

'I know,' she replied. 'But I couldn't lose you.'

For a moment there was only them in the whole world.

Then Gram gripped Romara's throat and wrenched her into the air. She dangled helplessly as he backhanded Jadyn away. For a moment, he might have done anything and Jadyn couldn't have prevented it. 'What the jagat is going on?' the trapper snarled.

Romara bared her teeth, Gram bared his, and knight and vyr faced each other with contorted faces, filled with hate. The orb on Romara's sheathed sword began to pulse.

'Get your hands off me,' Romara rasped, 'or lose them.'

'I could break your—'

Jadyn got his feet under him, moving slowly so as not to provoke anything rash. 'Gram, I freed you to give you a chance to prove your story—'

'Shut up,' Gram snarled, squeezing Romara's windpipe. 'I didn't lie, and I *will* prove it.'

Romara's right hand went to her orb, light pulsed and she threw him off with glyma-strength. Panting hard, she croaked, 'You touch anyone of my mine and I'll *gut* you. Understood?'

Jadyn dreaded seeing her eyes turn bloodshot. He put a hand on her shoulder, willing her to calm down. 'Rom, please,' he murmured, 'we've got to get out of here.'

She growled at him – then abruptly shuddered and grabbed Jadyn, pressing her forehead to his. 'Oh jagat, I'm going under,' she whispered despairingly. 'I'm losing *everything*.'

'Breathe, just breathe,' he murmured back. 'I'm here for you.'

She exhaled and sagged, then put her hand on his chest. 'It's okay,' she said. 'I'm fine.'

Jadyn turned his head and saw both Gram and Aura staring at them. The big trapper was exhaling in gusts, going through the same self-calming rituals as Romara, and Jadyn was struck by how alike they'd looked in that brief confrontation – that either might have been the vyr. It was a chilling insight – or vision of the future.

'E dramatica, verite,' Aura commented. 'But go now, si? Aura knowing way.'

A moment later, the bells inside the bastion began to peal, sounding the alarm.

'Yes,' Jadyn said, 'let's go.'

5

Shifting Winds

The Vyr

A coin has two sides. So too has magic. Glyma is the gift of the gods, a powerful tool for good. But tools can be misused, and there are those who corrupt magic for their own purposes. The monstrous vyr were once men or women, with the same potential for the glyma as a Vestal knight or mage. But in the vyr, madness and bloodlust rule.

THE GLYMA PATH, C. 1320

Port Gaudien, Vandarath
Summer 1472

Romara reached the end of the filthy alley and stopped abruptly, flattening herself against the wall as swinging lanterns ahead revealed a Watch patrol. Jadyn, Gram and Aura melted into shadows too, just as someone shone a tiny, ineffectual lantern past them, illuminating the stinking puddles and rancid garbage. They cursed the stench and moved on.

Massaging her bruised throat, she glared at Gram Larch, hating the way she'd felt when dangling in his grasp. Their eyes locked again, his anger clearly still there. As was hers.

Aura hissed impatiently, 'Why stopping? This way, Vestals.'

The Nepari took the lead, darting across a winding channel of mud just a handcart's width, and Romara went after her, followed by the two men. At the next corner they all paused as another patrol of City Watch jogged past, boots thumping and armour jingling.

She covered the orb on her flamberge, aching to use glyma, but resisting. It was too dangerous for her now.

'Rom, you don't have to do this,' Jadyn murmured. 'Leave us, pretend to join the search and salvage your reputation. They might not realise you were part of this—'

'I brained Elan Sandreth. Believe me, *everyone* knows I'm involved.'

He winced, but she patted his cheek. 'I'll never leave you.' Then she turned to the Nepari thief and the big trapper and asked, 'How the jagat do we get out of here?'

'Have no plan?' Aura asked incredulously. 'Tu en serio, no plan?'

'I wasn't *planning* on being locked up,' Jadyn snapped.

'I've never been here before,' Gram put in. 'I just want to get out into the wilds.'

'Not wilding, go sea,' Aura countered. 'Faster, harder for chase.'

'Jagat,' Romara cursed, cringing inside at the tolling bells and the shouting of the guards echoing through the lanes. 'I don't even know which way we're going.'

Aura poked her face into Romara's. 'How much pay for help?'

'*Pay?*' Romara hissed. 'Pay? Why you—'

Jadyn clapped a hand over her mouth and whispered, 'Shh! Hear her out.'

Romara ripped his hand away furiously, but managed to lower her voice. 'We are victims of injustice,' she snarled at Aura. 'How dare you try to extort money from us?'

'Especially as we don't have any,' Jadyn put in.

Aura gave them a disappointed look. 'No money.' She looked at Romara's flamberge. 'But nice orb. Is valuable, am thinking. Get good price.'

'You touch that sword and I'll be the one who cuts your hands off,' Romara snapped.

'Maybe take from Vestal's bodies?' the Nepari sniffed. 'Am thinking goodbye, then. Buena fortuna. Aura find ship, sail home.'

Romara grabbed her arm. 'Wait – you can get onto a ship?'

'Si. No problem. Have friends . . . Not like you.'

Romara exchanged a fraught look with Jadyn. Time was burning and patrols were closing in on all sides. 'Fine,' she exclaimed. 'We'll reward you.'

'With what?' Aura asked doubtfully. 'No money, no helping.'

Arghhh! 'I give you my word as a Vestal knight,' she said.

'What is word worth?'

'*Jagat!*' Romara swore. 'House Challys will stand you a hundred aurochs for our return.'

'Five hundred.'

'*What?* Two hundred and you get to keep your hands, you greedy little tart.'

Aura pouted. 'Four hundred. No less.'

Romara's face swelled up in outrage, then Jadyn touched her arm and shook his head, and she realised that she was going to explode again. 'Fine,' she groaned, wrestling her rage down. 'Fine . . . Holy Akka, for four hundred aurochs I could *adopt* her!'

'E Cara, we be sisters,' Aura cooed. 'So happy. Come, this way.' She darted up the alley, and Jadyn hurried after her, clearly suspecting trickery, but Romara hesitated, turning to Gram again.

The tension between them instantly began to simmer. 'What about you?'

'Your man said he'd let me guide him to Nilis Evandriel. I'm with him. You're the one who needs to work out where your loyalties lie, Knight-Commander.'

Her hackles rose, but she was one breakdown from turning into something just like this animal. 'Then we're in this together,' she told Gram. 'But I'll be watching you.'

Jadyn waited with Aura, conscious that behind them, Romara and Gram were renewing their barely contained, seething spat. Another patrol had just gone by, and now they heard others, searching alleys on either side. The poor sheltering in these squalid, run-down houses were huddling behind shutters and barred windows, surely aware of the fugitives, but so far no one had given them away. The ground was strewn with foetid rubbish. Dogs snarled at them as they blundered into their territory, and pigs grunted as they made their way past unseen pens, until even Aura was no longer sure of her way.

'You think Aura live here?' she snapped, when Jadyn pointed this out. 'This way . . . no, this.'

They stumbled on through the dark.

But the sound of the waves on the shore was growing louder and a few furtive, frantic minutes later they were in the docklands. Here the locals were still wide awake and drinking with abandon. Copper-skinned Nepari and turbaned Zynochi sailors were dancing with alcohol-flushed Vandarai prostitutes of all ages and states of undress to the music of maltreated instruments. Jadyn caught sight of Vestal Guard tabards and realised men of various centuries – yes, even the Falcons – were carousing here. Alcohol fumes, laughter and singing filled the air, violence lurked – and the Watch were still nowhere to be seen. The bells from Tar-Gaudi Bastion could be heard, though, and the revellers were starting to look around anxiously.

They will be here soon, Jadyn thought anxiously.

Aura led them to the lee of a tavern, then ran off, returning moments later with two presumably purloined cloaks. She handed them to Jadyn and Romara to cover their tabards. 'Disguise, si? We find friend, have ship. Be gone, next tide.'

They ignored their guilt over the stolen goods and followed her to the back door of a seedy inn behind the wharfs, where she negotiated a private dining room and food and drink – without having to flash coin, Jadyn noticed – before vanishing upstairs. Just when they were beginning to worry they'd been abandoned – or traded in – she reappeared.

'Sier Jadyn,' she said brightly, 'you come, si?'

Gram and Romara looked unhappy at splitting up.

Jadyn asked, 'Why?'

'Because docks be man's world,' Aura said briskly. 'This story: you my lover, no longer Vestal or virgin. Is why need boat.' She tossed him one of the purses she'd stolen. 'You be man and pay, si?'

Jadyn was appalled, but Romara snorted. 'It's mildly plausible. Other knights have done similar things. Go on, your reputation's jagged anyway.'

Put like that ... Jadyn rose and looked at Aura properly, in good light, for the first time.

She was pretty, her perky face framed by long black ringlets, her clothing tight at the waist but otherwise baggy and ornately dyed, with copper and brass jewellery sewn into it, poor quality but polished. There were traces of some brutal life lessons too, in the nicks and scars on her cheeks and jaw. But she brimmed with irrepressible spirit. *Tough, beaten down but indomitable*, he thought, with some approval.

He was prone to believe the best of people. A naïve innocent, Romara often told him. But Aura had kept her head in this fraught half-hour, and he sensed more to her than avarice. 'I'm in your hands,' he told her.

'Exciting,' she trilled, wiggling her fingers. 'Come on, Vestal. Follow Aura, we find shippings.'

The moment Jadyn and Aura were gone, Romara turned and regarded Gram Larch. Under his shaggy hair and beard, he looked younger than she'd thought, maybe thirty or so, like her. He had deep brown eyes and weather-beaten skin, and the granite solidity of a man that lived by his own terms.

She realised that he was dealing with something akin to what she was going through – the teetering on the edge of losing all control. But he was also a vorlok's son, and she didn't trust anything about him.

'Listen, vyr-man,' she snapped, 'I'd do anything for Jadyn. That includes protecting him from himself. The moment I think you're trying to corrupt him, I'll have your head.'

He met her threat with equanimity. 'We need to convince people like you, if our rebellion is ever to succeed. I will guide you faithfully, and give you the answers you need. And the name's Gram. You can call me that.'

His calm annoyed her. 'Yes? And you can call me *Lady Challys*.'

His face hardened, but he touched his forelock. 'Milady.'

They fell silent, waiting for what felt like too long; then stiffened, hearing boots on the stairs.

They both rose ... as the door burst open, and two men and one woman with drawn swords burst in – Order flamberges with glowing orbs, and white Vestal tabards, with a red lion on the breast. She knew them all.

'Well, well, here's the traitors,' Sier Morden Warnock drawled. 'What do you think, Halyn?'

The woman, Siera Halyn Crayle, smirked. 'That the Chickens are trying to fly the coop.' She balled a fist, conjuring light, and jabbed a finger at Romara and Gram. 'Kneel, like you're already on the block.'

Jadyn followed Aura down a corridor, through a curtained door into a taproom, which appeared to be in some kind of uproar over a cockfight, then upstairs to a landing, where a red-bearded sailor barred their way.

'This 'im?' he asked, eyeing up Jadyn. 'Is he *really* a fallen Vestal?'

Aura took Jadyn's arm and melted against his side, stroking his chest in an unsettling way. 'Is Aura's man. Handsome, strong, can level buildings.'

Redbeard snorted. 'Sure. Gimme your sword, matey. No weapons in there.'

Jadyn pulled the leather covering from the orb and made it glow. 'I'm keeping it, "matey".'

The man's nerve broke. 'Uh, yeah, sure, no problem, uh, Sier.' He looked at Aura with new respect. 'You really did a knight?'

'All men be fascinated by Aura,' she remarked. 'Is known fact.' She tugged Jadyn along the corridor to the third door, which she flung open, calling, 'Capitano! Is me, your Little Rum Raisin!'

His little what? Jadyn thought, as chairs scraped and boots thumped in the gloom ahead. He conjured light into the orb of his flamberge, lighting up the room. 'Hands where I can see them,' he called, as he entered the poorly lit chamber, where three men sat round a table, a flickering lantern hanging over it.

Two were common Vandari thugs, but the third was a rotund Khetian with jet skin, a braided beard and robes big enough to double as a trader's pavilion. His gold chains and rings spoke of illicit goods. 'Auranuschka,' he rumbled. 'Aren't you supposed to be locked up?'

'Butamo bebe, pleased to see Aura?' the Nepari asked, fluttering her eyelashes like a cheap actress. 'Am still your favourite mameena?'

The Khetian guffawed humourlessly. 'You took half my jewellery.' His eyes went to Jadyn's flamberge. 'I didn't believe Roux when he said that you'd come back, and with a knight at your beck and call.' His eyes flicked to Jadyn's face. 'I am Butamo Gulhambu, Sier.'

An opium smuggler, Jadyn guessed. That was the only way an independent trader could afford the gold this man wore. But that was none of his business, right now. 'Aura says you can offer passage out?'

Butamo frowned. 'The tide's in two hours, at midnight. But I don't sail after dark.'

Sure you do, if the price is right. 'Smugglers do it all the time,' Jadyn countered. 'My first assignment was hunting the likes of you in the Sea of Erath.'

Butamo glanced at his bodyguards, who shuffled nervously. 'Why would a Vestal knight need my services?'

'I've left the Order, for . . . uh,' Jadyn managed, then Aura stepped in smoothly.

'E Cara, we having bebe,' she said, rolling her eyes as if she couldn't believe her bad luck.

'You're pregnant? To a Vestal?' Butamo touched a finger to his nose in some ritual gesture. 'Holy Akka!'

'From just one copulation,' Aura exclaimed, throwing up her hands. 'Unbelievable! Now Aura must live in castle. Akka laugh at her.'

Jadyn clamped his jaw to stop himself blurting denials, while the bodyguards gaped and Butamo stroked his chins, assessing. 'I thought laying with a Vestal knight was fatal?'

Jadyn coloured. 'Um . . .'

'There be ways, if careful,' Aura declared cheerily. 'Was brief copulation, but fruitful.'

Jadyn winced, and pulled out the stolen purse. 'We can pay.'

Butamo's probably wondering if he should delay me while sending a runner to the bastion. But he must know that the first person to die if we're assailed would be him.

'Decide now,' he said firmly. 'And decide well.'

Butamo's eyes narrowed, then he nodded slowly . . .

. . . as the door swung open behind them and a Vestal knight, one of the Lion pentacle, stepped through, with a florid magus at his back. Butamo's redheaded doorman, Roux, was hovering behind them like an anxious investor.

'You're not going anywhere, traitor,' the knight said.

'Except to the axeman's block,' the mage added, kindling light in his stave. 'Yield, or die.'

The docklands of Port Gaudien were a maze where those familiar with its ways could vanish like the rats that plagued the place. Finding someone who didn't wish to be found was nigh impossible.

But following Vestal knights is like tracking a herd of phaunts, Obanji Vost mused, as he walked down the corridor he'd just seen three Lions enter. He heard raised voices. That there were three was troubling; he didn't overestimate his own skills. But if he could take one down quickly, the other two might panic.

He'd been in the dormitory with Elindhu when the alarm bells began ringing in the bastion, and they'd swiftly divined that Jadyn had escaped. They realised equally quickly that someone would assume they were involved, and having no faith that it would end well, had gathered their gear and left. Seeing the Lion pentacle heading towards the docks, they risked following them, until their quarry split up, three going right and the other two left.

'What now?' Obanji panted in Elindhu's ear. 'Who do we follow?'

'I'll follow the pair – the Lion's mage is with them,' she whispered. 'You take the others. Be careful, my friend.'

She quickly vanished, while Obanji crept after Morden Warnock and his two comrades. *I'm stalking knights of my own Order*, his conscience nagged, but he knew he'd not hesitate to kill them to save one of his comrades. He edged closer, in time to hear Siera Halyn Crayle say loudly, 'Kneel, like you're already on the block.'

Through the doorway was a sparsely furnished dining room, where he saw Romara Challys and Gram Larch facing Sier Morden and his two comrades.

Neither Romara or Gram had drawn weapons, but the three Lions had their flamberges out.

He shifted his weight, preparing to move . . .

. . . and a floorboard squeaked beneath his foot.

The nearest knight spun, a swarthy, olive-skinned Mutazan who must have seen Obanji's silhouette, as he called, 'Hey, you – stop there.' He aligned his flamberge as the others turned, succumbing to reflex.

'*Abutha n'epuna!*' Obanji bellowed, sweeping out his own blade and lunging forward.

After a tense hour hiding in the bastion's stables, having failed to find Obanji, Soren had just about resolved to slip away when the alarm bells began ringing, someone shouted about a prisoner escaping, and moments later, Obanji and Elindhu scurried past.

Elindhu was an unnerving presence, with beady eyes that saw too much, but Obanji was a good man, and they were racially akin. That was as far as thought went for Soren. He darted after them, well used to moving silently to evade the roaming packs of bullies on Avas, or his father's gnarled fists.

He was only a few paces behind Obanji in the tavern when violence broke out and he reacted on pure instinct.

Romara looked along the blade pressed to her throat, measuring its wielder: she'd encountered Siera Halyn Crayle, a burly lump of sheep-scat, before. Even in a holy order of knights, birds of a feather found a way to flock together. Morden Warnock and Halyn Crayle were kindred spirits, a pair of arrogant strutting bullies.

Everything Jadyn and I tried not to be.

But the recognition went both ways, for she and Siera Halyn had been rivals for a long time, often crossing paths in Order tournaments, with wins on both sides.

'Siera Halyn,' she greeted her mockingly, watching her eyes, waiting for a blink.

'I said kneel, Romi, dear,' Halyn replied, 'or I'll slash your Challys throat and see just how blue your blood is.'

She has no intention of taking us alive—

But that was as far as she got, for Obanji appeared out of nowhere, bellowed, '*Abutha unending!*' in his own tongue, and launched himself at the Mutazan beside the door. Siera Halyn couldn't stop her gaze twitching behind her – and Romara moved instantly, battering the woman's blade aside with her forearm, then slamming her fist into Halyn's blowsy face. Her knuckles crushed the bridge of her nose with a satisfying crunch, Halyn reeled and Gram snarled, rearing up . . .

. . . but Halyn had the glyma ready, and so did Morden. Halyn thrust her splayed fingers at Romara, gasping, '*Pulso*,' hurling her backwards, while Morden drove a short-arm smash with his pommel into Gram's temple. The big trapper went down like a poleaxed steer, while at the door, Obanji's assault was repelled by the brown-bearded knight's instant parry and counter.

The escape bid was disintegrating even as it was launched.

Halyn's flamberge flashed after Romara, the tip almost carving her cheek open, while Morden closed in on her other flank. 'She's mine,' Halyn spat, wiping blood from her face. 'I've been waiting years to jag her over.'

Romara snatched up a chair in time to block the first blow – which demolished the seat – then another concussion of force smashed her into the wall. She sagged, horribly winded, as Siera Halyn moved in for the kill . . .

Soren launched himself into the room, going round Obanji's left and lunging at a bearded southerner, forcing the Lion to back up – but when the vicious riposte came at him, he suddenly realised exactly what he was doing – taking on trained glyma-knights with no experience or magic of his own.

With a wave of the hand the bearded Mutazan casually threw him at the wall before going after Obanji again. Pain shot down Soren's arm where his left shoulder hit, but he ignored it, for the trapper was down and Romara was on her own and unarmed.

'Falcons!' Soren shouted, for distraction, then he went for the nearest foe: the same Sier Morden who'd bullied him at the barracks.

His earlier humiliation turned to fury, and as if in response, the orb on Ghaneen Suul's blade blazed – but Soren had no idea what to do with the power, so he fought as if it wasn't there, launching a naïve overhand blow that the older knight actually sneered at, even as he went to parry . . .

. . . *Fool's Feint*, Pa used to call the blow; one of his favourite moves, it had been forced down Soren's throat like a holy sacrament. He spun out of the feint and launched a roundhouse slash, and if Sier Morden hadn't been shielded with glyma, he'd have had his throat torn out. As it was, he managed to deflect Soren's blow, but only by giving ground, too off-balance to riposte. Soren battered at him again, driving him away from Romara, then spinning towards the blonde woman – Siera Halyn, Morden had called her – as she tried to lance Romara in the chest. She reacted too slowly, pulling out of her blow but unable to parry, and the wavy edge of the flamberge caved in her already bloodied face, sending gore and teeth flying as she fell.

Sier Morden howled in fury and came at Soren, while in the corner Obanji was busy driving back the defiant Mutazan, but Soren followed his pa's rule, keeping his eyes on his attacker's blade and feet, as the bigger man launched into an efficient chop-chop-lunge while trying to grip him with glyma-energy, aiming to pin Soren in place and skewer him . . .

. . . but Soren had moved seamlessly into *The Flow*; a falling block that evaded the jaws of air seeking to grip him, followed by a roll and counter-punch up into the belly, turning an apparently doomed position into victory. Any ordinary foe would have been cut down, but Morden's enhanced power and speed enabled him to batter Soren's killing blow aside . . .

. . . just as Romara slammed a blade onto the back of his helm, bursting it and the skull apart, and the knight crashed to the ground. The Mutazan lost all composure, tried to bull his way out and instead ran onto Obanji's thrust, the blade entering the chest and coming out his back. His face aghast, he shuddered to a halt and fell onto his back, rapidly falling still.

'Oh jagat,' Romara moaned. 'Now we're killing our own.' Then she stared at Soren. 'Who taught you, boy?'

'My pa,' Soren panted. 'Imperial Army. What do we do now?'

'Where's Jadyn?' Obanji asked Romara.

'This way!' she panted, running for the door, bellowing, '*JADYN!*'

Obanji clapped Soren's shoulder. 'I guess you're with us after all. Go after her. I'll look after this vyr-man.'

I'm in, Soren thought, heart soaring, as he dashed for the door. *I'm a Falcon.*

He heard Romara's boots thudding on the stairs to his right and pelted after her.

No one had ever accused Jadyn of being a blademaster, but he did have the glyma, which he drew on as he interposed himself between Aura and the two Lions. The knight came to meet him, the red-faced mage conjured energy and the treacherous doorman, Roux, whipped out a cosh and went for Aura.

Jadyn blocked the knight's rush, as the sea captain Butamo backed up, shouting for his bodyguards to protect him. But Aura, shrilling abuse in her own tongue, had snatched a dagger from the table and sent the spinning blade hammering into Roux's chest. The doorman staggered and fell, the look of disbelief on his face turning to drowsy death.

She's done that before, Jadyn thought, as he battered his foe's next swing aside. Then the Lion mage's staff filled the room with blue light: something lethal was imminent . . .

. . . until a little woman with a foot-high pile of grey braids appeared behind him and jammed her own elobyne-tipped staff into the man's back, reversing the current of power with a lethal *crack*. The mage went down in a boneless heap, shuddering like jelly.

At the sight of Elindhu, Jadyn's hopes surged.

The Lion knight, suddenly realising he was alone, panicked, flinging a force-pulse at Jadyn as he spun and tried to go through Elindhu – but his blast met Jadyn's shields and dissipated, so all he achieved was to expose his back to his deadliest foe. Jadyn hardened his heart and drove his blade in, the glyma-energy punching it through smoothly. The man was dead before he crashed to the floor.

Aura gaped, Elindhu winced and Butamo muttered a prayer to his gods.

Jadyn heard Romara calling his name just before she crashed into the room and saw him. Elindhu quickly stepped aside as Romara threw herself at him, clasping him to her. Jadyn ignored everyone else and hugged her tightly, overwhelmed by his love's palpable relief.

We're alive, his heart drummed out while he kissed her forehead. *We're alive.*

'I love a good reunion,' Elindhu commented. 'It's its own reward.'

Then, to Jadyn's surprise, Soren var'Dael dashed in. 'I'm with you,' the young man said, taking in the three dead bodies in awe. Then he saw Butamo and his two men. 'Who're they?'

'We're the passage out of here,' the Khetian trader rumbled, then he asked Soren, 'Chinjama wi Mbixi, umfana?'

'Aye, but only a little,' Soren replied. 'Father forbade it.'

Jadyn had reluctantly let Romara go. 'Captain Butamo has agreed to give us passage.' He faced the trader again. 'Someone will have heard all that, so best take us to your ship, right now.'

Butamo nodded, clearly agreeing. 'Follow me.'

Descending the stairs, they found Obanji supporting a dazed-looking Gram Larch. 'Thank Akka,' the Abuthan exclaimed when Jadyn appeared, then he peered at Aura. 'Who's this, then?'

'Am Aura, be friend,' Aura replied. 'Butamo, friend, have big ship, way out.'

Obanji and Butamo exchanged some rapid-fire Mbixi, then nodded warily at each other. The Khetian trader studied the room, where three Vestal knights lay in bloody heaps, his eyebrows raised at the carnage. 'The price just went up, my friends,' he rumbled. 'I'll never be able to come back here.'

'You've got nerve, *friend*,' Romara sniffed. 'But fine, whatever: let's go.'

Aura was looking at Obanji, Soren and Elindhu curiously. 'These come also?'

'This is my mistake,' Jadyn said, gazing from face to face while trying to contain his emotions. 'You don't have to—'

'We're a pentacle,' Obanji interrupted. 'We're with you to the end. It's in the vows.'

'Who's she?' Elindhu added, looking hard at Aura.

Romara sighed. 'Unfortunately, she's with us. Her name's Aura.'

'These are my comrades in the Vestal Order,' Jadyn told her.

Aura peered dubiously at the ring of faces, then stuck out her chest. 'Hello Virgins, nice be meeting you.'

The next hour passed in a blend of tumultuous haste and crawling tension, as the Watch poured into the docks, backed up by Sandreth soldiers and men-at-arms in Vestal tabards. All manner of chaos was breaking out, every opium-smuggling, prostitution or pirate gang believing themselves the Watch's quarry, and scattering to the winds. But Butamo's men had Romara's pentacle safe aboard the ship long before the rioting broke out.

Theirs was far from the only vessel surreptitiously hoisting anchor, Romara noticed.

'Ah,' the Khetian rumbled, joining her at the railing. 'It will be good to be back at sea.'

She gave him a curious look, for the captain was obese in a way few sailors were. 'With respect, you don't look much like a seaman.'

'But I very much am, Siera,' Butamo replied. 'I love to travel, but I hate riding and carriages make me sick. The sea, though, is for ever a mystery and a fascination. And I have good stomach for it.' He patted his giant belly. 'I have a good stomach for everything.'

'What do you trade?'

'All things.' Butamo looked her up and down. 'Better not to ask, hmm?'

We're all outlaws now, Romara reminded herself wanly. She found herself already missing the Order, where everything was black and white – or had been, until tonight.

'How do you know Aura?' she asked instead.

'She and Sergio were business partners, but he abandoned her:

I looked after her for a while, but she stole from me – nothing of real value, mind. We lost touch a few months ago.' He shrugged. 'I forgive her, romantic that I am.'

Romara winced. 'You were . . . um . . . lovers?'

'No,' the Khetian snorted, 'just friends, for a time.'

'Sorry I asked. It's none of my business.'

They fell silent as the sailors got the ship underway, most rowing while a few hoisted black sails, though there was no wind to speak of. On shore, some kind of running battle was going on, judging by the torches streaming past and racket of rams battering down doors. No one would be sleeping in the docklands for the rest of the night.

Elindhu joined them, lowering her hood and asking, 'Would you like some wind?'

Butamo gave her an assessing look. 'I was counting on it, Magia.'

'Be thankful I don't sink you when we're done, opium trader,' Elindhu flashed back, before brandishing her staff and waddling off towards the stern like an imperious mother hen.

Romara surveyed the decks, feeling both grateful and sad that her pentacle were mixed up in this mess. Obanji and Soren were in the bow, discussing something. It was regrettable that the young man had been dragged into it too, but Obanji said it was his choice – and having seen the way he fought, he'd be no liability.

Jadyn had gone off with Butamo's quartermaster to arrange practical matters, like sleeping quarters and bedrolls. Gram and Aura were at the rails, and she wondered for a moment if they knew each other already, but she didn't sense any camaraderie.

The sooner we can ditch the Nepari, the better. This has nothing to do with her, and I doubt we can trust her.

As the rowers turned the bow towards the open sea, Elindhu's staff sparked to life and the wind rose, filling the sails. They were swiftly in motion, picking up speed as they headed for the open seas.

Romara found herself thinking of her Falcons, the ordinary men-at-arms who'd served her and the Order so well, and hoping they wouldn't be punished for their pentacle's transgressions. She'd miss them all.

Port Gaudien and the Vandarath coast were soon just a silhouette against dark skies. Other ships were also leaving, trailing in their wake; she hoped they'd be overlooked among the crowd. She sensed spells veiling them, thanks to Elindhu, preventing anyone from scrying them magically. Their escape was almost complete.

But we've betrayed our Order and slain our brother and sister knights, she thought numbly. *They'll hunt us down until we're dead. They'll never relent.* That her pentacle had been forced to kill other Vestal knights sickened her, as did the knowledge that the Order's archon had allowed himself to be drawn into Elspeth Sandreth's webs. *Jag them all.*

With the ship well underway, Elindhu joined Romara as she headed for the hold, where Jadyn had arranged for them to rest. It was largely empty, as Butamo hadn't had the chance to take on cargo for his return journey. He was talking about making purchases at the next port, though with Vestal bastions all down the coast, that might prove impossible.

Thinking about that gave Romara an unpleasant foretaste of what life on the run would mean: guarding tongues and hiding faces, living with false names, subterfuge and fear. But saving Jadyn from the cells hadn't been a choice: she loved him, and couldn't live without him.

The swell was moderate; even so, Gram had been ill, but her pentacle were used to sea travel and had no such discomfort. Irritatingly, Aura was also fine. There was something about the Nepari woman that set Romara's teeth on edge; seeing her vomit would have cheered her right up. *She treats this like it's a game, but it's our lives.* Right now she was currently perched on a beam and batting her eyelashes at Soren, who looked rather confused.

Is she an idiot? Doesn't she know what we are? Romara sighed inwardly. *Well, time to start working out what we're doing.*

'All right, Falcons, listen in,' she began, and her comrades, new and old, looked up. 'Butamo says he'll take us to Solabas – it's outside the empire, but the Order does still have bastions and shards there, through the Church. So it's not safety. From there we'll have to plan the next steps.'

'Solabas? That's a fair way,' Obanji commented.

'About seven hundred kylos, I'm told,' Romara agreed. 'This vessel is big enough to handle high seas, especially with Elindhu helping with the winds. The captain estimates he can do the journey in roughly ten days.'

'Can we trust him?' Obanji asked. 'In Abutha, we say the word of a trader is worth a camel's fart.'

'Ney, ney,' Aura put in, 'Butamo is good friend. Putty in hands. He like me.'

'He'd better,' Romara said. 'He's getting every coin I can spare, and I won't be able to get us any more – my family all hate me for joining the Order.'

'Money come, money go,' Aura said airily. 'Just make sure promised coin come to Aura.'

'Do we have a destination, or are we just running?' Elindhu asked.

'We're looking for someone,' Gram put in. 'Nilis Evandriel.'

'*Nilis Evandriel?*' Obanji snorted. 'You want to *meet* that fraud?'

'He's no fraud,' the trapper retorted.

'You sure about that?' Obanji looked at Elindhu. 'What do you think?'

She shrugged expressively. 'I'm a specialist on erlings, not heretics. I haven't studied Evandriel's claims, but I am curious about them. Either he's the world's biggest liar, or its greatest truth-teller.'

Obanji rubbed his stubbled chin. 'Why are we looking for him?'

'To learn the truth about the vyr,' Jadyn replied. 'Gram says they're in the right, and that it's elobyne destroying our world. I want to hear this first-hand.'

'So we're going to try and find Nilis Evandriel, a condemned heretic our own Order has been hunting for – for what? Decades? While the same Order hunt us?'

'Pretty much,' Romara sighed.

'Assuming we even find him, how will we know he's telling the truth?' Obanji asked.

'He's a great man, a prophet,' Gram protested, but everyone ignored him.

'We'll demand proof,' Jadyn insisted, 'and once we look him in the eye, we'll know.'

'You'll *know*, will you?' Elindhu teased. 'Jadyn Kaen, who can't tell when he's having his leg pulled?'

'What is "leg pulling"?' Aura asked. 'Do Vestals do such things?' They ignored her, too.

'Jadyn,' Obanji said, 'I love you, but you're the most gullible man alive. Nilis Evandriel will have you believing night is day.'

'But *you'll* all know,' Jadyn replied earnestly. 'Obanji, Romara, you know how to see inside people's heads. And Elindhu will read the truth in his soul.'

Romara grimaced, thinking, *I don't want to meet Evandriel. I'd rather kill him.* Then it occurred to her that this might solve all their problems. *If we brought back his head, surely the Order would forgive us?*

But she tucked that thought to the very back of her mind, instead outlining for Obanji, Elindhu and Soren what had taken place inside the bastion, leading up to her breaking Jadyn – and Gram and Aura – out of the dungeon. 'There was no justice in any of this, and no seeking of truth,' she concluded sadly. 'It was entrapment and victimisation by our own leaders, in collusion with a noblewoman who should have had no say in there.'

'Sickening,' Elindhu commented.

'Sucos cerdos,' Aura growled – *dirty pigs* – which was the first thing she'd said that Romara agreed with.

'So that's why we're going to see this through,' she said. 'Because if the Order can act like that, then suddenly the possibility of Evandriel being right isn't so impossible.'

Obanji answered for them all. 'We're with you, boss.'

'Thank you,' Romara said, shifting uncomfortably. 'There's another thing. As you're probably aware, on Avas I suffered a . . . well, to be frank, I lost control of my glyma and almost died. My intention, before that outrage happened to Jadyn, was to retire. I'm putting that on hold, obviously, but right now, I can barely touch the glyma without bursting into flame.' She found herself trembling, with a lump in her throat, as she faced her comrades: Obanji's weathered, wise visage; Elindhu's inscrutable but kindly face and Jadyn's beloved, gentle eyes. All of them radiated concern. 'I'm going to practise restraint and minimise my use of the glyma. This is a matter of life and death. I'm teetering on the edge, and every moment of stress is like dousing myself in oil, then entering a burning house.'

She accidentally caught Gram Larch's glance and saw something unexpected: *sympathy*. It occurred to her that more than the others, a vyr would know what she was going through. It was an uncomfortable realisation.

'So I have decided to take a step back,' she went on. 'This journey . . . this quest, I suppose we must call it . . . was prompted by Jadyn's actions: it's his vision, so I'm passing command to him. While we're on this journey, he's in charge and even if I disagree with him, his decision is the one which matters.'

She looked round, seeing sadness but not disagreement, except from Jadyn himself. 'It's necessary,' she assured him. 'I need to learn to control myself before I think about anyone else.'

'As you will,' he said thickly.

She rose, then knelt before him, presenting her flamberge hilt. 'Knight-Commander Kaen, I pledge you my obedience and service, henceforth. Ar-byan.'

The others followed suit, echoing her blessing.

Jadyn looked embarrassed, but he didn't argue. After the pledging, he faced them, shuffling awkwardly. 'I see this as temporary,' he said. 'And as for our journey – our quest – I truly believe in it. Whether Evandriel can prove Gram's claim or not, these claims need to be investigated. In any case, I see no other choice: we must go forward, because if we stop, we'll be captured and killed.'

Gram gave Jadyn a heavy, thankful nod, but Aura pulled a sour face. 'Is not good,' she muttered. 'Aura be against dying.'

Jadyn faced her. 'We are grateful for your help, but you're under no obligation to stay with us. You're free to leave as soon as you like.'

'Sooner, even,' Gram muttered, and Romara nodded in agreement.

Aura pouted. 'Aura stay, until paying.'

'We're going into more danger,' Jadyn said. 'This is nothing to do with you.'

'You promise Aura four hundred aurochs. Am wanting.'

'You'll get them,' Romara replied. 'Then you'll go.'

Aura looked at her truculently. 'Making sure, Virgin, or I steal coin, and boyfriend as well.'

Jadyn stammered a denial and Gram roused angrily. 'Shut the jagat up,' he put in, jabbing a thick finger at Aura. 'This is a vital mission. Stay out of our way.'

'Maybe steal your boyfriend, too,' Aura pouted, then she stood and headed for the upper decks. 'Bored of talk-talk. Find nice sailor, drink rum, sing song. Adios, virgins.'

They sat in silence a minute, reflecting.

'I don't trust her,' Gram muttered after a moment, 'but perhaps that's just me.'

'No, I'm with you,' Romara told him, though it rankled to be agreeing with the vyr.

'Me too,' Soren added. Then he bowed his head. 'But I'm just an initiate.'

'You still have a voice,' Obanji told him. 'Lad, I'm sorry you've been dragged into this. But we'll look after you, and we'll make a full knight of you, I promise you that.'

Soren nodded mutely, as if too overwhelmed to speak.

Jadyn turned to Gram. 'All right, you'll guide us to Nilis Evandriel and we'll learn whether elobyne is really killing our lands, because if that's the case, we must tell the world. This is about standing up for truth – if truth it is – even if all our own people are against us.'

He believes that, Romara knew, for Jadyn had always worn his heart on his sleeve.

'Can you deliver us to Nilis Evandriel, trapper?' she asked.

The Avas man faced her, his rugged face resolute. 'A few years ago, a woman from far away visited my mother's village. They treated her like she was Elysia herself. Agynea, her name was. She's one of Nilis Evandriel's acolytes, a former scholar persuaded by his arguments to go rogue. She visited to my mother's coven to persuade them too.' He looked skywards, as if asking some divinity for forgiveness, then added, 'She came from a village on the Neparia side of the Qor-Espina, the alps that divide Solabas from Neparia.'

'Solabas and Neparia are both outside the empire,' Romara noted, 'but the Church is strong in both, and therefore, so is the Order. We won't be safe there . . .'

'We'll find a way,' Jadyn said. 'Akka will guide us.'

It was so *very* Jadyn, to be caught up in the ideals, irrespective of the practicalities. *You stubborn, foolish, lovely man.* 'Fine,' she sighed, looking to see how the others were taking it all.

'We're with you,' Obanji reiterated. 'And on the bright side, we can still replenish our orbs in Solabas and Neparia, so that's something.' He gave Romara an awkward look. 'You won't need to use the glyma, Romara. We'll cover for you.'

Elindhu's bright eyes were lit with a strange hunger. 'We will seek the truth, as our vows require,' she said. 'This is a chance to ask what no one else dares.'

Gram raised a hand uncertainly. 'About replenishing your powers . . . Agynea claimed that near her village, there was an "old place" – that's what she called it – dedicated to a lost power called *aegis*. Perhaps that might help?'

Jadyn opened his mouth, then closed it again, his eyes softened by wonder. The aegis was the magic of the Sanctor Wardens, the heroes of his childhood.

'It's just fairy tales,' Romara said firmly. 'The aegis was a myth. It *is* a myth.'

'Not according to Agynea,' Gram replied. 'She said the old place was called "Vanashta Baanholt", if that means anything to you?'

'Really?' Jadyn exclaimed. 'Vanashta Baanholt was apparently the heart of the Sanctor Warden order. Legend says it disappeared when the last Wardens died; it's never been found.'

'I know nothing of that,' Gram said. 'It was just a thought.'

Or a hook, to keep Jadyn interested, Romara thought angrily, though how Gram could know of Jadyn's fancies, she couldn't say. 'It doesn't exist,' she insisted. 'Forget about it.'

'I agree with Romara,' Obanji put in. 'It's a shame, but the Sanctor Wardens were just men who went bad in the end, lest we forget.'

Romara nodded emphatically, but she knew Jadyn: he'd follow that lead like a faithful hound.

This is going to kill us, she worried. *We should be hiding, not setting a lance against the gods.* But everyone else appeared willing.

'I've never been to Neparia,' she groaned, 'and I already hate it.'

At that, the trap door above them flew open and Aura's head popped through, upside down. 'Neparia be beautiful! Aura knowing! Guide you, si!' She flipped down into the hold like a tumbler, landing and striking a pose. 'Aura help free Neparia from imperial bastidos.' Then she remembered who she was speaking to. 'You not bastidos, no, you is legit . . . what is word? Proper birth, good people.'

'I suppose you were listening the whole time?' Romara sighed.

'Virgins talk more if Aura not here. Is no problem.' She danced a jig. 'Aura be going home.'

The Day Court

The Left Hand of God

It is said that the Night Court is the right hand of the Hierophant, and the Day Court the left. The Night Court is where strategic decisions are made. But the Day Court is the forum where matters of commerce, justice and the minutiae of society are adjudicated upon. The Devourer will swallow the ruler who neglects such details, but our Hierophant gives equal attention to both.

EVERARD LUFTAN, GUILDMASTER, PETRAXUS, 1411

Petraxus, Talmont
Summer 1472

Eindil Pandramion III, the Hierophant, God-Emperor of Talmont, sat on the Throne of Pearl and wondered whether he had the patience to deal with one more moment of this damned day. As ever, the Sunburst Crown weighed abominably on his neck and shoulders, despite the braziers, the cold was seeping into his joints, and the noise of the giant hall, the shuffling feet and carping voices, the discontented murmurers and the whining supplicants had given him a headache hours ago.

Elysia, have mercy. Just let it end.

Today, he presided over the Day Court, the forum for secular matters, the laws and daily doings that shifted men and money around his empire. It was filled with the lords of the land: greedy dynastic boors who ruled their territories like little emperors. Nothing he did for them was ever enough. Envy rolled off them in waves as they knelt before him, men and women who'd grown up with everyone grovelling to *them*. It made him wish he could grind their faces into the floor until they were nothing but bloody smears.

He consoled himself with the knowledge that, year by year, he was breaking them down, crushing their insolence and the threats they posed to his rule. The Night Court had devised a myriad of constricting coils that shifted wealth, power and authority from the regions to Petraxus, because of the ever-present threat of rebellion. The primary business of a ruler was to stay in power, and to secure that power for his heirs. Everything else – morality, justice, tradition or even honour – was secondary to that burning principle. Even self-destructive acts could be countenanced, so long as they hurt his rivals more.

For these Day Court grandees are certainly my rivals and I must never forget that.

Another supplicant finished his plea – Ostaban, Duke of Bravantia, demanding compensation for crops burned by the vyr, and the right to levy more soldiers to protect his granaries. He would be refused, for he was a brother to the King of Bravantia, an egotistical prick who wanted his daughter to marry a Miravian lord, a dangerous alliance that couldn't go ahead.

Stentor Robias read Eindil's finger gestures and spoke his will. 'The Throne of Pearl hears your plea, and sympathises for your loss,' the herald said smoothly. 'But the security of a lord's lands against his own subjects is his own issue. The precedents are clear on this, and the Hierophant sees no special circumstances here. Moreover, the loss of the shards entrusted to you must be compensated. However, the Hierophant does agree to posting an additional Vestal century on your lands to help secure your people. Duke Ostaban, you may go.'

The puce-faced lord swallowed his reactions – disappointment, and unease, because he certainly didn't want more Church military in his province – then kissed the step below Eindil's feet, rose and backed away, hatred in his eyes as he emitted a pious babble of gratitude.

That's what you get for wasting my time, you whining cock, Eindil thought, with some satisfaction.

'Next, the Day Court welcomes Lady Elspeth Sandreth of Vandarath,' Robias announced.

The masses packed into the Day Court peered about, then grudgingly parted as a distant, slender figure in green silks and wolf fur appeared at the doors and slowly approached the throne. She was grey-blonde, mature, shapely, artfully made-up, and she carried herself with straight-backed grace. A maidservant, a mousy girl with blonde curls, accompanied her, holding a leather satchel.

Eindil gestured to Robias, who dutifully leaned in. 'Remind me?'

'The wife of Lord Walter Sandreth, a duke from western Vandarath. Old house, perennially broke, and her husband's thirty years older than her. She's linked to the archon.'

'How so?'

'By the boudoir. She's here about some dispute over some domestic matter.'

'Why her? Where's her husband?'

'He's too old to travel. Milord, House Sandreth are useful supporters of imperial interests, often siding with Petraxus against their own neighbours – for reward, of course. She's worth indulging if her request is reasonable.'

That was all they had time for, because by now Lady Elspeth was kneeling and kissing the footmark of Jovan Lux, preserved on the lower step. Her expression was suitably awed and she'd chosen a high neckline, which was to her credit. Eindil was tired of 'ladies' trying to sway him with ridiculously presented cleavage and even glimpses of nipples, as if he didn't have a palace full of wives and concubines already.

'Lady Elspeth, please present your supplication,' Robias invited.

'Great Ruler, Lord of All, I come to you with a plea for clemency,' the noblewoman said in a clear, composed voice. 'I kneel on behalf of my daughter-in-law, who is wrongfully beset.'

Eindil glanced at Robias, who was looking a little puzzled. 'Clemency?'

'Indeed,' Elspeth replied. She reached for the satchel her maid carried and produced a document, which a servant took and handed to

Robias. 'These are marital papers for my son, Elan, who two weeks ago married Romara Challys, in Port Gaudien. But almost immediately, she was kidnapped by rogue Vestal knights.'

There was a sharp intake of breath and Eindil shot a glance at Sier Fidelus d'Arenberg, the Vestal Order's representative in court today. *Privacy*, he signed to Robias. This smacked of unwanted scandal.

Robias thumped his stave and shouted, 'Erect the Pavilion of Concord. This is a matter of imperial security and must be conducted *Ensus Privatus*.'

There was a delay while the indoor pavilion of heavy tasselled fabric, thirty paces square and almost as tall, was swiftly erected around the throne. During this time, Eindil studied the composed Lady Elspeth. She had the air of someone entirely at ease in the arts of manipulation and persuasion. He was reminded of a Sharifan cat, an exquisite breed with silky white fur; it would shred the hand of anyone foolish enough to try to stroke it.

Once the pavilion was erected, only Stentor Robias and Sier Fidelus d'Arenberg, a thickset former Exemplar now running to fat, were permitted to remain with him, facing Lady Elspeth.

Eindil gestured for Robias to recommence. 'This is a sacred space, where only Truth may be spoken,' the herald intoned. 'Lady Elspeth Sandreth, speak your truth.'

The noblewoman was composure itself. 'Great Ruler, Descendant of the Most High, I swear that my words are to be the whole, unvarnished truth,' she said smoothly. 'Two months ago, my son Elan proposed to Romara Challys, a Siera of the Vestal Order, and—'

Eindil interrupted with a curt gesture. 'Robias, is this the same knight-commander who lost us Avas Isle? I thought I had commanded an investigation?'

'Your Majesty recalls correctly. That investigation was held in Gaudien a few days ago,' Robias replied. 'Siera Romara was exonerated by a Judicial Forum conducted by Lictor Yoryn Borghart. Her seneschal, Sier Jadyn Kaen, was found guilty of consorting with the vyr.'

'Just so,' Lady Elspeth said emphatically. 'This lowborn brigand deceived even his commander, but Lictor Borghart saw through him and took him into custody. That same night, her spirit broken by this deception, Romara retired to the chapel to pray. My son Elan, who once courted her in their youth, consoled her, and they rediscovered their love and agreed to marry. She sought permission to leave the Order, and as it happened, Archon Corbus Ritter was in town. I have the signed attestation from Lord Corbus here,' she added, producing more papers for Robias to peruse. 'These are her completed discharge papers; as well as the marital certificates: they wed that very night.'

'An irregular courtship,' Eindil commented.

'Great Ruler, they had been very much in love when they were young, but the discovery of her Gift had compelled her to enter the Vestal Order. My Elan vowed that he would wait for her, even if it took a lifetime. This reunion is the culmination of their dreams.'

What's really going on, here? Eindil wondered. The crown compelled him to stay above dynastic rivalries, but it was requisite for any sensible ruler to stay abreast of them. The Challys family were one of the oldest and richest dynasties of cultured, conservative Miravia and if he recalled correctly, whoever wed this Romara would inherit in time.

'You spoke of clemency? And a kidnapping?' he asked. 'Explain.'

Lady Elspeth wrung her hands with apparent anguish. 'Dear Romara has been kidnapped by her former comrades, who have gone rogue. But the Justiciary are pursuing her as if she were a rogue knight herself.'

Eindil looked at Fidelus d'Arenberg. 'Sier Fidelus, you represent the Order here. Is this so?'

Fidelus looked flustered at being put on the spot. 'Aye, a lictor named Borghart has invoked pursuit. But we were told that Siera Romara had assaulted Lord Elan and colluded in rescuing Sier Jadyn Kaen – indeed, we believe her entire pentacle has gone rogue, escaping with two vyr prisoners. They are being pursued, Siera Romara included.'

Eindil gave Lady Elspeth a stern look. 'Well, Lady?'

'Sier Fidelus is mistaken, as is the Judiciary. Kaen and his vyr friends did escape, and kidnapped dear Romara. Elan is helping Lictor Borghart – a fine and diligent investigator – to rescue her and bring them to justice. I am here to correct this error, and to protect Romara's honour.'

And preserve your son's claim on this very rich noblewoman, Eindil mused, smelling rats by the dozen. *If we declare her marriage void, through her being a rogue and a vyr, she'll have nothing. I wonder how long this woman's son's 'love' for her would last after that?*

He gestured to Robias to attend him. 'Well?' he whispered in the stentor's ear.

'Given what we know, the documentation could equally well be genuine or fraudulent,' Robias murmured. 'Archon Ritter is consorting with this woman and was present; forging House Challys' signet is simple enough and we don't know the young woman's signature, so she may or may not have signed any of it.'

'But ... ?' Eindil asked.

'But Lady Elspeth is a staunch ally of the empire, while House Challys has traditionally been separatist. If we declare this marriage void or fraudulent, we annoy Archon Ritter and a diligent supporter, and help preserve the future of an independent-minded dynasty in Miravia. But if we support Lady Elspeth's claims, we gain leverage against the Archon and future control of House Challys, while bolstering a regional ally.'

As usual, it felt like an excellent summation.

'Then our decision is obvious,' Eindil agreed. 'We support her claim.'

Robias hammered his stave thrice into the marble tiles. 'Here is the judgement of Eindil Pandramion III, Hierophant of Talmont: we uphold the marriage and loyalty of Romara Challys, and the right of her and her husband, Elan Sandreth, to inherit the lands and titles of House Challys in due course. We command that the Vestal Order acknowledge Lady Romara's innocence, and assist all efforts to recover this beloved daughter of the empire. Before Akka and Elysia, we declare this to be. Ar-byan.'

'Ar-byan,' Lady Elspeth echoed, her face quietly radiant as she kissed the footstep of Jovan Lux again, before gazing up at Eindil with gratitude all over her fine-boned, if ageing, features.

It was tempting to invite her to his palace that evening, to see what she was made of – and make a cuckold of the archon, which would be amusing. But it would be too great a reward for her connivance, and the only woman he truly desired was thousands of kylos away.

Vazi, he thought longingly, *hurry back to us*.

He watched Lady Sandreth's face as she rose with serpentine grace, resolving that he would keep a greater eye on her and her weavings in future. She felt like a dangerous ally.

Part Two
HUNTERS AND HUNTED

6

Pirates in Port

The Triple Empire

The Edict created a tripod, based upon mutual benefits and dependencies, that united three rival powers. Previously Zynochia dominated knowledge and natural resources, but Abutha and Khetia had the gold and manpower to challenge them. The rise of Talmont under Jovan Lux altered that balance. Talmont needed Zynochian lore and goods and Abuthan gold, and the Zynochi and Abuthan royalty craved elobyne. Dynastic alliances formed, uniting these rivals in the new Triple Empire, which rules us still.

ANNALS OF TALMONT, 1448

A tripod is inherently unstable.

NILIS EVANDRIEL, RENEGADE SCHOLAR, 1470

Solabas
Summer 1472

'Wait, is *two hundred kylos* to Neparia?' Aura wailed, looking around the stony beach. 'And *over* Qor-Espina? Why no sail around?'

'We'll get horses,' Jadyn told her. 'We've still got a little coin.'

The longboat was already rowing back to the ship, as Butamo was leaving Solabas and heading for a haven in Foyland, to avoid any pursuit.

A good man, for a criminal. Jadyn wasn't sure how he felt about that; life outside the Order was confusing.

'Dusa cento kylos,' Aura said, looking ruefully at her sandals. 'Why no Foyland, be closer?'

'Foyland is chaos,' Jadyn replied. 'Solabas is outside the empire too, but it's at peace. This is the safest place to disembark. If you leave us, you may never get paid,' he added.

'Si, is why staying,' Aura agreed. 'For promise of man. What could go wrong?'

It had taken them nine days after escaping Port Gaudien, only putting ashore to refill the water barrels before kissing goodbye to land at Cape Foulair and sailing due south. They'd struck the coast of Foyland, a lawless mess of feuding kingdoms, and followed it westwards to here, an inconspicuous inlet west of Slaver's Bay.

'Solabas be bad place,' Aura complained. 'Mucho piratos.'

'Only in the ports,' Elindhu replied. 'We're going inland. Hardly anyone lives there, so it should be safe.'

'The hinterland is heavily forested, rugged country,' Obanji agreed. 'It's not heavily populated, but there are towns and villages where we can re-supply.'

'Wonderful,' Romara said wryly. 'I can't wait to explore it.'

Jadyn wasn't overjoyed with the route either, but he saw little choice. Solabas was independent of the empire, though the universality of the Akkanite Church meant that there would be an Order presence, but it was the fastest route into Neparia and finding Nilis Evandriel.

The sky was deep purple-blue and the sun was considerably warmer here. His comrades were already shedding layers of clothing and girding themselves for a hard journey.

Just days ago we were intimates with governors, housed in bastions and given the best of food and drink. Now we're outlaws, and anyone we meet could be dangerous. Who of us will bear up, and who'll break? Jadyn wondered.

Obanji and Elindhu he could rely on. Romara was fragile right now, and he was terrified she'd lapse again, this time fatally. And Soren, Aura and Gram were unknowns.

Time will tell, I guess.

They set out on a dirt track that followed the coast, seeking a road into the hinterland. Butamo had told them to seek the nearby Serena River and follow it upstream; the delta where it met the sea should be no more than a day's walk west, the Khetian had said.

Obanji walked with Soren, drilling him in the four combat runes, *Potentas*, *Salva*, *Flamma* and *Pulso*, while Elindhu, looking like a walking tent, moved in a waking trance.

Jadyn quickened his pace to walk beside Aura, hoping to gain a better understanding of who she was. 'How did you come to leave Neparia?' he asked.

Aura fluttered her hand over her face. 'Aura meet handsome sailor, make her tremble, body and soul. Face like angel, heart like devil. Become quiver for his arrows, fall in love. Then he sail away, abandon her in Gaudien.' She pulled a sour face. 'Now I knife, slip throat.'

'Slit,' Jadyn corrected reflexively, though he was taken aback by her fierceness.

'Si, that.'

'What was his name?'

'Jagat Heart. Liar Prince. Flea Dog.' Then she ground her heel into the dirt. 'Sergio.'

'I see. Aura, thank you for agreeing to guide us in Neparia.'

'Is no problem – you pay Aura, she help, si?' She eyed him up offhandedly. 'And you free her, is good. If you handsome, would reward with inedible making of love, but you is Virgin Vestal. No fun.'

He couldn't tell if she was joking. 'Inedible?'

'Si – this mean "amazing", "wonderful", neya?'

'Ah, more the opposite. The word you want is "incredible".'

'E Cara,' she spat. 'Stupid language. Anyway, you Vestal knight – all impotent, si? Dull. Gram is bear. Inedible. No fun for Aura.'

Jadyn bit his lip, not sure he should be raising the next question, much less that he wanted to know the answer, but if he wanted to truly understand her . . . 'What did Borghart do to you?'

'Strangeness things. Like coin toss: I call wrong, he cut.' She showed him an arm laced with a dozen recent lacerations, only now scabbing over. 'Or make walk in room of broken glass with blinding fold.' She shrugged. 'Aura avoid all, make him crazy. Is madman . . .' She pulled a disdainful face and gestured forward. 'Come, Virgin, this way. Must find river.'

Jadyn stared after her. He'd been expecting worse – but what she'd been through smacked of some kind of arcane test, though not one he'd ever heard of. Maybe Elindhu would know.

He let Aura walk on and dropped back to join Romara. 'How are you doing?'

'Fine, though my boots are already wearing thin and we've barely started walking.'

'Butamo said we'd find a village before dusk. We can buy horses and supplies there.'

'Thank Akka for that.' She glanced back at Gram, sweltering in his Avas furs. 'I couldn't get a word out of him.'

'Did you try?'

She looked at him, her face unrepentant. 'He's a vyr, Jadyn. I know you think he can help us, but he's still a murdering arsonist.' When he went to protest, she snapped, 'Yes, yes, I know in *here*' – she tapped her skull – 'that it's more complicated. But in here' – she tapped her heart – 'that's how I feel.'

She'd never been the most tolerant. That'd been his job, as her seneschal. He gave her a wry, sad smile, clapped her shoulder, then dropped back to speak with the others. Obanji was his usual phlegmatic self, and Soren barely said a word, dazed by all he'd gone through. Elindhu, on the other hand, was in a talkative mood, full of speculation about Gram and his tale.

'You know he's almost certainly deluded,' she started. 'Nilis Evandriel is said to be a mad deviant.' Her beady eyes twinkled. 'Though of course, when someone challenges the orthodox, sordid allegations always fly, don't they?'

Jadyn bowed his head. 'We're probably already being proclaimed as monsters.'

'Absolutely,' Elindhu agreed. 'But we're still ourselves.'

He gave her a fond look. 'Thank you for staying.'

'Oh, I'm as curious as you about all this.'

Remembering his questioning, he asked, 'The lictor said that the vyr give their coven powdered elobyne – he said that's what causes the non-Gifted in the vyr covens to go berserk. Have you heard of this?'

Elindhu frowned. 'I've heard rumours, but nothing official. It's said that the Order experimented with giving knights powdered elobyne, and they basically self-immolated – the combination of elobyne orbs and the powder was too much, and they burned themselves to cinders.' She shuddered. 'But I suppose the non-Gifted, without an orb, might gain something?'

'Maybe?' He turned his mind to practical matters. 'Do you have enough water? Are your boots sufficient?' he asked, seeking safer ground. 'I know it's a cliché that a mage can't cope with the hardships that knights can, but you know . . .'

Her timeless face crinkled into a smile. 'I'm very adaptable. Don't worry about me.'

'Good to hear. But listen, Aura says she was subjected to some kind of cruel testing regime by Lictor Borghart – making her guess on a coin toss, and cutting her if she failed, and the like. Have you heard of the like?'

Elindhu shook her head. 'Never. Lictors, eh?'

Jadyn asked her to check in on the Nepari woman and learn more, then dropped back to the rear, where Gram, red-faced and sweating, trudged along. 'You should just ditch those furs, friend. They'll be the death of you.'

'I trapped and skinned them all. They're a mark of prowess on Avas.'

'We're in Solabas now,' Jadyn reminded the trapper. 'Those furs tell a story you mightn't want told.'

Gram glowered at him. 'They're my heritage, and all I have from home.'

You helped burn your home, Jadyn almost retorted, but he bit his lip. 'Tell me about the vyr. I need to know what your capabilities are, in case we run into trouble.'

He frowned, but answered, 'There are ceremonies, and some kind of potion. Everyone is told to join in, and most are changed by it. That's where the vyr potential is opened up, even for people without the Gift. But it's overpowering, and none of them can control it. When the coven's leader demands it, everyone in the coven goes feral. That's always scared me, and I wanted to protect Ma, so I have always fought to remain in control.'

Jadyn remembered what Borghart had said about powdered elobyne being used to make more vyr. 'That's reprehensible: turning ordinary men and women into wild things.'

Gram flinched. 'Aye, but desperate people do desperate things. Without the vyr's magical power, they'd be quickly crushed. To have any chance, we have to dare the unthinkable.'

Jadyn thought about his own recent experience of speaking out. After ten years fighting what had seemed such a black and white war, suddenly everything was now fraught with doubt. 'So you swear you're not a vorlok in your own right?' he asked.

'No . . . but I do feel the potential lurking,' Gram replied uneasily. 'I've never been tested for the Gift, but maybe . . . But I fear what I might become.'

Jadyn proffered his sword hilt. 'Touch the orb, if you want?'

Gram paused, then shook his head. 'Better not to know.'

The test only works if the person wants it and opens themselves up, Jadyn reflected. *I can't force him to do it.* He decided he'd heard enough for now, and changed the subject. 'Tell me more of this Agynea?'

'You ask me to reveal sworn secrets, but our goals are aligned, for now, so I will tell you of her. Agynea is old. Young. Wise. Childish. You will understand, when you meet her.'

'How did she get all the way to Avas from Neparia?'

'Perhaps she flew on a broomstick?'

Jadyn couldn't tell if he was joking. Knights and mages of the Order had access to portali gates, magical doors that enabled rapid travel between distant places, and Jadyn wondered if the vyr had similar things.

'How will you find her in a place you've never been?' he asked.

'There are secret signs,' Gram replied. 'I know how and where to look.'

Jadyn met the man's eye. 'Then we're in your hands,' he admitted.

'But there isn't a trap you could walk us into that we couldn't cut our way out of.'

'You don't have to worry about that,' Gram replied. 'I want this journey as much as you.'

For Romara, the blisters she was developing on her feet turned what might have been a pleasant walk into painful torture. She felt every step of the barren, rocky piece of shore.

Obanji had taken the lead, being the most experienced outdoors man among the pentacle, and he'd taken Soren with him, to further his induction into pentacle life. By mid-afternoon, with the sun dropping into a cloudy haze to the west and the weather finally cooling, they returned with excited faces.

'Chief, there's something ahead,' Obanji told Romara. '*Erlings.*'

Romara blinked, a sense of unreality descending. She'd never seen an erling in her life; she didn't think any of them had. 'Where?'

'Not far,' the Abuthan replied. 'They're below the next bluff, in the rocks.'

Romara waved Elindhu forward as her comrades gathered; she had studied erlings – the 'old folk' of Hytal who'd been supplanted by humanity. The few remaining erlings were supposedly confined to their homeland in faraway Tyr, and the Order had mandated that any erling found outside their reservation should be captured or killed.

She wasn't sure she could do that, not when seeing an erling was something she'd wanted all her life. It would be a fine tale for her grandchildren. She looked at Jadyn, whose grandchildren they would also be. 'You're in charge now,' she reminded them. 'What do you want to do?'

Jadyn had a look of childish wonder on his face. 'Ah, we should see what they're up to,' he proposed, in a dazed voice. 'Verify that it's really them.'

'Aye, we must,' Elindhu said, her beady eyes aglow. 'This is a gift from Elysia.'

They shared a look of understanding, then Jadyn turned to Gram

133

and Aura. 'If we all go forward, we may be detected. You'll wait here. Soren, will you stay with them? I take it you've already seen them?'

The young man looked disappointed, but nodded.

'It's all right, let Soren guide you forward,' Obanji said. 'I've seen them before, when I was younger.' He looked at Gram and Aura. 'I'll get to know our new friends better.'

Gram gave the Abuthan a resigned look, while Aura pouted and sat on a rock. 'Not wanting see, any ways,' she griped sarcastically. 'Erlings. Dull dull dull.'

Jadyn grinned at Soren. 'Take us in, Initiate.'

They left their helms with Obanji – they didn't want the steel glinting in the sun – and followed Soren around to a rocky headland, dropping to hands and knees and crawling to a spot overlooking a tiny gravel beach. Waves foamed in with a hissing sound and the air was rich with salt and seaweed.

At first, Romara couldn't see anything, until Soren pointed to a cluster of rounded rocks, covered in greenish brown weed and half immersed in water. Staring at them, she could see they had oddly human shapes – then she realised that the rocks themselves were the erlings, and sucked in her breath.

Erlings were said to vary wildly in size, but these were smaller than humans, with mottled dark brown skin, amber eyes and features that looked like they'd been crudely moulded from clay. Their lank hair was more like vegetation, while what little they wore looked like hide. There were four of them, sitting in a circle, chanting softly while holding hands.

'Akka on High,' Jadyn breathed in her ear. 'I never thought to see one.'

'Me neither,' she replied. 'What are they doing?'

Elindhu leaned forward excitedly. 'They're shifting skins,' she whispered. 'Just watch.'

What she meant quickly became clear: the erlings were altering form. Their skin was changing hue to bluish-green, their faces were becoming less bulbous and their bodies sleeker. When one raised a hand and spread its fingers, there was webbing between. All the while they sang, a soft keening that struck Romara as a lament.

'It's like they're in mourning,' Soren murmured.

'Perhaps they live here, but have to leave?' Jadyn suggested.

'These aren't their lands,' Romara muttered. 'The Order says that erlings are aiding the vyr. We have a duty here, even if it doesn't feel right.'

Elindhu looked appalled. 'You can't assail them. And we're not in the Order now.'

'I don't think they're vyr allies,' Jadyn said, not looking at her. 'We should leave them alone.'

Romara knew her Farm Boy: Jadyn had been raised on the old tales of erlings granting wishes and rescuing injured hunters. Vandari farmers still left them offerings of milk and offal. But those legends also had monsters in them.

She looked back at the erlings, seeing that their strangely formed faces had slitted gills in the cheeks and that the group – now clearly identifiable as a male and three females, two of them children – were naked, with skin of opalescent scales. The two adults had leather satchels slung over their shoulders and knotted to their waists.

The Codex says we must capture or kill them, she fretted. *Though I don't want to . . .*

Jadyn abruptly stood – and the erlings saw him instantly. Their amber eyes bulged in fear and they splashed into the foam, vanishing into the spume.

'Oh, they got away,' he sighed. 'What a pity.'

It was typical Jadyn to do the 'right' thing instead of the regulated thing, and damn the consequences. It was also the main reason he'd gone through his entire career without ever being given command of his own century.

'You're your own worst enemy, Jadyn,' Elindhu commented drily, but she gave Romara a pleased, grateful look. 'He's a good man,' she murmured. 'Worth waiting for.'

They clambered down and examined the tiny inlet. Ragged clothing had been left behind, and a few copper trinkets glinted on the sand; these, they hastily grabbed. 'Imagine being able to change form, to adapt to any environment,' Jadyn marvelled. 'What a remarkable race. There are only a few thousand on the reservations, but perhaps there are many more in the wild?'

'There probably are, if soft-hearts like you keep letting them go,' Romara said wryly. 'But I suppose they looked harmless. I thought erlings were tall and beautiful?'

'They take many forms,' Elindhu replied. 'Once they had cities and they ruled the north.'

Erling ruins still dotted the north, eerie reminders that empires could also fall. The link between erlings and the vyr was unproven, but treated as fact by the imperial court. The reservations in Tyr were reputedly dismal places, and Elindhu had told them that the erlings would probably be extinct in a decade or two.

They returned to Obanji, Gram and Aura. The two men were chatting reasonably amiably – Obanji had a way with people – and Aura was bathing her feet in the sea, still clearly cross at not being allowed to see the erlings.

'Let's go,' Jadyn said. He was still sounding unsure about being in command.

They walked along the cliffs for another hour, by which stage Romara felt like she was walking on nails. But Elindhu had a look at her feet and applied some salve, then padded her boots out with extra cloth. After that, walking was more comfortable.

They were starting to think about finding a place to set camp when they approached a low ridge, and Obanji came trotting back. 'There's a settlement ahead,' he warned.

'Elysia be praised,' Romara groaned. 'First up, I'm getting new boots.'

'I'm not sure this is the place for that,' the Abuthan replied. 'It doesn't look safe.'

'We need horses,' Jadyn reminded them. 'Let's get the lie of the land, then decide.'

Keeping low, they climbed the ridge and surveyed the little village. There was a tiny stream feeding a surprisingly large sprawl of tiny mudbrick houses, clustered together like a fungal growth around a rocky inlet. Scrawny cattle moped about the fringes, but this didn't look much like a farming community. Sailing ships, seven in all, were either docked at a rickety wooden wharf, or anchored in the small bay. All of them were war galleys, with archery platforms and metal rams on the prows. But they flew no flags.

Pirates.

Jadyn felt his stomach tighten at the sight of the ships, the kind he and the Falcons had hunted for four years along the Aquinium coast before they'd been transferred to the islands. They were the plague of the shipping lanes, but resources were stretched so thinly that successive Hierophants hadn't managed to eradicate them.

This village was clearly reliant on piracy, but it didn't look exactly prosperous. Former fishermen, driven to it by desperation, Jadyn suspected. Recently, whole shoals of fish had been washing ashore, days dead – something to do with the temperature changing in the deep oceans, according to the scholars, affecting the currents and the migration and breeding of water life. Catches were plummeting, which meant those who lived off the sea were starving.

'This is a dangerous place,' Obanji warned. 'We should go on.'

'It's the only place we know of, and we need supplies,' Romara countered. 'And the next village will be exactly the same, or worse.'

Jadyn nodded. 'I agree. We've got about half a day's food and water left, and this place is unknown to us all. We'll have to get what we need here.'

'They won't sell us anything,' Gram predicted. 'They'll be living hand to mouth as it is.'

'Then we'll take what we need,' Jadyn growled. 'This is an illegal operation and anything that causes pirates discomfort, I count as a blessing.'

The others nodded emphatically, except Elindhu. 'Any trouble could put the Order on our trail,' she said.

'Then be not seen,' Aura said. 'Be indivisible.'

'Invisible,' Romara corrected waspishly.

Jadyn touched her arm placatingly. 'Aura's right, this is a situation requiring stealth.' He faced the others. 'Here's what we'll do. We'll wait for twilight, so there's light to work with, but enough shadows to hide in. We need water and food, horses and saddlery. They should all be in the same place – the stables. We'll approach from inland . . . See, over there? That's an Akkanite Church, so we'll enter during evening orison, while the village is at prayer. That'll hopefully allow us to slip in and out without a fuss.'

That decided, they settled into what shade they could find, and Obanji took the first watch, stringing his bow and stabbing arrows into the ground in a line, including one of his rare elobyne-tipped shafts. But the next few hours passed quietly, and Jadyn took over sentry duty.

'How's Soren settling in?' he asked, as Obanji went to leave.

'He's still in shock, trying to come to terms with new abilities, and being a fugitive.'

'I feel terrible about that. He was innocent of all this.'

'Right up until he joined us and made those Lions look like fools,' Obanji replied. 'He came in out of nowhere, and even against the glyma, he was deadly. He's a natural, and well-drilled, too. His father was imperial army before he got invalided out, and a top swordsman, by Soren's account.' The Abuthan sighed heavily. 'I get the sense his father was also a bully who took out his frustrations on the boy.'

'I'm grateful you've taken him under your wing.'

Obanji's face crinkled into a sympathetic smile. 'Jadyn, you've got the weight of the world, right now. Let me worry about Soren. It's the least I can do.'

Jadyn shifted uncomfortably. 'It should be you in command.'

'No, I back Romara's decision,' Obanji replied. 'In my land, there is a thing called a dream-quest. Men and women have crossed the deserts in search of themselves. This is your dream-quest, my friend. It's right that you should lead.' He clapped him on the shoulder. 'Trust yourself.'

I'm lucky to know you, Jadyn thought, heartened.

Obanji went to rest, and Jadyn settled into watching the village. The sailors came ashore, settling down to drinking and queuing up at curtained booths; he guessed they were for the local women. Ragged snatches of music reached him, carried on a brisk off-shore breeze. There looked to be two classes of people here: those who tended the crops about the huts and those from the ships, whose purpose while ashore appeared to be exclusively concerned with debauchery. He doubted it was a happy or safe place.

An hour before sunset, Aura joined him, settling nearby and watching the town intently. She might come across as flighty, but she clearly paid a great deal of attention to planning.

'What race are the pirates?' Jadyn asked. 'Are they local?'

She shook her head. 'When village go bad, go pirate, then bad men move in, first to teach ways, then to rule. Be like invite wolf to home. Pirates be Pelas men.'

The Pelas archipelago was vast, hundreds or even thousands of islands, most of them too small to be inhabited. Centuries ago, they'd been a major naval power, terrifying the coastal settlements of the south. Eventually the Aquini built a navy and crushed them. Soon after, their capital was destroyed by a volcanic eruption, from which they never recovered. Now the islands were a backwater, riddled with old secrets and strange legends.

'Pelasians, eh?' Jadyn mused. 'Let's not worry if one or two get hurt, then.'

Aura perked up. 'Aura like this, Farm Boy.'

Only Romara called him 'Farm Boy'. It felt odd to hear another use the nickname, but he didn't mind. *I am a Farm Boy, at heart. And once we've done what we must, I will be again.*

She remained with him throughout the watch, unsettling company with her flirting manner and odd speech. There was more to her than met the eye, he judged; she was proving to be a careful planner, despite her apparent flightiness. He decided that he liked her spirit.

Together, they studied the village, working out how it functioned. The large buildings around the wharf and square were dominated by the sailors, while the primitive thatched huts were inhabited by the Solabi natives, probably the original inhabitants. The poverty of it all was evident from the stench of rotting fish and human waste; it came from a dumping ground not far below his position, wafting towards them on the warm wind. Whatever wealth piracy brought in, it obviously wasn't shared equally.

Parasites, Jadyn thought grimly. *I wish we had our full century here.*

Finally, the burning sun went down, kissing the steeple of the church before vanishing. They rejoined the others just as the call they were waiting for rang out: 'Kalefar, Kalefar . . .'

'Dear Elysia, I miss the orison,' Romara muttered.

As the populace drifted towards the church in the square, Jadyn led his little group down the slope to the edge of the village. Those who still wore tabards had them covered by cloaks, and their helms were tucked under their arms, so there was nothing in sight marking them as Vestal.

Chants and responses carried from the inlet, and Jadyn felt the ache Romara had expressed, not just for the replenishing of their elobyne orbs, but for community, and the sense of belonging to the greater whole.

Before they entered the maze of empty huts, they glimpsed the pale glow of an orison gem-cloth, being renewed by prayer for any Vestal knight who might need it. It was strange how the orison persisted, even without knights there to benefit.

We'll recharge if we can, he resolved. *It might be our last chance for a long time.*

With the brief orison done, the villagers began returning, as Jadyn's party neared the stables. Music rose again from the square, blending with the cooking smoke and the reek of the midden.

They were skirting a pig pen between low-roofed hovels when a male voice came from the shadows. 'Min an ghurab?' it asked, in a guttural voice.

Jadyn's heart thumped, but Aura spoke up. 'Albhara,' she chirped. 'Nahn tayihun?'

The unseen man spat out some words in a disdainful voice, and Aura thanked him, then led them on, shooting Jadyn a superior look. 'Aura say; we is lost sailors, ask direction. This way.'

Jadyn found himself admiring her wit. 'I'm right behind you,' he told her, in case she needed reassurance.

'Enjoy,' she tittered, jiggling her hips as she led the way through the maze of huts. Yes, she had grace and a shapely body, but Jadyn looked away, because increased libido often presaged a loss of glyma-control.

Another minute took them to the edge of what passed for the main road, where they halted in the shadows. To the left lay the church and the square, where most of the villagers had congregated. Fiddles shrieked, rough male voices sang shanties, and the smell of cooking filled the air. It looked like the crews of all seven ships were ashore, at least a hundred men.

Jadyn drew them into a huddle. 'We'll head for the stables. We want two horses each, and food and water and travelling gear. And we'll need it fast.'

Aura spoke up. 'We be too many. Must suppurate, or people make alarmings.'

'Separate,' Jadyn corrected. 'What does everyone think?'

Romara shook her head, but Obanji nodded. 'Two pairs, one trio,' he suggested. He eyed Gram and Aura. 'Keep these two apart.'

Jadyn agreed. 'All right, Obanji takes Soren and Elindhu. Romara, take Gram. I'm with Aura. She and I'll go first, for the language.' Before anyone could object, he pulled Aura up and they stepped into the road, while the others shrank back into the shadows.

Aura plucked at his sleeve. 'Walk normal. No sneaky-sneak. Be, uh . . . braised? Brassy?'

'*Brazen*. I thought we didn't want to be seen?'

'Right now, many eyes see. Walk with belonging, be no problem.'

Jadyn looked about and realised she was right: some villagers were returning, mostly older folk, and the huts weren't so deserted as he'd thought. He and Aura needed to look like they belonged, so he straightened and walked openly towards the stables. The men eyed him appraisingly, while the women and children darted aside.

We're pirates in port, he tried to project. *Don't mess with us . . .*

But then a young Solabi with a scarred face detached from the shadows and confronted them. 'Not know you,' he said, in halting Talmoni. He wore a curved sword and had an air of violence.

Aura stepped between them, swaying flirtatiously as she replied.

They conversed, then the man stepped aside, fluttering a hand over his heart.

'What was that all about?' Jadyn asked, as they walked on.

'He not see me in square,' she replied. 'I say am new ashore, he believe, offer money for me, tell me am beautiful.' She grinned. 'Is true am beautiful, but not enough money.'

She sashayed onwards, and Jadyn had to hurry to keep up. They were nearing the stable, for he heard hammering on metal and saw a deep red glow inside the wide open doors. Presumably the smith was repairing harnesses and gear for the next march into Foyland.

Jadyn couldn't risk hesitation, so he strode right in, with Aura behind him. He'd hoped the smith would be alone, but hope cheated him: there were at least a dozen men inside the dimly lit building, which was full of tools and half-finished implements. They all looked his way and began to rise, hands going to weapons.

'Hey, who're you?' someone asked.

But then another man spoke, and to Jadyn's horror, he knew the voice.

'Jadyn? By all that's holy, Jadyn Kaen?'

Huddled in the alley of the wretched village, full of the stink of animal waste, cooking-fire smoke and the ordure of packed human- ity, Soren found it hard to breathe. At least on Avas they had cold air and cleansing rain, but here the reek of rotting garbage and the miasma of the cooking smoke permeated the air. Inside the huts, people coughed repeatedly.

Avas, he now realised, had been a kind of paradise, a wonderful dream he'd once had – until the vyr burned it all. For a moment he was overcome with missing it, and Ma and Enid.

To calm himself, he ran through the runes Obanji had been teaching him, readying his mind for whatever might lie ahead, even though he had little control right now. He couldn't even draw energy consistently from the pommel-orb. He would master it, though, he knew that.

I will be a warrior like my father never dreamed possible.

Obanji tapped his shoulder and he realised that Romara and Gram had already gone. He, the Abuthan and the unsettling Elindhu were the only ones left. 'Is it time?' he asked.

Obanji nodded. 'Aye, let's—'

Elindhu's eyes flashed open. 'Yes, we must go,' she said tersely. 'Jadyn's in trouble.'

She darted from the alley into the dusty road and began to run towards the stables. Obanji and Soren went after her, as the village came to life . . .

Jadyn stopped, stunned, as the dozen men in the stables, variously rubbing down horses or swigging from tankards, faced him. Then his eyes went to a burly bald man in their midst, clad in rough leathers but wearing an Order flamberge over his shoulder, with the orb on the pommel glowing softly.

Tevas Nicolini. Of all the damnable luck . . .

If Jadyn had been any good at bluffing, he might have concocted a story, but nothing came. Instead he just gaped at his old blademaster and wondered at the cruelty of fate. The last time he'd seen Tevas had been at his retirement ceremony. He'd put on weight since then, and his skin was tanned darker, but it was truly him.

There's no good reason for him to be here, and that sword is illegal. So he's a pirate now . . .

'Jadyn,' Nicolini marvelled, 'what the jagat are you doing in this hole?'

'Uh, we just rode in,' he stammered. 'On Order business.'

It didn't even ring true: if he'd truly been here on Order business, he'd already be killing people. But lying was something he had little to no experience in.

Tevas shook his head. 'No, you haven't. The grandmasters know to leave this patch alone.' He spat on the ground. 'Why are you really here?'

Jadyn's brain froze, while Aura edged backwards.

'What do we do?' one of the men, clearly Pelasian, asked Tevas.

'Well,' the former knight drawled, lifting a hand over his shoulder and gripping his hilt, 'if my old student doesn't lay down his sword in six seconds . . . we kill him.'

Jadyn held up his hand. 'I am a Vestal knight and sanctioned to use the glyma,' he warned. 'When you left the Order, you lost that right, Tevas.'

His former tutor just shrugged. 'Out here, rules don't matter.' He drew his flamberge, the blade glittering in the smithy fire; and Jadyn had no choice but to do the same.

'What about the woman?' the smith growled, hefting a hammer. 'Like the look'a her.'

'She say you be ugly turd,' Aura replied, pulling out a dagger.

'I'll brand your arse,' he replied, placing an iron in the fire. 'So everyone'll know it's mine.'

Tevas pursed his lips sourly, as if this were a sadly necessary task, like butchering a knackered horse, then he sent pale light running down the blade. 'Let's do this,' he growled.

He levelled the blade at Jadyn and slammed a burst of energy and force straight at him.

Jadyn had seen Tevas do just that a thousand times and was already moving, drawing on glyma and going for the nearest Pelasian. Dodging the energy pulse, he rolled under a sweeping hatchet, coming up under the man's guard. His flamberge plunged into the man's belly and he swung him round to catch Tevas' next bolt. As the hatchet dropped, he caught it and hurled it into the face of the next closest man.

Aura tried to bolt for the door, but a man dropped from the rafters and, leering toothily, blocked her exit. She backed up – towards the hulking smith.

Jadyn headed for her, shielding against Tevas' next bolt then firing his own blast of energy – into the glowing coals of the smith's fire, which sent them flying. Everyone else ducked the fiery missiles except the shielded Tevas.

Aura pulled a dagger, but two men were blocking Jadyn from reaching her, closing in on either flank to bring him down before he could bring his glyma to bear . . .

•

Her escape route blocked, Aura stumbled back, feigning fear. She dropped her dagger as the Pelasian pirate came at her, reaching for her throat—

—as she flashed her right hand up her left sleeve and produced another dagger, whipping it round and slashing the pirate's face, making him shriek and stagger back, clutching at his cheeks as blood sprayed.

But others were closing in, led by the giant blacksmith . . .

Her body moved as if of its own volition, as if she were outside it, looking on and shouting instructions. The horrific details – the stabbing and the blood and the shrieks – made no impression on her, reflexes and the survival instinct taking over. She felt as if her body knew exactly what to do, and in this hyperaware state, nothing was impossible. She spun to face another man who came in on her right, kicked him in the face and staggered him, tried to run but the smith reached out, grabbed her arm and swung her, sweeping her off her feet and slamming her to the dirt.

She gasped, half-winded and momentarily stunned. A few paces away, Jadyn was fighting three men in a blur of sparks, the hammering of steel on steel deafening in this confined place. Then the smith loomed over her, holding a massive hammer.

His boot slammed into her side, she almost blacked out in pain and lost her blade, then the giant dropped down on top of her, one hand gripping her throat and the other ripping open her blouse . . .

The village had realised that something was wrong, shouting and pointing at Romara and Gram as they hurried for the stables, a burgeoning crowd closing in. Obanji, Soren and Elindhu were out of sight somewhere behind them.

Then Romara heard steel on steel and felt the invisible pulse of the glyma.

'Come on!' she shouted at Gram. She wasn't sure he'd follow, but Jadyn was in there and that was all that mattered. She drew her blade as she ran, but left the elobyne quiescent, frightened of losing control. *I've got to do without it, starting now.*

That resolution lasted only as long as it took to burst through the wide open doors and see Jadyn and Aura cornered and fighting a dozen men at least. Aura was down, with a huge man in smith's leathers throttling her. Although fearing it would be the death of her, she flung a burst of energy that forced the smith off the girl, then ploughed on towards Jadyn, cutting down a Pelasian as she went – and then she saw Tevas Nicolini. Her heart thudded, but she swallowed all her tangled memories of the man and roared, 'Back off, Tevas!'

Nicolini turned, his face falling. 'Oh, Rom, not you, too?' But he came straight at her, preventing her from reaching Jadyn.

'Jag off, old man,' she snarled back, her blood rising despite herself.

His flamberge was lit; if she didn't match him, she'd be blown away . . . and Jadyn's life was at stake. So she drew on her elobyne, a moment before their blades, now both lit by glyma-light, smashed together . . . and something inside her *howled—*

For a moment she was back in training as that hard, smooth-pated head bobbed behind a wall of moving steel. They smashed at each other, staggered and slammed together again, and she went from dread to wonder, because somehow she'd improved – and Tevas had got *old.*

But the other combatants had recovered from her surprise appearance and were flooding towards her.

If we're going to die here . . . we'll take these scum with us . . .

Her vision went scarlet again, and her body rippled with an overload of glyma-energy . . .

Aura was pinned, crushed and airless, helpless and despairing – until an explosion of force hit the blacksmith, throwing him bodily away. She gasped down some air and rolled away, smacking against the smith's anvil, even as he rose again and snatched up his hammer, bellowing in fury. He swung, the massive steel head cracking down an instant after she'd shot sideways.

She got the fire-pit between them, but he reared up on the far side, his face lit by the molten metal boiling in a stone trough. Acting on instinct, she seized a big ladle and somehow knowing *exactly* what to do with it, in one motion scooped and flung—

—the liquid metal into the blacksmith's face. He screamed, the most hideous shriek she'd ever heard, and went down, flailing.

She spun as two more men came at her, just as her imagination conjured a new way out. She fled for the back door, hurdling tangles of old saddlery and piles of coal, then shooting out into the yard. The pair pursued, as did others seeking easier prey, and suddenly she had half a dozen men on her heels . . .

When Romara ran ahead, Gram was caught on the back foot and left behind, facing a growing number of villagers, some of whom produced weapons and closed in, shouting questions he couldn't understand. He took to his heels and ran to the stables, where the sounds of combat were getting louder.

Then glyma-energy flared wildly – and somehow, it triggered his own potential, the burning core he'd always resisted. His mother was gone now, and these people meant nothing to him. He only knew he had to get into the fray, so for the first time, he surrendered himself to the urges inside him.

The result was almost instantaneous – as if it had been waiting for this very moment. His gums swelled inside his elongating jaws, his spine stretched, crunched and bent, and lengthening nails burst bloodily from his thickening fingertips. He staggered on, bulging muscles stretching his furs, then he came down on all fours and ploughed into the stables.

At first all he could see through strangely blurring eyesight was the lanterns and the glowing coals – and Romara's auburn hair streaming like a banner. She was screaming, engulfed by a typhoon of light, and he could somehow *feel* that agony.

Instinctively, he *pulled* it from her, ripping it away, and his vision went scarlet. His hands were now talons and he roared like a mountain lion. Heads turned his way, wide-eyed and fearful, but all he saw was Romara, with a pirate lining up a blow at her unprotected flank. In a bound he was on that man. Hurling him aside, broken, he waded into the rest. A sword turned on his thickening hide, so he tore the man's throat out with his right claw, then battered the next blade aside, snapped the man's neck like it was a twig and hurled the corpse at the next man.

Romara's eyes no longer flashed scarlet but her normal pale blue, momentarily wide-eyed and stunned – but she recovered, throwing herself at a bald-pated man wielding an Order flamberge . . .

Soren, Obanji and Elindhu burst through the growing crowd of Solabi villagers almost before they were aware of them. A crowd had gathered outside the smithy, some holding spears and knives, but they looked hesitant about intervening.

Inside, steel clanged and shouted battle-cries were interspersed with shrieks of pain. Something like an invisible hot wind was pulsing inside it.

That must be the glyma, Soren realised.

Elindhu raised her staff and blazed light, and the villagers scattered from her path. Obanji and Soren flanked her, the Abuthan veteran with his bow drawn, heading towards the fray. Behind them, a bell began tolling in the church tower. Glancing over his shoulder, Soren saw Pelasian sailors brandishing cutlasses appearing along the central road. 'There they are!' one shouted, breaking into a run, the rest following fast behind him.

At the cry, Obanji twisted and shot an arrow, striking the man mid-chest. To their left, three men with bows were taking aim themselves.

'Move!' Elindhu shouted, making the villagers scatter in alarm, then she raised her staff and shouted, '*Salva*—'

The archers fired, but their arrows shattered. That made them all recoil, but then a spearman rushed in, intent on skewering her in the back. Soren intercepted him, catching the spearhead one-handed before breaking the man's jaw with his cross-guard and knocking him senseless. A hurled dagger grazed his cheek, and he felt a sudden flash of rage.

'*Calm*, lad,' said Obanji, appearing beside him, in the same breath shouting, '*Pulso*,' and pushing another man out of their way.

Elindhu followed up with, '*Flamma!*' Crackling heat and flame surrounded them; a defensive swirl that made the remaining villagers scatter fearfully, gaining them some respite.

'With me,' Obanji shouted, pounding towards the stables, where the glyma-energy now felt like the radiating heat of a furnace.

Cut off from Tevas Nicolini and Romara, Jadyn found himself facing two men who somehow knew – *Thanks, Tevas!* – how to ensure a glyma-user didn't get to conjure. They were hounding him with fast jabbing thrusts and stabbing blades. That kept him off-balance and unable to pause and gather the energy to truly cut loose and use the one advantage he had.

He was terrified for Romara – neither of them had ever managed to beat Tevas Nicolini when he was their blademaster, and he could feel her growing rage.

Gram Larch waded into the mêlée, his unexpectedly leathery hide turning blades and his claws tearing at the pirates, scattering them as blood sprayed.

He is a jagging vorlok after all, Jadyn thought. *Or maybe he's just become one.*

Either way, Gram's rampage was breaking the pirates. Jadyn shouted at him to stay close, but the trapper, now a giant thing somewhere between wolf and bear, caught the scent of fear and charged after the fleeing pirates, leaving Jadyn and Romara to fend for themselves . . .

Even as Romara fell into the maelstrom of the glyma, the fires inside her were again ripped away, a bewildering experience she couldn't fathom. But it kept her from succumbing to madness, and that meant everything in that moment. She needed all her concentration and skill right now, or she was done.

She had no desire to kill Tevas Nicolini, a man she'd once been in love with, or so she'd thought. He had taught her how to fight, given her the skills to survive in what was primarily a man's world, turning a feckless high-born debutante into someone who could fight – and best – most men she faced. That'd been so empowering, so uplifting, that she'd fallen for him desperately. And with her libido newly starved, having lost Elan Sandreth, she'd *hurled* herself at the older man.

Tevas Nicolini had not just refused her, he'd beaten it out of her in the training arena.

Akka on High, he was brutal. But it had been what she needed, if she wasn't to be cast from the Order or destroyed by her lack of physical and emotional control. He'd once almost drowned her in a horse trough to cool her ardour – all for her own good.

He saved me . . .

Once they'd got past her embarrassing infatuation, they'd become proper friends. She *owed* him, not just because he'd taught her how to survive and win a fight, but how to deal with temptations and forge proper, adult friendships. He, alongside Jadyn and Obanji, her other role models, had been a big part in her becoming herself.

So she could barely bring herself to attack, which was her undoing . . .

He pulled a *Fool's Feint*, which had *always* fooled her, that fake sweep of his flamberge luring her into over-committing and exposing herself. Tevas dashed her blade aside and stabbed at her unguarded waist—

Aura hurtled out the back doors, just ahead of the men chasing her, while Jadyn, Romara and Gram, who was looking more beast than man, turned the tide at the entrance. She lost sight of her companions, dodging and feinting around water-troughs, hay-ricks and broken-down fences, left then right, rolling under the grasp of one man and sidestepping another. Some kept on running, clearly unnerved by the fight inside, but two stayed with her, and she evaded one, darting round a broken-down old shed, only to blunder into the other . . .

She shrieked in horror, but to her amazement Gram appeared behind the man blocking her way, roaring in fury. Both men forgot her in that instant, terrified by the towering vyr, whose face was now bestial, his talons like daggers.

Whipping out her last two hidden knives, she slipped behind the nearest pirate and plunged them into his back, impaling him from left and right. The pirate staggered, gurgled bloodily and fell on his face, as Gram ripped the other man off his feet and threw him at a wall – and right through it. A moment later, the vyr was rearing over her, his eyes blazing green and weeping blood. She realised that he was so far gone he barely knew friend from foe.

'Nice vorlok!' she squealed, as she kicked herself backwards . . .

Soren was younger and faster than Obanji and Elindhu, and the glyma-energy in the air was somehow filling his limbs and lungs. He erupted through the stable doors and saw a bald man outwit Romara and open her up for a killing blow.

He was too far away to attack physically, so he shouted '*Pulso*,' blasting an air-punch at the man, just as Obanji had been teaching him. It slammed the man sideways into a pile of the blacksmith's tools, and by pure luck, his skull struck into the anvil.

Shields flashed, turning the worst of the blow aside, so the man only convulsed painfully. But Soren stormed on, desperate to capitalise before the man recovered . . . when suddenly he felt like every bone in his body had turned to hollow straw, and his muscles to jelly.

He was falling even as his vision blurred and winked out . . .

Romara's life flashed before her eyes, but instead of ending it, Tevas Nicolini went flying sideways and hit the smith's anvil. His wards protected him from serious harm, but he was still down. Realising he was still conscious, she scrambled towards him and slammed her hilt into his temple, before he could react. He went down like a sack of meal, helpless.

She hefted her flamberge, but already knew she wouldn't kill him. He meant too much to her. She lowered the weapon again, thinking, *I'd rather stab myself.*

The surviving pirates were running, and in moments they'd all vanished from the stables – those who could. Jadyn, panting hard, blazed a weak energy bolt over their heads, just to ensure they kept running, then faced the room.

Elindhu was standing in the open doorway, her staff's orb ablaze, fiercely intimidating for a five-foot-tall woman with a pillar of grey braids. Obanji was helping Soren sit up – the boy had collapsed, but he didn't look wounded. *He just used the glyma in combat for the first time*, Jadyn guessed, remembering what that was like. Everyone overdid it in their maiden fight.

'Wha' wassat?' Soren mumbled, wincing at the fluid Obanji was feeding him from his hipflask. Obanji's lethal homebrew was the perfect elixir for those 'over-extending' moments. But outside, voices were still shouting, and the church bell was still ringing wildly.

We have to go, or we'll be trapped in here . . .

He hurried to Romara, standing like an angel over Tevas Nicolini's prone body. That his old blademaster still breathed was a relief, even if he'd gone renegade.

So have we, in a way . . . I wish he could join us . . . But this was a quest for volunteers, and if he refused, they'd be obliged to deal with him. *Better we leave him behind.*

Aura reappeared through the rear door with Gram. The Nepari's face was pale, but she'd fought with real athleticism and no little skill. Either she'd had training, or she was like Soren, a natural to this bloody game. He made a mental note to find out which.

As for Gram, he was in vyr-form, with a slavering, bloody maw and talons like daggers, but he was hovering protectively over Aura. The vorlok – if that was what he was – gazed back at Jadyn, his eyes now green and weeping blood. Then he exhaled, contorted and shrank into himself, his monstrous form giving way as it had from his mother in death, leaving the same large but ordinary-looking man, in torn furs. He dropped to his knees and retched.

'Gram lied to us,' Romara exclaimed. She hefted her blade again. 'I'll deal with him.'

Jadyn went to stop her, but her blood was still up, her control at the tipping point – he wondered if the only thing that had kept her inner beast at bay was coming face to face with Nicolini. She strode towards Gram, the orb on her flamberge powering up again—

*

152

Gram, reeling in the aftermath, saw Romara Challys coming, murder in her eyes, fuelling her body into something of focused ferocity. Her comrades were only just realising, and it was already too late for any of them to intervene – if they even wanted to.

He did the only thing he could: he reached for that power inside her, not knowing if he could rip it from her as he'd done before, but trying, with desperate alacrity . . .

As he did, he experienced *something*, so visceral that it filled all his senses: he tasted, smelled, and felt her, all of her, tasted her mouth, her saliva . . . A wave of physical desire smote him, driving him to his knees . . . then the beast inside him rose again, surging to his defence . . .

But he refused to channel it this time, instead hurling it away again, blasting that energy into the blacksmith's fire. It erupted, blasting upwards so high it scorched the roof beams, then all his senses stalled, he crumpled and fell onto his belly—

—as did Romara, whose face had changed from fury to bewilderment, her eyes glazed. She stumbled as her legs gave way and fell limply on her side.

Then darkness flooded in and he feared he'd killed them both . . .

'He's fine,' Elindhu reported tersely, kneeling over the prostrate trapper. She'd already seen to Romara, who was also breathing, if semi-conscious. 'He's waking.'

Obanji prodded Gram with his boot. 'Hey, vorlok, what'd you do to her?'

'No . . . I . . . she was . . . attack,' Gram babbled, sounding as stunned as Romara. 'I took her rage . . . into me . . .' He buried his face in his shaking hands. 'I've never let that happen to me before. I never wanted to become this.'

Elindhu, snorting in disbelief, turned to Jadyn. 'Now what?'

The others stared, waiting for their commander's decision.

We're all here because of Gram's story, Jadyn thought, his mind racing. *Does this mean he lied?* He remembered what Gram had told him. 'Perhaps he leeched energy from Romara, like he did with his mother on Avas?'

'I'm not his jagging mother,' Romara, who was sipping Obanji's homebrew, rasped. Her face was white as snow and her eyes glazed. 'I want answers.'

'So do I,' Jadyn answered. 'But not here. We need to move.'

As if to emphasise the point, Soren called from the doorway, 'There's lots of folks outside.'

Jadyn joined him, and saw dozens of villagers milling fearfully. The pirates, realising they faced glyma-users, were hanging back, but he doubted that'd last.

'Saddle up, people,' he told his pentacle. 'Take what we need.'

They responded by plundering the smithy and stables for travel gear. 'The pirates were preparing to travel overland,' Elindhu remarked, when they found a pile of already packed saddlebags. 'These saddlebags are full already. We're in luck.'

Noble-born Romara, who knew horseflesh, selected their mounts and they all worked frantically to saddle up and lash on the baggage. They even found riding boots, and Romara was swift to replace her own worn-out footwear.

Romara indicated Tevas Nicolini, who was still out cold. 'What about him?' she asked Jadyn. 'If we took him with us, he might . . .' Her voice tailed off hopefully.

Jadyn shook his head, remembering the coldness with which Nicolini had ordered his death. 'Leave him. He's gone bad, Rom. I'm sorry, I know he's important to you – and me too – but he's left the Order and he's still using the glyma. That's a capital offence.'

'We're not exactly in the Order any more ourselves,' she reminded him.

'I know. And we owe him, which is why we let him live. Hopefully, he won't come after us.'

Then Soren called from the doors, 'More men are coming!'

That spurred them all into motion.

Soren mounted up and taking the reins of the other spare, told Jadyn, 'I've ridden before. We had a horse on the farm.'

'Jagat, it's good to be in the saddle again,' Romara said as she mounted. 'I didn't fancy walking in unbroken boots.' She still looked pale, but she was steady as she nudged her mare towards the doors.

Jadyn turned to Aura. 'Do you know how to ride?'

'Have not. Is easy?'

'No, it's not. Romara, take the reins of Aura's horse. She can ride with me for now.' He kicked his foot from his left stirrup. 'Aura, come here. Put one foot in here, then swing up behind me, grab my shoulders and hold on.'

Aura hesitated, until a trumpet blew from the direction of the bay.

'Move, you jagging nuisance,' Romara shouted, clearly still on edge.

Shooting her a venomous glance, Aura did as she was bid, while Jadyn fought to keep the unfamiliar beast steady. It took a couple of goes, then she scrambled up and plastered herself to Jadyn's back. He steadied the horse when Aura squeaked and almost lost her grip and trotted calmly for the doors.

Soren took the lead, followed by Elindhu, perched side-saddle on her mare like a bird on the back of an Erathi river buffalo. They brandished sword and staff respectively, their elobyne crystals lighting the scene. The villagers had fled to the cover of the huts, but the pirates, sixty men or more all armed to the teeth, were arrayed before them, blocking the path to the cove. Clearly, going to the church and using the orison cloth to recharge would cause more bloodshed, and the risk of losing someone.

'We'll move out,' Jadyn told his comrades. 'There'll be other shards.'

Then he said to Aura, 'Hold on, tight,' and kicked his heels into the horse's flanks, breaking into a canter, and the rest followed, moving up to a gallop, tearing along the moonlit dirt road and out into the night.

'E Cara,' Aura gasped, jolting at each hoof-fall. 'Horse ... Bad ... Ow – *ow!*'

There was no question of slowing down for her comfort. In minutes, the nameless port was cut off by the first ridge, and before them the road wound into broken hills. On the crest of the rise, they reined in and took stock. Aura sagged against Jadyn's back, groaning in discomfort, but until they could find the time to teach her the basics, she'd have to stay where she was.

Tired they might be, but the escape had lifted their spirits. '*Woohoo*,' Soren whooped. 'Now *that* was something!' He punched the air. 'I used the glyma – did you see me shielding? I stopped some of their arrows, and—'

Obanji clapped him on the shoulder and interrupted, 'Yes, but you also overextended and fainted. That lack of control can kill you. You must drill, drill, and drill again. Understand?'

Soren looked crestfallen, but he nodded obediently.

'Anyone hurt?' Elindhu asked, and when they'd all chorused their status – fine, basically – Obanji looked at Aura.

'Which way now?'

Aura pointed inland. 'Follow road, find river, mountains. Cross for Neparia.'

'There you have it,' Jadyn said.

Elindhu gestured towards the village. 'Too bad we couldn't replenish our elobyne orbs,' she said regretfully. 'That church's orison cloth could be the last we see in a while.'

Obanji and Soren nodded in agreement, but Romara just winced and looked away.

'We can't go back,' Jadyn replied. 'Listen up. Tevas said, "The grandmasters know to let us alone." That means these damned pirates have cut a deal with the local authorities, so we can take it as read that our presence will be reported. We've got to move on. No rest until dawn, I'm sorry. We ride all night.'

The eerie Skull moon rose, followed by the Dragon's Egg with its fractured surface, then the red-limned Eye, the three moons lighting their way so they didn't need torches. Descending from a small huddle of low hills, they reached a flat plain, and the road stretched out before them towards the shadowy mountains of the Qor-Massif, a hundred kylos or more to the southeast.

'Hold on tight,' Jadyn told Aura. 'Falcons, the road is before us. Let's ride!'

7

Divided Paths

The Gift, Glyma and Vyr

The Gift – a natural capacity to use magical energies – is bequeathed by Akka according to His inscrutable will. Those who use it to wield His holy fire must maintain their discipline, lest they succumb to rage, and become vyr (a Qoroi word for corruption). For this reason, all glyma-wielders must put aside sinful urges and live chaste, wholesome lives, dedicated to serving Akka and Elysia, and their living descendant, the hierophant.

CLAUDYNE VULKER, FIRST FEMALE EXEMPLAR, PETRAXUS 1352

Solabas
Summer 1472

As the hours passed, the Falcons slowed their pace to conserve the horses. Finally, the sun rose, sending shafts of golden light across the landscape before softening to reveal stark, barren hills of broken rock.

For Romara, the night ride had been tortuous, physically exhausting because she'd been drained before they even began, and with her control of the glyma all but gone, she couldn't draw on her elobyne orb for strength. And then there was the terror of what Gram had done.

He stole my power and left me helpless!

How he'd done it eluded her, and she had no idea how to resist – and if one vorlok could do it, then potentially they all could, and that would render the Order helpless.

Almost as worrying, the act of sucking out her glyma had been accompanied by the most unsettling blast of physical and emotional feelings she'd ever experienced. At times, using glyma in combination, she'd felt a sensation of *simpatico* with another, usually Jadyn, but this had been *much* more powerful. Even now she could remember the taste of Gram's mouth, and the musky smell of him, as if they'd just made love. Humiliatingly, for a moment she'd desired exactly that.

It's going to drive me insane.

As soon as Jadyn signalled a halt, she rode fast at Gram, whipping her horse's head round just in time so her beast's shoulder rammed into his mount, making it stagger and knocking him from the saddle to the stony ground.

He knew enough to roll away from the kicking hooves, but she gave him no respite, leaping down and striding towards him, her fists clenched, and raged, 'What did you do?' She grabbed his hide jerkin. 'What did you do to me?'

'I don't know,' Gram managed to choke through the dust – but then he looked up into her eyes and suddenly he was doing it *again*, pulling her glyma away, draining her like a leech while burrowing into her soul.

'Stop it,' she choked, reeling dazedly away. 'Someone, stop him . . .'

Jadyn dismounted hurriedly, thrusting his reins into Aura's hands, and ran over, grabbed Romara and turned her to face him. 'What's happened?'

She didn't want to explain what she'd experienced because it felt like admitting to some deep-rooted flaw. And somehow, Jadyn – her faithful, devoted love – wasn't the right person to tell. *It's like confessing to an infidelity*, she thought wildly. *And that's ridiculous, because I want nothing to do with that vyr monster . . .*

Instead, she turned to Elindhu, who was analytical enough not to be hurt by this. 'In the fight last night, Gram drew my glyma-energy out of me,' she said. 'How can that be?'

Elindhu blinked like an old owl. 'I've not heard of such a thing before. And surely, if this was something the vyr did often, we'd know.' She turned to Gram. 'Explain yourself.'

Gram's face clouded. 'It just happened . . . I wanted to stop her from hurting me – and because I'd spent years pulling energy from my mother, I suppose it came naturally.'

'Can you do it to me, now?' Elindhu asked, offering her staff-orb.

They all stiffened, but no one objected. Gram sat up, frowning, then made a reaching, pulling gesture. The orb didn't falter. 'Hmm . . . No, from me, not the orb,' Elindhu told him.

He tried again, and they both frowned. 'A little, sort of,' the trapper said.

'I agree,' Elindhu said thoughtfully. 'I certainly felt something, but it was very minor.'

Gram frowned, staring at the rocky ground. 'My mother always said I'd get her killed – I'd leave her weakened at the wrong moment. But she also said it helped keep her sane.'

'Akka on high,' Romara groaned. 'I'm not your mother, and I don't want this.'

He looked up at her sullenly. 'Nor do I.'

His brown eyes pierced her, and she could taste his fear and grief, the inner turmoil of a man who'd lost everything and lived now only on the sufferance of enemies.

'Can't you *do* something?' Romara demanded of Elindhu, turning away before Gram's compelling gaze twisted her mind. People said the vyr could beguile the unwary. Perhaps this was what they meant?

Elindhu knelt in front of Gram, who flinched. 'I could bind his powers, locking them inside him,' she mused, 'but that's hard work on both of us, and it would mean he would be helpless if we're assailed. I'd rather not do that.'

'You've got to do *something*,' Romara snapped. 'It's intolerable.'

'Tell me more about it,' Elindhu said to Gram, ignoring Romara's fear.

Gram's face took on a look of heavy concentration and his voice softened. 'It's like I've already told you: a vorlok has a bond with their coven. I had that bond with Mother, but I refused to embrace it, because I needed to stay aware, to keep her safe. When she drew on the glyma, it was as if a bell was sounding in my chest – I could sense her in her entirety. It was like being thrown into deep water, but I learned to swim it, and resist. And now, with her gone, it happens to some degree whenever anyone nearby radiates power.' He looked at Romara. 'But especially you, Siera Romara. I don't know why.'

'And you've never been tested for the Gift?'

He hung his head. 'No . . . but I don't need to be tested. I already know.'

He does have the Gift, Romara realised. 'So you really are a vorlok?'

'He's a potential vorlok,' Elindhu corrected her, 'as are we all, if you think about it. And therefore, he's potentially a Vestal knight as well.'

That silenced them all, but Gram shook his head. 'Never that,' he stated. 'I believe in the vyr cause, but I don't want to die in a berserk fit, like all vorloks and draegar eventually do.' He stared at the ground. 'Perhaps I'm a coward?'

Romara blinked at his stark words, finding herself forced to reappraise him.

He's no coward, but he's on the edge of the same precipice as me. And I was about to fall over it, but he pulled me back. Suddenly, she could no longer wholly condemn him. *He's lived with glyma-rage as long as any of us, and he's still sane, even without any Order training. That's incredible.*

Everyone was looking at her, waiting for her judgement, but she was glad not to be in charge. 'It's too hard,' she mumbled, looking at Jadyn. 'You decide. It's beyond me.'

He gave her a puzzled look, because she seldom abrogated decision-making. But he decided swiftly. 'We need Gram. This Agynea woman isn't going to talk to us without him, even if we can find her without his help. He kept Romara safe and retained his own self-control. He's earned my trust.'

'At the least, let Elindhu bind him,' Obanji urged.

'I can if I must,' Elindhu replied diffidently. 'But for what it's worth, I think it's better for Romara that I don't, in case she needs him again. I think that's vital.'

Despite her fears, Romara agreed with Elindhu, knowing that without Gram, she'd lose herself the next time she used the glyma. 'I can live with that,' she told Jadyn.

'Then it's decided,' he said. 'Get some rest, everyone. We ride again in a few hours.'

Romara risked meeting Gram's gaze again. She saw honest worry. 'Unless we're under direct attack, stay out of my way, vyr,' she told him, and he nodded, and mercifully looked away.

She went to her horse and picketed it, then sought solitude.

Jadyn watched Romara leave, feeling helpless, but he resisted the urge to follow. Everyone was his responsibility right now, not just her. So he saw to his mount and the spares, directed the setting-up of the camp and tried to clear his head after the long night's ride.

Damn, all I want is to sleep.

Only once they were settled in did he go looking for Romara, finding her in the lee of a boulder, gazing east where the darkness was lifting, ahead of dawn. The moonlit landscape was undulating pasture, interspersed with wooded hills. Even out here, the smell of smoke, the reek of a burning world, never quite left their nostrils.

'We need Gram,' he said softly, settling beside her. 'And what he says feels true.'

Romara gave him a stricken look. She still had blackened eyes, giving her a corpselike look. 'It's bad enough that he can do that to any of us,' she said. 'But there's more. That leeching effect is *intimate*, Jadyn. It's like being raped . . . no, that's not fair, because it wasn't aggressive and he's probably just as much a victim – and I've never been raped, so how would I know? But it was like being forced to eat each other's brains. Do you understand?'

She *needed* him to understand, that was very, very clear. So he put an arm around her and kissed her forehead. 'I think so. I'm sorry it happened.'

'I don't want to be that intimate with anyone,' she whispered. 'Except you.'

'What, you want to eat my brains?' he quipped.

She chuckled weakly. 'Mmm, with a nice red wine.'

He laughed, and after a moment, he felt her anxiety recede. He wished they were already in the future, living somewhere safe, and they could take this turmoil to their bed.

Finally, she nudged him away and asked, 'How does no one know about this? Not even Elindhu knew.'

'Perhaps Gram's unique? We kill vyr on sight, so the question's probably never come up. And I hate to say it, but it probably suits the Order to keep things black and white. It's easier to kill something "evil".'

'They are evil, Jadyn – they burn and kill.'

'Aye, but clearly there's more to it. How can we uphold the "Sacred Truth" when we're forbidden to ask difficult questions?'

She responded by plucking at the badge on her travel-stained tabard. 'This emblem was my whole life, Jadyn. What are we now? Being a Vestal knight is all I've known. I don't know how to be anything else.'

'Nor do I,' he confessed. 'But we've got to learn the truth. We swore to uphold Justice and Truth. That's all very well, until the truth turns out to be something our superiors don't want to hear. Let's make them hear it.'

'You're a dreamer, Jadyn. They won't listen. They never do. We can only do our best with the time we have – and Akka knows, mine is running out. I get *angrier* every day. Until I'm purged forever of the glyma, I'm on the edge of self-destruction, and a danger to us all.'

'It's just a phase,' he replied. 'In a few months, you'll be purged entirely and free.'

She touched his face, made him look at her. 'Can't we just stop now? Before this quest destroys us both?'

His reaction was telling, for he looked away. 'Rom, there's nothing in the world I want more than to do just that, but I will never find peace if I don't follow this road with all the strength I have left. Our whole world may be at stake, everyone who's drawing breath, if Gram's right. I have to know.' He swallowed the lump in his throat. 'But afterwards—'

'There won't be an after,' she blurted. 'Jag you, Jadyn Kaen. Jag you.'

She rose and stormed away again. Before he could follow, Obanji appeared.

'Ah, there you are.' Then the Abuthan saw Romara's receding back and added, 'Sorry to interrupt.' Jadyn went to go after her, but he caught Jadyn's shoulder. 'Let her go, lad.'

He didn't want to, but he trusted Obanji's judgement better than his own. 'Am I wrong to want to go on?' he asked. 'With everything at stake, I can't turn aside ... but I also feel that if I do go on, I'll lose her ...'

Obanji grimaced, looking his age in the stark sunlight. 'Son, I've always admired your idealism. Old cynics like me are too ready to accept the imperfections of the world, but you don't. Morally, you're absolutely in the right. But morals are naïve things. They can strengthen your sword, but they can also break it. We've all been in service long enough to know that one day we'll do as our predecessors did and hand our causes over to others. Make sure you do so before you outlive those you love.'

Jadyn bowed his head. 'You should be our commander. You've always been the best of us.'

Obanji grimaced wryly. 'There's never been a pentacle commander who isn't from the noble houses, you know that. I was an orphan, born of indentured labourers and raised in an Akkanite orphanage. "Vost" isn't my family name: it's the Aquilani word for orphan. I'm content to follow Romara – and in her absence you, Knight-Commander Kaen.'

'It's not right,' Jadyn said.

'But it's the way of the world. I just hope that by the time Soren's ready to command a century, our Order will be ready to let him.'

'I hope so too,' Jadyn replied, studying the Abuthan. 'Hey, you'll be forty soon. What's your secret? How have you managed to control the glyma so long?'

Obanji smiled wryly. 'By avoiding the stress of command.'

Gram Larch was afraid. In truth, he'd been frightened for months now, so long he couldn't remember not being scared. All the grief and loss ... watching fires he'd helped ignite swallow up the hills and valleys and woods he'd hunted all his life was torture, even if they were almost lifeless by the time the torch was lit. He'd hated it, even though that's what it took to shatter the hated shards. 'Life will return,' the wise ones kept saying, but it was a leap of faith.

Then there was losing his mother Fritha, first to madness and then to eternity. She'd been all he truly knew, the pillar of his life. Her absence was a hole in his heart.

But his greatest fear was what was happening to him right now. Once he knew he had the Gift, becoming a vorlok himself felt horribly inevitable. But now he was giving in to it, it was also intoxicating, a storm he couldn't contain. *Every battle I'm thrown into now, I lose control – and I feel so powerful.*

The only thing he could see holding back the madness was that he relied on others for the glyma-energy. A true vorlok was their own source of power, drawing from the furnace of life, but for now he needed others, at least until he learned how – if he ever did.

Right now, Romara is that source . . . and it's helping her stay sane, too.

That was a comfort, but it too came with pitfalls. He couldn't get her out of his head, since he'd unwittingly created this symbiosis they shared. Her battered, bereft and beautiful face haunted him. Without having kissed her mouth, he knew her taste. He could even call up fragments from her past: meaningless glimpses, out of context, but as vivid as if he'd lived them himself. Many were too intimate for him to deal with.

With such a maelstrom swirling inside his head, the last thing he wanted was to find himself sitting cross-legged, facing the pentacle's mage. If these Vestals did decide to execute him, it would probably be on her say-so. Mages were generally the brains of the Order, the guiding hand to the ruthless knights, and certainly Elindhu was very different to her athletic, muscular comrades. Grey-haired, with a pot belly, beaky nose and waddling gait, she hardly radiated menace. But he didn't underestimate her.

'When you draw on glyma-energy, what do you feel?' she asked, her beady eyes boring into him. 'Rage?'

'I feel powerful.'

'Can you tell friend from foe?'

'Aye,' he replied hoarsely. *Mostly.*

'Where does the power come from? You have no orb.'

'It just comes; it seeps into me all the time – ever since my mother

164

and I were initiated into the coven – but most of it comes from others of power.'

'Your coven's vorlok gave you something containing elobyne dust, yes?'

Reluctantly, he nodded. 'Aye. It killed some and turned most of them into half-beasts. But me ... I have the Gift, so I have a measure of control. I resisted and found ways to dissipate that energy. Until yesterday.'

'What changed yesterday?'

'Being thrown into direct danger, for the first time since my mother died. With her dead, it feels like my restraint has gone. And I desperately want this journey to be successful. So when everyone drew on their elobyne orbs, it was like being drenched in fire.'

Elindhu's eyes glinted. 'Why Romara?'

'I don't know.' He shrugged helplessly. 'Perhaps because she's in the same danger as me?'

That was true, but since this weirdness began, it felt as if he had a gaping wound that only she could salve. She was inside him now, and he wanted her, body and soul. All he could see now was her, the most passionate, strong-willed, and yes, *jag it*, desirable woman he'd ever met.

Even though of them all, she most wants me dead. And she's in love with another man ...

Elindhu pursed her lips thoughtfully, as if sensing his thoughts, but she changed the subject. 'Do you truly know how to find Nilis Evandriel?'

'I know where to look.'

'And that's where you're taking us?'

'Yes.'

She stroked her chin before leaning in and asking, unexpectedly, 'Is there an alliance of the vyr and the erlings?'

He blinked in surprise, then remembered that her field of expertise was the erling race. 'None that I know of,' he said. 'I've honestly never seen an erling.'

She smiled enigmatically. 'Are you sure?' Without waiting for an answer, she rose. 'I'll speak for you, Gram Larch. Hopefully, that will be enough. Don't betray our faith in you.'

As she walked off, he saw Jadyn and Obanji were returning from another private conversation, while Romara was sitting on the ridge above, silhouetted like some tragic heroine against the ruddy dawn. As Elindhu passed Aura, who was already asleep, she paused to drape a saddle blanket over her. Soren had started a tiny cooking fire, the flames well-concealed by banked sand and rock, and was readying a pot of tea.

These are decent people, Gram thought. *I've hated and feared them all my life, but they aren't evil. Just misled.* He renewed his resolve to guide them to Nilis Evandriel and the truth.

Then his eyes were dragged back to Romara Challys, who was stalking back into the camp, her pale aristocratic face timelessly beautiful, framed by that luscious tangle of auburn hair.

His throat went dry, then she saw him and glared back with big, wounded eyes that pierced his soul, until he had to look away.

She's going to destroy me, one way or the other.

They had decided that travelling at night while the moons shone and the skies remained clear was the most sensible option. The road had remained empty, and they'd seen no sign of pursuit.

'Gather in,' Jadyn called, 'all of you, not just the Falcons.'

They obeyed curiously, his pentacle surrounding him, with Aura and Gram outside the circle.

'Last night, Romara and I discussed something important,' Jadyn began. 'She made the point that we've left the Order, and I've been thinking about that. The more I do, the more I become convinced of this: *we haven't left the Order, the Order has left us.*'

He watched their eyes open wider as they took that in, and what it meant.

He tapped the Akkanite blazon, a blazing sun, on his tabard. 'This represents the Light of Truth. Truth is what we are seeking. Lictor Borghart tried to have me killed for seeking that truth, encouraged by our Archon, Corbus Ritter, who is committing adultery with Lady Elspeth Sandreth. These are *not* deeds of the righteous. So I refuse to put aside my tabard, even if for a time I must conceal it. I am no outlaw. I am a Vestal knight, a seeker of truth, and I will go on being one, even if the whole Order comes against me.'

They all looked troubled, but he saw Obanji slowly nod, and then Elindhu and Romara. Soren puffed out his cheeks hopefully, blinking hard. And Gram and Aura were listening intently, outsiders, but bound to them.

'The only people I want with me,' Jadyn went on, 'are those who want to seek that truth too. Anyone who doesn't, this is your chance to stand aside. This quest won't get any easier. The closer we get, the harder they'll try to stop us – and if it does turn out that everything Gram has said is true, then we'll have the whole might of the Triple Empire arrayed against us. So choose well, but choose now. I won't judge you, and I won't stand in your way.'

'I'm with you,' Obanji said, immediately. 'Falcons Eternal.'

'Me too,' Soren added instantly, following his mentor's lead.

'And I,' Elindhu said, with surprising vehemence. 'This is a chance to right many wrongs.'

Romara remained silent.

Elysia, have mercy, Jadyn thought wanly. *Please don't take her away from me.*

But he'd said his piece, and unlike the others, she couldn't safely use the glyma now, so she was more vulnerable. He couldn't blame her if she opted out of this journey.

Her face was downcast, her eyes on the stones between her feet, but finally she shrugged. 'Of course I'm in,' she said. 'I'm a Falcon, to the very end. Falcons Eternal.'

But she looked like she'd just chiselled her own headstone.

'Thank you,' Jadyn said, hiding his relief. 'Thank you all.' He rose to his feet, anxious to resume travel with dawn approaching. 'Saddle up, everyone.' He looked at Aura. 'Can you ride on your own?'

She winced. 'Lady not ride. Riding be for brutes. Ride with Jadyn more.'

Romara gave her a dubious look. 'You'll ride with whomever we tell you.'

'Aura ride with nice Jadyn. Or handsome Soren,' she added, giving the young initiate an alluring glance. 'Wanting ride, e muchacho?'

Soren looked confused, then he went scarlet. 'Um . . . I . . . vows . . .'

'You be not vowed yet,' Aura noted. 'Can still be man, not virgin.'

'Aura, with me,' Jadyn said tersely. 'Come on, Falcons, let's ride.'

The Nepari clambered up behind him, muttering that he was absolutely no fun. So he deliberately made his mount trot as they set out, making each bounce worse, to shut her up. It worked; after a time she was reduced to throaty grunting, then she sagged against his back, unable to speak except in stifled, inarticulate moans.

'Are you all right?' he asked her, when she groaned as if in pain.

'Mmm,' she managed, in a dazed voice. 'Muchos buena. But slowing now, grafia?'

Thank Elysia for that, he thought, a little puzzled, as he relented and set a gentler pace, while she melted against his back, until it was one giant wet sweaty patch of heat. At times she nuzzled the back of his neck, moaning in Nepari.

It was rather odd.

Riding under moonlight in the wilderness of Solabas was a starkly beautiful experience. As they left the coast, they wound into hills initially coated in olives and tall cypresses, later supplanted by tall pines. They passed through a number of tiny hamlets and villages, some burned out and abandoned, and found several patches of burnt forest as well, desolate stretches of charred stumps and ash-covered ground. He wondered if the vyr rebellion had reached this remote area, even though there were no shards in the region.

They found a large river near dawn, refilled their water bottles and rode on, following the river road upstream towards the southeast and the higher peaks.

'This be Serena River,' Aura told Jadyn, having regained her poise. 'Serena flow from Regio Lago – Lake Regal. Lake be border to Ferasto kingdom. Cross Ferasto to Neparia. Is good.'

They rode cautiously now, always with one of them scouting ahead to give warning, and stopping frequently to water the horses. The

Serena River was slow and silty, but offered shelter along the banks in the form of occasional rows of weeping willows, drinking deeply of the water. They were mainly riding through farmland now, though again, they found many burned-out abandoned homesteads.

'Those are vyr symbols,' Gram admitted, pointing out etchings on gate posts. 'These fires were deliberately lit.'

'Why?' Jadyn asked. 'I thought you said the vyr only set fires to destroy elobyne shards?'

The trapper gave him a grim look. 'So did I. But for some people, a war is a chance to unleash their worst side. I'm sure not all of your Order are saints, and I've heard of atrocities by regular troops and mercenaries on the people they're supposedly protecting.'

'Aye,' Jadyn sighed. 'So have I.'

As the sun rose, they reached a low wooded rise with a view of the river plains below and realised that there was a large settlement ahead. The true size of it only became apparent when the sun rose on a fortified keep, dominating a sea of mudbrick houses, ringed by a sandstone wall several kylos in circumference. It looked large enough to house ten thousand souls, but many more were camped outside; a sea of tents and lean-tos that covered the floodplain.

'Refugees,' Obanji said. 'Thousands of them. Things must be bad in the hinterland.'

Having ridden most of the night, they needed to rest the horses, so they worked their way down the river's edge, two or three kylos short of the town, and set up camp in the shelter of some handy willows a little way from the road winding by. Obanji was their best cook and with Soren his willing helper, they conjured up a decent meal of the fried bacon and eggs Elindhu had brought from the pirates' village. The magia took the first watch, sitting cross-legged on a rock, her grey hair gleaming like silver filigree in the sunrise.

After the meal, they sought rest, but Jadyn couldn't settle, so he took over the watch from Elindhu and made himself comfortable, well used to long, tedious stints of sentry duty.

Ten minutes later, Aura slipped from her nook and sat on the rock nearby, throwing him a tired but still vivacious smile. 'Not be sleeping,' she complained. 'Bad place, Solabas. War with Neparia, many time. Neparia victory, always, but not wanting to keep.'

It wasn't how the annals told it: Solabas had a forbidding, largely forested interior, but the southwestern coastal plains were rich and populace, and Neparia, the larger country, had tried and failed many times to invade. But the Solabi were resilient and remained unconquered.

Jadyn wasn't interested in debating the point. 'Once we've crossed the mountains into Neparia, we'll leave the wilderness and see you to a town or city,' he promised. 'You'll be safe among your own kind, I'm sure.'

'Is good. Not liking wilder-nest. Is not Aura's . . . um . . . habitat, si?'

He smiled. *I'm sure it isn't.*

Boots crunched and Romara trudged by, heading upstream. When she saw Jadyn with Aura her frown deepened. 'I'm going to see if I can find a waterhole to bath in,' she said sourly. 'I can't sleep until I'm clean.'

'That one have broomstick up tushi,' Aura muttered, when she'd gone.

Jadyn coloured. 'She comes from an old noble line. The Challys family have ruled great lands, fought in famous battles. She's far above us all.'

Aura chuckled gently. 'Poor Jadyn not so highly born, eh?'

'Not I,' he admitted. 'It was a fluke my Gift was ever discovered – a friend in my village found an elobyne sliver on an old battlefield and it glowed when I touched it. I showed the local priest, and the Order took me in. The other initiates despised me. They used to call me—'

'Farm Boy?' Aura chipped in.

'Aye, as you've noticed. The masters said I was a plodder, but Romara shielded me from all the hazing.'

'What is "azing"?'

'Bullying. Pecking orders. Putting "lesser mortals" in their place.' He was surprised at how the memories still rankled. He'd entered the Order naïve enough to think that he'd joined a brotherhood of noble souls, but what he'd found was a cauldron of seething rivalries and uncontrolled egos. 'It was hard for someone like me, with no lineage and no outstanding talent. But I wasn't the only one in that situation. The Gift can manifest in anyone, so in many ways the Order is more egalitarian than most of society. The acceptance of women and people of other races into the Order as equals has permeated through society. Even though it was hard for me, it was still a dream come true.'

'Better to be least Vestal, than not Vestal, si?'

'Of course. But I wanted to be like the old Sanctor Wardens.' He thought about what Gram had said about the aegis. 'Perhaps they weren't just a myth?'

'You die disappointing, I think,' Aura sniffed. 'Aura help though, Jadyn Kaen. As thanking for rescue.'

'Thank you, Aurana . . . um . . .'

'Auranushka,' she corrected mockingly. 'So sweet, brave protector can't say name.' She patted his shoulder. 'Shame you be lackwit, otherwise nice man.'

Jadyn frowned at the teasing. 'I noticed that you have a skill with throwing knives,' he replied, remembering that he'd intended to ask about that.

She shrugged. 'Sergio show me; he say "Aura, tua tresa accomplia." Sometime if concentrate, can see path of knife, always hit. Perfecto.'

'Interesting,' he mused. 'I sometimes get the same feeling – not around throwing knives, but when I'm fighting. It's like I can see the other's move coming – not anticipating, but actually *seeing*. It doesn't happen often, but it's saved my life a few times.' He gripped his sword-hilt and poked the orb towards her. 'Have you ever been tested for the Gift? Hold the crystal orb and let your thoughts drift.'

She pursed her lips doubtfully, then reached out. 'Will do,' she said. 'For you.'

She stroked the orb, gazing into his eyes in a way that was disconcerting, as if she was trying to beguile him. The orb didn't light up, even faintly, and she released it with a sly titter. 'Was nice holding your weapon, Sier Knight.'

Sensing mockery, he coloured. 'It was worth trying. Um, has Elindhu spoken to you about . . . um, things . . . ?' he asked weakly. 'What Borghart did, I mean.'

Aura gave him a condescending look. 'Try to. She be odd. But not knowing, ney. But anyway, Borghart is past now. Forgetted.' She took his hand in hers and gave him a direct look. 'Aura never look behindward, only forward. Is how survive.'

'But—' He floundered, and tried again. 'What Borghart did to you . . .'

'Is forgotted. Back of skull, compreno?' Her eyes hardened and her hands curled into claws. 'Until moment come . . . *Atacar!* Revenging. Make him pay. Then forget forever.'

He was somewhat awed by all that, and squeezed her hand, to soothe her unsettling show of fangs. 'No one should have to go through that, especially from a member of the Justiciary. I wish I knew what to say or do to make things right. What he did was cruelty.'

'Life be cruel, Farm Boy,' she replied. 'But you pay Aura money as promise, all be good.'

Their eyes met and he felt the strangest *frisson*, one he'd never felt before, not even with Romara. It wasn't sexual or romantic, but a sense that they were somehow bound together; that she belonged on this path every bit as much as he and the others.

Just then, Romara reappeared, clearly wet. 'Hey, Nepari,' she called, glaring at their linked hands. 'There's a pool upstream. Go wash.'

'Wash? Tresa buena!' Aura rose and ran off the way Romara had come from.

Settling beside Jadyn and wringing out her auburn hair, which gleamed like rich honey, Romara curled her lip. 'What did she want that required hand-holding?'

'We were just talking,' Jadyn replied defensively. 'She's been abused, remember.'

'That doesn't make her a damsel in distress, Jadyn. Be careful.'

That struck Jadyn as harsh. 'She's had a horrible time, stranded in a foreign land, ending up before a lictor who tortured her. But she's resilient. Some of what she said made me think she might have the Gift, so I tested her.'

Romara blinked. 'And?'

'Nothing. But she says she sometimes feels like the world goes slow, the way it does for me, when I'm fighting. I know you've always said that I imagine that sensation, but it's real. There's something about her.'

'Besides a pretty face?' Romara sniffed. 'Look, I'm sorry if she's been abused, and impressed that she's got the gumption to put it behind her, but I still don't trust her. Decent women don't latch onto men like this Sergio of hers.'

'What do decent woman do, then?' Jadyn prompted, feeling irritable.

'Marry and have children – unless they have a God-given talent, like me, in which case they use it to make a difference. I don't just mean a talent for the glyma,' she added. 'Women with a gift for business, for scholarship, for art – for anything – should be free to make their way and contribute to society. But Aura's a thief – a parasite – and she can't be trusted. We should leave her in the next town. Surely she can make her way home without us.'

Jadyn loved Romara, but she really could be a highborn prig at times. 'I doubt she'll leave us until she's been paid. Four hundred aurochs mightn't be much to you, but it's salvation for her.'

'I'm not trying to cheat her, but where we're going, she won't survive anyway,' Romara said. 'For her own safety, she should leave us. I'll get her the money somehow, on my honour.'

It sounded reasonable, but Jadyn doubted leaving Aura in a foreign land was a good idea. So he changed the subject to the road ahead, speculating as to what they might find at the border into Ferasto, how they'd travel through the brigand kingdom, and which route might best get them into Neparia undetected.

'It's a good thing we've got a Nepari guide to help us,' Jadyn remarked, when Romara confessed she knew nothing about the region. It was petty, but he couldn't help it.

Romara's expression hardened, but just then the stillness was broken by a shrill shout. It came from upstream and was cut off mid-cry.

'*Aura!*' Jadyn came to his feet with his heart suddenly pounding.

The riverside pool wasn't large, just a place a few paces wide behind some boulders that divided it from the main flow, a haven of still, clear water just a few feet deep.

Aura knelt and drank, groaning with exhaustion. It was tempting to just hurl herself in and sink to the bottom. Her skin felt filthy, overheated and desiccated. Her lips were cracking and her hair was a greasy mess. Right now, cleanliness would be wonderful.

Reasoning that these honour-bound Vestals were no threat to her person, she untied her hair and stripped, then immersed herself, sighing for sheer pleasure. The water was a little cold, but it rinsed away the grime of travel and refreshed her parched senses. Settling on the silty bottom, she scrubbed at her body and face, marvelling how such a place could be as glorious as a feather bed, just as a scrap of food when hungry was as succulent as the freshest glazed fruits.

Then she turned her mind to her situation. Grateful though she was to have been rescued from Borghart, she had to ditch these virgin knights and their suicidal quest and find her Sergio again – whether to cut his throat or kiss his lips, she still couldn't decide. Maybe he'd had no choice but to leave her behind in Gaudien and flee . . . but maybe not?

I'll know when I see him, she decided. *When I look into his eyes, I will see his soul.*

Those beguiling eyes had been how it all started – a melting glance across the room in a Nepari taverna, charming his way to her table, and then into her bed. She'd been down on her luck and out of plans. But Sergio, for all he was a rogue and a dreamer, dazzled her. *Blinding me.*

That he might have left her to die tore at her, heart and soul.

With an effort, she pushed him from her mind and just enjoyed the moment, closing her eyes and listening to the river's cool murmur, the morning sunlight and the droning winds, and the lonely cry of a circling eagle, far above. It had an entrancing quality, a way of blending into music that lifted her senses from her body. She sank onto her back and let her black hair fan out around her as her thoughts drifted away.

Must we go on? I could stay here forever, just floating . . .

But just then she felt a prescient sting behind her eyes, a flash of danger.

Her eyes flew open as the water rippled – and a big hand grasped her ankle. Something large and oddly shaped rose from below the surface, water streaming over it, and she thought for a moment one of the knights intended to betray his vow . . .

Then she registered the face – and screamed.

It was a creature like nothing she'd ever seen, a seven-foot trulka with a bulbous body and pebbly hide, deep-set amber eyes either side of a rudder-like nose. When she convulsed in its grip, its mouth opened to reveal flinty teeth. Its grip on her leg tightened.

She lashed out with her other foot, still shrieking for help, but went under mid-cry, then a massive fist smashed through the surface, grazing her face. She tried to kick free as her throat filled with water, causing blinding panic. She thrashed and twisted, managed to get her face above the churning surface, spraying water from her mouth and sucking at air. She glimpsed that hideous stone face and amber eyes then she was smashed down again by a punch that exploded into the water and struck her belly, knocking the wind from her lungs again . . .

Then just as abruptly, the creature let her go, and she was jerked bodily from the water to land on the pebbly ground, where she crouched, vomiting.

The mage, Elindhu, was standing at the pool's edge, her eyes glowing like the crystal on her staff and her face angry. She was speaking rapidly in a language Aura didn't know.

The giant creature could have broken Elindhu with one fist, but instead, it backed to the river's edge, ducking its head like a child caught misbehaving, then sank so that only its big eyes and bald crown showed.

Someone shouted and boots crunched: Aura recognised Jadyn's voice, calling, '*Aura – Aura?*' Gratifyingly, he sounded worried.

'Eloda keeya nie,' Elindhu shouted at the creature. 'Vantai, sha!'

The rock-monster cringed, then went under. Ripples swirled away, out into the river's current, and vanished. Elindhu lowered her staff, the crystal dimming. 'Estas bien?' Elindhu asked Aura in Nepari.

'Si, si,' Aura babbled, scrambling away from the pool. 'Che va, e Cara?'

Jadyn and Romara burst into the dell, swords drawn and faces flushed. 'What's happening?' Jadyn demanded, placing himself between Aura and the pool. Romara flanked him, giving Aura an exasperated look when she saw that she was naked.

'The danger is gone,' Elindhu answered. 'Dress now, child.'

Aura scooped up her clothing and threw on her over-shirt before they got too good a look at her tattoos, some of which were for lovers only to enjoy. But she remained by the pool, wet cloth clinging to her curves, to annoy them and maybe show off. *Enjoy the sight, virgins*, she thought defiantly as Soren appeared, stopping with mouth open, drinking in her bare, bronzed legs. She gave him a wink, because he was handsome, though a little too young for her.

Maybe I'll corrupt you anyway, she mused. *Just for fun.*

Then Elindhu stepped between them, giving her a sharp look. 'Dress, Aura,' she repeated. She turned to Jadyn and Romara. 'It was nothing,' she told them. 'There was no real danger.'

That surprised Aura, who'd felt very much endangered. But she held her tongue, intrigued.

'There was a nayade in the pool,' Elindhu said. 'It was curious about Auranuschka, but I scared it away.'

It wanted to eat me, Aura thought. *And she didn't scare it with spells – she talked to it.*

'A nayade?' Romara snorted. 'I was here before Aura and I never saw it.'

'Perhaps your visit roused it, so that it was awake when Aura arrived?' Elindhu replied. 'Or perhaps it sensed your glyma and was afraid?'

Aura had heard of nayadai: water-creatures whose males were like trulkas, big and brutal, though the females were said to be sultry, seductive predators. They were known throughout the continent by many names, but sightings were rare and seldom proven.

'According to our oaths, we must roust it out, then slay it,' Romara started, before rounding on Aura. 'For Akka's sake, get dressed, harlot!'

Aura thrust her thinly covered breasts out in response. *See these, you sour spinster? All men dream of them.* Only once that point was made did she sashay away, picturing Jadyn and Soren staring at her bottom and burning up inside. As they should, if they were men at all.

She dressed in a copse of olive trees, still shaky from the frightening encounter, then rejoined the knights. Obanji gave her a sip of his evil liquor that burned all the way down to her stomach, but left her feeling much better. 'Is good. You sell, make mucho lucre,' she told him.

'When I retire,' he chuckled. 'It'll be my nest egg.'

Jadyn, Romara and Elindhu arrived back in camp, still arguing over the encounter with the nayade, when Romara reeled and collapsed, gripping her skull . . .

Port Gaudien, Vandarath

Yoryn Borghart believed in rising before dawn, and was always at his desk by sun-up. But this morning held a surprise: Elan Sandreth didn't normally rise until midday, yet here he was, already in the lictor's office, sitting in his chair.

'What is it?' Borghart asked tersely.

In reply, Elan wordlessly handed him a short loop of twisted leather.

Borghart saw it had a lock of auburn hair woven into it. 'What is this?'

'Romara Challys' hair,' Elan replied, with a sly smile. 'Ideal for tracing her.'

Borghart gestured, and his office door slammed shut. 'It's a dozen days since they fled and you bring it to me only now? I was told they'd left nothing personal behind.'

The trail had gone cold since Jadyn Kaen had betrayed the Order and fled with his entire pentacle. *A true knight would have stood his ground, faced his perfidy and accepted the just punishment*, Borghart mused. *But Kaen is lowborn dross.*

'This is my personal property,' Elan Sandreth replied, unperturbed by Borghart's annoyance. 'She gifted it to me well before the Order took her. I'm surprised she graduated, though perhaps she sucked her assessor's cock. Her skill in that art was remarkable.'

Borghart eyed the nobleman with distaste, although the thought of a naked Romara Challys kneeling before him was a stirring vision. 'Your mother mentioned that you courted her.'

'*She* courted me – it was very much that way round – when we were young. She thought by surrendering her virtue, she might become a Sandreth. I accepted what she offered, but she was never worthy of my lineage. I was about to be rid of her when she gained the glyma and was hauled off kicking and screaming to the Order.'

Borghart heard sourness in the young man's taunting. *He envies her Gift*, he guessed. He also knew that House Challys was richer than the Sandreths these days, so he mistrusted the man's account.

'You could have remembered sooner,' he grumbled.

'I'd quite forgotten I had it, but when I did recall the trinket, I came straight here, knowing of your skills.' Elan stood lazily and bowed, as if bequeathing Borghart his own chair. 'Make yourself comfortable, good lictor. I'm excited to see your powers in action.'

Borghart disliked being indebted to the louche brat, but this was a real boon. Anything that was personal and precious to a particular person resonated their essence and provided an anchor for scrying spells, enabling penetration of any veil spells protecting the subject. So Borghart drew on the glyma, enduring the exquisite longing to *howl like a wolf* when the power flooded in. He had to ration glyma use at his age, but his control remained iron-clad . . . most of the time.

Romara Challys, he thought hungrily, picturing that haughty bitch with her glorious mane of red hair. '*Inveni*,' he murmured, invoking the rune of seeking. *Where are you, Romara?*

For a time his inner sight saw only darkness, then it surged across land and sea, flashing over troughs of water until it struck another land, darkly forested, yellow-brown, arid and sweltering, to a rocky outcropping, where seven people were milling about among horses, beside a river . . . One had long red hair . . .

Ha! I have you!

Romara's pale face, her eyes bruised and expression strained, swam before him – and the sight of the *treacherous bitch* made his temper flare. His fingers formed a knife and he slammed the ethereal blade into the heretic's head, right between her eyes, then cursed himself and reined in his anger.

The woman's face contorted in shock and she fell, then he heard someone, another woman, shout, '*Valeo!*' and his scrying fell apart, hurling his awareness back into his office, but leaving a palpable sense of distance and direction.

Elan Sandreth was staring at him, his eyes filled with longing. On the table, an inch or so of the bracelet was smouldering into ash. 'Hey,' he complained, 'I treasured that token.'

Borghart quickly ground out the embers with the heel of his hand; in all likelihood he'd need to use it again. He strode to the map on the wall, pulled it down and spread it across the desk, pulled a compass from a drawer and aligned it with his recollection of where Romara had been.

'Due south of us,' he told Elan. 'The interior of Solabas, judging by the landscape.'

'That's a long way,' Elan muttered.

Borghart contemplated his options. His role here in northwest Vandarath was relatively junior, but capturing a pentacle of heretics could elevate his career considerably. They were outside his current jurisdiction, but a legal pursuit across territorial boundaries was a well-established precedent. *I have the right to go after them.*

'Was she alone?' Elan asked.

'The vision focused specifically on her,' Borghart replied, 'but I sensed others, seven people in all: almost certainly her pentacle, the missing Avas half-breed boy and the two escaped prisoners: the vyr and the Nepari. Perhaps she is also a vyr, and guiding them.'

He knew that wasn't so, but he had other reasons to find Auranuschka Perafi. She was perhaps the most interesting of these fugitives.

'Then we must hunt them down!' Elan exclaimed. 'I can provide funds, anything you need.'

Borghart was a little surprised at Sandreth's enthusiasm. His family were old money, not the sort to go gallivanting across the continent when they could stay at home and play at politics. 'What's your interest?'

'Exactly as it was: to reclaim Romara – and her family's remaining fortune. I might ask you the same?'

'You met the archon. Do you know how Corbus Ritter became head of the Order? He hunted down the Badgers, the last full pentacle to rebel. He was elected archon two years later.'

Elan grinned. 'So you're aiming high, then?'

'Always.'

But he had a deeper reason to take up the pursuit. When he tortured prisoners, it could get very intimate: often, when he touched a victim, he received visions concerning their past and future. During her initial questioning, when he'd intended merely to maim her and maybe use her body for pleasure, he'd realised that Auranuschka Perafi had almost exactly the same talent as he: a kind of precognition.

He'd started exploring that, with quite astounding results: she could guess a coin toss with incredible accuracy, in a hundred tosses, she called only eleven wrong, even when threatened with mutilation. She could dodge thrown blades and avoid broken glass while blindfolded, and call dice throws with uncanny accuracy. It had been fascinating, even alarming, because that was more than he could do, though he'd never had to use his secret talent under such duress.

When, after a week of such explorations, he'd had a precognitive warning of his own – that his testing was making her dangerous – he'd scheduled her maiming and death.

She escaped the night before. *A coincidence . . . ? I think not.*

'It suits me to pursue them,' he told Elan. 'And with your mother's success in ratifying your "marriage" to Romara Challys, it's in your interest, too. We can use a portali gate to reach an Order bastion in Solabas in a few hours. I'll requisition aid there and we'll be only a day or two behind them. You'll get your "wife" back, and I'll get the rest of them.' He ran his eye over the nobleman. 'But I'd be wary of such a wife, were I you.'

'Our marriage won't last long,' Elan smirked. 'One night, then an awful accident involving something sharp. That's all I need for her family's wealth to be mine.'

Serena River, northeastern Solabas

A few minutes after the psychic assault, Romara had recovered, apart from a bruised rump, dusty clothes and a splitting headache. And the embarrassment, which was the worst part.

'You're saying we've been found?' Jadyn asked, keeping his voice calm.

She groaned, clutching her head. 'Aye, Borghart scryed me.'

'How?' Elindhu asked. 'I was sure we left nothing personal behind us in Gaudien.'

'I don't know, but his scrying went right through our veils like they weren't there. So somehow he has something physical of mine . . . I don't understand how, though.'

Only the least competent knights couldn't veil, but it took a mage's skill to scry, and even then it was easily repulsed unless anchored by some physical item, which was damaged or destroyed by the spell.

'If they've got something tied to you, veils won't work,' Elindhu said.

Jadyn gave Romara's shoulder a squeeze. The others had gathered anxiously, even Gram and Aura. 'What happen?' the Nepari woman asked. 'We be found?'

'Yes, through magic,' Jadyn replied.

'Did you get any sense of where Borghart was?' Obanji asked Romara.

All Romara had seen was Borghart's face, before that searing lance of pain had made her black out. 'None at all.'

'Scrying is a one-way contact; you get to see your target, and you get a vague idea of where they are, but you can't communicate.' Elindhu reminded them. 'You were veiled, which is why you were aware of his attempt. Attacking you gained him nothing; that was just arrogance.'

'He probably couldn't help himself, the vindictive prick,' Romara said, rubbing her temple.

'Probably,' Elindhu agreed. 'But as it's the first scrying attempt you've felt, he's probably still in Port Gaudien. But now he knows roughly where we are and using a portali gate, he could reach one of the Solabas coastal bastions by sunset. We need to keep moving, and hope whatever he's using to find you burns out quickly.'

Jadyn grimaced. 'Aye, you're right. Let's go.'

It wasn't ideal: they'd been riding all night and neither they nor the horses had managed any real rest since the previous day. But they made ready, quickly repacking their gear, refilling water bottles and saddling up. Romara found herself shaky at first, scared another spell might strike at her, but as the minutes passed, she began to breathe again. They were soon ready to go, leaving just enough time to relieve bladders. Romara headed into a copse of olives, pocketed a handful of ripe ones, found a private spot and dropped her pants before squatting and gratefully freeing her waters.

'Skirt be easier,' a female voice commented, and she almost jumped three feet.

Aura appeared, hoisting her skirts and squatted. 'Man pants, good if man,' the Nepari chuckled. 'Not so good for woman, heh?' Then she groaned as her urine flowed. 'Oh, so better.'

Romara gritted her teeth. 'Can you just shut it?'

'What, mouth or tushi?' Aura giggled. 'One good thing: when ride, bam-bam on tushi, is nice, si?'

Romara finished and rose, hauling up her trousers. 'It doesn't happen if you sit properly.'

'Have big . . . what is word? Orgasmus . . . Jadyn not notice . . . But maybe he do?'

'You're disgusting.'

Aura stood as well, her expression teasing. 'Maybe riding be only fun Lady get, mmm?'

That's it . . . Romara launched herself at Aura, grabbed her throat and slammed her back against the boulder, hard enough to rattle her teeth. The Nepari's eyes bulging, she went for a knife, Romara grabbed her wrist, then thrust her face into hers. 'We're knights of a sacred Order, sworn to serve Akka and empire. You will not slander us!'

Aura sagged sullenly. 'So, you be stronger. Talmoni bully victorious again. All hail!'

Romara pressed her nose to Aura's. 'No, I'm telling you that if you want respect, you give it. We're trying to save our world, and I will not let you endanger us. Understood?'

Aura wrinkled her nose. 'Si, is understand. Am sorry.'

To Romara's surprise, the Nepari's apology sounded genuine.

She let go abruptly, caught the girl when she almost fell and exhaled her anger. 'Jadyn says he tested you for the Gift?'

'Si. Am not special, like Romara be special. Happy?' Aura stamped away – not back to the camp, but deeper into the trees. 'Need shitting. Privata, si?'

Romara ground her teeth, then took a breath and let her anger dissipate, annoyed at herself for that momentary flash of temper. *I'm going under*, she thought miserably. *I'm a danger to us all.*

She'd seen older knights succumb: they reached a certain point, usually in their thirties, when something snapped. From then on, the merest slight turned into a brawl, and a skirmish could quickly become a massacre. That was why most knights retired to non-combatant roles by thirty. You didn't see many older knights like Obanji.

Not that I'll grow old anyway, not with the whole Order hunting us.

'Aura,' she called, 'come back, we've got to go.'

There was no reply.

She wavered, then decided she was the problem and left the Nepari, hurrying back to camp while wishing they could abandon this 'quest' and just hide. But Jadyn wouldn't do that, she knew. Stubborn, tenacious, idealistic; the qualities she admired most in him. He'd follow this road until the end, wherever it led.

I could walk away from this, but chances are I'd never see him again.

'Siera,' a gruff voice called and Gram appeared through the trees, already mounted on the largest horse. 'We've seen riders on the road – armed men. Come quickly.'

Romara eyed up the vyr nervously. She couldn't shake the smell of him from her nostrils or the taste of him from her spittle, despite having never touched him. But she wasn't going to show him her unease.

'Let me see,' she said brusquely, leaping onto a rock for a better vantage. She shielded her eyes and gazed towards the road, which ran parallel to the river, just a few hundred paces away.

'Ah, jagat!' she swore.

More than fifty riders were paused along the track, just a few hundred paces away, while those in command debated their route forward. Then the lead riders turned off the road and began cantering towards their concealed camp. The newly risen sun glinted off the bald pate of the lead man; she didn't need his familiar shape to tell her who he was.

'It's Tevas Nicolini,' Romara cursed. 'Let's get the jagat out of here.'

She leapt down and went to run, but Gram offered her his big hand. She swallowed and took it, but to her relief there was no sizzling connection of energy and empathy, just hard callused skin and a muscular grip that pulled her up behind him. He slammed his heels into the horse's flanks and then burst into motion, thudding back towards where the others waited, hopefully already mounted and aware of the enemy.

It wasn't until they reached the camp that she realised that she'd left Aura behind.

8

Scattered

Imperial Scholars

Knowledge is power, therefore a ruler must accumulate and distribute all knowledge. Some truths are too dangerous for the ignorant masses to comprehend, so we must protect them from such intellectual storms. Therefore the primary role of the Imperial Society of Scholarship is not to seek knowledge but to control it.

HIEROPHANT EDDAXA I, PETRAXUS 1328

Southern Hytal
Summer 1472

Gram Larch's horse pounded into the argofyl copse, with Romara clinging to the trapper's back. He was shouting, *'They're on us! Ride!'*

Jadyn cursed and echoed the order, grateful they were ready to go. From his vantage, Jadyn could see a cloud of dust and the silhouettes of riders racing towards them. He considered standing and fighting, but there looked to be too many.

'Scatter!' he shouted. 'Make for Lake Regio!' He pulled his mount's head around, prepared to dig in his heels, and then realised that Aura's mare was untended. He grabbed its reins, shouting, 'Where's Aura?'

'She's back that way,' called Romara, pointing back the way she and Gram had come. She dismounted as Gram reined in and ran for her own mare, shouting, 'My fault, I'll get her!'

'Push on!' Jadyn called. 'I've got her horse – I'll go!'

With that he shot off, pulling Aura's mount behind. He swept around a tangled copse and lost sight of his Falcons – but an alarmed Aura was running towards him.

'Climb up!' he shouted, bringing his horse to a halt, then he bent and grabbed her under the armpit and hauled her up. Trained to the sword and the orb as he was, she felt light as a bird to him as he swung her up. 'Hold on,' he shouted. 'You fall, you die.'

Then he slammed in his heels and launched both horses into a furious gallop, hammering northeast, away from the river, seeking a way back to the road.

Romara swore as Jadyn pelted away, but all she could do was swing into her saddle as the first of their enemies appeared and arrows started flying. One whistled past her rump as she clung to the saddle-bow, scrabbling for the reins.

The others were already in motion. Obanji and Soren were vanishing into a cutting, heading downstream, but she went after Gram instead, heading southeast along the riverbank. Elindhu's mount followed, the saddle empty.

Jagat, where is she?

But there was no time to go back and find her, not when their pursuers were bearing down on them and the air was filled with arrows. A shaft grazed her thigh, carving a bloody tear, but she hung on as fear gave her mare wings. She went to shield, but shied away for fear of the glyma, concentrating instead on just staying in the saddle.

When a shallow tributary appeared before them with a game trail running along it, they veered upstream, away from the Serena, hooves thumping like her heartbeat. More arrows flashed by, but horse archery was an art and with the path proving bumpy and the vegetation growing thicker, the shafts were flying wide; as the shooting was slowing the pursuers, the gap between was widening.

'They've split up too,' Gram shouted, looking backwards. 'There's about a score on us.'

Pelting alongside the stream, Romara couldn't spare more than a glance back; the uneven, twisty path required all their skill, and their horses were snorting and spraying in the heat. *Twenty enemy behind us, more or less*, she estimated. It felt too many to fight, especially if any had the glyma.

The trees suddenly thinned and then ended, and they burst onto a hillside of dying sunflowers. Moments later their pursuers emerged behind, closer than she'd hoped, shouting encouragement to each other. She and Gram dug in heels again, working up to a gallop, praying their beasts wouldn't stumble as they mowed through the dead plants, heading towards a large barn straight ahead.

Now they were clear of the trees, arrows began to fly again, hissing shafts slashing past, alarmingly close. She felt a desperate urge to shield, but drawing on the glyma now, with her blood and fear pounding inside, felt suicidal. Then Gram dropped back a few paces to come up alongside her, crowding in, shouting at her, waving his hand behind him as he forced his horse across her path, slowing them both and shouting, 'Burn the field!'

She reined in, gasping at the harm such an act could cause – then the cold, analytical part of her, inured to killing and death, took over. She drew on her elobyne orb, trusting the vyr to draw the power away before it became too much for her.

'IGNIS FLAMMA!' she roared, and sent a torrent of pure flame into the parched field behind them – and reeled in the aftermath as the beast now lurking inside her bared fangs. Somehow she fought it down, helped immensely because Gram was there, pulling the glyma and rage from her as if sucking poison from her body.

The dead sunflowers caught fast, sending flames shooting up into the sky. She heard cries of horror, glimpsed several dark shapes rearing up then crashing down, but only one man broke through, pelting blindly towards her, his clothing alight. Aghast but acting almost without thought, she hefted her flamberge and cut him down.

'Ah, jagat,' she groaned, fighting her urge to conjure more power, 'Gram, let's go!'

But before they could escape, half a dozen riders were coming round the left edge of their fire, and there were as many again on the right, trapping them between the barn and the burning field.

Their leader, a Bravanti with long greased hair and moustaches, wore ramshackle mail, a cobbled-together mix of chain and plate, but he was wielding an Order flamberge. Beside him was a tawny-haired woman sporting a Foylish bronze torc, holding a stave tipped with elobyne. Their men, mostly archers, were Pelasians, the usual motley mix of light and dark skins from the islands who welcomed all nations.

'A rogue knight-commander and a vorlok,' the Foylish woman drawled. 'I could buy a castle wit' bounty fer this lot.' She levelled her stave at Romara. 'Mind you, I'm a renegade too, so I'll have t'be careful how I collect.'

'Maybe we can make a deal?' Romara panted.

She pealed with laughter. 'Oh, no, lass. You'll die here, sure as night follers day.'

The mounted archers lined up shots, with cold efficiency.

'I'm going down fighting,' Romara muttered to Gram. 'Keep me sane as long as you can.'

Gram nodded and went to dismount, but she signed for him to wait.

'No sense mucking round, eh?' the Bravanti drawled. 'Archers – cut 'em down.'

Soren followed Obanji's galloping horse down a defile and onto a mudflat that broadened out into the river's floodplain. Behind them, the cutting filed with armed riders, only some three dozen paces or so behind.

'Hee-yah!' Obanji bellowed, spurring his mount onwards, and Soren followed, clinging to his mount, his skills as a rider being taxed heavily. The plodding farm horse he'd grown up with couldn't run like these beasts; all he could do was cling on, keep his head low and pray.

Their pursuers, at least a score of Pelasians, stayed on their tail as they fled through tussock and boggy pools. Arrows were flashing past or cracking on the Obanji's wards; they maintained the gap, but it couldn't go on. Sooner or later they'd run out of luck.

Obanji had somehow picked out a barely discernible trail weaving between giant flaxes and swamp trees, thick-trunked giants with splayed limbs, and at last the footing became firmer, a solid path leading towards the riverbank.

'Where're we going?' Soren shouted, but Obanji kept pounding on, as their pursuers reached the raised track and followed.

Moments later, they were at the water's edge, where Obanji sent his horse straight into the river, and Soren yelped as he followed, slamming down in an eruption of spray and almost going under. But somehow, their surefooted steeds found the bottom and they surged on again, saddle-deep in water and fighting the current.

'Hold on,' Obanji shouted, keeping his mount's head pointed towards what Soren realised must be a sandbar. As they emerged onto the narrow band of dry shingle and sand, Obanji drew his bow, strung it and reached for an arrow – one of his elobyne-tipped ones.

The land they'd just left was only thirty paces or so away and the first of the pursuers had just appeared. While they waited on the high bank for their fellows, those with bows took aim.

'Prepare to shield,' Obanji told Soren, facing their enemies steadily. 'You know how.'

The rune was *Salva*, but by now Soren knew the words were just memory-enhancers, a way of tuning one's thoughts to an action learned by rote. He'd been practising by lying on his back, tossing pebbles straight up and deflecting them away before they fell on him. A slow, controlled release could keep you safe for several seconds. But there were a dozen archers, whose shafts would take just an eye-blink from bow to striking him, and he had no idea when they'd fire.

'This isn't good,' he hissed. 'What's the plan?'

Obanji chuckled grimly. 'Winning.'

'How?'

'Not sure yet.'

The archers on the riverbank raised their bows in unison, while those wielding swords nudged their mounts down the bank. 'Fire!' one of the archers shouted, and the arrows flew.

Jadyn kept one hand wrapped in Aura's reins and the other clutching his own as they descended one slope and climbed another, praying the others had got away. They'd fled northeast, riding away from the river, hurdling fallen trees and skirting impenetrable copses, their horses constantly switching from smooth gallop to lurching canter as the terrain shifted. Every second, the dozen men pursuing them were drawing closer.

His mount was hampered by having to bear Aura's weight as well as his own, and towing her horse was also slowing them down. Something had to change, and as they reached a patch of open ground, he realised this was their one chance.

She either swims, or we both sink . . .

'Aura, you have to ride by yourself,' he called over his shoulder, slowing and pulling her mare alongside. 'Let me go!'

She might not have known what he was planning, but she obeyed at once, releasing her grip on him and seizing the cantle behind her. He dropped the reins onto the beast's neck – *and the world slowed . . .* He saw exactly the force and trajectory needed, and the approaching moment, kicking his right leg free, lifting his foot to the saddle, then propelling himself sideways . . .

For an instant he was airborne, then he slammed down onto the saddle of the horse cantering alongside. Gripping the pommel, he swung his left leg over; the horse lurched and almost stumbled as he hauled himself upright and groped for the reins. Beside him, Aura was screeching as she was thrown about wildly, unable to find the swinging stirrups. Then she kicked her feet forward and miraculously thrust her toes straight into the stirrups – and then she was in control, riding the fast-moving horse like a veteran.

How'd she do that?

But his own leap from horse to horse had probably looked just as impossible, he realised. His mind flashed back to what she'd said about Borghart testing her, and how sometimes when throwing knives, she couldn't miss. It wasn't the Gift, but it was surely a talent – one they shared.

'You're doing well,' he shouted. 'Let him run, but turn his head inland!'

She complied, shooting ahead of him, which allowed him to cover her back as their pursuers burst from the trees behind them and swerved to follow.

'*Salva!*' he shouted, *knowing* it was the right moment – and his spell slapped away a sharp volley of arrows, and on they went. Aura was lying almost flat, her knuckles white on the reins, and emitting a continuous wordless wail, but she was doing all the right things – staying on at a gallop was easier than when the beast was cantering or trotting.

'You've got it,' he encouraged. 'Press your thighs inwards and lean forward.'

'E Cara mia, es locura!' she shrieked – and it *was* crazy. But it was working.

Their enemies were still with them, though, and now Jadyn could see the nearest was Tevas Nicolini himself, only forty or fifty paces behind. He and his men were whipping their horses now, and they'd be in range of a glyma-bolt at any moment.

But the track suddenly struck the trail he and the Falcons had turned off to find rest beside the river. They burst into the open and shot between towering, overloaded wagons, forcing startled drivers to rein in sharply. He glimpsed another track on the far side, vanishing into bushland of argofyl and olives, and took it in desperation, glancing back past a shrieking Aura to the chaos behind.

Their sudden appearance had spooked horses and drivers alike. One wagon, failing to complete an evasive manoeuvre, had tipped, spilling barrels and bales onto the road, where many rolled or split – right in the path of Tevas and his men. Jadyn grinned at the shouts, screaming and crashing sounds.

They gained precious seconds, as their pursuers tried to dodge angry wagon-drivers and panicked horses; they were out of sight through the trees, but they could hear Tevas roaring at his men to push on through.

Jadyn looked about feverishly. *We need to lose them properly*, he thought, but the woods were thick on either side and he saw no way into the tangled undergrowth.

'Not liking,' Aura wailed. 'Not able – will die!' She was shaking, dripping sweat and terrified – and correct: this *would* kill her, for she was a novice facing trained fighters.

They rounded a curve and Jadyn saw the end of the track coming, a T-junction below a high bank topped by thick pines. A small flat bridge over a creek led west and a low wooden gate barred a path eastwards, his preferred direction. As they pounded towards the juncture, he hauled on his reins, throwing a look backwards – the twisting path had Tevas and his men out of sight for a few seconds.

Now, or never, he thought, pulling up and waving for Aura to do the same as an improvised plan unfolded. '*Pulso*,' he shouted, shattering the wooden gate, while Aura brought her mount to a halt. The gate track led to what looked like a ruined farmhouse in a small clearing surrounded by spindly saplings, where the forest was beginning to reclaim the land.

It's the obvious direction we'd take.

'Dismount,' he told her, doing so himself. 'Forget your gear.'

She fell from the horse, and he slapped both on the rump, adding a burst of glyma energy. The two horses fled through the shattered gate and vanished down that track, while he grabbed Aura, threw her over his shoulder, leaped from the banks into the creek and rolled them under the wooden bridge.

'Breathe in, deep, and hold your breath,' he told her, and once she'd complied, he pulled her with him under the stagnant water. She began to struggle – then she went rigid against him as the ground shook and moments later horses pounded onto the bridge, right above them.

Jadyn dimly heard Tevas shout, 'Whoa!' and prayed to Elysia for mercy . . .

'Which way, boss?' said someone just a few paces above them.

Jadyn willed strength into Aura as they shivered there, petrified, soaking wet and coated in moss and filth. *If they see the imprint of our landing in the reeds and mud, we're done . . .*

But Tevas shouted, 'That gate – look, the breaks in the timber are new. And I hear hooves!'

They pounded away, at least a dozen men, by Jaden's count.

He sagged, let Aura go and lifting his head out of the water, exhaled in relief. 'We've got about three minutes before they find the horses and get back here,' he told her. 'Get up, move.'

Aura showed her spirit by straightening her shoulders and following him out from under the bridge without complaint. They crept up the bank, relieved to see no one in sight.

'Which way?' she asked. 'Back to road?'

'No, we'll not get a hundred paces. We'll head into the woods.'

He helped her into the trees, a dense thicket of pines, tangled up with climbing ivy and undergrowth. It wasn't long before they heard the riders return, shouting to each other. But they were well out of sight and hurrying deeper into the trees.

The undergrowth thinned out quickly, increasing their visibility but making it easier for them to run unimpeded, although there were twisted roots and fallen branches everywhere. Jadyn took Aura's hand, which was callused from past manual labours; she was a lot fitter than he'd anticipated, too. And there was no despair on her face, only purpose.

She's a survivor, he thought approvingly, knowing her legs would be jelly right now, from the hard riding – *Mine are!* – but he couldn't spare her. He pulled her up a slope, then through a sharp defile, seeking obstacles to put between them and pursuit. He thought he heard Tevas shouting his name at one point, but inside ten minutes the noise of pursuit was gone.

They were soaked, sweating and filthy, with no supplies and no gear, in a forest he didn't know. 'Sorry,' he told Aura, 'but we have to keep going.'

She gave him a wordless look of exhaustion, but bared her teeth. 'Not stopping. Soy una pera dura.'

He knew enough Nepari to translate that one: *I'm a hard bitch.*

'Hey, we've found a nickname for you, Peradura.'

She laughed in delight. 'Come on, Farm Boy, let's see if you're hard as me!'

They faced the wooded slope and ran.

As the Bravanti ordered his archers to fire, Romara saw the Foylish magia was conjuring, and knew exactly what they planned: she'd counter her shielding wards the instant they formed so the volley of arrows could slam into Gram and her before they could react.

Even if by some miracle they all missed – and that really would be a miracle – she'd be flooded in glyma-energy and the beast inside her would rip her apart from the inside out. This was death, either way . . .

So be it.

'*Down*,' she snapped, pulling on her elobyne crystal. Her senses were flooded even as she jack-knifed over the back of her horse, putting its solid frame between her and the archers – and Gram, attuned to her as only Jadyn had ever been, mirrored her moves. Even as they moved he was pulling on her glyma energy, enough to turn a torrent into a trickle she could manage . . .

. . . at least for a few seconds.

They hit the ground as arrows swept the space they'd occupied, thudding into the horses, staggering the poor beasts as they convulsed, too stricken even to scream as they toppled . . .

Then Gram, already halfway through his transfiguration, grabbed his dying mount, roaring as his frame expanded and contorted, and hurled the dying beast into a spinning arc into the archers behind them. It took down three of them, leaving them stunned or broken.

The Bravanti renegade and his mage gaped, but Romara felt like she'd grasped a bull's horns: now she had to ride or die. She heard her voice become a howl as her inner killer invaded her body, a scrabbling, shrieking presence roaring in triumph—

—until Gram wrenched most of that twisted power into himself and went bullocking towards the enemy. She went with him, clear-headed again, but with virtually no magic.

Six strides and they were on the pirates. The sorcerous bond between her and Gram was almost visible, a tension of push and pull: she gave and he took, and with that exchange came a deluge of awareness, as if she knew every move he'd make, the way she could with Jadyn. As Gram went for the Bravanti, she went at the mage, but they were met by a pair of Pelasians brave enough to try and shield their leaders.

Gram slapped aside a blow from the first Pelasian, tore him from the saddle and broke his back, then hurled his body at the next.

Romara parried blades aimed at his back, her skill formidable even without the glyma. Four men were cut down in seconds – and as the others broke and ran, they reached the enemy captains.

Gram took on the Bravanti, while Romara went for the Foylish woman, somehow staying cool-headed even as glyma crackled through her. She shouted, '*Salva*—' an instant before the mage tried to shred her with an energy blast, then she was inside the woman's guard and ramming her blade up into her belly, punching it through shields and out her back, as Gram, utterly in tune with her, reached the Bravanti, ripped off his sword-arm and broke his neck. For a few more glorious seconds they hacked down the few pirates who still fought, spinning and slashing in a union of instinct and survival—

Then with their captains down and facing a Vestal knight and a vyr, those left pulled their mounts' heads around and kicked them into motion. In seconds they were pounding away, leaving Gram and Romara alone by the burning field, surrounded by corpses and crippled horses and men.

Jagat, Romara moaned. The link between them had faded, which felt like a vein running to her heart being severed. She staggered and would have fallen, had Gram, still immense and splattered in blood, not caught and held her up.

That embrace anchored her, but roused her inner beast again, as residual energy flowed between them. Her mind filled with the sights and emotions of those torrid moments as she and Gram had danced on the edge of the volcano, utterly in tune, fighting as one.

It now felt miraculous.

She was utterly aware of him, too: his muscle-corded body and heaving chest, torn furs and tunic, his arms wrapped round her, head thrown back as he howled out the last of his battle-rage. Heat was radiating from him, and for a moment she was her younger self, a girl with no self-control and a needy libido ...

... until Gram's voice dropped from a throaty moan of desire to a groan of denial ...

Realising nothing would now happen doused her own heat – for which she felt as much regret as relief – but she felt safe too, secure enough to keep hold of him, grateful for his strength because her legs felt wobbly as a newborn colt.

'It's done,' she groaned, once she felt able to stand on her own. 'You can let me go.'

He released her, his bestial features giving way to his normal face and form. She made herself watch, studying the horror of it; somewhat disturbingly, she felt no repulsion now. He'd taken his own inner beast on to protect her and somehow stayed the right side of sane himself.

What a Vestal knight he'd have made, she thought. *One of the greats.*

But they needed to move, to leave this carnage. Corpses – the men they'd killed, dead and dying horses too – were scattered about the clearing. Some were still breathing, trying to still their sobs so as not to draw her attention.

More enemy could arrive at any moment, so though it felt cruel, the wounded weren't her problem. Nor did she feel regret. 'We did . . . what we . . . had to,' she managed.

'Is it the same for you?' he asked hoarsely. 'Do you just want to tear down the world when it grips you?'

'Aye,' she whispered, 'but you kept me here again. We fought well together.'

'I could sense your every move,' he agreed. 'I felt unstoppable.'

The way we moved together was like nothing else, she thought, then corrected herself. *Except fighting alongside Jadyn.*

It felt like a betrayal, and abruptly she felt ashamed and needing to reassert her distance.

'Don't touch me like that again unless it's life or death,' she told him sternly. 'We have to find another way to fight. Take that Bravanti prick's flamberge. Learn to use it and draw on it, so you don't need me.'

Gram looked hurt, but he stumbled silently to the Bravanti's body. He lifted the orb-blade and examined the crystal – then he threw it away. 'I've got elobyne in my blood and that's bad enough. That thing would be too much for me.'

'Fair enough,' she muttered. She looked down at her bloodstained, torn clothes and wrecked chainmail shirt. 'Dear Akka, I'd give anything to wash again . . . provided there's no jagging nayade lurking in the pool.'

Gram picked up a dropped bow and a quiver of arrows. 'This is a weapon I can use while I'm in control.' He looked back at Romara. 'Jadyn said something about a lake?'

'Aye, somewhere upstream, to the southeast. We need to head towards those mountains.' She pointed towards distant ramparts of jagged stone, a hazy purple serration on the horizon.

'These aren't my lands, but I've hunted and trapped all my life,' Gram said. 'If we need to, I can catch us fresh meat. We must stay away from the river, for the pursuit will focus on it.' He examined his own blood-soaked furs and skin and shuddered. 'I too desire greatly to wash.'

Romara felt again the queasy sense that Gram was a fine man – for a vyr. He wasn't just a beast – but then, neither was she. But they would both become something monstrous if they continued down this path.

Unfortunately, for now at least, that was no longer a choice.

'Let's see if we can find a couple of sound horses and move on,' she suggested.

Gram looked around at the battlefield and shuddered. 'Maybe if we'd stayed together we could have beaten them all?' he suggested.

Romara shook her head. 'There were too many. Splitting up gave us a fighting chance. And Tevas Nicolini led them: he could have beaten any of us, one on one.'

'Then you should have killed him back at the village.'

'I know, but I couldn't,' she admitted. 'If you die at his hand, I give you leave to haunt me.'

Gram smiled humourlessly. 'That's great consolation, Siera Challys. I will make your life a misery.'

'You already do,' she said tartly, but then she winked, to show it was a jest.

At his answering smile, she had to look away, before she lost herself in it.

*

'*Salva!*' Soren shouted, and his paltry, poorly formed balloon of energy pulsed out – and was engulfed by Obanji's shield, which slapped the volley of arrows away. He drew again on his elobyne orb, his flamberge flashing as he prepared to meet the mass of riders picking their way into the river, blades lifted and ready. In seconds they were wading through the deepest part of the flow, between the high bank and the sandbar.

Above them, the archers readied another volley.

'Behind me, lad,' Obanji murmured. 'Be ready to shield again, but get it right. I'll not be helping you next time.'

Soren felt his nerves jangling. *I'm not ready* . . .

The Abuthan kindled the elobyne chip that formed the arrowhead of his shaft, but he hadn't taken aim, though the riders were close enough that they could see the whites of their eyes.

'Charge!' their captain roared – and everything happened at once.

Obanji shouted, 'Now!' and drawing his bow in a flash, he shot the *elobyne-tipped* shaft into the water in front of the leading horse.

'*Salva!*' Soren shouted simultaneously, as the enemy archers loosed. Their volley tore his shielding to ribbons . . . but though some punched through, they'd lost momentum and fell harmlessly into the current. Meanwhile, Obanji's arrowhead exploded, radiating a blast of heat through the water around the phalanx of riders.

The result was instantaneous: steam billowed, blinding and scalding the riders, while the horses started shrilling horribly, suddenly up to their chests in boiling water and tipping armoured men into the bubbling cauldron.

'Now go—' Obanji roared.

Soren barely heard, for he was staring in horror at screaming men with blistered skin, thrashing horses and tumbling bodies.

'*Soren!*' Obanji shouted, '*move!*'

This time the command got through. Soren hauled his mount's head round, urging it to the far bank while they both pulsed out shields – but no one was shooting at them now, for the archers were too caught up in the horror unfolding below. As the current swept the boiling patch of water away and the steam lifted, it revealed scalded men and beasts floating motionless, others screaming, thrashing about. All he wanted was to get away from the hell he'd helped to create.

He lifted his eyes to the archers on the bank, fearing another volley, but none were paying Obanji and him any attention, instead focused on trying to help those who could be saved – except for one lone archer, who began firing arrows at them, screaming imprecations to Akka. His shafts went wildly astray; he fell to his knees and buried his face.

Soren felt like doing the same. For a moment he was overwhelmed. 'How could we?' he panted, his eyes stinging. 'It's not right . . .'

Obanji drew alongside and grasped his arm. 'Lad, look at me.'

When he forced himself to look up, he no longer saw the fatherly man who'd saved him and was giving him what he needed to survive. He saw a ruthless killer.

'Jag off,' he blurted. 'Leave me alone.'

Obanji grasped his tunic and held him in place, making him face him. 'Lad, battle isn't glory. It's winning, by whatever means. That's today's lesson. When you fight, it's kill or be killed. *Never* forget that.'

Soren pulled away, and then convulsed, his stomach rebelling. He jerked his head around and bent over, spewing a bitter stream of brown gruel over his right boot and into the river.

'We're monsters,' he groaned, 'just like the vyr.'

'At times,' Obanji replied distantly. 'It's one of the reasons I believe Gram's tale.'

Soren winced, then spat his mouth clean, and straightened. 'Don't tell the others I was sick', he mumbled. He straightened in the saddle and nudged his mount up the bank, and Obanji followed, his phlegmatic face turned away, gazing at their enemies. No one was following them.

'They've all done it, many times,' the Abuthan knight said in a gentler voice. 'I still feel that way sometimes, even in my dotage. No one would condemn you.' He gave Soren a comforting pat on the arm. 'You did well, lad. Come on, let's go and find the others.'

Camaris Bastion, Solabas

Borghart and I just walked six hundred kylos in a few hours, Elan San-dreth thought numbly, vomiting on the floor of the tower room. He thanked Elysia that he'd survived his first journey through a portali gate; he wasn't eager to experience another. They'd stepped through an ordinary door in Tar-Gaudi tower into a dark landscape of distant peaks and misty valleys. Borghart lit his elobyne orb and led the way through misty vales, following a path like a glowing thread of spider silk, while ghostly voices whispered and taunted them. Just when Elan had despaired of ever escaping the horribly unsettling semi-void, Borghart had led him out of the mirk, up a hill to a peak, under night skies carpeted by glowing stars and through a stone arch into a room atop the highest tower of this place, Tar-Camar, the Camaris bastion, on the coast of Solabas. Both of them had been violently ill within seconds of arriving, unable to react as alarms rang out and boots thudded on the stairs below.

If the men who found them had been enemies, they'd have been helpless – but this was an Order bastion, and Borghart knew the local grandmaster. They were given rooms for the night, and when their stomachs settled, food and wine. Horses and men were swiftly promised, and a full Vestal century with which to hunt Romara's renegades. The reward for the capture or death of the Falcon penta-cle was rising by the day.

Before turning in for the night, Elan paused outside his room and asked Borghart, 'Where's Romara going? Neparia?'

'More likely Ferasto,' the lictor replied. 'It's an independent king-dom, with no shards or bastions. They may think they'll be safe there.'

'Can't we just use the portali gate and get ahead of them?' Elan wondered, even though the world beyond the gates had been thor-oughly unpleasant. 'Or use one to appear in the middle of their camp and take them unawares?'

Borghart sighed. 'If only it were that simple. For one thing, you can only enter and exit that "half-world" through an established gate; and second, there are no portali gates in Ferasto. Neparia has a few, but not Ferasto.'

'Why not, by Akka? They're damned useful.'

'Milord, in truth, there have been no new portali gates created since the Order was founded. We inherited them from the Sanctor Wardens, who destroyed or concealed most of them. We have only a few dozen, less than half of what they had.'

Elan whistled. 'I didn't know that.'

'Most people don't, and we like to keep it that way. The Wardens were much more than the Order's official stance on them suggests, and the power they wielded was very real.' Borghart scowled. 'We have no choice but to ride, but hopefully it will be a brief pursuit.'

'For my part, I am more than happy to continue,' Elan assured him. 'Romara and her family fortune are worth pursuing to the very end. And of course, I'd like to remind her of a few things we enjoyed in our youth.' He patted his crotch. 'Surely there's some way I can enjoy her, without being damaged by her glyma?'

Borghart smiled crookedly. 'There are ways. I want the Nepari woman alive, myself. There's something about her . . .'

The nobleman raised an eyebrow. 'I've always heard you lictors like to finish off the pretty ones that way?'

'Yes, but I've got more than that in mind,' the lictor said musingly. 'I've often wondered if the glyma-gift is not the only talent Akka gives us. At times I feel like I know what's going to happen before it does, and that the forces that guide the world are speaking directly to me.'

There was a curious madness in his eyes that Elan found both fascinating and repulsive.

'What's that got to do with the girl?' he asked.

Borghart's face lit up. 'I think she's the same. To understand it better, I wish to dissect her, body and soul.'

9

In This Together

The Enemy Within

Since its union, the Triple Empire has not faced a credible external enemy. Instead, we face a rising tide of internal threats from separatists led by the elusive vyr. In Talmont and its provinces, in Zynochia and Abutha, the tide of rebellion rises. But it does give us license to crush dissent, in the name of unity.

ARCHON BRES LANNARD, TAR-NARETH, 1443

Regio Lago, Solabas
Summer 1472

The interior of Solabas was a mix of populous valleys where crofters grew grain and managed cattle and rugged uplands forested with pines and cypresses. Jadyn and Aura were able to drink and wash in the many streams and tiny tarns as they slogged along, staying under the forest canopy, which was a considerable relief and helped lift their spirits.

But by dusk, they were exhausted and their bellies were crying out for food. They'd left all signs of pursuit behind, but had very little idea where they were. Jadyn was hopeful they were still walking broadly east towards Regio Lago, their agreed rendezvous.

If any of the others make it.

Elindhu carried personal items belonging to each of the pentacle, so in extremis, she could scry to find them. The protocol in these circumstances was for the mage to find each group and guide them to the others. He hoped she'd made it out of the attack and was now doing exactly that.

'E Cara,' Aura groaned, as they stumbled down another slope and found a small lake, set in ancient pines. 'Be night soon, si? We stop, am begging.'

'Don't worry, we're resting here,' Jadyn told her, after scanning the lakeshore for hazards. The sun was close to setting behind the hill they'd just descended, but there was a noisome smell here he didn't like, and it was growing as they approached the stagnant-looking body of water.

Aura had limped past, but she pulled up, wrinkling her nose. 'What be stenching?'

Jadyn was longing to quench his thirst, but this lake felt wrong. There was no birdsong either, and below the surface he could see tangles of rotting weed. The pines on the far side of the water were all dead, too, their needles brown and the branches silver-grey.

Then a gleam caught the light of the setting sun on the opposite ridge, and silhouetted against the sky he saw three elobyne shards planted in a triangle.

Three in one place? I've never seen that, he thought, walking to the edge of the water. There was sludge floating in it, which stank like excrement. *Are we close to a settlement?*

'We can't drink this,' he told Aura. 'We'll have to move on.'

She groaned, as thirsty as him, then glanced up at the shards. 'Them did this, am thinking,' she said. 'Be as Gram say: shards killing land.'

It wasn't the only explanation – but he'd never seen three shards planted together, either. 'Let's have a look.'

Aura hesitated. 'Neya. Am sensing dangers.'

He paused – Aura's instincts were good, and he felt uneasy too – but he shook his head. 'I think we need to see this.'

They tramped wearily round the reeking lake, finding nothing living at all. When they reached the trio of shards on the ridge, the air was thrumming with energy, teasing Jadyn's skin like an unseen wind, but in an unsettling, debilitating way, as if it were pulling the marrow from his bones. The entire hill was covered in dead trees – and worse, the neighbouring peaks were also topped by clusters of shards, and those slopes were just as lifeless.

'Hey, you up there, stand still!' a voice rang out.

Aura shot Jadyn an 'I told you so' look.

Before they could react further, three men appeared, below them on the northern slope. Two wore mail and had elobyne swords over their shoulders; the third carried a stave. They weren't wearing white Order tabards, however, but grey tunics with a hand holding a gleaming sun, marking them out as Lighters: members of the Order of Akka's Light. The Lighters were the only people permitted to handle shards, or mine the elobyne on Nexus Isle, and they answered only to the Hierophant.

Jadyn touched his flamberge to the nearest shard and felt it fill with energy – a precaution, but also a demonstration of what he was, for his tabard had been lost with their horses.

'Sier?' called the mage, a pompous-looking man with long Bravanti moustaches and mournful eyes. The two knights, one Talmoni and the other Abuthan, drew their own swords, watching carefully. 'Who are you, to hold a flamberge but wear no tabard?'

Jadyn knew that he and Aura looked frights, and they were too tired to run. But these men were in the wilderness and had likely been here for some time. They might not have heard of the Falcons going rogue.

'I am Jadyn Kaen, of the Falcons,' he replied, unable to lie, even here. 'We're hunting vyr.'

The three men exchanged glances. 'Are there vyr nearby?' they asked anxiously. As the Lighters' roles were the creation and siting of shards, the vyr were the bane of their existence.

'Aye,' Jadyn replied. 'My pentacle are working out of uniform, trying to unmask vyr in the nearby villages. But some pirates got wind of us. I was lucky to escape an ambush.' He gave them a rueful shrug. 'It's a relief to meet you, in truth. We only just escaped with our lives.'

The three men seemed to relax, but they hadn't sheathed weapons. 'Who's she?' the taller of the two knights asked, gesturing at Aura.

'Was pirate's woman,' Aura put in, spitting contemptuously. 'This man, Vestal knight, rescues. Is good, si.'

'Can't she speak proper Talmoni?' the knight snickered. 'Though I guess she's just a whore.'

His contempt was another reminder of the Gifted's disdain for lessers. Jadyn wondered if it had always been this way and he'd not noticed, or whether it was getting worse. 'She warned me of the attack,' he replied in a reproving voice. 'I owe her, so I'll see her safe.'

'Do not succumb to temptation,' the mage said, in a censorious voice. 'Her kind know only one way to show gratitude. Beware her wiles.'

Aura's eyes narrowed and she went to reply, but Jadyn cut her off. 'She's a pious girl. It's not her fault these animals kidnapped her. Her home town isn't far, but we've had to enter the wilds to escape those hunting us. If you could point us back towards civilisation, and perhaps spare us some food, it would be much appreciated, brothers.'

The three Lighters conferred, then the mage said, 'Of course, Sier Knight. Come ahead. Our camp is a kylo or two north of here, outside the dead zone.'

The two knights finally sheathed their weapons and Jadyn followed suit, then strode forward, offering his hand. The knights were Valbert, the Talmoni and Silomon, the Abuthan, and the haughty Bravanti magus was Brondello. They shook his hand formally and offered blessings; all the Lighters were ordained priests as well as fighting men. The two knights led the way, Valbert offering an arm to Aura with a mocking show of chivalry, but Aura pretended not to notice his condescension, instead clutching his arm and prattling about how grateful she was that such 'heroes' would protect her.

Jadyn fell into step with Magister Brondello.

'I've never seen clusters of shards before,' he commented. 'Nor even heard of it.'

The mage smiled complacently. 'We don't do it anywhere except foreign wilds. The Solabi don't do anything important out here, so the Order of Akka's Light pays for the right to plant shards. Three at once speeds up the extraction of energy – of course, it means we're constantly having to move them, and we go through indentured workers at a ridiculous speed. But the energy we can send back to Petraxus is worth the cost and more.' He shrugged amiably. 'If we're going to ruin land, we destroy a foreign place first, eh?'

To have Gram's allegations admitted so glibly was a real gut-punch.

If they did this inside the empire, it'd be impossible to conceal, Jadyn realised. *They'd be forced to admit that the shards really are dangerous.* No wonder the vyr hated the empire.

Striving to keep his reaction muted, he forced a disinterested shrug. 'As long as the power keeps flowing, eh? Though I thought the shards were harmless, that they only took ... um ... excess energy?'

'There's no such thing as a free meal, Sier Jadyn,' Brondello chuckled. 'Energy must come from somewhere. What we extract here empowers your sword, and every other Order flamberge, and you lot keep millions safe from eastern barbarians and the jagatai vyr. We're doing Akka's work here.'

'Indeed you are.'

Brondello clapped him on the arm. 'Glad to allay your doubts. But I wasn't joking about there being no free meals, Sier. You must pay for yours in news. We've been stuck out here for six months – we've barely seen an outsider. So what's been happening in the north?'

Jadyn gave him an account of those recent events he was aware of, as they descended into the valley and emerged into a clearing hewn from the forest, where two cohorts of Lighter men-at-arms were supervising hundreds of indentured labourers. Jadyn could see they were being treated like slaves as they dragged shard pillars up the slopes, cut down trees, fetched water or unloaded supplies. They were housed in crude pens, exhausted men trying to sleep on the filthy ground. The stench of their open ablution pits was as atrocious as their conditions. He had to fight to hide his revulsion.

How is this legal? he wondered. He'd heard that as the rich got richer it was growing more and more common for the poor to be treated badly, but he'd never really considered what that might mean. That the indebted ended up like this was horrifying.

It was hard to remain civil, but somehow, he managed. Brondello apologised that his knight-commander and seneschal were absent, but promised a good meal. Jadyn and Aura were shown to small tents set side by side. Sier Valbert made a show of offering to guard Aura while she washed in the nearby stream – something Jadyn thanked him for, but did himself, because there was much about the man he didn't like. Valbert looked surly, until Brondello sent him away on some trumped-up errand.

'Valbert's a boor and Silomon's no better, especially around women,' the mage told Jadyn. 'I'm constantly having to clean up after them, if you know what I mean.'

Jadyn did, and resolved to keep more than an eye on these men, but the remainder of the evening was amiable enough. Magister Brondello, determined to show off his sophistication, produced a bottle of Solabi red to accompany his regaling Jadyn and Aura with his accomplishments and service history. As that included an account of going to Nexus Isle and the elobyne mines, it wasn't at all boring.

'Not many realise, but there's actually only one piece of elobyne in this world,' the mage told them. 'Every shard, every orb – it all comes from one great stone that crashed into Coros, millennia ago. Each fragment calls to the rest – that's how the energy is shared.'

'I didn't know that,' Jadyn admitted. 'How is it mined?'

'It has to be indentured labour, because prolonged exposure to the original stone is lethal,' Brondello replied blithely. 'Scores die, every month. The funeral pyres are burning constantly there, so most folk think it's a volcano.' He shook his head, awed at the recollection. 'There's not much else on Nexus Isle, in truth, except a fortress on the highest peak. It's inaccessible by any road, but the most beautiful tower I've ever seen, gleaming like it's made of marble.' He made a reverent Akkanite fist. 'I tell you, at night I've seen the silhouettes of winged Serrafim against the night sky, coming and going. Some say Jovan Lux was granted eternal life by Elysia and that he dwells up there, with the angels.'

It sounded like a fairy tale, but the mage's face was piously serious. Brondello was happy to talk on, clearly grateful for an attentive audience, and Jadyn learned more about elobyne and how it worked than the Vestal Order had ever taught him. Much of it chilled him, because every word was echoing Gram's claims.

Finally he couldn't help but ask, 'How is it that the Hierophant permits all this? How does the general populace not realise that our shards are dangerous?'

'The Hierophant permits it because it's in his interests, and you and I help him because it's in ours. And the populace ... well, wealthy folk don't care, because this is all for them, indirectly. And the rest are either ignorant or in denial. More fool them.'

'But surely we're all in this together?'

'Are we?' Magister Brondello asked airily. 'Not really. Jovan Lux was a wise man. He knew he needed Zynochi resources and Abuthan gold if Talmont was to rise and become those nations' equal. He could have declared war, but the Order was tiny back then, as Hytal is far less densely populated than the equatorial empires. So instead, he seduced the great of both empires with promises of eternal power – and so the Triple Empire was formed. Now the Gifted of every nation are loyal only to him and his descendants. We have no external enemies, only a vast peasantry to suppress, lest they destroy his peace and return us to the Dark Age. Our duty as Gifted is to serve that purpose.' He gestured expansively, taking in the morass of exhausted indentured labourers. 'These scumbags are all worthless drunkards and thieves, leeching from good people's hard work. Here we teach them the discipline of labour and a touch of piety. We save their souls, I'd go as far as saying.'

Dear Elysia, this man is vile, Jadyn thought numbly, as he sipped his wine. It was tempting to return to his tent, retrieve his flamberge and ram it down the man's throat. Tempting, but stupid.

'Surely the end-game of planting shards on a lifeless world benefits no one?'

Brondello shrugged complacently. 'Frankly, Sier Jadyn, every land on Coros could burn and the Hierophant and his court wouldn't notice the smoke. But regardless, it won't come to that. We only need enough peasants to serve our needs for food production and labour, so the sooner the excess die off, the sooner we can relax our grip. Overpopulation is our enemy, as much as the damnable vyr. Soon we'll triumph, and men like you and I will live like kings and enjoy the spoils of victory.' He raised his wine cup. 'To Eindil Pandramion the Third: long may he reign.'

'To Eindil,' Jadyn echoed, managing to just about sound sincere.

The rest of the wine tasted like blood and ash.

Despite the uncomfortable evening, Jadyn and Aura were able to sleep unmolested and in relative comfort and were sent onwards with a horse each, laden with bedrolls, water bottles, feed and supplies. Brondello directed them to a forest track heading back towards the main road, and they made sure they were seen taking it, in case the Lighters subsequently found out they were renegades and pursued them.

'These be *horrible* mans,' Aura said, when they were finally free to talk. 'Speak of "lesser people" like insect.' She fixed Jadyn with a stony stare. 'Empire not glorious, be seeing?'

He faced her. 'No, it's not glorious. There has to be a better way.'

The Nepari nodded slowly. 'Is learning now. Good Virgin. Eyes opening.'

He found himself smiling at her with genuine affection – tired and clearly afraid, yet plucky and clear-sighted. *A good person*, he decided again. *Brave and true*.

'I had an imaginary friend when I was a child,' he found himself confessing. 'An erling, about two feet tall, who looked like a squirrel. She played with me when no one else would.'

'Mmm?' she said quizzically. 'Why is telling?'

'I don't know,' he said, then he realised that he did. 'Her name was Ora, for her gold fur.'

'Ah! Farm Boy had imaginary friend named Aura!' she trilled, grinning. 'Is sweet. But Aura not imaginary.' She poked his side playfully. 'See!' When he jumped at the ticklish sensation, she poked again. 'See!'

He caught her hand the third time, and found himself staring into her eyes.

'Aura having imagined friending also,' she said seriously. 'Akka and Devourer, they speak to her, tell her this or that, all of life. Akka in right ear, Devourer in left. Verite, is so.'

He went to laugh, then realised she meant it. 'Never listen to the Devourer,' he advised. 'Only hearken to Akka.'

She shrugged. 'Sometime, only Devourer be speaking sense.'

The morning they eluded Tevas Nicolini's men, Romara and Gram left the forest and walked into the refugee camp they'd glimpsed from the hills the previous day, reasoning that one way to hide was among other people – and because Gram insisted he'd be able to find them help.

The tent city surrounded a walled Solabi river town, named Riokastella. Barges came and went on the Serena, big-hoofed horses walking a track on the far bank to haul them upstream, while those heading downstream were poled down the middle of the current. Roads from several directions converged here, and the main thoroughfare east was much busier than any they'd seen so far.

Romara wrapped her Order flamberge in her cloak before they trudged through the crowded tents, Gram looking around for something familiar. Suspicious-looking Solabi travellers, refugees from the south where the vyr were raiding, gazed at them with speculative eyes and before long they were being paced by a group of young men, who soon closed in on either flank.

Romara nudged Gram. 'We're going to have a fight on our hands,' she warned.

But Gram waved at a large hide tent before them. 'They'll leave us alone now.'

He made a complex hand gesture to a lean, tanned Solabi woman slouched against the entrance pole. She was pretty in a feral kind of way, which was accentuated when she leaned in and sniffed Gram, then inclined her head. 'Welcome, Xaltos.' She eyed up Romara, then touched her forelock respectfully. 'Xaltia.' Then she disappeared inside the large tent.

'What did she call us?' Romara whispered.

'Exalted, it means,' Gram told her. 'It's a title the vyr use for vorloks or draegar.'

'We're neither,' Romara snapped.

'Aren't we?'

The Solabi woman returned, holding the tent flap open respectfully. 'El te vera ahora,' she said in a reverent voice. *He will see you now.*

They entered, to find a surprisingly large space, with roof flaps opened for light and fresh air, though in the miasma of the camp that meant little. An incense-laden fire burned brightly. Sitting, using a saddle as a chair, was a dark-skinned, grey-haired man, his beard and hair braided in the fashion of Pelasi from the southern islands. He wore a loose blue-green shirt over roomy leather trousers, and his bare feet were chapped. To Romara he was big-eyed and twitchy as a predatory bird, and radiated a subtle sort of madness.

But he strode up, sniffed Gram and embracing him, roared, 'Bienvenido! Habla Solabi?'

'Only Talmoni,' Gram replied. 'I'm Gram Larch, of Avas. This is Romara.'

'Xaltia!' the man greeted her, throwing his arms round her and pressing her to him, sniffing at her neck and hair, then growling, 'Foylish, I'm guessing, by your gorgeous red hair?'

'Miravian,' Romara answered, pushing him firmly to arm's length, but clapping his shoulders and forcing some warmth into her face. 'You are?'

'Killian Modesto. I've brought my coven here to mingle with these refugees and get close to the enemy.'

Holy Elysia! Romara's every instinct was to warn the local Order grandmaster, if there was one, but she curbed it, at least for now. 'Don't you fear exposure?'

Modesto shook his head. 'These people believe in us more than they believe in lords who allow imperial shards to be erected in fertile valleys.' He grinned toothily. 'They shelter us and we feed them – we raid caravans and bring all the supplies here. This is a refugee camp now, but in a few months it will be an army.' He stepped back and indicated his mats. 'I'm sorry, I have no chairs – but I do have beer.'

Romara's stomach moaned in anticipation.

He introduced the woman as Fatima. 'A Zynochi name, chosen by her sailor father. Her mother was a port girl from Camaris.'

'A dumb tart, I'd guess,' Fatima said, 'but I suppose I should be grateful. Y'know, to be born and all.'

'I myself am also a mongrel, being Pelasian, a race of stray dogs,' Killian Modesto put in. 'But what is "purity", anyway?' He filled tankards from a wooden barrel in the corner and toasted them, then turned to Gram. 'So, Gram Larch of Avas, what brings you to Riokastella? Have you come to join our struggle?'

Gram shook his head. 'We have another task, for Agynea.'

Killian's eyes widened. 'Disappointing. We could use your help, I won't deny it, but we don't presume our little fight is of great moment to the High Ones.' He slurped his beer. 'And I know not to ask. But please, tell us what you can – we are starved of news of the greater world.'

An hour or two passed amiably, occasionally interrupted by boys entering to mutter in Killian's ears, of this or that wagon arriving, travellers of possible interest passing through, or rumours from the town. But then one such runner rushed in and whispered urgently in Fatima's ear, and she looked at Gram. 'Some Pelasians have arrived, coming from the west. They are enquiring about a band of criminals. Some of the descriptions match you.'

Romara laid a hand on her bundled cloak. 'How do you know that?'

'The Watch are in our pockets,' Killian said.

'These newcomers claim the people they are hunting are rogue Vestals,' Fatima said, baring yellow hackles. 'Led by one Romara Challys.'

When Fatima laid a hand on Killian's arm, Romara could feel energy tingling between them, along with repressed tension.

'That's me,' Romara confirmed, making a decision. She drew her flamberge from the cloak and drew the most minute trickle of glyma she could ... and as Gram instinctively tempered the rush, she let her newly released inner beast seep into her. It was painful, in a chilling, numbing way, her core temperature dropping as her hands became claws, her mouth filled with icy prickling and her skin rippled weirdly ... then she stopped it, before it went too far.

Killian and Fatima stared, then grinned savagely. 'A corrupted Vestal,' the Pelasian rasped.

'Magnificent,' Fatima added, as if she'd just sprouted Serrafim wings. 'Xaltia, we are eternally yours. How may we serve?'

'Few of the Fallen join us, Siera,' Killian said reverently. 'We are honoured.'

'I'm still learning what it means,' Romara admitted. 'It's happened all at once.'

'You will become great among us,' Killian enthused. 'A draegar, a foe even the Order's champions fear. I am truly proud to meet you.'

Romara, profoundly uncomfortable, sought words that wouldn't commit her to evil. But they were interrupted when another youth burst in, crying fearfully, 'Pelasians and soldiers, coming right here—'

'Ach,' Killian snarled. 'So we do have a rat.'

They rose, and Killian ushered Gram and Romara out, as dozens of men and women crowded into the pavilion to defend it, if need be. Fatima took charge, while Killian led Gram and Aura away with calm alacrity.

They reached the river without being intercepted, where a barge rode at anchor, almost as if it was waiting for just such a moment. Killian took them aboard and into the cabin, where a narrow window looked back at the sea of tents. Romara thought she saw Tevas Nicolini himself, surrounded by many red-clad soldiers, with refugees crowding around to see what was happening.

'This will take you upstream, Xaltia,' Killian said. He seized her shoulders and kissed her cheeks. 'It has been too short a time, but it's best you move on now. This barge will get you to the next town. In the cabin you'll find a purse, enough for passage or to help fabricate a disguise. Urghul be with you,' he added, with a wry smile.

'You pray to the Devourer?' Romara asked, startled.

'It's a joke,' he chuckled. 'There is no Devourer, just as there's no Akka or Elysia, or any other god. There's just us, so only we can save our world.' Killian turned to Gram. 'Remember us to Agynea. We badly need her guidance and wisdom.'

The vorlok disembarked and the bargeman clambered onto one of the horses and nudged it into motion. Romara and Gram waved their farewells as the great barge moved upstream at walking pace. The Pelasian saluted them, then galloped off.

They watched anxiously, but after an hour, they were well past the tent town, Riokastella was lost in the trees, and no one had come after them.

Once she felt safe enough to leave the deck, Romara explored the vessel. It had one cabin with a narrow bed and a well-stocked pantry. When Gram followed her in, he filled the room; he looked as edgy as she was, to be alone together after sharing such traumas. She looked round the cramped space uneasily, wondering what the night might bring. That Gram was a threat to her virtue was something she'd felt bubbling uneasily beneath her surface emotions for several days now. *But my love is for Jadyn*, she told herself. *Only him.*

She swallowed, then asked, 'What did I look like, when I changed, back there?'

Was I hideous?

'Your hair deepened to the colour of blood,' Gram replied softly, as if trying to minimise her alarm. 'Your eyes turned deep purple. Your veins bulged, deep blue, but your pallor increased, your skin turning almost translucent. I could see the sinew and muscle beneath. Your teeth sharpened, and there's a vestigial horn that will come if you let it – a single prong in the middle of your forehead.'

'It sounds horrible,' she said morosely.

He looked at her frankly. 'It had a kind of beauty – but then, I'm used to such things.'

She swallowed and looked away. 'We Vestals take a vow of chastity to protect our partners. You vyr are playing with the same energies; so I presume you face the same issue. Let's avoid temptation, eh?'

That she'd acknowledged that temptation existed felt like a betrayal of Jadyn and their love, but the reality was undeniable. She and Gram had spent too long inside each other's heads to pretend otherwise.

'Aye,' Gram agreed hoarsely. 'I'll sleep above. Get some rest, and I'll take the first watch.'

10

Bhokasta

Three Thrones, One Ruler

While establishing the Triple Empire, Jovan Lux married into every major noble House in Hytal, Zynochia and Abutha, taking ten wives from each. He also established an annual rotation of his court, maintaining Petraxus as his primary base but spending every second year in either Bedum or Dagoz, a wise practice that continues to this day. As the generations pass, his descendants now rule four-fifths of the known world.

RYSTAN GABRIEL, SCHOLAR, PETRAXUS 1389

Regio Lago, Solabas
Summer 1472

Despite being hundreds of kylos inland, Regio Lago, or Lake Regal, was filled with seabirds nesting during spring and summer. It was more inland sea than lake, rimmed by steep cliffs and rocky beaches, the surface glittering beneath the wheeling gulls and azure sky. A light westerly was rippling through the stately pines and gleaming argofyl trees on the shore, and not even the distant smoke plumes from villages dotted along the shore could spoil the beauty.

Jadyn and Aura had been travelling for two nights and the best part of two days, a reasonably amiable journey, especially now Aura was riding with a degree of confidence. She still belittled him at every opportunity, but she was also worldly, observant and slyly funny. At times, she felt like a friend – but Jadyn was still mildly surprised each morning when he woke to find her there, wrapped in her blanket on the other side of the fire. He wasn't sure if it was the promise of money or fear of their pursuers that kept her with him.

Even so, he never came close to feeling relaxed. He'd seldom been without his pentacle, and never for long, but all he could do was pray they were alive and well and heading for Regio Lago and that somehow Elindhu would be able to reunite them all.

It'll be a relief to be together again, he thought, as they headed for a lakeshore village they'd spotted, hoping to get provisions and maybe even shelter and rest.

There were a number of beached fishing boats, and a few dozen huts clustered together beside an Akkanite shrine which looked not so much a church as an altar for sacrifices, a fusion of orthodoxy and older pagan traditions.

Dear Gods, I'd give anything to wash, Jadyn thought, gazing longingly at the water. 'Will they help us, do you think?' he asked. 'We can't even speak to them.'

'Is no problem,' Aura replied. 'Mu'ena vasi Solabi.'

'Huh?'

'I say, "I speak Solabi." Much trade over border.'

Another language she knows, Jadyn realised. 'You're, um, surprising,' he admitted.

'Am beautiful, intelligent and stupidous,' Aura said loftily.

'Er . . . stupendous?'

'Si, that. We go, Aura talk. Today am "Lady Nushka" and you be servant.'

'Shouldn't I be the lord and you the servant?'

'Not dressed like that.'

He snorted and let it go. She was probably right. They nudged their horses into motion, descending the slope while he ensured his orb was out of sight. 'We still look like mercenaries,' he warned her. 'We can't expect a friendly welcome.'

Sure enough, the moment the villagers spotted them, the men started snatching up weapons.

'Sodakos, sodakos,' Aura greeted them, before launching into a musical flow of Solabi, and soon the suspicious villagers were genuflecting reverently, helping her dismount and even calling for wine to quench her thirst.

'Do servants get to drink?' Jadyn murmured hopefully, as he swung from his saddle.

'No,' she replied, wincing at the taste. 'This place be Bhokasta; is dump, but does for rest. Estuary be for washing, drinking of water. Is good.' She waved airily as a crowd of dark-eyed Solabi women ushered her towards the huts. 'No trust,' she called, as she went. 'Be awaring.'

Jadyn turned to confront the men, still holding knives and fishing spears. They murmured among themselves, then one asked, 'You Talmoni?'

'I'm Vandari,' Jadyn answered. 'I'm the Lady's guard.'

'Ah, Vandari,' his interrogator repeated. 'Why Lady here?'

He had no idea what Aura had told them, so played it vague. 'Travelling.'

'Travelling,' the man echoed doubtfully. 'Just she, you?'

Jadyn faced him squarely, his hand concealing the elobyne orb as he drew power from it. Puissance surged through him, and a flash of hot temper. 'I am more than enough.'

'You sure ... Vandari pig ... ?' The man's eyes were flickering over Jadyn's right shoulder.

Right then ...

Jadyn's right uppercut smashed into the chin of the spokesman, snapping his head back and dropping him, even as he kicked backwards – sight unseen but straight into the groin of the man standing behind him, jack-knifing him over. Hands were grabbing at him, but he lashed out, left and right, his glyma-strength enabling him to break noses and jaws, sending blood and teeth flying. He scarcely felt the few blows that did land. When the fishermen raised knives and spears, he whipped out his sword, chopped a spear-haft in half and whirled, carving a space.

'Who's next?'

But at the sight of the orb they were already backing right off.

'No one be next,' Aura called, reappearing, one hand holding a scarlet-robed woman by the hair, the other pressing a knife to her throat. 'Is true, all Solabi be thiefers.'

Jagat, are we going to have to kill the whole damned village?

The first man he'd slugged groaned, clutching his jaw. 'Please, she's my wife—'

'This be wife?' Aura asked, eyebrows raised. 'Have pick of village?'

The wife snarled something and Aura said, 'Really? So sad.'

The woman tossed her head, then she caught Aura's left elbow and pulled up the sleeve, revealing a faded tattoo of a snake emerging from a lamp, on her inner arm.

'Sabbahi!' she hissed.

The entire village took another step back, while Jadyn gaped. *Sabbahi? She's an assassin?*

Aura let the woman go, pulled her sleeve back down and assumed a haughty stance, snapping out orders, and this time there was nothing but fear and obedience on the villagers' faces.

Aura smiled and called, 'Hola, servant Jadyn. Bring baggings.'

She turned peremptorily and headed for the biggest hut, the only one larger than a horse's stall. Jadyn kept his sword drawn as he hefted one saddlebag, then gestured with his blade for the fishermen to bring the rest.

The inside of the hut was surprising: carpets covered the floor, black and scarlet, intricately patterned, and cotton hangings covered the walls, embroidered with words and images from the local interpretation of the Akkanite faith. A skinny girl huddled by the smouldering firepit, stirring what smelled like a curried fish stew. She cowered when she saw them.

'We sleep here,' Aura told Jadyn. 'Is chief man's house.'

'Will they attack us again? Shouldn't we move on?'

'No – Sabbahi be respected here.' She bent over the skinny girl and murmured soothingly, ignoring the villagers who were carefully stacking the other saddlebags before backing away.

On a whim, Jadyn gave them a copper each, purloined from the pirates, and suddenly they were smiling at him and kissing the coins as they bowed their way out.

'Solabi,' Aura sniffed. 'Beggar by blood, thief by nature.'

'No, this is what poverty does,' Jadyn answered. 'Having nothing is dehumanising.' He gave her a hard look. 'Are you *really* a Sabbahi?'

Aura gave him a coy smile. 'Is fake tattoo. Old trick.'

'It's not real?'

'Is real tattoo . . . But Aura not Sabbahi. Just pretend, for surviving. Am full of tricks.'

'You know how to use a knife . . .'

'Have told already – Sergio teach, Aura learn. Am good pupil,' she added grimly.

This chilling little glimpse into her psyche did nothing to allay his suspicions. He remembered what she'd said of imaginary friends: Akka and the Devourer, sparring for her soul. *Is she really a trained killer, after all?* But he put his doubts aside and set about unpacking the needful.

Aura gave the serving-girl two coppers, which vanished into the folds of the girl's filthy robe. 'Va se,' Aura told the girl – *Go* – and she scurried out the door and vanished.

'How do we cross the lake into Ferasto?' he asked, once they'd unpacked.

'Ferasto, closed kingdom,' Aura replied. 'Must go Baluarte, buy warrant, then travel be legal.'

'I hadn't counted on that.'

'So, now you count.' Aura wrinkled her nose and said, 'Smell like horse. Must bathing.'

She was right; after just a few minutes the air in here was ripe, so he followed her to the estuary she'd pointed out earlier, where a stream entered the vast lake. A dozen naked copper-skinned women of all ages were bathing there, many pregnant. They squealed when they saw him, snatching up colourful clothing and scurrying off.

Aura laughed, then peeled off her own robe – and all the breath left his lungs.

He'd seen her naked once before, but he had immediately looked away. This time he found himself gaping at her lean but curvaceous body, her thick black hair falling to her waist, her high, firm breasts.

A cobra tattoo coiled round her right thigh, the cowled head adorning her buttock, echoing the false – *or not?* – Sabbahi tattoo on her left forearm. Her right breast was etched with Zynochi lettering.

Of course she noticed that he was struck dumb.

'Have said, Aura esa tresa bella,' she said, gesturing carelessly. 'No see woman before, Vestal? Enjoy to look, is great privilege.' She turned and swayed into the water. 'Come, we wash.'

Once she was fully immersed and largely out of sight, his limbs loosened enough that he could move. But rather than join her, he walked a few dozen paces downstream, stripped there and immersed himself in the water, which was cold but refreshing. He splashed round for a few minutes before setting to scrubbing his body, then his clothing, with his flamberge thrust into the stones at the water's edge, close at hand.

At last, he waded ashore and sat nearby while she basked at the water's edge, immersed to her hips but her upper torso brazenly visible. 'Ah,' she sighed, wringing out her thick dark hair. 'This be Elysium, si? Or would be, if you proper man with big libido, not stupid vow.'

He was getting sick of that mantra, not least because she was the most beautiful sight he'd ever had the intense discomfort of seeing. 'Is nothing sacred to you?'

'Sacred?' she sniffed. 'Love. Children. Laughter. Sun on skin. Love-makery. Friends. Kindness. All sacred . . . Forsaking all these to please priest; *not* sacred.'

'I thought you believed in Akka?'

'Believe? Maybe. Agree, maybe not? Akka is Talmoni god, Edict god: too much rules. *Dull*. Khetian people say, "all is god", no rules. *Confusing*. Kharagh say "horse is god". *What?* Pelasi say "god is fish". *Silly*. So, why choose?'

'But the Edict teaches us right from wrong—'

'No, it compel, waving finger. Only heart teach right and wrong,' she said, tapping her left breast, which he stared at – then jerked his eyes away. She laughed gaily, threw herself backwards underwater, then rose in an explosion of spray. 'You funny,' she gusted. 'Like child.'

'We have our vows for important reasons,' he told her firmly.

'Like what?' she asked, with a mockery of innocence.

Stupidly, he tried to explain. 'The glyma goes badly wrong when we become, erm, *involved* with someone. Magic requires discipline, but lust, love, desire . . . those destroy our control . . . and can result in killing your partner . . . uh, Aura?'

She was now staring round-eyed. 'E Cara! Sexing with Vestal can kill? Had heard, not believing!' She covered her breasts and loins with her hands. 'No looking, Vestal. Not wanting Aura! Sexing bad!'

Finally, I'm getting through to her.

'It is a very real risk,' he told her, averting his eyes. 'All magic requires energy, and during . . . erm, congress . . . male glyma-wielders risk flooding their partner with energy and killing them. Women magicians do the opposite; they drain energy. Either can be fatal.'

'E Cara,' Aura gulped. 'Can you even . . . ?' She made a crude gesture.

He felt himself go scarlet, even though all Vestal knights learned to live with such teasing. 'Uh, you can . . . but it undermines your personal discipline. Conquering physical desires prolongs your career . . .'

She looked at him with appalled sadness. 'So longer career, longer misery. Am sorry for Jadyn Knight.'

'When I retire, I'll make up for lost time.'

'Si, you must. If crazy quest no kill, you marry, have mucho bebes! Si?'

'Yes, I will marry,' he told her firmly. 'I'll marry Romara.'

She grimaced and was her subversive self again. 'Bad choice! Angry temper, all hard, no soft. Jadyn need laughing woman, make happy.'

'I know my heart,' he said. Deeming himself dry enough, and eager to escape the awkward conversation, he rose and headed for the huts . . .

. . . just as Romara appeared from the village, travel-stained and weary, and yet somehow still a lady of noble blood. A very irritable noblewoman. Gram was trailing her, still clad in his torn and soiled furs. They began to call greetings, then realised he was naked, and Aura also, and lost track of their words.

Oh, no . . . Jadyn ran for his cloak and hastily wrapped himself in it, his face burning as he blurted, 'You found us!'

Romara and Gram didn't respond; both were staring at Aura.

'Hola, friendlies,' she declared, wading ashore. 'Clean is good. Am blissing now.' She sauntered past, swept up her clothes and walked on, wiggling her behind. When they just gaped, she snorted, 'Nice see you, too, Virgins,' and headed for the village.

Gram choked back laughter, but Romara glared at Jadyn. 'You two look . . . companionable.'

'We were washing,' Jadyn retorted. 'I couldn't let her out here alone. The villagers tried to knife us earlier.'

Her face was still stony. 'Did they?'

'It's resolved now'. *Kind of* . . . 'How did you find us? Did Elindhu guide you here?'

'No, it's just good fortune,' Romara replied, relaxing now that Aura had gone. 'Tevas is still hunting us, but his men aren't terribly enthusiastic. We evaded them easily enough. We reached the lake a little further down the shoreline, and this was the first village we found.'

'And Gram?' he asked, dropping his voice. He'd been worrying that they'd come to blows.

'He's been proper and courteous,' she replied, with a surprising degree of respect. 'I think we can trust him, at least as far as this vyr village he's taking us to. What of Aura?'

'I've had no problems from her.'

'I still say we cut her loose as soon as we can.' She looked out over the lake. 'From here, we cross into Ferasto, then head for the passes into Neparia, right?'

'Aye, but Aura says we'll need a royal warrant to move freely in Ferasto, and we can only obtain that at Baluarte, an island fortress near here. So that's where we're heading as soon as Obanji, Soren and Elindhu catch up.' He indicated the estuary. 'I'm done here, but I suggest you wash – you'll be sharing her hut, and she's not one for bad smells.'

'Neither am I,' Romara said, looking down at her tunic and shuddering. 'I suppose you're right: this is no time for niceties.' She walked down to the estuary and waded in, fully clothed. A moment later, Gram did the same, the pair conversing in low voices, then laughing.

223

Jadyn dressed, then stood guard, a little troubled by the obvious camaraderie that had grown between Romara and Gram. There was no doubt in his mind that their bond of shared glyma-energy was keeping them both alive and sane, but it was unsettling to see them shyly disrobe while bathing, decorously apart but subtly together as they washed.

He realised with a shock that he was jealous. He and Romara had been like brother and sister for a decade; having outsiders around was strange and unsettling.

Nothing will come between us, he vowed. *She is still my only love.*

They had to endure only one uncomfortable night in Bhokasta before Obanji and Soren rode in from a nearby settlement with Elindhu, who'd found them the same day they'd separated. They'd retained the spare horses, and had plenty of provisions remaining, too.

'I lost my own horse during the initial attack,' Elindhu told Jadyn and Romara as she hugged them both. 'The men hunting us are close behind, though, so we need to move on, quickly.'

They left immediately after warning the fisher folk to hide, and the villagers swiftly had vanished into the thin bushland around the lake. By then, Jadyn's party were in the saddle and moving on.

He kept them moving rapidly, but close enough together so they could brief each other about their journeys. They were all troubled by his report of triple-shards in the hills, and the effects it was having on the Solabi landscape, vindicating Nilis Evandriel's accusations against the Order. But as Elindhu pointed out, there might be other explanations. 'Though it doesn't look good,' she admitted.

'The mage said it was all a temporary measure, and once the vyr were defeated, they'd dismantle it,' Jadyn answered, still reluctant to condemn his Order. But even he wondered if he was being naïve.

Another few hours' hard riding saw Baluarte hove into view, an island fortress on the outflow of the Serena River. 'See, am true guider,' Aura trilled, tilting her face to the setting sun. 'Virgins be lost, elsewise.'

'Hardly,' Romara replied. 'We can find our own way, I assure you.'

Maybe, Jadyn thought, *although there's finding your way, and there's doing so without bringing the world down on your head*. 'Aura, please,' he said, before Romara upset the girl, 'will you tell us more about Ferasto?'

'Si, Aura know Ferasto well,' the Nepari declared, puffing up. 'Come with Sailor Boy Sergio. We play tricks, make money. Good time.'

'Are you saying you're an outlaw here?' Romara asked sharply.

'Neya, not outlaw. People not know Aura. Too clever, si. Get travel warrant, no problem.'

Jadyn feared there was a lot more to her story she'd left unsaid – but Ferasto remained their best option for reaching Neparia and finding Nilis Evandriel. 'Tell us about the warrant?'

Aura waved her hand knowledgeably. 'King of Ferasto have many enemy, si? Neparia, Solabas, Foyland. King be fearing. So he make rich with opium. Money-money-money, buy many soldier. Control trade, make tariff, si? For control of lands, make warrant. No have warrant, no enter, nada. We buy, all good.'

'So we can just buy a warrant?' Romara asked. 'What do we need you for, then?'

Aura shrugged. 'Must have sponsor, local person.'

'What?' Jadyn asked. 'How will we get that?'

'Is easy. In Baluarte, Aura has other name, fake person, si? She buy as local, no problem.'

'You've got a false identity in Ferasto? That you used to commit crimes?'

'Ney, ney, Aura have many personality. Is still good reputing.'

'Good people don't do such things,' Romara grumbled.

'Vestal know nothing,' Aura sniffed. 'World is cruel.'

Her light, flippant tone belied her face, unusually solemn and moody. Jadyn sensed genuine suffering lurking behind her words. *We who have the glyma don't know how the powerless live*, he reflected. *Who are we to judge her?* Aura was, he was starting to think, a kind of miracle, although he wasn't denying she could also be trouble.

'We'll try it,' he said. 'But if you're known in Ferasto, you could endanger us.'

'Elysia on high, I wish we could just use a portali gate to reach Neparia,' Romara grumbled.

'What is portali?' Aura asked.

Romara clammed up, but Jadyn couldn't see the harm in telling her. 'Some bastions have a special gate that enables our people to travel hundreds of kylos in just a few hours.'

Aura looked somewhat appalled. 'Not liking. Vestal Order be bad people.'

'No, we aren't,' Romara retorted. 'We represent truth, justice and honour.'

Aura spat and said, 'Could tell of Order honour. But I spare glory detailing.'

'Gory details,' Romara corrected. 'When will you learn to speak properly?'

Aura faced her, eyes flashing. 'Aura born, learn Nepari. Learn Solabi from traders, Bedumi and Mutazi also. Also Pelasi, fluent. Not need Talmoni until now. Ke passa dos Nepp, Cunya?'

'What did you call me?' Romara flared.

'Learn Nepari, find out,' Aura retorted, urging her mount on and leaving them behind.

Romara cast her eyes skywards, but to his surprise, Jadyn found his sympathies were with Aura. 'That's five languages she has,' he noted. 'And she can make herself understood in ours, too. Cut her some slack, Rom.'

'Talmoni is the imperial language,' Romara countered. 'If she was smart, it'd have been her first priority.' She glared after the Nepari, then exhaled morosely. 'Sorry, she just sets my teeth on edge. And while I'm apologising, I'm sorry I implied that you might be tempted by her. It's just . . . well, you know that not every knight keeps his vows, and you and she were naked.'

'We were washing, on a public beach, in a place where we couldn't afford to be separated.'

'Aye, I know. Sorry. I spoke hastily, and wrongly.'

'That's enough apologising,' he smiled. 'It'll make me giddy. Did Gram behave?'

'He's a vorlok,' she snapped, but then her face softened. 'But he's also a decent man. Honestly, he might be redeemable. I trust him more than Auranoo-whatever.' She gave him a taut look. 'And right now, that thing he can do, that drawing out my glyma-energy . . . that's important to me.'

He shot her a worried look. 'Is the glyma-rage getting worse?'

She looked away. 'I'm managing it.'

No, you're not, Jadyn realised. *You're barely holding on . . .*

'We'll be in Neparia soon, Rom. We'll find Nilis Evandriel and resolve this.'

Romara gave him a hollow-eyed look. 'I see two outcomes: in one, Nilis Evandriel is a truth-speaker and we end up dying for him. In the second, he's a liar and we take his head. Frankly, I'd prefer the latter.'

Tevas Nicolini paced along the line of kneeling Solabi villagers, people they'd spotted lurking near a deserted village on the lake. They'd resisted when his men attacked, but hadn't stood a chance. The surviving men numbered fourteen; seventeen others lay dead. He'd had the women and children corralled in the animal pens, with those of age being used for sport. A few had got away, but he wasn't worried about them. He just wanted information.

'Was Talmoni here?' he shouted in the face of the tallest man, a greybeard with a scarred face. 'Talmoni? *Talmoni*, you jagatai moron!'

The galling thing was, these animals seemed willing to talk, but none spoke Talmoni. Apparently those with a little were already dead. So whatever these wretches knew was locked inside their heads. He punched the man anyway, venting his frustration before the elobyne made him do worse, then nursed his grazed knuckles as he watched the man squirm at his feet, spitting out teeth and blood.

'Do we kill them and go?' asked Vitch, his sergeant. 'I don' reckon they was here.'

'Nor do I,' Tevas conceded. The chance of claiming the reward for Jadyn Kaen and Romara Challys was receding by the day. *We should abandon pursuit and cut our losses.*

As if sensing his doubts, Vitch dropped his voice and muttered,

'The lads don't know why we're still chasing 'em, Tevas. We ain't the Order – it's not our job to hunt down renegades.' *And when we fought them, we got our arses whipped*, his expression added.

Vitch was a thug, but he was Tevas' most reliable man. If he said the Pelasians were getting mutinous, it paid to listen. Renegade Vestals were worth a king's ransom in bounty and the men had been keen enough at first, but when they lost a dozen men on encountering the Falcons, that enthusiasm had understandably waned. But they were still with him, because the bounty would be enough to retire in luxury . . . if they survived to collect.

Vitch didn't look like he cared much for the money any more, though. Like any good mercenary, his first thought was getting out alive, and he'd been downgrading those odds as they travelled, clearly.

'Think how good it's going to feel when you're lopping these traitors' heads off,' Tevas said. 'And there's that pile of gold you'll collect. Me, I'll head for the Mar-Eras and buy up a palace. What about you?'

The sergeant brightened a little, pulling out his hipflask of Shyll whisky and sipping. 'Well, it won't be this hole,' he snickered. 'I'll make for the Nepari coast. A bit of sun, and that rich port wine they make, oh yeah.'

They'd ransacked the village for anything of value, leaving the gulls to tear at the piled-up corpses, their shrieking almost enough to mask the lewd laughter of the soldiers and the rhythmic grunting coming from the huts they were using the women in.

'Speaking of holes,' Vitch grunted, 'I'm gonna take a turn on one of them whores.'

How did I end up with these scum? Tevas wondered, missing the Order's imposing bastions, spotless uniforms, and the semblance of honour and decency. But it was a rhetorical wondering. He'd almost made it to forty by the time he'd retired, a longer career than most in the Order, but that meant longer exposure to the glyma, and a deeper need for that feeling of potency. So he'd joined a pirate gang and taken control. He'd known the sort of men he'd be working with and he'd told himself he'd change them, but he'd never really tried.

I wouldn't have picked Jadyn Kaen to go renegade, he mused. *He drank honour and pissed loyalty.* But maybe he'd felt the tramp of time too? Or stolen a trove of elobyne crystals and run? Or lost his cool and bludgeoned some young tyro to death over some stupid remark? That happened to the best. Maybe he and Romara had finally broken their vows and screwed? Or he'd been seduced by some trollop and killed her in the throes of passion. That was also an old, old tale. The Order broke everyone, eventually. The standards and ideals were too high. He could see that, now he was out. Still, whatever it was, the price on Jadyn and Romara's head made killing them worth the guilt.

I can still take them both down, all else remaining equal . . .

One last big payday, then he'd finally retire properly and purge the glyma from himself. Then he'd take some lithe Bedumi girl to wife and settle down to enjoy the rosy sunsets, while the rest of the world burned.

Next morning, there was uproar: some drunken fool had missed something, because all the surviving Solabi men, women and children had been untied and slipped away in the night, leaving Tevas' men fuming. Only one prisoner remained, the man he'd concussed the previous night, who hadn't regained consciousness, and probably wouldn't.

Infuriated, he lined his men up and began berating them – until he glanced inland and saw a line of horsemen, clearly Order from their colours, coming from the north.

'Jagat, who are these bastards?' he wondered. The last thing he wanted to see was a Vestal century. He hurriedly concealed his flamberge's tell-tale orb beneath his leather hilt cover. 'Forget this mess,' he muttered to Vitch. 'Losing those women is punishment enough for the lads.' He raised his voice. 'Smarten up, you scum! We got Vestals comin' in.'

He saw curiosity, fear and awe on the men's faces as they formed up with an alacrity that was usually missing. They were still a filthy, ragged and motley array, but they stood up straight as the Vestal cohort trotted in, a phalanx of Solabi men led by a hard-faced knight-commander. With them were two Talmoni, one a lictor – and unfortunately, Tevas knew him.

He hurriedly saluted, fist to chest. 'Lictor Borghart! Welcome to Solabas. I—'

'Tevas Nicolini, by the gods,' drawled the tall, shaven-skulled cadaver that was Yoryn Borghart. 'Well, well . . . I trust this is a coincidence?'

Behind him, a richly dressed younger man, handsome, but fast going to seed, also dismounted and joined them. 'Is what a coincidence?' he asked. 'Lictor, do you know this man?'

Akka on high, isn't that Elan Sandreth? Tevas thought, groaning inside. *What're these pricks doing here?* Then he realised they were here for the same reason: the lictor was also hunting Jadyn and Romara.

'This is Tevas Nicolini, a former blademaster of the Order,' Borghart said softly. 'Retired . . . and now operating outside the empire – and still using an Order flamberge, I'd warrant.'

'It's grey area of the Code,' Tevas replied meekly.

'Hardly,' the lictor sniffed. 'Didn't you surrender your weapon on retirement?'

'Of course,' Tevas lied. 'I found this one in a market—'

'I don't care,' Borghart interrupted, with a glint in his eye that suggested that as long as Tevas was useful, it wouldn't matter. 'As blademaster at Tar-Millmont, you must have known Romara Challys and Jadyn Kaen? The Falcons were among the centuries that based themselves there.'

So he is chasing them, Tevas thought, kissing goodbye to the bounty. Lictors didn't share.

'I know them,' he admitted. 'They showed up at the village where I've . . . uh, retired, on the coast. I realised they had turned renegade and demanded their surrender. We came to blows, they escaped, but as a loyal imperial citizen I felt the need to pursue—'

'Spare me the boar-shit,' Borghart interrupted. 'Since you retired you've gone mercenary. See, we lictors keep our fingers on the pulse. We know the renegades we pursue took ship from Vandarath to Solabas. Did they come to you for aid?'

'No, no, they just walked in,' Tevas denied frantically, before Borghart decided to torture him for the 'truth'. 'They were as shocked as I was, I swear.'

Fortunately, that was true, and Borghart, a strong mage, must have sensed that, for he gave a nod of confirmation to the nobleman, then surveyed the carnage that had been wrought on the village, with intent, approving eyes. 'Were they here?'

'Um, maybe, Milord,' Tevas mumbled, wiping his sweating brow. 'The villagers don't speak Talmoni, so we can't question them . . .'

His voice trailed off in the face of Borghart's icy stare. 'Fortunately I speak seven languages,' the lictor replied. 'Where are your prisoners?'

'They . . . ah, escaped.'

Borghart stared at him, while Elan Sandreth closed his eyes and shook his head. 'Whose fault was that?' asked the lictor.

'I . . . um . . . one of the Solabi must've had a knife and cut them all free after nightfall. But it could have been anyone's fault, so I can't single out one—'

'Can you not? These guards of yours presumably had an officer supervising them?'

Tevas' skin flushed cold. 'Aye.'

'Who was that?'

Oh, jagat . . . 'Sergeant Vitch,' he mumbled, then repeated louder. 'Vitch.'

'Vitch,' Borghart repeated, his eyes glinting dangerously. '*Sergeant Vitch, report!*'

The sergeant froze, wavering as if he might run – but he knew better than to try, instead stepping forward with commendable courage and saluting. 'Sergeant Jan Vitch, reporting.'

'This man is valuable,' Tevas muttered to Borghart. 'He's ex-imperial army, one of few I can trust. Most of them are ex-army but he's my best man.'

The lictor gave no sign he'd heard. 'Who was responsible for searching the prisoners, Sergeant Vitch?'

If the sergeant named names, he might be condemning other men to death. If he took responsibility himself, it could be suicidal. Or Borghart might simply reprimand those responsible and move on.

'Milord,' Tevas blurted, to save Vitch from the dilemma, 'ultimately, everything is *my* responsibility.'

Borghart rounded on him, black eyes boring in, and for a moment, everything froze in a breathless tableau, the gulls hanging in the air, the smoke from the village unmoving, his dripping sweat freezing on his face and neck.

'Do you consider yourself above punishment, Nicolini?'

'No,' Tevas managed.

The lictor tilted his head, considering. 'While it is true that ultimately all responsibility devolves upwards, are we then to blame the Hierophant for all sin? Or Akka? I think not. A commander gives orders and expects them to be obeyed. A sergeant relays them and expects the same . . . and he checks, and follows up . . .'

Tevas never even saw Borghart kindle the glyma – one moment the man was immobile, pondering the philosophies of command; the next, he'd spun and a bolt of energy blasted Vitch's face. There was a hideous *crack!* – and a moment later, the dead sergeant was lying ten feet away, the front of his skull blasted away and what was left of his head blackened and smoking.

'*AND WHEN FAILURE OCCURS,*' Borghart was suddenly screaming, '*EXAMPLES MUST BE MADE.*'

Another blast of energy struck Vitch's torso, charring cloth, then flesh. The body started roasting . . . until the bones burned, and at last, crumpled to glowing ash. It took less than a minute. Two of his men had passed out, and Tevas had to fight his own mad impulse to retaliate, but a slight movement – an almost non-existent shake of the head from Elan Sandreth – brought him back to his senses.

Instead he stood silently, breathing hard, as the lictor stalked along the lines of men.

'We are hunting renegade Knights of the Vestments of Elysia Divina,' Borghart barked. 'Such a prey requires discipline and resource. I'm told you men have military training. You possess discipline, even if you have let it lapse. Archon Corbus Ritter has authorised a reward of ten gold talents – to be shared *equally* among those involved in the capture or death of the Falcon pentacle. That's enough for *everyone* here to retire in luxury.'

Borghart paused to let his words sink in, and Tevas saw fear replaced by greed and longing. It was fivefold the bounty he'd told them they'd receive. *By Akka, I could use that sort of wealth myself . . .*

'So,' the lictor went on, as his glyma rage faded and calm returned, 'we have incentive, skill and experience. Failure will not tolerated, but that is the way of the world when one hunts dangerous prey. Are you with me?'

Whether from greed or dread, every man shouted, *'AYE!'*

'Aye,' Tevas echoed.

'Excellent,' Borghart replied. 'So, we must retake your prisoners and question them.'

Tevas remembered the concussed man. 'There's one left, but he hasn't regained consciousness.'

The lictor's eyes lit up. 'Ah. Bring him to me.'

In minutes, the grey-bearded Solabi was dumped on the beach at Borghart's feet. As the lictor knelt over him, hands weaving, Elan Sandreth drew Tevas aside.

'So you know the fugitives?' the young lord asked him.

'Aye. After I was promoted from the field, I became an instructor at Tar-Millmont, in Vandarath,' Tevas answered. 'Kaen and Challys were my pupils for a couple of years. We remained in touch, until I left the Order.'

'So they're your friends?' The young man's smile didn't reach his eyes. 'Some might find your failure to apprehend them suspicious, in the light of that fact.'

This snake is as vicious as Borghart, Tevas realised. 'Not friends. I didn't befriend initiates.'

'Mm, one must always be cognisant of rank,' the young peer mused. 'Lessers are to be commanded, or even *used*, but not associated with, don't you think?'

'The Order is a meritocracy,' Tevas replied stiffly, not liking this turn in the conversation, 'based on skill.'

'I doubt that,' Elan Sandreth observed. 'Those born and bred for command are natural leaders, elevated by their excellence. Cohort leaders are only ever nobility, yes? Whereas those rising from the fields will always wear dirty boots, don't you think? This Jadyn Kaen is a peasant oaf, but Romara was gentry.' He eyed Tevas. 'Well above the likes of you, I warrant. Nicolini ... a mercantile name, yes? A money-grubbing shopkeeper from Aquinium, mayhap?'

'Yes, Lord.' Having to mumble platitudes to this silken shit-bag – when he could cut him in half with one blow – was hard to take.

'Yet there you were, in a position of power over your trainees.' Elan went on. 'Did you ever use that difference in authority, Master Nicolini? Did you ever *abuse* it?'

Somehow, Tevas kept his voice even. 'No.'

'Romara must've been a temptation, though?'

'Nothing happened.' *Though Akka knows, I had to fend her off in the early days.*

The young noble looked at him intently, then barked a laugh. 'Just as well. She's my wife.'

Tevas blinked, startled. *'She's what?'*

'We married, just before she went missing,' Elan declared. 'I'm officially her husband, and all she has is mine. Remember that, Blademaster. She belongs to me.'

Tevas was too stunned to know how to react, but before he could ask any of the multitude of questions flashing through his brain, Borghart provided an interruption.

The lictor hunched over the comatose prisoner, his right hand lit up and gripped the villager's skull in a claw-like grip, at which the man started babbling in his own tongue, a terrified stream-of-consciousness. His voice reached a crescendo, then Borghart gestured and the man flopped, his body deflating, exuding a corrupted meat smell as it decayed into a desiccated corpse.

Tevas shuddered, though he'd seen such things before. Necromancy was officially forbidden, but lictors had leave to do pretty much what they liked, so long as it got results.

Borghart straightened. 'They rode towards Baluarte two days ago. That Nepari whore is an assassin, by the way. How amusing: our renegades are travelling with a vorlok and a sabbahi assassin. What-ever next?'

'It smacks of some larger conspiracy,' Elan Sandreth replied, with the air of one who enjoys such things. 'Good to meet you, Master Nicolini,' he added. 'We must chat again.'

'To Baluarte, then,' the lictor said. 'As you say, when such enemies combine, something larger is afoot.' He surveyed the village dispassionately, fully in control of his emotions again. 'Burn this wretched place as punishment for harbouring criminals. Their boats, too. Such scum don't deserve a home or a livelihood.'

Baluarte, Regio Lago, Solabas

Jadyn's group arrived too late for the last ferry to Baluarte Island. With their purses light and not sure if word of their flight had already reached the ferry town, they camped a kylo away, at the water's edge.

Baluarte was a fortress built on an island in the Serena, where the river began its journey from Lake Regal to the sea. It oversaw lake and river traffic with spear-hurling ballistae and giant catapults for lobbing burning pitch at transgressors. On the far shore lay their next destination, the port of Huestra in Ferasto, twinkling in the sunset.

Romara felt several scrying attempts on her, but this time her veil spell blocked them. The nagging attacks kept her on edge, but she took comfort that Borghart couldn't be using whatever memento he'd used before to find her that first time, as he couldn't penetrate her veil spell.

They spent the evening seeing to small things: washing and repairing clothes, and setting the camp. Obanji took Soren through his drills while Elindhu went into a meditative trance. To Jadyn's surprise, Gram volunteered to cook, and Aura helped, chattering non-stop while the trapper ignored her.

Jadyn joined Romara in rubbing down the horses, singing Talmoni ballads, and presently Gram joined in, in a deep basso. Soon, they all were bellowing out songs, while Aura danced a Nepari aronda. Jadyn smiled; it was moments like this that bonded a pentacle as deeply as any shared peril. Banter, teasing and laughter was a glue for holding them together. Since escaping Gaudien, they'd been in constant turmoil, but tonight, he felt like he was getting his family back – and that it was growing.

'Hey, Elindhu, what's a Pentacle when it becomes six or seven?' he asked, in a rush of enthusiasm.

'A Hexagon or Heptagon – and ironically, "Hexen" is an old Vandarai word for witches,' she replied.

'There's only five Vestals here.' Romara put in stiffly. 'We're a pentacle and that's all.'

Her reaction sobered Jadyn, but he covered his gaffe by starting a new song. Then Gram declared the meal ready; he'd roasted a pair of hares Obanji had shot that evening, stuffed with herbs and some mashed roots he'd found near a burnt-out farmhouse. While they ate they watched the sunset paint the lake and the forbidding island-fortress in hues of purple and scarlet.

After the meal, Obanji prepared to put Soren through his paces with a blade again – and this time, Gram said, 'Show me, too.'

Jadyn looked at Romara, who nodded her approval. She took her flamberge, removed the orb from the pommel and handed it to the trapper. 'If he can learn to fight without drawing on the glyma, well and good,' she commented.

'Fair enough. But let's keep it calm,' Jadyn told Obanji.

'All right then, Big Man,' Obanji said to Gram. 'Let's see what you've got.'

The Abuthan arrayed Gram and Soren side by side, while he demonstrated a series of basic parries and blows. For Soren they were now second nature, but Gram found them hard, his bulk working against him. Soon he was stripped to the waist despite the cold, already slick with sweat, and his teeth set in anger at himself. The more he tried, the more ponderous he was, especially beside the slick footwork and deft movements of the younger man.

'You're like a laggy with a sledgehammer,' Soren teased. 'Move your feet.'

'What is laggy?' Aura asked.

236

'A labourer,' Jadyn told her. 'It's an insulting term, implying stupidity.'

Aura raised her eyebrows. 'Foolish boy.'

Gram rumbled in anger, then exhaled forcibly and tried again, with no better form. 'You'd be better with an axe or hammer,' Obanji commented. 'Give you one big enough and the fight's over in one blow.'

'By who?' Soren scoffed, a streak of cockiness emerging. 'He'd be down before he could swing.'

The boy shouldn't boast like that, nor put a comrade down, Jadyn thought, *although maybe it's insecurity.*

He went to caution Soren, but Gram snarled, 'Yeah? Show me – head to head.'

The atmosphere took on a frisson of danger. Jadyn looked at Romara, expecting her to veto it, but she shrugged, so he gave his approval. 'Use sheathed blades – no naked steel. First touch only, best of seven.'

The combatants stalked to either end of the little beach, while the rest of the pentacle made casual bets; all were in favour of Soren except Romara. Aura cheekily called for Soren to strip to the waist too – which he did. He was trim but well-built, a contrast to Gram's shaggy immensity.

'Right, Big Man,' the initiate said, twirling his blade, 'this is how it's done.'

He swept in, feinting high left and right, then thwacking Gram in the belly, a perfect rendition of the movements Gram had been failing to execute. 'One,' he counted, as the big man bent over, gasping: though the blade was sheathed, it was heavy and the blow had been hard.

To prove it no fluke, Soren did it again next time, while Gram chased feints. 'Two.'

Gram snarled.

'No,' Romara snapped. 'None of that.'

Her words calmed the trapper, but he still got smacked in the chest a few seconds later by Soren, who was a blur of motion. 'Three.'

'*Nrgghh,*' the giant fumed.

'Last chance,' Soren crowed, twirling his blade theatrically. 'See if you can land a blow.'

Gram stalked towards him, his face contorted in fury, and Jadyn thought of intervening – but next moment, Gram's wild swing flashed over Soren's head as the initiate ducked, then the young man rammed his sheathed sword point-first into the giant's belly and Gram jack-knifed, folding with an explosive grunt and collapsing to his knees, spilling his sword.

'Four,' Soren crowed, and placed his scabbard against Gram's throat. 'Did you follow that, Big Man?'

Gram looked up at him, his eyes flashing – then he smashed his right fist into Soren's groin.

For a moment the tableau froze – until Soren made a whimpering sound, his stricken face bulging as he dropped his weapon and clutched at himself in utter agony, his legs giving way as he folded.

Gram watched him fall with a look of sour satisfaction, growling, 'Nah, missed it. Can you show me again?'

Obanji grabbed Gram and slammed him onto his back, snapping, 'Don't get up.'

Soren was sobbing, but still trying to make a point. 'If . . . real fight . . . he dead . . . Gonna . . . kill . . .'

'You stay down, too,' Jadyn advised, bending over him. 'There's a lesson, for sure: don't assume a foe is down, just because you think you've landed a killing blow. Now let it go.'

'Can't . . . breathe . . .'

'Try harder.' Jadyn straightened. 'Show's over, people. No retribution, no follow-ups.' Once they all nodded, he looked down at Gram. 'You'll take Soren's watch as well as your own. And you owe him a beer.'

'Find me a battle-axe,' he growled, thrusting the hilt of Romara's flamberge into her lap. 'That thing isn't for me.'

'We'll do that, but you'll still have to learn to use your feet,' Jadyn told him. 'There's no substitute for hard work. Soren, pour cold water over your cods. That usually works for me.'

There was some resentful posturing, as Obanji helped Soren to his knees and tended to him. Then the young man showed some spirit by pulling out Obanji's seldom-used lute and belting out a vengeful version of 'Burning Wood', a vyr-slaying anthem from the Talmoni heartland.

Gram bunched a fist when he recognised it, but calmed at Romara's urging.

With that song out of his system, Soren settled down and sang 'Lady of Shivers' and 'Rose Heart', his voice filling the dell, and everyone relaxed, especially after Gram went back to the road to keep watch.

They settled in for some sleep, but Jadyn woke around midnight to relieve the trapper. 'Keep your temper, friend,' he advised. 'Using the glyma isn't easy, and all of us struggle to hold ours.'

Gram bowed his head. 'I'm sorry . . . He was just pissing me off, the flash young prick.'

Jadyn smiled. 'Naturals like him piss everyone off – he'll outshine us all, one day soon. But he'll also learn to sing low. Humility is a virtue, if you're a glyma man. Keeps you calm.'

'I'm surprised he's still got an unbroken nose,' Gram grunted.

'That'll come. Go on, get some rest.'

Gram slouched off, and Jadyn relaxed, not too concerned. Flare-ups in a group of fighters always happened, and Soren and Gram were unused to living cheek by jowl with others.

They'll be fine. And maybe we'll become a hexagon or whatever, despite what Rom said.

In Neparia, there was a saying: *Akka a deracha, Devorador a skerda* – Akka on my right, Devourer on my left. Both were out tonight, sitting on Aura's shoulders as she lay beneath the moons and stars, trying to sleep. She wished they'd shut up, but they just went on and on and on. Apart from Jadyn, on watch, she was the only one awake. The ground was cold, and despite her exhaustion, she just couldn't sleep. This infernal beach was all stones and it reeked of ash, and every distant noise jarred her awake.

Finally, she rolled onto her back and watched the stars, who took on the faces of Akka and the Devourer as they debated her future. She hadn't been joking when she told Jadyn that she had imaginary companions . . . if imaginary they were. Some nights they felt very real indeed.

We're only days from Neparia, Akka was saying. *Once she's home, all will be well.*

Well? the Devourer scoffed, her dry, feminine voice amused. *Neparia's a shithole. Aura burned her bridges when she left – if she goes back, she'll be lucky if she isn't locked up in a convent and left to rot.*

My convents are holy places, Akka protested, in a wounded voice.

Ha! They're prisons for free spirits like Aura. She'd die like a caged canary.

I would, Aura put in.

The higher powers ignored her.

At least she'd die shriven of sin, Akka stated. *That's the most anyone can hope for in life.*

Ha! You think your convents free of sin? the Devourer answered. *Clearly you haven't visited one recently. Your nuns are a pack of money-grubbing chocha-licking flagellation fiends! No, Aura must be free. There's nothing in Neparia for her . . . But Ferasto holds a world of opportunity for those cunning enough to make the most of it.*

Ferasto? the Great God sneered. *A pagan backwater with—*

—dozens of opium-rich warlords who'd welcome a nice piece of rump like our Aura.

Hey, I'm worth more than that, Aura exclaimed indignantly.

The giant faces in the sky turned and peered down at her. *You think so?* they sniffed. *You're just a slut with no prospects and nowhere to go. You need a protector to keep you safe from maniacs like Borghart.*

Tragically, Aura knew they were right. Her whole life had taught her that this was a man's world, where only women with the glyma or great personal wealth got to live under their own terms. For the majority, the equation was simple: you had ten years of youth and beauty – at the most – in which to secure a protector and the coin to live on, and even then all you were likely to get was some wife-beating brute who'd treat you like a slave. But if you couldn't snare such a prize in time, you had no prospects but penury and a miserable death.

I'm nearly twenty-three, she fretted. *My days of beauty are almost over.*

Ridiculously, these men she'd fallen in with, super-warriors who should have been perfect as protectors and providers, were no use, because of their damnable chastity. All her skills of seduction, from her enchanting smiles and witty jests to the darker arts of the boudoir, were useless against Jadyn and his foolish knights.

They can't lie with me without killing me, she worried. *So how can I control them?*

Charm them with your smile, Akka suggested.

And maybe the odd hand-job, the Devourer suggested. *That should be safe, surely?*

No, Aura replied. *They're too pure for that. I've got nothing they want.*

Then cash them in, the Devourer urged. *Think of the bounty. Enough to buy your way into the bed of any man you want. You could find Sergio and buy his ship, make him your servant. Live the high life for ever.*

There is no for ever, Akka replied. *Only Eternity – in my Paradise or your belly, Devorador.*

Oh, I'm sure Aura knows where she's going, the Devourer purred. *She's already mine.*

No, she whispered despairingly. *Go away.*

She rolled onto her side, banishing Akka and his enemy from her mind, and stared miserably into the dying campfire, while the others snored and snuffled through their own dreams.

I'm nothing to them, she reflected. *So they should be nothing to me . . .*

11

Lady Juanita

Ferasto

Ferasto is a bandit kingdom peopled with Foylish, Solabi and Nepari migrants. Hemmed in by mountains and a giant lake, Regio Lago, it was an impoverished backwater for centuries, until they realised that it was ideal for poppy-growing. It is now one of the empire's largest suppliers of opium, and has a strong army. Even the Vestal Order must sing low in Ferasto, where shards are forbidden.

INCHALUS SEKUM, MUTAZI SCRIBE, 1469

Baluarte, Regio Lago
Summer 1472

The ferries to Ferasto left from Canas, on the Solabi side of the Serena River's headwaters. From sunrise, sailors began pushing out barges and rowing boats, most going directly to Huestra on the other side of the lake, taking those with a valid travel warrant. But Jadyn's group had to join those going to Baluarte to obtain such a warrant.

By dawn they were queuing with hundreds of merchants, gypsies and refugees. There'd been further vyr attacks nearby – at Riokastella, Romara wasn't surprised to learn – forcing yet more people to abandon their lives and seek a haven in Ferasto. Most would be turned away; she could almost taste the desperation in the air.

Hoping they were still ahead of whatever arrest notices had been posted for them, they approached the ticket booth for Baluarte. But the Ferasti ticket-sellers were interested only in their money. From there it was on to the docks, where they queued yet again, this time for the Baluarte barges. Those were drawn from the shore to the island-fortress and back by hundreds of indentured labourers, men of all races chained together and visibly suffering. It made their blood boil, but there was nothing they could do.

When Akka created the world, Romara thought, *He got a lot wrong.*

She had a more pressing concern than wrongs she couldn't right: the nagging feeling that she herself was the greatest danger to the group. The vyr-thing she would become was a lurking presence inside her now, pacing the interior of her skull, hissing and snarling as it sought release. For now, she could hold it in check, but if trouble broke out, she wasn't so sure.

What happens if I lose control, here in this town?

Hours in the queue crawled by, fretting while the inadequate ferries battled with the unusually high number of refugees, until they were able to board a barge large enough for their horses. They gathered in the stern, watching the Canas dock recede and the island fortress grow closer. Their mood was pensive, even tense.

Jadyn asked Aura to explain again how she intended to gain the warrant.

'Is no problem,' Aura insisted. 'Have obtain warrant afore. Am known, have money. Is easy.'

'Who are you, here?' Obanji asked.

'Am grand lady: Juanita Casameria della Markez. Everyone know family.'

'Then how will you pass yourself off as her?' Elindhu enquired, scratching her big nose.

'Juanita be recluse. Widowed, live in country. Aura use name before, no trouble.'

They all looked dubious.

Soren blurted, 'There must be a better way, surely?'

'What you want?' Aura snorted. 'King of Ferasto come and row you himself?'

They all threw in comments – unfavourable ones – until Jadyn held up a hand. 'We'll try it. If it works, well and good; but if not we'll return to Canas and opt for another route.'

'Not needing,' Aura exclaimed. 'Aura not fail.'

Frowning, Jadyn said, 'I'll go with you to keep you safe.'

'Neya,' Aura protested. 'Is white man. Here, serfant always brown, never white.'

'Servant,' Romara corrected. 'How can that be? The Edict demands equal treatment of all before the law.'

'You think old man in Petraxus can make local love foreigner?' Aura sniffed. 'You stupider than looking.'

Romara felt a flash of temper, but Gram's hand on her arm deflated her anger to just a hiss of annoyance.

'Then I should go with Aura,' Obanji suggested, 'seeing as I'm the right colour.'

'Ney-ney, is black Abuthan; so should be dressed like merchant, hung with gold,' Aura objected. 'Not servantile.' She looked at Soren. 'Not him, neither. Too young.'

'What about me?' Gram growled. He had dark brown beard and hair and deeply tanned skin from living in the wild. 'I've seen brown-haired Ferasti here. I could pass as one.'

Aura gave him a thoughtful look. 'Not thinking so. You be bear, not man.'

'What about a woman servant?' Romara demanded. 'I could be your maid.'

Aura sniggered. 'Is tempting, but no. Must be man. Or nobody . . . Si, better if nobody—'

'Then it's Gram,' Romara interrupted. 'I'm sure you're right: no woman can go anywhere without a man in this world.' She glared at Jadyn, because *everything* was his fault, just now.

'No trusting?' Aura sighed, as if hurt.

'Damn right, no trusting,' Romara replied. 'You want trust, you earn it: by going *with* Gram and bringing back that warrant and not a squad of Royal Guard.'

Aura spat into the water. 'Feelings hurt.'

'Too bad. Gram, at the first sign of betrayal, break her skinny neck.'

The trapper growled in assent.

Aura sniffed at Romara. 'Is jealous bully.'

'I'm not jealous of anything about you.'

'Is so. Jealous of freedom. Jealous of beauty. Jealous of happy. Jealous because Aura *lives*, while Romara just *exists*. Jealous-envy sour-pussy.'

It took an effort not to punch her. 'You know nothing about what I feel.'

'No? You feel angry. Always angry. Am wrong? Ney, am right!'

Romara felt herself colouring and lost her words, because yes, right now anger dominated everything, due to the glyma-energy and her precarious condition.

Damn it, I can't even win an argument with this trollop!

Fighting down the urge to lash out, she hissed, 'Elysia on high, fine . . . *fine!* Just don't you *dare* betray us.' She tapped Gram's chest. 'Watch her like a hawk.'

'Aura, slow down,' Gram hissed as he hurried after her, through the crowded docks of Baluarte Island. Everywhere there were refugees, families dragging their possessions, foreign words washing over him but their stories clear, because he'd seen the same on Avas: failed farms, droughts and wildfires. They were filing miserably towards the castle, where royal officials waited like vultures to receive the bribes that *might* secure a hearing. Fortunately, he and Aura wouldn't have to wait behind such people, as they had money and status, however fictitious.

Gram could feel Romara's anxious eyes on his back all the way up the road, until they turned onto Regulus Way and lost sight of the waiting barges. His gaze was locked on Aura's back, from her luscious black tresses, glittering with copper trinkets down to the sway of her hips as she made her sinuous, strutting way. She'd bared her shoulders and midriff to blend in, an outfit unthinkable in his native north, but commonplace here: a southern beauty in her element.

Despite that, Gram was unmoved: Aura had nothing he wanted. His only concern was getting this damned warrant and getting off the island whole. *This will tell us if she's truly with us, or acting for herself . . .*

His own motivations were crystal-clear. He'd been completely honest with his captors-turned-allies: elobyne was a cancer that must be excised, and Nilis Evandriel would convince them of that truth. He still marvelled that these Vestal knights had been prepared to make this journey, which he credited to Jadyn Kaen. He genuinely admired the man's open-mindedness.

But emotionally, it was Romara who bound him to the Falcons. Her struggle spoke to his own, and the intimacy of their glyma bond drew them together. *I pull her back from the madness and she gives me a reason to stay sane.* He still couldn't see this ending in anything other than a bloody wreck, but for now, they were prolonging each other's lives.

Aura was a chance companion, though, and as shifty as a weasel. And in this bewildering place, where people teemed like ants, it was all he could do to keep up with her. 'Slow down,' he called again, to no avail.

Regulus Way, a boulevard running up to the royal fortress, was a sea of bodies flowing to its own tide. Ferasti Royal Guard stood on every corner, watching the refugees pass with bored eyes. But all of them stared as Aura approached, moving as if courting their attention.

'Keep your head down,' he growled.

'This be Ferasto, Bearman,' she replied. 'Powerful woman, she strut. Only servant cowers.' She exchanged a lingering look with a moustachioed Bravanti swordsman in a rakish hat, then passed onwards, whispering, 'Handsome, but Bravanti smell like cheese.' By the time they were halfway to Capito Mons, the fortress, he had her opinion on the merits of men from every land. Naturally, only Nepari men rated well.

'Except in honesty,' she growled. 'Nepari men be liars, all.'

'What of Avas men?' Gram asked, mostly just to ensure she stayed in earshot.

'Avas?' she frowned. 'Not knowing. Only meet you, Soren. You be typical, hmm?'

'No.'

'Good, else island be full of bears,' she snickered. 'Is Avas women like bear, too?'

'Not at all,' he growled. 'They have milky skin and long brown or sometimes red hair. Lovely eyes, brown or blue. The most beautiful women in the world.'

'Red hair, blue eye,' Aura echoed teasingly. 'Like Romara, si?'

He felt himself go red. 'Let's keep moving.'

She laughed. 'Before, you want slow walk. Now want hurry. Make up mind, Bearman.'

She sashayed onwards, twinkling her eyes at a rich-looking Mutazi on a white horse, who touched his right hand to his heart and made a pounding gesture: *My heart beats for you.*

She peeled with laughter and waved as she passed, clearly enjoying herself immensely.

But then they were at the gates of Capito Mons, where they joined the traders' queue. Officials were working the line, picking out 'priority cases' – those prepared to pay a bribe to be bumped up the list – and one approached Aura. 'Are you here to see Simon Ponte?' a sweating velvet-clad man asked, speaking Talmoni, the language of commerce, while feasting his eyes on Aura's cleavage. 'I'd pay well for your time myself, chica.'

'Not Simon Ponte,' Aura snapped. 'Am not whore, not wanting whoremaster. Mi nombre esa Juanita Casameria della Markez. Si, *Markez* family. Seeking travel warrant for friend.'

The official coloured. 'Sorry, Milady, my error.' He looked at Gram doubtfully. 'This is your friend?'

'No, this be mutt-headed servant,' Aura sneered. 'Trader friend waiting in Canas. Go there next.' Then she launched into a stream of Solabi, gesturing dramatically, and in moments the florid official was caught up in her tale, nodding with his tongue hanging out.

'Priority case, si,' he assured her. 'I'll get the duty captain. He will convey you straight to the magistrate, who will process the warrant himself.'

The man scurried away and Gram, his nerves frayed, muttered, 'Who is Juanita Casam . . . er, who is she again?'

'Juanita Casameria della Markez. Daughter of rich man. Aura resembles. Have pretend so afore, is easy.'

'But won't the magistrate know her?'

'Neya; her family in country, she be invalid.'

'Holy Akka. But how can you prove—?'

'Shh,' Aura interrupted, as the official returned with a captain. 'Capitano, so please we enter?' she said, offering her right hand to the newcomer, displaying a gold signet ring Gram was sure she'd never worn previously on the journey. Considering she'd been in a dungeon only a few weeks ago, he wondered where she'd concealed it.

The captain, a moustachioed, rakish man with grey curls, looked her up and down appreciatively. 'Milady Casameria,' he said, in accented Talmoni. 'Welcome to Capito Mons! I am Capitano Juan Dernas. But surely you have servants who could attend to these matters?'

Aura giggled. 'Of course, but wish to visit Baluarte, see friend.' She touched her nose, the universal gesture of discretion. 'This errand is . . . "excuse", si?' She twinkled her eyes at him.

'Of course,' the captain smiled amiably. 'Well, please, come this way.' He offered an arm, which Aura took.

'Come, oaf,' she told Gram. 'Is new man, barbarian,' she apologised to the captain.

The captain gave Gram a pitying look. 'Where's he from?'

'Barbarian place, not caring,' Aura shrugged. 'Please, brave Capitano, lead on.' She thrust out her bosom and pressed herself to his side. 'Love your uniform. Tresa modo, bravo.'

Gram fumed at their backs, trailing Aura and the captain into the fortress, through a maze of corridors, up some stairs and into a foyer, where Dernas bade Gram wait. He was reluctant to let her go, but had no choice; the door was guarded.

When they admitted Aura, he caught a glimpse of carpets and a desk and a man in a red felt cap, then the guards pulled it closed and he was left alone facing the pair of armed men, with no idea what Aura was doing or saying inside.

Romara said not to let her out of my sight, he worried. *I've already let her down.*

When you see a chance, take it, the Devourer reminded Aura.

That had been the lesson of many of Aura's experiences, especially since Sergio dumped her in the north. And now, trapped by another pair of powerful men, she had no choice but to hearken.

This is your one chance, the Queen of Evil reiterated. *Act now, and you'll walk away rich, instead of sharing those doomed knights' fate.*

Akka remained silent. He'd given up on her.

Aura readied her story: *Milord, I've been kidnapped by renegade Vestal knights and a vorlok – there are prices on their heads. I can lead you straight to them! How much is the bounty? Why, that's generous! You pay half now, half later, si?*

The words teased the tip of her tongue as Capitano Dernas led her into the big office, up a red carpet to the desk, where a fat man in a frock coat and a tasselled velvet cap played with stacks of papers.

'Sir, this is the woman I spoke of,' the captain said warmly.

'Milady Juanita, yes?' the fat man said, looking up and stripping her clothing away with his eyes. 'It's a pleasure, indeed.'

She opened her mouth to speak and earn her freedom, then floundered, struck by an unexpected attack of conscience . . .

. . . when the captain seized her from behind and slammed her to her knees, gripping her chin and wrenching it halfway round. 'Move, and I'll break your jagging neck,' Dernas growled.

Her skin went slick and her bones began to tremble, as all the previous times she'd been forced to her knees by a man flashed before her. *Ney, ney,* she wailed silently. *Not again.*

The fat man rose, walked round his desk and sat in an armchair facing her. 'So, this is the one with Lady Casameria's signet?'

'I *am* Juanita Casameria,' Aura blustered. 'This is outrag— outre— Whatever is . . .'

'I have met Lady Juanita Casameria,' Dernas chuckled darkly in her ear. 'She is bedridden.'

E Cara, Aura groaned inwardly. *E Cara mia . . .*

'Last year,' the fat man said, 'a certain Don Rodrigo desca Varro and his friend Juanita Casameria visited Huertas and Canas, and perpetrated a string of jewel thefts of a particular kind: one would seduce the target, while the other robbed the strong-box. Sound familiar, "Milady"?'

Sergio and Aura had taken so much, she'd thought she'd never be poor again. They'd fled to the coast and bought a ship, becoming smugglers, plying the trade-routes for months ... until her lover abandoned her in Gaudien.

'Ney-ney, not knowing nothing,' she protested.

Dernas wrenched her face round and made him look at her. 'I went upcountry to seek Juanita, and found a bedridden invalid. The poor girl couldn't even walk. And the real Rodrigo desca Varro died as an infant.'

Aura tried for innocent confusion, while her mind raced. Her neck was hurting abominably and she was terrified she was a wrong answer away from death. But these were the moments when hesitation cost everything.

'Is not me—' she began, but Dernas clamped a hand over her mouth.

'Where is "Don Rodrigo"?' the fat official demanded. 'Who are you really? And why are you here? Are you so stupid you thought you could come back and peddle the same lies?'

Uh ... si, am that stupido, she thought, as her plans to cash in the Falcons collapsed.

Jag these pigs. They won't believe me anyway. She cast about for a new story. 'Please, not thief. Just Nepari girl, kidnapped, made to serve bad man. Sergio Landanez, his name be, make me sin for him. Just wanting home.'

'You're saying you're a kidnapped whore, trying to get back to Neparia?' the captain clarified sarcastically. 'Is that what you are, slut?'

'No, no, am good girl, good girl. Wanting be nun, si, but kidnapped was! Must believe!'

'How did you get Lady Juanita's signet?' the magistrate demanded.

'Sergio found, made me wear.' She managed to burst into tears, wailing, 'Was all Sergio—'

'What other trinkets did he give you?' the fat man drawled. 'Show me.'

Shaking in genuine fear, she fumbled inside her bodice – making sure to flash a nipple – and brought out the gold filigree chain that was her only nest-egg, while Dernas took her belt-pouch, containing the last of the money stolen from Lictor Borghart. The captain tossed it from hand to hand, then threw it to the fat man.

'A start,' he told her. 'But not enough.'

'Have more,' Aura wailed. 'Pay when get warrant.'

Dernas snorted, reaching round from behind her and unbuttoning her next button, licking her ear repulsively. 'Oh, you'll pay,' he told her. The fat man gloated over her humiliation, while she quivered in rage.

'Take her to the back room, Dernas,' the magistrate purred. 'We'll squeeze every last drop from this one.'

'But ... warrant,' she protested, her stomach curdling.

The captain chuckled and pulled her upright, and for a second she felt a torrent of images and sensations, as if what they intended had already been experienced, in all its sick horror ...

You deserve this, Akka condemned her, his stern voice filling her right ear.

Fight! the Devourer blared into her left.

Aura's pulse began to race, but her vision seemed to slow, as if time had halved in speed, except for her. She sent her right hand flashing out and yanked the captain's dagger from its sheath. He'd been too complacent, got too close, and though he tried to grab her, his fingers only caught flying hair as she slashed the stolen blade sideways in one brutal motion, opening his throat from ear to ear.

Te gusta, bastido?

Dernas staggered backwards, yanking out a tress of her hair, then hit the desk and slid to the carpet, convulsing weakly with blood spraying in a graceful arc. But Aura hadn't stopped to watch; she'd spun and hurled the dagger like a crossbow bolt, slamming it into the middle of the fat man's chest. He gasped in shock, clutched at the quivering hilt, tried to rise, but instead slumped into the armchair, legs kicking weakly.

Then his head fell sideways and he too went still.

Aura's heart *thump-thump-thumped*, her blood felt like acid and there were lightning bolts going off in her head – then normal time reasserted itself and she felt like a holed bucket, emptying helplessly.

She had to catch herself on the desk to hold herself upright on jelly legs, until survival instincts took over, and she found the strength to stand.

What just happened? she wondered, but neither Akka nor the Devourer knew. *I saw it all as it unfolded . . . I knew what to do and how to do it . . .* Before this journey, for all her escapades, she'd never killed. But she could feel herself changing.

It's this journey, she realised. *It's Borghart and what he did to me . . . He woke something. He knew it, I knew it.*

Suddenly, it came to her in a flash of recognition – or precognition – that she'd been a heartbeat from making a foolish, tragic mistake. Because the Falcons' journey was also her own. Why, she had no idea. But it was utterly clear to her now that she had to go on.

If I stop or turn aside, Borghart will find me, and I'll be too helpless to resist.

This quest was like riding a horse: you stayed in the saddle, or you fell.

The captain was still silently shaking, caught in the grip of a palsy as his blood soaked away into the carpet; he went still without managing a sound. Still hyper-aware, she listened to the sounds of the castle, and heard no reaction outside the door. Part of her wanted to vomit, and Akka was in her right ear, disowning her forever. But the Devourer was whispering in her left ear that there'd be gold as well as warrants in the fat man's desk, and who knew what else?

When you see a chance, take it, the Queen of Evil urged, and this time, she was right.

Gram sagged in relief when finally the door opened and a flushed Aura emerged. He went to her side as she pulled the door closed behind her and handed him a bulging carpet-bag.

'Where's Capitano Dernas?' one of the pair of guards asked.

Aura gave him a sultry, slightly dazed look, but Gram wasn't fooled. He knew her well enough by now to see that she was battling shock, not lust. Suddenly the lengthy wait felt far more sinister.

What did they do to her?

'They is ... how say ... cleaning up,' Aura said, licking her lips. 'Two men at once, is ...' She managed to turn what Gram recognised as a shudder of revulsion into overwhelmed eroticism as she finished, '... is amazing.'

Gram felt the beast inside his skull growl.

Smirking, one guard said, 'Want to earn some more money?'

Aura giggled, though her eyes were utterly cold. 'Had all can take,' she replied, fanning her face. She glanced at the door, as if reliving a wondrous memory. 'They ask thirty minuto, for enjoy brandy. Privato, si?'

The men rolled their eyes at each other. 'Sure.' They looked her up and down again, clearly picturing all they imagined had gone on inside. 'Do call again,' they snickered, winking.

Aura took Gram's arm and he felt her trembling, but she trilled, 'Dream of me, muchachos.'

Gram laid a big hand on her to steady her, helped her to the stairs and away from their eyes, where he murmured, 'Aura, what happened?'

She looked up, her face momentarily naked, and he saw he was right: she was barely holding herself together. 'Story go wrong, they know, want to lock Aura, radish her.'

'Um, ravish?'

'Si, that. Murder her. Bad men.'

'The bastards,' he growled, contemplating going back and seeing what fists might achieve.

She dangled the carpet-bag. 'Stupid men. Aura kill already.'

He froze. '*You what?*'

'She kill,' she repeated, her bravado returning. 'They deserve. Come, we go.'

Oh jagat! he thought, as they headed for the exit.

Each minute passed like a lifetime. He was sure the alarm would sound at any moment, and it took all his self-control to maintain a steady gait as they walked out of the main gates and were swallowed up by the crowds.

'We have to hurry,' he murmured.

'No, hurry draws attention. We walk.' She was cooler now, while he was trembling on the edge of eruption. 'So,' she added, 'Gram trust Aura now, si?'

He met her eyes, deciding she was, finally, part of them. 'Aye,' he conceded. 'I trust you.'

'Tresa buena,' she said, meeting his gaze properly for perhaps the first time. 'This Aura swear; she be with you, si? Comprenez? Am with to end.'

She actually sounded like she meant it, but Gram wouldn't be convinced until Romara was.

Jadyn was leaning on the railing, drinking in the sights and sounds of the docks, a mixture of the familiar and the alien. Ferasto was a cosmopolitan place where people from all over the world came, lured by opium wealth. Most were Solabi and Nepari, but he saw Bravanti, Foylish warriors with bronze torcs round their necks, Mutazi and Bedumi traders, stately Abuthans weighed down by gold chains, brightly dressed Khetian merchants, and austere, turbaned Zynochi traders all in white. On the balconies of brothels, women of every nation called invitations to the men passing below. Horses, oxen and even camels were hauling loads from the ships' holds, produce from near and far.

He'd also noted royal Ferasti warships moored off the island, and the ballistae and catapults in the towers onshore. Seizing a ship and sailing without the warrant would be suicidal. They'd have to enter Ferasto legitimately, or not at all. Nevertheless, he'd hired this ferry to Huestra in anticipation of success. He'd lose the deposit if Aura failed them, but it felt wise to secure instant departure.

If Tevas or Borghart do show up, seconds will matter.

He'd sent Romara and Soren out for provisions, and they'd just returned, bearing fresh gear and supplies for the road. They stowed their new purchases, and were now all waiting anxiously, their eyes on the road to the castle.

Then Aura and Gram came hurrying towards the docklands, and

Jadyn immediately sensed trouble. 'Here's our friends,' he said to the barge's master, a shifty Bravanti who smelled weirdly of cheese. 'Prepare to cast off.'

'Must see warrant first,' the master replied.

Jadyn gave him a placatory wave and went to greet Aura and Gram as they scampered aboard. 'Were you successful?' he demanded. 'What happened?'

Aura fished a bronze royal seal from a carpet bag. 'Have warrant, no problem.' She posed like an actress at the finalé of a show – but Jadyn recognised that she was in the throes of post-combat shock.

Just then, alarm bells began to peal, the sound rolling down from Capito Mons. The bargemaster threw Jadyn an anxious look. 'Nothing to do with us,' Jadyn assured him. 'Ten more silver to deliver us to Huestra, right now.'

An already lucrative crossing was now even more so. The master immediately shouted for his crew to speed up.

'The alarm's been raised,' Romara hissed, glaring at Aura. 'You know about that?'

Aura spat over the side, as if removing a vile taste from her mouth, and said, 'Si.'

'If you tipped them off—'

Aura faced the taller woman. 'No tip-off. They unmasked, be helpless. Wicked Capitano, nasty offish . . . oafish . . .'

'Official?' Jadyn tried.

'Si, that. Dead, both dead.'

Romara flinched, then gave her a suspicious look. 'You killed two royal officials?'

'Si,' Aura answered, looking to Jadyn for support. 'Had no choice. But am true, true to Falconers. Asking Bearman, he know.'

Jadyn's skin prickled at the thought that 'helpless' Aura had killed again. But Gram nodded in support. 'They separated us, but she got us what we needed.'

Romara threw him an exasperated look. 'You were supposed to keep her out of trouble.'

'That's not so easy,' Gram mumbled, hanging his head.

Isn't that the truth? Jadyn nudged Aura's carpet bag. 'What's in there?'

She thrust it at him. 'Oafish seals, papers, money. No need thanking Aura. She be loyal.' She looked at Romara defiantly, then stamped away, muttering about injustices.

Gram gave Jadyn and Romara an eloquent shrug, then found it wise to be elsewhere. The ferry pushed off and began spidering across the water; in minutes they were hundreds of paces from the island, carving a path for Huestra, on the Ferasti side of the river mouth.

Romara nudged Jadyn. 'Do you believe her?'

'I think she's passed the point of suspicion, Rom. She's with us now, for better or for worse.'

'She killed two men on her own,' Romara noted, 'and she has sabbahi tattoos. She's not just a simple thief. If that's all she was, she'd be dead by now.'

'Perhaps,' he conceded, gazing down the vessel at Aura, whose long black hair was now flying loose like a banner. Her perky, plucky face was upturned proudly, but he sensed that she was struggling to maintain that front. It moved him, somehow, to admiration, and pity. And he was thinking about what she'd said about perceiving the world differently when stressed, about seeing the path through mayhem, just as he sometimes could.

I'm beginning to think I was fated to meet her.

'She could have betrayed us,' he told Romara. 'Give her the benefit of the doubt.'

'Sometimes you're an idiot,' she replied, then she too stamped off.

It was clearly his day for pleasing no one.

'Six hours,' Yoryn Borghart fumed quietly, looking around the closed-up office in Baluarte, where the murders had taken place. There were still bloodstains on the seat and carpet. 'Six *jagging* hours.'

That was how long it had been since a woman had walked brazenly into this office, murdered a magistrate and a captain of the guard, then walked out with a dozen different warrants and a strongbox full of coins. Then she'd vanished, probably on a ferry to Huestra.

They had arrived to find Baluarte in uproar. He'd presented his credentials as a lictor and promised the Ferasti officials arcane help in solving the crime. It'd taken a good deal of bribery, because these pagan scum refused to let the Order operate inside their kingdom, but he'd finally gained access to the crime scene. Tevas Nicolini, who had a knack of garnering information from commoners, had learned that a group of seven had crossed into Ferasto that morning: Jadyn's pentacle and the other two fugitives, almost certainly. But that only confirmed what Borghart had already intuited. The Nepari woman, Auranuschka Perafi, had done this.

She's somewhere ahead of us. I can feel it.

Lictors were trained to ignore intuition and concentrate on facts, but Borghart placed great weight on his own guesses and instincts. If he listened hard enough and looked deep enough, he just *knew* what was right.

'The guards thought she was a whore, come to service the good bureaucrat,' smirked Elan Sandreth, who'd accompanied him here.

'Does this amuse you, Milord?' Borghart asked frostily.

'Does it not you?' Elan laughed. 'I rather suspect these fools got the comeuppance they deserved. This Nepari woman is beginning to intrigue me.'

'She's mine,' Borghart reminded him. 'And I find nothing here amusing. She took a sheath of travel warrants, a royal seal and Akka knows what else. And now they're loose in jagging Ferasto, where we can't go.'

The Ferasti king forbade the Vestal Order and all its offshoots from entry to the kingdom – but without revealing those links, he'd never have been permitted to investigate the murders. It was a cleft stick that had him fuming.

'Is it possible that they're aiming to cross Ferasto into Neparia?' Elan asked.

'No, Ferasto is their destination,' Borghart answered sourly. 'With no Order presence there, it's an ideal refuge for all manner of scum.' He clenched a fist. 'I refuse to abandon the hunt.'

Elan pulled a face. 'I've put hundreds of aurochs into this pursuit, Lictor. I expect a return.'

'I am well aware of that, Milord,' Borghart snapped. 'That bracelet of yours is good for one, maybe two more scrying attempts on Romara, but unless we can actually pursue her, that's no good to us.'

'We'll get into Ferasto,' Elan assured him. 'Money talks here, and I have plenty.'

Somewhat mollified, Borghart bent over the bloodstained carpet, hoping . . . and then he got lucky. There was a tangle of black hair caught in the dried blood. He extracted one hair and invoked a scrying spell. As the hair burned away, he glimpsed a dusky copper-skinned face, somewhere across the lake in Ferasto proper, a momentary vision before the strand of hair was consumed and the link broken. But it was enough.

'It's her,' he confirmed, dangling the remaining strands of hair. 'Auranuschka Perafi. I'll find her now. There's nowhere she can hide from me.'

I cannot wait to get you back, he thought, knowing he would. He'd never failed before.

'Where are they?' Elan asked, jealous, as always, after a demonstration of sorcery.

Borghart pointed in the direction he'd glimpsed. 'They're east of us, on the main road, heading for Murallo and the pass into Neparia. We can be on them inside a day, if we ride hard.'

Elan licked his lips sourly. 'Point me at the right official and I'll purchase our passage.'

He was as good as his word. Within the hour, they'd gained access to Ferasto for all of their Vestal century, who were waiting in Canas. They had to remove all Order insignias, and were made to promise to return the fugitives to Baluarte for justice, but what mattered was that they and their men got to cross to Huestra.

An hour later, near to sunset, they were mustered outside Huestra.

A second surreptitious scrying told Borghart that the Nepari was only some twenty kylos to the east.

'We ride until sunset,' he ordered his riders, comprising twenty of Nicolini's mercenaries and a hundred Vestal guard, led by Sier Rohas Uccello and his pentacle. 'And tomorrow, we'll rise before dawn, catch them unawares and end this.'

12

Ferasto

Serrafim

The Book of Lux teaches us that Coros is a battleground between the forces of Light and Darkness, Good and Evil. Only the holiest of souls endure, and those ascend to Paradise, where they are armoured in light, becoming Serrafim, the Angels of Akka. The Serrafim are the protectors of humankind, and lead the struggle against the armies of Darkness. Many claim to have seen them, and speak ever of their beauty and might.

TELVYN ARGO, IMPERIAL SCHOLAR, PETRAXUS 1457

Ferasto
Summer 1472

The barge deposited Jadyn's party across the river mouth in Huestra, on the eastern shore of Regio Lago. They left immediately, taking the road eastwards towards the mountains and the pass to Neparia. They rode hard; although they now had travel warrants, the hunt would be on for Gram and Aura, to bring them to justice for the killings at Baluarte.

Mid-afternoon, a royal Ferasti courser pounded past, galloping like she was in a race with the wind. Once she was gone, Jadyn pulled his comrades off the crowded road into a grove of wild olives, fearful that the guards at the next waystation would have descriptions of Aura and Gram.

'We can't continue on this road,' Jadyn said. 'We need a new plan.'

'But this is the only road,' Romara protested. 'That courser might have been nothing to do with Aura's blasted killing spree.'

'Not my fault,' Aura wailed. 'You prefer Aura submit to filthy men?'

'No one's suggesting that,' Jadyn replied, giving Romara a warning look.

'We should never have entrusted her with the task,' she muttered, looking away.

'She was our only way to gain a warrant,' Obanji reminded her. He gazed east, rubbing his chin. 'The real question is, how long before patrols start working these roads, looking specifically for Aura and Gram?'

'Actually, there's a bigger question than that,' Elindhu put in. 'If we extrapolate on Borghart's earlier scrying of Romara, he's probably on his way to Baluarte, if he's not there already. So that courser might have been taking news of more than the killings. She might have had descriptions of all of us.'

'Jagat, she's right,' Obanji groaned. 'Almost certainly.'

'Borghart can't enter Ferasto,' Jadyn reminded them.

'You think?' Romara sniffed. 'The only thing that's sacred here is a man's purse.'

'Si,' Aura put in. 'Ferasti pigs, only love poppy and gold.'

'I think we can count on that bargemaster giving up our descriptions to the highest bidder,' Romara added. 'It seems to me we've got one option: to reach Murallo Pass before it's closed to us. We need to press on.'

Elindhu shook her head, making her pile of braids wobble. 'I disagree. That courser will be in Murallo well before we are. To go on this way now is wrong-headed.'

'Then we need another way into Neparia,' Obanji said. 'Surely there are others?'

Jadyn looked at Elindhu, who knew more about maps and geography than him. 'Is there another way?'

The mage looked thoughtful, scrunching up her outsized nose and squinting at some imagined map in her head. 'Well, yes and no. Murallo is the only pass used by traders, because it's the easiest and has inns and waystations, and because it's the only one travellers with warrants are permitted to use. If we leave the main road, we're fair game, and the high-country Ferasti aren't shy of slaughtering outsiders. Most of them are still the same brigand families that founded this damned place.'

'We can handle that scum,' Soren declared.

'Probably,' Elindhu said agreeably. 'But the passes into Neparia are all fortified, because the Ferasti are rightfully paranoid about attempted invasions. And the upland valleys are the property of the opium lords; it's where they grow their crops. Those fields and roads are heavily watched.'

'This damned kingdom is a dead-end for us, then,' Romara muttered. 'Quite literally.'

Jadyn peered at Elindhu. 'So by "yes and no", did you really just mean "no"?'

She flashed him a toothy grin. 'Ah, someone who listens. There is one other option: a valley called Semmanath-Tuhr, with a difficult crossing into Neparia. But no one ever goes there.'

Everyone's face turned suspicious. 'Why's that?' Obanji asked, for them all.

'Because it's erling land.'

'You mean a reservation?' Jadyn asked, as they all caught their breath.

'No, those are only in Tyr,' Elindhu replied. 'Erlings have been all but eradicated outside of Tyr, but as we've seen, there are still erlings in the wilds. Some band together and form hidden communities. A shaman in Tyr told me of several such places: Semmanath-Tuhr is one. I believe I can find it, and get us through.'

'This sounds too easy,' Romara commented.

'It's not. Very few people know of it, and the erlings work to keep it that way: they kill any who enter – or they melt away if the trespassers look dangerous. The Ferasti and the Nepari have both tried clearing them out, but they found nothing.'

'Then they'll kill us,' Romara said. 'This sounds worse than our other options.'

'Don't you think we look dangerous, Rom?' Obanji smiled. 'They'll leave us alone.'

'I concur,' Elindhu said. 'And if they do accost us, I can deal with them. Remember, I've lived on the Tyr reservations, and I have tokens of friendship all erlings will recognise.'

Jadyn looked at Romara. 'What do you think?' he asked, feeling inadequate for the decision.

'I left you in charge,' she replied tersely. 'I trust your judgement.'

'We all do,' Obanji added.

Grateful for the show of support, Jadyn cast his eyes around the circle, taking in Elindhu's willingness; the ambivalence of his knights and Aura's haunted expression. But it was Gram's attitude that interested him most. The Order believed that erlings were in league with the vyr, but the trapper was showing no enthusiasm at all.

'Do vyr work with the erlings?' Jadyn asked him bluntly.

'I've never seen an erling. I wasn't even sure they were real until recently.'

Jadyn made his decision. 'If we try to cross at Murallo or anywhere else, we'll probably face men of the Order. We'll put innocent lives at risk, and we'll bring Borghart down on our heads. But if we can slip across this valley . . . ?'

'Semmanath-Tuhr,' Elindhu reminded him.

'Yes, that. I think it's worth trying.'

'Thank you, Jadyn,' Elindhu beamed. 'I've dreamed of seeing it.'

'This isn't a scholars' research jaunt,' Romara reminded her. 'If we end up massacred by erlings and vorloks, my ghost is going to nag yours for the rest of eternity.'

Elindhu mock-shuddered. 'That sounds worse than the Devourer's Maw.'

'It will be, I promise you,' Romara told her, with a hint of a smile. 'My mouth or the Devourer's Maw – basically they're the same thing.'

'Then it's settled,' Jadyn chuckled. 'Let's get some rest.'

They set out well before sunrise, still yawning and rubbing grit from their eyes. They retraced their route to a crossroads they'd passed, then struck out on a rural road going south, riding through hamlets and villages that were struggling to survive, in lands where the soil was thin and conditions unforgiving. There might be money in Ferasto, but it wasn't here. Even the castles they saw were pitiful affairs, motley piles of brick and stone, barely large enough to shelter a cohort of thirty. Most were empty, falling into ruin.

Their passing didn't go unnoticed, though. Children ran to watch them, and farmers paused to lean on their forks and peer from under their wide-brimmed hats. But no one hailed them, or tried to stop them.

Midday saw them watering their steeds in a muddy creek in the foothills of the Qor-Espina, when Jadyn noticed Aura suddenly come over dizzy, slumping against her horse's flank.

'E Cara,' she swore blearily. 'Be not . . .'

He caught her arm as the others turned their way. But this wasn't some attention-seeking ploy, because Jadyn felt a crackling when he touched her that was all too familiar: the sensation of a scrying spell coming apart on his veil warding.

'Ach,' he grunted, 'they've got eyes on Aura.'

'*What?*' Obanji asked sharply.

'I just felt a scrying, targeted on Aura,' Jadyn replied, steadying her. 'It's over now.'

'Head sparking,' Aura said blearily. 'Feel strange.'

No further attempts came – whoever had scryed her was too wily to try again, so soon after having their spell disrupted. 'Has this happened before?' he asked her.

'Last night, this morning,' the Nepari woman replied hesitantly. 'Think be sicking.'

'Did you drop anything in that magistrate's office?' he asked.

She shook her head, then muttered, 'E Cara mia—' She poked gingerly at her head. 'Capitano grab hair, afore I slip his throat. Hurt still.'

Jadyn gently parted her billowing black hair, examining her scalp and finding a torn patch, scabbing over. 'Someone with the glyma found Aura's hair,' he surmised.

'Akka Excelsior,' Romara groaned. 'Everyone *knows* that you don't leave such things behind.'

'Not everys one,' Aura shot back. 'Only holy bitches.'

'Keep it civil,' Obanji put in.

'That means both of you,' Jadyn put in. 'Not *everybody* knows that, Romara.'

'Ferasto doesn't permit the Order to operate in their borders, so who did the scrying?' Elindhu mused. 'A lictor we know, maybe?'

Jadyn groaned, and turned back to Aura. 'You'll ride double with me again, so you're within the ambit of my veil spell.'

'Lictor be watching me?' Aura asked, her expression both fearful and angry. 'Is disgustable! Spying on innocenta femina, e Cara! Glyma, vorlok, all magica be evil!'

Obanji said wryly, 'To be fair, he's investigating the murder of two officials you were trying to cheat out of a royal warrant.'

'Don't care. Is not fair, not nice. Indigestible!'

Jadyn saw the others pulling amused sneers and felt a flash of protective anger. 'Hey, she's right. We live in a world where some people have powers others don't, and you've lived your adult lives on the favourable side of that imbalance. You've always had an edge she hasn't. So climb down off your high horses, and . . . er . . . mount up . . .'

'. . . on your high horses again,' Elindhu finished for him.

They all laughed, but a little sheepishly.

'The road's before us, Falcons,' Jadyn concluded. 'Let's ride.'

Yoryn Borghart stroked his goatee thoughtfully. His last scrying had indicated that the Nepari woman and those with her had made an unexpected move. She was now due south of their current position, well off the road to Murallo and the Nepari border.

Where are they going? he worried. The last of her hair had burned in that scrying, leaving just one more chance to scry them: Romara's last few strands from Elan Sandreth's bracelet. He was running out of ways to track his quarry, though his fear was mitigated by a certainty that should he wish to, he could find Auranuschka Perafi without the glyma.

We have a bond, a shared talent. She can't hide from me.

They were on the main road from Huestra to Murallo, close to where he'd detected the Nepari woman before dawn, catching her asleep. They'd reached the spot a couple of hours later, hoping to find that their quarry had slept late, but they were already gone. After a fruitless search of the road nearby, he'd resorted to his latest scrying – and discovered that they'd been evaded.

Around him, the Solabi Vestal guards and Nicolini's Pelasian pirates were taking on water, the two groups ignoring each other. Borghart signed for Elan Sandreth, Tevas Nicolini and Sier Rohas Uccello to join him. After bringing them up to date, he turned to Sier Rohas, a hard-faced Solabi with a shock of black hair and leathery tanned skin.

'What's south of here?'

'Nothing,' Sier Rohas replied, in clipped, accented Talmoni. 'Dying farms. Burnt-out lands.'

'Are the vyr active there?' Tevas asked.

'Ney, they've moved on,' the Solabi replied. 'Those left are too stubborn to leave, too proud to work the poppy fields, too sentimental to leave their ancestral lands. The walking dead.'

'Why would Romara go that way?' Elan Sandreth wondered.

Sier Rohas scowled. Borghart suspected the man was more than half peasant himself, despite his eloquent Talmoni. 'They can only be passing through,' the Solabi knight answered. 'All the mountain passes south of here are guarded by Nepari lords, and they all have Order bastions. It'd be a risky crossing for fugitive knights.' Then he scowled thoughtfully and said, 'Except Semmanath-Tuhr.'

Borghart gave him a sharp look. 'What's that?'

The Solabi made a pagan gesture with his fingers. 'An erling haven.'

Tevas Nicolini started. 'Elindhu Morspeth, the Falcon's mage, is a scholar whose specialty is erlings,' he commented.

'I thought erlings only lived in Tyr?' Elan asked.

'There are hidden enclaves here and there,' Borghart answered, his thoughts flying. 'Always in the wild. Small numbers, unobtrusive. Impossible to wholly eradicate.'

'And dangerous,' Sier Rohas put in. 'Semmanath-Tuhr is a place no one goes, especially after dark. Large forces sometimes cross in daylight and see no sign of them, but I've heard of whole centuries destroyed if they make camp overnight.' He spat again. 'If that's where they're going, they're dead already.'

Borghart pondered his words, increasingly certain they were on the right track. *Auranushka Perafi went that way, I'm sure of it.*

'If they've realised we're on their trail, they may be desperate enough to try it.' He patted the pouch, where the leather bracelet containing Romara's hair was now their only connection to their quarry. It was an asset they couldn't afford to squander. For now, they had to use logic, sweat and perseverance to hunt down their prey, not magic.

'We must ride hard,' he told them. 'There'll be no bounty for any of us if they get away.'

The climb into the mountains was arduous. They lost the sun's heat as the clouds clinging to the Qor-Espina swallowed it up, and the road dwindled to a dirt track and then to nothing at all. They were forced to pick a path through a tangle of broken hills, giant rock mounds that looked, as Obanji put it, as if they'd been shat from the arse of a gunaku.

'What be goon-a-coo?' Aura asked.

'A stone giant of the desert.' Obanji chuckled. 'Pray we don't meet one. We Abuthans say the gunaku stands a kylo tall and their farts can wither forests.'

The last farm they'd passed was far behind them and little but spindly brushwood and occasional patches of rye-grass grew in the foothills. Vultures circled high above, and apart from one small flock of tiny deer, the only other creatures they saw were lizards and snakes.

It was mid-afternoon now, and Aura was drowsing, pressed to Jadyn's back, clinging on even while semi-conscious, as if their bodies were slowly fusing into one.

A thought struck him and he nudged his mount alongside Elindhu, still perched side-saddle like a nesting bird. 'I'd been meaning to ask you,' he said. 'Remember that nayade? The one which attacked Aura in the pool beside the Serena River?'

She gave him a sharp look. 'Mmm? What of it?'

'Well, I've been thinking about those erlings we saw at the coast, who changed shape. Their skin changed, even their breathing changed, from mouth and nose to gills. Is it possible that the nayade we encountered was actually an erling?'

Elindhu pursed her lips, as if reluctant to discuss it. 'It is possible that many "mythical" creatures – trulkas, nayadai, scarabae and the like – are all erlings,' she replied. 'Erlings have mutable bodies, and often alter form to some degree – within the confines of the humanoid shape – to better survive their environment. That's how they can appear to vanish into any landscape, and survive in places we can't.'

'They're better adapted for survival than us,' Jadyn remarked. 'How dangerous is Semmanath-Tuhr, then?'

'Perilous,' she conceded. 'But as I said, I have tokens of erling friendship, and I know their ways. We should be able to pass unmolested . . . But be aware that erlings can vary widely in intellect, as well as shape and size. The wildest ones can barely speak, and may not recognise my tokens, so we must still go cautiously.'

'I envy you meeting them. What are they like?'

'They're like us in some ways, but not in others,' Elindhu replied. 'Some are as intelligent as us – but most are like children, easily distracted or duped. Simple beings who exist only to fill the basic needs: to eat and drink, to breed, to enjoy simple pleasures.' Her voice was sad.

'How did they build cities, then?' Jadyn asked.

'The clever ones oversaw, the others laboured. But when humanity came, in numbers vast as the sea, the erlings were swept away. Few now remain, and most are in Tyrland reservations, where they're dying out. That makes places like Semmanath-Tuhr precious. I hope we can pass through without doing harm.'

'Or being harmed,' Jadyn replied. 'Romara's right, this isn't a research trip, Elindhu. There's too much at stake.'

She sighed. 'I know, but I dearly hope to at least see a few—'

'Maybe on the way back?' Jadyn suggested.

They topped a rise and paused, looking the way they'd come. They'd climbed a long way and had a panoramic view of their trail through the badlands of Ferasto, all the way to the distant glimmer of Regio Lago.

Aura woke, and peeled herself from Jadyn's sweating back. 'E Cara, am melted,' she said, looking disgusted. 'Why is stopping?'

Jadyn went to reply when Soren made a strangled sound, and pointed: there was a dust-cloud below, in a valley five or six kylos away. 'Someone's behind us,' he said anxiously.

'It's Borghart,' Obanji said. 'Who else can it be?'

'*Damn him*,' said Romara. 'Elindhu, how far to this erling valley?'

'I only know roughly, from old maps,' Elindhu answered, her voice anxious. 'We need to find a conical mountain; it marks the southern end.'

Aura perked up. 'Can help. Is famous mountain: Henina-Mons, shape like steeple.'

Elindhu's eyes lit up. 'That's the one. A henin was an old-fashioned pointed hat noblewomen used to wear. If we can get a glimpse of the peaks through this cloud, we'll be able to find it.'

Jadyn clapped Aura on the knee. 'Well done. Let's ride, Falcons. The road is before us.'

Soren was becoming convinced that all this riding would kill him. Obanji said it would get easier as his body became accustomed, but after another long day in the saddle, his thighs were screaming, his buttocks felt like they'd been flayed and the cramping was almost constant.

But he refused to complain, because right now, what mattered more than anything else was impressing the pentacle – not because he feared they'd cut him loose, but because their approval had become everything to him. *See, I'm worthy*, he thought, every time he got something right, be it riding, a sword drill or the glyma-exercises Obanji was teaching him. *Potentas*, for strength. *Flamma* for energy. *Salva* for physical shields and *Pulso*, for force. He was improving on all of them. And the Abuthan had begun teaching him *Valeo*, the veil. 'If they know your face, they'll hunt you down magically, lad. This is how we hide.'

He hadn't thought a Vestal knight would ever have had to hide from anything, but he set about his lessons with a will.

When he slept, he still dreamed of his father's nagging voice, railing about keeping his guard up and his feet moving; and when he woke, he wept for his mother and sister. Enid should be in an orphanage in Beradin by now, but he doubted a poor foreign girl would be treated well.

After this, I'll rescue her and we'll go somewhere where it's okay to be a poor man's mixed-race child.

Since spotting their pursuers, they'd been climbing hard, following a stream that tumbled down a narrow cleft between two peaks. It was difficult, like ascending a stair in places. Soren found himself at the back with Elindhu, just behind Jadyn, who had Aura pressed behind him, her cheek against his back.

When she saw Soren watching, she winked with exaggerated sensuality, and he flinched, confused by the Nepari woman's behaviour towards him.

'Don't let her get to you, boy,' Elindhu murmured. 'She's just teasing.'

'Why?'

'Because she's desperate to belong, and that's the only way she knows.' Elindhu often rode side-saddle, but was currently astride, so steep was the path. 'It's just a survival reflex of hers. And don't worry about Jadyn – his heart's been set on Romara for years. He's just too kind to let Aura cope alone.'

They were topping the rise, entering a narrow gorge where the stream ran along the bottom, with a tiny goat-trail alongside. Fortunately it was summer, as marks on the rocks suggested the stream would be a torrent in the wet season, and the cleft unpassable. The view behind them shrank as the walls closed in.

Soren took a last glance behind him – just as six riders pelted into view, just a hundred or so paces below. The lead man was a knight, who jabbed an arm upwards, and began surging up the slopes, the others following. Two of them drew bows. 'They've caught us,' he warned Elindhu.

'Jadyn,' the magia called, 'they're on us—' Then she reined in and looked at Soren. 'Dismount, boy. You're my protector here. Send your horse on; they're no use to us here.'

Maybe, but those bastards aren't dismounting, Soren thought, watching them surge up the slope. But he obeyed, sliding off and drawing his flamberge, then slapping the horse's rump to send it on its way. Elindhu did likewise, then she raised her staff.

'Shield me, boy!' she snapped, chanting rune-words he didn't know. Her eyes rolled back in her skull, then began to glow as white as the crystal orb on her staff.

The archers loosed and Soren shouted, '*Salva*,' pulsing energy that slapped the arrows away. But the knight and three other riders were now in the narrow defile, pounding up the slope towards him, their swords drawn.

The knight was wearing a white tabard.

'Hurry,' Soren begged Elindhu, who was lost in her spells.

Two more arrows came and he blocked them, if raggedly. A third flight flew before he could regain his composure and one broke through, ripping at Elindhu's robes.

Her voice didn't falter.

The arrows stopped as the lead riders came closer, making archery too risky. Soren could see the horses were straining now, struggling up each step, their muscles bulging.

'What's happening?' Obanji called back down the cleft.

'I've got this,' Soren replied, and he'd have to, because the cleft was too narrow for anyone to climb past him and Elindhu. '*Pulso! Flamma!*' he shouted, unleashing first force, then fire, trying to fling the Vestal knight back down the slope. But the knight's shields were too strong, and Soren became increasingly frantic. '*PULSO!*'

Then the Vestal knight filled his vision. He wore an open-faced helm, revealing a bronzed, flat-planed Solabi visage, lit with purpose. He'd effortlessly outstripped his men and his flamberge was crackling with energy.

'Jagatai,' Obanji cursed, from somewhere behind. 'Shield, boy—'

Soren fearfully strengthened to his wards, just before the knight blazed energy at him. It crackled on his wards and broke them, making him stagger. Then with a bellowing cry, the knight launched himself from his saddle and flew fully a dozen paces, landing right in front of Soren, already swinging . . .

Their blades slammed together, vibrating madly on impact, then the Solabi cracked a blast of energy at Elindhu, which sparked impotently off her wards, even as he swung a vicious slash at Soren's neck. The initiate blocked through muscle memory, reading the blow subconsciously, then smashed his hilt at the knight's face, striking unseen shields and smearing sparks across the air, then tried to force-push him away. But the Solabi withstood easily, while his men filled the cleft behind him.

Unable to give ground without disrupting Elindhu, Soren planted his feet and threw himself into every parry. He was far less bulky and the man's full weight and force had him reeling as their blades clashed again and slid until their hilts locked – and for an instant they were face to face . . .

'*Ena luki hewir nas!*' Elindhu shrieked, and slammed her staff's heel into the ground.

A deafening *crack* resonated, accompanied by a hideous lurch in the ground at Soren's feet – which suddenly gave way. He had a moment to register the Solabi knight's sudden alarm, his eyes bulging as they both fell . . .

But something gripped Soren and jerked him back upwards to sprawl at Elindhu's feet. He almost fell again as that piece of ground also gave way, but Obanji had already reached past Elindhu and grabbed his collar, hauling him up with glyma-enhanced strength. Above him, Elindhu shrieked again, and the walls of the cleft below her collapsed inwards with a horrific crunching sound. Choking, blinding dust filled the air.

Soren held desperately onto his flamberge as Obanji dragged him away from the crumbling edge, while Elindhu cackled like a demented hen. He was hauled a dozen paces, until they staggered clear of the dust cloud and fell to their knees, panting for breath.

From behind and below, they heard agonised cries and the rage of despair, blended with the sound of sliding rocks and rolling boulders impacting somewhere in the murk.

Holy Akka, he thought, looking at Elindhu with horrified awe.

She had a quietly pleased look on her face, as if she'd just solved a tricky equation. 'Well done, boy,' she told him. 'You kept him off me. No mean feat, that.'

Obanji hauled him to his feet and hugged him, and to his surprise, so did Gram, a rare smile cracking his grim visage. Even the aloof Romara gave him an approving nod.

As the dust settled, Jadyn made his way back along the shattered defile. Soren followed him to the new lip of a now-precipitous drop. Together, they peered over the edge.

At the bottom, a hundred paces below, lay a pile of newly shattered rocks. Forty or more men were scrabbling about it, trying to pull their comrades free. Then a dust-caked armoured man in a filthy tabard wriggled up out of the debris and staggered to his feet, turning to glare up the precipice at where Jadyn and Soren stood.

'*Jagatai putasi scamagi!*' the Solabi knight raged. '*Putasi mensas!*'

'That doesn't sound polite,' Jadyn remarked. 'Any idea what he just said?'

'No idea. My ma wouldn't let me swear.'

'Good to hear it,' Jadyn chuckled as he assessed the slope. 'They won't make it up here. They'll need to find another way. How difficult that will be, I don't know, but let's not waste time. We have to keep moving.'

He had turned to go, when a voice rang out from below.

'Jadyn Kaen,' Lictor Borghart shouted, 'you will not escape me!'

Jadyn turned back. 'No, Lictor, you won't escape the truth,' he called. Then he turned his back and led Soren back up the defile. On the way he said, 'Well done, Initiate var'Dael.'

It was Soren's proudest ever moment.

They rejoined the others and once mounted, climbed a few hundred paces further to a small plateau littered with boulders but dotted with clumps of hardy grass.

Then Aura shrilled, 'E vasa! Jadyn Knight, see!'

The clouds had broken enough to reveal a conical peak, silhouetted against the eastern skyline, snow-tipped and streaked red by the setting sun. It was visible between two rounded hills about a kylo away, topped by at least a dozen poles, stark against the darkening sky. Even from there, they could see that flocks of large birds were swarming about them.

'It be Henina-Mons,' Aura shouted.

'She's right,' Elindhu exclaimed. 'And those two round hills should be the entrance to Semmanath-Tuhr.'

They all gave a low cheer, except Obanji, who noted that they had about an hour of daylight left. 'We've found it, but you said that no one should enter at night, Elindhu,' he rumbled.

'We may have no choice,' Jadyn replied. 'There might be a dozen other easier ways up here than the one we took. Elindhu, do you have any idea?'

The mage laughed drily. 'Darling, I'm flattered by your faith in my omniscience, but I've only had this place described to me. I have no more idea about the geography than you. We must either take our chances at night, or try and find a defensible place to hide for the night. It's your choice, Commander.'

Soren watched Jadyn consider, thinking, *One day, I want to be just like him . . . and Obanji, of course. I want to be looked up to, and trusted.*

Jadyn glanced at Romara for reassurance, as he always did in such moments, then he faced them. 'If we try to find a safe place this side of the valley, Borghart might prevent us from entering. We'd give a good account of ourselves, but we'd fail. So we're going to enter Semmanath-Tuhr and trust Elindhu's erling-lore and our own prowess to prevail. Ready yourselves, Falcons. There's a dark road before us.'

Have we chosen rightly? Romara wondered, as they trotted towards the two rounded hills. Behind them the setting sun was lost somewhere behind clouds on the western horizon and the light was fading fast.

Jadyn had that composed look he always wore once the decision was made and he could concentrate on seeing things through. The others, taking their cue from him, rode with watchful calm, including

Aura, who was restored to her own mount, now that being scryed was more or less irrelevant. Borghart knew where they were, and all they could do was stay ahead.

Romara noticed Gram sniffing the air like a hound. 'What is it?'

'Rotting meat,' he growled.

A few minutes later, they could all could smell it. As they reached the beginning of Semmanath-Tuhr, raucous crows shrieked and flashed about, jealously guarding the two big conical mounds crowned by what looked like dead trees. They could now see the steep-sided valley, thick with mist-shrouded trees, with a rushing watercourse that fell to the valley floor.

'Follow the river through and we'll reach Neparia,' Elindhu told them. 'It should only take us a few hours.' She fished into her saddle-bag, produced a handful of primitive-looking necklaces made of shells, bones and feathers and began handing them around.

Romara nudged her horse up the nearest mound, to see what was at the summit. What she found made her stomach churn. Thick pine branches, long, straight and sharpened at the tip, had been driven into the ground. Most were empty, a few were festooned with old bones, but three had fresh corpses impaled on them, probably just a few days old. The bodies had been lowered onto the stakes so that they were pierced through their buttocks, with the points emerging from their backs or chests. Carrion birds the size of cats were busy with the remains.

'Akka on high,' she gasped. 'I hope they were dead before they were impaled.'

Elindhu appeared beside her. 'That's not the tradition, I'm afraid. Only the living go to the stake.' She handed her a necklace of finger-bones and feathers. 'Wear this, Siera, and you might not share those poor wretches' fate.'

Well, Tevas Nicolini thought dourly, *it's exactly what I would have done: keep moving, causing new problems for those following.* It was of little comfort. Once again, Romara's pentacle had made things harder for them.

He watched the lictor conferring with Sier Rohas, who'd finally calmed down after his discomfiture earlier. That only pure luck had saved him from being crushed to death seemed to have made the Solabi knight angrier.

They'd found another way up to the plateau and the entrance to this erling-haunted place, which was called Valao Sombras in Solabi, or Semmanath-Tuhr in the erling tongue: an evil-sounding place in either language. But their quarry had gone in.

Do we follow? Or do we go round and potentially lose the trail?

Elan Sandreth sauntered up, raising his voice above the shrieking crows to ask, 'What do you think, Nicolini?'

'We'd be mad to go in there,' Tevas answered. 'I've heard rumours of such places. If you're lucky there's only a handful of erlings and they'll just hide. But Sier Rohas thinks there's a whole tribe down there, so we're better to wait until morning, when they drag out Jadyn and the rest and impale them.'

'There's more than a hundred of us,' Elan replied. 'Surely they wouldn't take us on?'

'Maybe not, but we'd take casualties, and in any case, we'll probably blunder straight past Jadyn's lot in the dark. It's easier to hide when you're just a few. We're better to await daylight, when we can travel faster and in greater safety. We'll not lose much ground by waiting, and we'll be a whole lot safer.'

'You speak of this Jadyn Kaen a lot, but isn't my Romara their leader?' Elan asked.

'Aye, but I was closer to Jadyn. All the other knights at the academy thought him weak, but he was diligent, steady and sensible. I knew he'd go from strength to strength.'

'You like him,' Elan accused.

'What of it? I'll still take his head for that Akka-be-damned bounty.'

They fell silent as Borghart and Sier Rohas stamped towards them.

'We're not going in there at night,' Borghart told them. 'Let those fiends do our work for us. If the erlings haven't staked their bodies by dawn, we'll ride through, and slaughter any who come at us.'

Tevas found himself nodding agreement. 'It's what I'd do.'

Borghart's cold glare skewered him. 'Do I look like I need your approval? Get your pirate scum rounded up, Nicolini: they've got the first watch.'

Tevas bit his lip to forestall a sharp reply and went to rise when they all heard the drumming of hooves – and a dozen horses, without saddles or harness but all shod, erupted into the middle of the camp. Shouting in alarm, the Vestal soldiers scattered as the beasts thundered past and down the slope. Even the crows stopped to watch, before resuming their squabbling over the impaled carcasses.

Borghart smirked. 'Those were the Falcons' horses, I warrant. It appears that animals fear this place. Sier Rohas, will we face the same problem tomorrow morning?'

'It's not something I've heard of before,' the Solabi knight replied. 'If necessary, we can blindfold and lead our mounts. Valao Sombras is only a dozen kylos long – we can do that in a day, even walking.'

'Agreed,' Borghart replied. 'I have a good feeling about this. Tomorrow, our pursuit ends.'

13

Semmanath-Tuhr

The Erling Twilight

There was no 'Erling War'. Wherever humanity encountered the Old Folk, they fled. As we tamed the land, these primitives slunk deeper into the wild. At the last, those few who remained were rounded up and given territory in Tyr. The erlings are now spiritless and in decline. Nature is pitiless to the weak.

CHRONICLES OF TALMONT, 1405

The Qor-Espina, Ferasto
Summer 1472

After only a few hundred paces into the erling valley, it became clear that the horses were terrified. Blindfolds didn't work, for their nostrils were flaring at some stench only they could smell, and in the dark, the footing on the valley floor was so treacherous that even leading them was likely to end in disaster.

'What's got up their noses?' Obanji wondered.

'Can't you smell it?' Gram replied. 'This place reeks of old death and live predators. It's cruel to bring them here.'

Jadyn could smell nothing, but the beasts' anxiety was clear. The light was almost gone, but they could see men and horses silhouetted against the dusk sky, five hundred paces above and behind them. There was no going back, and apparently no going forward. If they used a spell to light their way, they'd be marked, and maybe draw pursuit, but the horses absolutely refused to enter the trees, and the slopes on either side were sheer.

Maybe the horses are smarter than we are? he worried.

'Gram's right,' Elindhu murmured. 'It is cruel to drive them on, and probably futile in any case. We should let them go.'

'But we need them.'

'Do we? We had to walk them up much of the foothills, and the far side of the ranges won't be any gentler. And I gather the Eravandar region, where Agynea dwells, is also mountainous. We'll manage just as well without them.'

'E Cara,' groaned Aura, 'will have blister on blister.'

'At least there'll be no more saddle-sores,' Obanji grunted, clapping Soren on the shoulder.

The young man smiled sourly. 'I guess.'

'All right, let's do it,' Jadyn decided. 'Take whatever you can carry, prioritising bedrolls, food and anything personal Borghart might use to scry you. Remove the tack and leave it here.'

They tethered the horses and stripped them, dumping about a third of their stores and a lot of useful but not crucial gear – what Obanji called the 'nice-to-haves'. When they released the horses, they needed no encouragement; in seconds they were all pounding up the slope. As they reached the top, they heard Borghart's soldiers whooping in surprise and the crows shrieking in complaint, then it all went silent again.

Romara joined Jadyn. Her blackened eyes were healing and she had some colour back, but she'd lost weight and looked unwell. He chose not to mention that, her calm being fragile these days. 'Are you ready for this, Rom?'

'Are any of us?'

'Regretting leaving me in charge?'

She gave him a cool stare. 'It was the right call. But these are hard roads we're taking.'

'We've got Elindhu. What other pentacle has an actual erling expert? This is fated.'

'Sure, you keep telling yourself that,' she drawled, then dropped her voice. 'I'm going to have to stick close to Gram, in case ... you know what. But Jadyn, please don't get yourself killed protecting Aura. I know you and your sense of chivalry, but you need to be careful.'

'It's not chivalry, it's decency—'

'Whatever,' she interrupted. 'Keep yourself alive. Please.'

The old Romara would never have said such a thing, but he could see how frightened she was, so he set her words aside. *When this is over, the real Romara will come back to me.*

'All right,' he told them, 'Elindhu says the stream will lead us through. I don't think Borghart's going to follow us tonight, so once we're in the trees, we can risk some light.'

'Keep together,' Obanji added, 'eyes peeled.'

'That's a must,' Elindhu agreed. 'The erlings are wild and they'll take anyone who strays, but if we stick together, we should be fine. There's something I must do first, though.'

With that, she walked to the edge of the forbidding pines and raising her hands, chanted, '*Incalla syessa mai, consa Elindhu Morspeth, fraca a filla mai, kyndo sarai Tyrsia. Incalla fimbras o'brai, kynsa.*'

'So much for sneaking past unnoticed,' Romara muttered.

'They already know we're here. I've told them who and what I am: a scholar and erling-friend, known to the elders of Tyr. It will, I hope, be enough to allow us passage.' She flashed a wry smile. 'I do hope I pronounced it all correctly.'

'E Cara,' Aura groaned.

Jadyn patted her shoulder. 'It's all right, she's joking. Any other advice for us?'

Elindhu displayed her erling necklace. 'Yes – don't cover these necklaces. They're the only things keeping an erling from putting an arrow in your heart.'

'Is also joke?' Aura asked hopefully.

Jadyn shook his head.

As the last light left the western sky, Elindhu lit her staff-orb faintly, creating a little pool of light, and they set off into the trees, feeling their way until the ridge behind had vanished.

'Succeed or fail, I'm so happy,' she remarked, puffed up like a hen who'd just laid a golden egg. 'An actual erlhaafen! This is the most exciting moment of my life.'

The paths running either side of the small river were hunting trails, Gram realised, pointing out the signs to Romara: tufts of fur caught on twigs and patches worn into bark, suggesting deer aplenty, along with rabbits, squirrels, mice and voles. He spotted fox dens, badger setts and a beaver dam; the throaty cough of a mountain cat was followed by a wolf's howl, far off.

For all that, the woods had a watchful feel, and there were little runes etched into branches and rocks. He asked Elindhu, 'Is that erling script?'

'It is: a hunter's mark,' she confirmed. 'A warning to harm nothing. We're trespassing here.'

'Trespassing?' Romara snorted. 'The erlings are supposed to be confined to Tyrland.'

'Those living here are far older than humankind. They once ruled Hytal.'

'And now they don't.' Romara was drawing a little glyma so she could light her way, but even that was fraying her control and temper. When Gram brushed her shoulder, a reminder to remain calm, she flashed him a resentful look, as if scared of needing his aid.

Elindhu led the way, single file alongside the babbling stream that was skipping over rocks and winding through the tangles of gnarled trees festooned in moss. She was followed by Gram and Romara, then Aura and Jadyn, with Obanji and Soren at the rear. The atmosphere grew ever more oppressive. Sounds of skittering movement surrounded them; they glimpsed flashes of movement and caught the occasional whiff of rank, wet fur. But after half an hour they'd seen nothing more uncanny than a Leafman face, a Huirne, carved into a tree trunk.

Mist was rising over the stream, a wispy layer that undulated with the land, shifting in the faintest of breezes. Then they reached a waterfall, dropping twice a man's height into a small pool covered in livid green algae, with a few mossy rocks protruding. The Skull moon overhead brushed silvery light over the clearing, making everything glow faintly. On the far side they could see another stream cascading into the pool, but there was no visible outlet.

'It must go underground here,' Jadyn commented, surveying the place.

Obanji pointed east, above the trees, at the conical mountain, Henina-Mons, shimmering in the distance. 'It's a fine sight, and a sign we're heading the right way.'

Then they all caught their breath, because *something* had emerged atop the opposite falls – a rangy figure with long hair and an antlered brow, holding a drawn bow.

'Incalla syessa,' Elindhu called. 'Consa Elindhu. Orva tae?'

Moonlight lit the archer's face, so pale and gaunt it was almost a skull, dominated by a long nose and big amber eyes. When he responded, his voice was resonant and melodic.

Elindhu went to reply, but he was gone. 'He told us to be gone,' she reported anxiously.

They held their breath, the knights' orbs glimmering with latent energy pushing to be released. Gram stole some, to enhance his senses. His nostrils flaring, his vision sharpened until he could see the erling was now pressed against a tree trunk, his bow lowered.

'He's still there,' he whispered, 'but he's not taken aim.'

In a heartbeat, with the faintest of rustling, the erling had vanished again.

'He's gone. As best as I can tell, we're alone here.'

They all took a moment to shiver out some of their tension, then Jadyn turned to Gram. 'Your night-sight's clearly better than ours. Will you lead the way?'

It was as firm a show of trust as any he'd given. Gram climbed down to the pool to the left of the waterfall, and scanned it carefully. In this light, its depth was unknowable. *Two streams in, nothing out . . . the pool must drain into the ground.* He peered into the trees, glimpsing a fox waiting for the intruders to leave so it could drink. He sniffed the air: old decay and moss. They were still alone here.

Aura went to the stream on the far side, bending to drink . . . then she backed away, staring. 'E Cara mia,' she breathed, sounding incredulous. 'Ney posiba, ney posiba, shih ney—'

Gram joined her, not seeing anything untoward – until he realised the waterfall *was* the outflow from the pool – and it was flowing *upwards*.

Elindhu called, 'Get away from the water—!'

Too late.

One of the rocks in the pool moved, saucer-sized amber eyes flicked open and with a mighty splash, a giant figure erupted from below. Gram shoved Aura behind him, but a moment later an arm as big as a tree branch ripped him from the ground, and suddenly he was plunged into the water, swallowed by liquid darkness.

The giant's grip was terrifying, squeezing him like a strangler vine. He fought with all his strength to break free while trying to hold his breath, as his huge assailant blocked out the churning surface above him.

Another body crashed into the pool, bearing a bar of light, but Gram's lungs could withstand the constriction no longer. With a despairing wail of denial, his mouth burst open and bubbles exploded forth.

He blacked out as the beast drew him deeper . . .

Jadyn saw the creature – some kind of slime-encrusted giant with bulbous eyes and a maw like a toothy fish – erupt from beneath the algae. In an instant, Gram was torn from the water's edge, vanishing in a massive splash.

He heard Aura shriek and Romara gasp, light flaring from her orb, and dread gripped him, that she would panic and be lost to him forever. That thought drove him to the fore, ahead of Soren and Obanji – and a moment later he was swallowing a mouthful of air as he plunged into the water, energy flowing down his flamberge as he hefted it, hilt aloft and blade pointing down. Water engulfed him, sight and sound disintegrating into a churning silvery roar, but his feet struck something, a slippery bulk, and he saw a pair of glowing amber lamps beneath him.

He struck, jack-knifing his whole body to drive his glowing blade between those eyes, crunching through bone to bury steel in the skull. The water erupted in scarlet, a huge limb battered him against the rocky pool wall, but somehow he kept hold of the flamberge, ripping it from the monster's skull . . .

Then unseen forces gripped him and pulled him upwards through water into the air, until he came crashing down beside the pool. Convulsing, he vomited algae and water in sickening gouts, while around him, voices clamoured urgently.

Then sweet air reflated his chest and he found himself lying on his side, his vision slowly clearing. Bizarrely, Romara was kissing Gram with a strange rhythmic urgency, her head bobbing oddly. She'd planted her hands over his heart and looked to be pressing it, which struck him as very odd behaviour.

That's not in the Vestal Code, he thought dazedly. *She's gone mad.*

Then the big man convulsed, spewing water and blood, while Romara collapsed onto him, panting desperately, her face flushed as it went from terror to relief.

The trapper's eyes opened and he looked straight at Jadyn.

Jadyn closed his eyes and felt his mouth crease into a smile. *I got him out. Thank Elysia.*

The panic over, Romara crawled to the nearest boulder and put her back against it, still panting in relief. The technique – breathing for someone else, pumping their heart – was something Tevas Nicolini had shown her, when she found a fellow initiate who was in the process of hanging herself.

It felt good to save a life.

But the way fate kept hurling Gram and her together in life-or-death moments was tearing her apart. As she'd performed her miracle, she'd been inside his dying soul – she could feel it dragging her down. She could still taste his spittle; his heart still shuddered under her fingers – and every time she looked at him, she shivered with desire. *Need-want-take*, her body growled. *Seize, hold, possess.*

If she'd actually been virginal, it might have been easier, but she knew what she wanted: everything she'd done with Elan so long ago, and more. That she felt such a thing for a vyr and not Jadyn made her feel wretched and evil, but she couldn't help it.

I want this to be over, she groaned. *Let me be purged of glyma, and regain my true self.*

Her love for Jadyn had never been in question before, but now thoughts of Gram wouldn't let her be. When he'd gone into the pool, she'd thought her heart would punch a hole in her chest. She'd hurled Elindhu aside to save him, given him her breath and all her will to bring him back.

It's only because he can stop the rage from consuming me, she told herself. *That's all.*

'Are you all right?' Obanji asked, settling beside her. 'That was an amazing thing you did.'

'Something Tevas showed me once. It should be part of standard training.'

'Aye, that's the truth. You never stop amazing me, Commander.'

She gave him a wan smile. 'I'm just one of the lads now, Obanji. It was Jadyn who saved Gram, I just tidied up.'

Her eyes went back to Gram, who was gazing at her with grateful longing.

Damn, she thought, their glyma-rapport rekindling, *this is all wrong.* But she couldn't look away.

'All right,' Jadyn said finally. 'We should move on.'

His small group were visibly wrung out, and now the forest around them was full of watchful eyes and stealthy movement.

If that archer strikes, we'll be powerless.

His eyes went to the pool, where the giant now floated on its face. *If most erlings are like him, I can see why we need the reservations.*

Gram was sitting up, sipping Obanji's potent elixir. Romara was drained and shaky, looking at the trapper with a bleak expression. Elindhu was chanting her ritual greeting into the trees – until a skin-crawling screech presaged a mossy-skinned creature shambling out of the trees. The obese female was not alone: a pair of dark-skinned reptilian gargoyles with large bat-like ears and oddly formed baby faces trailed after her, whimpering. They ignored the humans as they splashed into the pool, swam to the floating body and clung to it, sobbing.

Akka on high, Jadyn thought in despair, *it had a mate and children.*

He looked helplessly at Elindhu, who looked stricken. 'What do we do?' he whispered.

She gave him a moist-eyed glance. 'There's nothing we can do, except leave.' She indicated the other stream, which was running *up* the hill on the other side of the clearing. 'Onwards, Falcons. The road is before us.'

After that fatal encounter, their journey became increasingly eerie and unsettling. By the time they topped the ridge where they'd seen the archer, the current of the stream water was flowing downwards again, which was a relief, but it felt as if the whole forest was aware of their passage now. A pair of oversized bats flapped overhead and hung from a branch, peering at them and chittering, as if discussing them. They glimpsed the horned archer again, lurking at the edge of their vision, watching silently. But strangest of all were the fish which broke from the water's surface and swam in the air above it, while birds dived into the stream and flew underwater.

Aura didn't know whether to stare in awe or drop to her knees and pray, but Akka's eternal love and Elysia's mercy felt a long way away, so she put her faith in Jadyn Kaen instead, because she knew he'd protect her. When he dived into that pool, she'd felt something akin to panic at the thought of losing him. That had never happened before, not even with Sergio.

What does this stupid Farm Boy matter to me?

She had no answer, but she knew to stay near him as they trod these strange paths, one hand on her belt dagger and the other fending off the branches crowding in like grasping hands. New rivulets were joining the stream, widening and deepening it. They gave the next pool a wide berth, and when Aura glanced back she saw a woman's head rise from beneath its surface, a sallow-faced girl with dripping black hair, who glared malevolently before plucking a flying fish from the air and taking a toothy bite out of it.

Get me out of here, she prayed, scurrying after Jadyn.

Hearing her footfalls, he threw her a calm look, and murmured, 'Stay close.'

Immediately her anxiety eased, though she kept imagining twisted faces with predatory amber eyes, lying in wait. But on they went, down an undulating slope, mist thickening over the water, which was fast becoming a river. She saw an eel swimming upstream a foot above the surface and catching a dragonfly. Then they reached another waterfall and stopped in awe as a glorious panorama unfolded below.

A large pool beneath them reflected the moons and stars. Beyond, they could see the river winding on through another belt of trees to a lake glistening beneath snow-capped ranges. It was breath-taking, gorgeous and chilling.

Movement caught their eye. A wolf, a majestic beast, an embodiment of this place's wild spirit, padded from the trees below and drank from the pool, moonlight kissing its fur with silver. Once it had drunk its fill, it stood on hind legs, its fur parting and peeling away from its torso until what remained was a wolf-headed woman with extraordinary musculature and beauty. She looked up, saw them, then dropped to all fours and in moments was entirely wolf again, bounding into the trees.

'Are we still in our world?' Jadyn exclaimed. 'Is this still Coros?'

'Am not knowing,' Aura replied, utterly amazed. 'These is also erling?'

Elindhu heard her. 'Anything more or less human-shaped is an erling,' she replied, her voice just as awed. 'They're far more mutable than even I knew. And the water and the fish . . . it's neither glyma nor vorlok-magic.' Far from looking terrified, she was intrigued. 'I could study this place for a lifetime.'

It would be a brief lifetime, Aura thought. *This place is not for us.*

At least they had some clear space ahead, and a clear path ran down beside the waterfall to the pool where the wolf-woman had drunk. There were stepping stones that looked suspiciously convenient. Elindhu led the way, testing each one with her staff – she smote the third one, which shuddered, then vanished below, trailing bubbles and muffled laughter. Those with the glyma managed the larger gap easily, but it was too far for Aura to jump.

'I've got you,' Jadyn said, smiling boyishly. He gathered her in his arms and leaped. Her heart was in her mouth, but he landed deftly, placed her down and bowed like some beau at the end of a dance.

Neya pasu, she thought. *Am impressed now.* She beamed her gratitude, but he blushed and looked away. *Poor boy*, she thought. *Am I under your skin, as you are mine?*

It was only fair.

Fool, the Devourer muttered in her left ear. *He's a Vestal knight, in love with another woman. You need to leave these imbeciles behind, before they drag you into an early grave.*

She's right, Akka agreed. *You're nothing to these people, remember that. You have to escape them, before they sacrifice you to their mission.*

That the King of Good and Queen of Evil agreed was chilling, and could not be ignored.

For Soren, the journey into the erling valley was a reliving of some of his oldest fears, of shadows, tall trees and lurking menace. The family farm on Avas had backed up against old forest, where Leafman carvings could still be found on the tree trunks. After dark it became too scary for his young imagination.

Following the eerie stream through the claustrophobic press of foliage, the worst of his fears came out to play. Every rustling leaf, every soft crackle of footfalls beyond their light, became a beast like that in the pool, stalking him alone. Worse, he kept hearing something like a song, a murmuring that was following him every step of the way.

The sound drifted in again, capturing him . . . and he heard a faint rustling to his right, too close. He turned – and was shocked to see amber eyes staring at him. In the undergrowth, just a few feet away, was a flawless female face, too predatory and perfect to be human . . .

Even as he went to yell in alarm, the music gripped him, pulling all thought and fear away, leaving him standing motionless as her mesmerising eyes leafed through his mind as if it were a book, murmuring entreaties and invitations in a melodic whisper. '*Runa a senesa, com peta nu*,' she purred, meaningless and yet somehow clear.

Come to me, beautiful boy . . .

Then a harsh voice, raucous as a crow, called, 'Soren, stay on the path!'

The erling blinked, Soren staggered as if breaking a cord between them and Romara stomped up, glaring at him impatiently. 'If you get left behind, you're screwed. Obanji, watch your protégé,' she called. 'He's your responsibility, Old Man!'

Soren flashed a terrified glance back into the trees, but the amber-eyed woman was gone.

It was the wolf-headed erling, he realised. *She was trying to lure me away. And I nearly went . . .*

Soren flinched guiltily as Obanji strode up, and went to explain, but the Abuthan clapped his shoulder and said, 'Just keep up, son. There's stuff out there no one wants to tangle with.'

Ashamed at his lapse, Soren clammed up, staying close to his mentor and keeping his eyes averted from the trees . . . where *something* was keeping pace with him. Then they broke from the woods, finding themselves on a flat expanse of stony grass where the river fed the lake. The silver-blue fish swimming above the surface dived suddenly as a heron swooped in. A beautiful olive-skinned girl with goat legs and horns emerged from a willow on the far side, gave them a startled look and scampered away.

'Are the reservations like this?' Obanji asked Elindhu.

'No, those are sad places,' Elindhu responded. 'Miserable. There's hardly any erlings left on them now.'

'Maybe they're all leaving to come here,' Soren suggested.

'No, they're becoming extinct,' she replied sharply. 'There are maybe a dozen places left like this in all of Hytal. Ten years ago there were twice that number. Erlings are dying out because our empire is destroying them.'

Soren saw Obanji raise his eyebrows at the vehemence of Elindhu's response, but scholars were passionate about their areas of expertise, he was beginning to realise, and her empathy with the erlings was clearly deep-rooted.

'Pa used to make us leave offerings for the Folk of the Trees, back on Avas,' he told them. 'But I don't think there were any erlings there. I reckon the foxes ate whatever we left out.'

'Probably,' Elindhu agreed, her face still sad. 'The erlings left the Isles long ago.'

They followed Jadyn down to the lakeshore, boots crunching on the stones. All three moons were high in the sky, Heaven's Belt glittered vividly and the snowy steeple of Henina-Mons was a pyramid of light, marking the far end of the valley only a few kylos away. But the way forward was unclear, as the heights closed around the lake, with high cliffs on either bank, topped by silvery shareth trees, tall, elegant towers of wood.

'Damn, it's beautiful,' Obanji muttered.

Soren could see that, but he was too worried about the wolf-woman to appreciate the view.

'I reckon we're halfway, give or take,' Jadyn told them all. 'And it's only midnight. We can do this. Any thoughts on the way forward from here?'

Obanji joined Jadyn, Romara and Elindhu in discussing which way around the lake looked more promising, while Soren stood with Gram and Aura. The big trapper was watching the woods behind them anxiously. His furs were sodden, his hair and beard dripping, and his whole stance was uncharacteristically fearful.

He almost died, Soren thought. *He's as scared as any of us.*

Aura was equally subdued, not at all her usual bubbly self. That was fine; she reminded Soren of the blousy, overacting women he'd seen in travelling shows. He didn't trust anything about her, but at least she'd stopped flirting with him of late, as if she knew she was wasting her time.

I'm going to be a Vestal knight. I have no interest in her.

He went to speak to Gram, when Aura gasped. He followed her gaze – and went rigid.

A line of heads had appeared in the lake, about sixty paces offshore. The water rippled as they advanced towards the shore, rising to reveal necks and shoulders, torsos and hips: a dozen slender figures with dripping clothes and hair, pointed ears or horns, all holding spears and long knives. The middle one held a Vestal flamberge, the orb aglow.

The Falcons drew weapons and formed up facing the newcomers – until Gram growled and they turned to see more figures had appeared atop the rocky shelf behind them. They included the horned archer they'd glimpsed before, and a dozen more like him, all aiming bows.

'Don't move,' Elindhu hissed. 'Let me do the talking.'

Soren gulped as the wolf-woman stalked into view, walking on hind legs but more wolf than woman, with a row of teats amid the pale fur on her belly. Behind her came a bulbous-faced ogress with a gargoyle child on either shoulder: the same creatures they'd seen mourning the giant that Jadyn had killed.

'Inshammach,' the ogress shrieked, pointing at Jadyn. 'Aja malkas inshammach!'

'Justice, she says,' Elindhu breathed. 'She wants justice for her loss.'

Romara was outraged. 'It tried to kill Gram. Jadyn had no choice.'

'You made a choice to be here,' a new voice called from the lakeside.

The speaker was the erling with the flamberge, clearly male. He had reached the shore, water dripping from silken garments. He wore a Foylish torc and gold rings, and would have been handsome, but for the tusks jutting from the corners of his mouth. 'These are erling lands,' he called. 'You should not have come here. And now you have killed one of us.'

He speaks Talmoni, Soren noted fearfully, *and he bears an Order weapon*.

His heart thumping, he edged closer to Obanji.

The knights looked to their defences, while Elindhu stepped forward and exchanged a torrent of melodic words with the erling, while the erling archers peered along their aimed shafts as if aching to let them fly.

The wolf-woman was staring straight at Soren, amber eyes gleaming. Then she smiled, her gaze caressing his face. His heart began to thud as he heard that subtle music again—

—until Obanji put a hand on his shoulder and growled, 'Don't meet their eyes.'

He looked away, and suddenly he could breathe again.

Elindhu concluded her debate with a hiss of temper, then reported, 'He's the herald of the Erlking of Semmanath-Tuhr. They want to put you on trial, Jadyn.'

'No,' Jadyn said flatly.

'The options aren't good,' she told him. 'They'll attack us all if they don't get their way.'

'Jadyn saved Gram's life,' Romara snapped. 'We had no idea the creature was there.'

'In their eyes, we're trespassing and we owe them a life as wergild for the widow.'

'Whose side are you?' Romara asked.

'Ours, clearly: I'm only relating what he's saying. Don't shoot the damned messenger.'

Romara raised a hand apologetically. 'Sorry, I misspoke.'

We're all scared, Soren realised. *Especially me*.

'We're a pentacle of the Vestal Order,' Jadyn snapped. 'Does he know what he's taking on?'

'He has one of our blades,' Elindhu countered. 'He knows exactly what we are. He says we are to follow him and face the Erlking's justice, or they'll kill us all.'

Jadyn shook his head. 'We do not surrender one of our own, and we don't submit to the justice of others. We can defeat them, for certain. We're Vestal knights.'

'Jadyn, no,' Elindhu protested. 'Such bloodshed would only bring many more of them – and it's unnecessary. I can make a case to their king. I know their kind. Please, have faith: if not in them, then in me.'

Romara was concentrating on keeping Gram calm, or maybe it was the other way round. Obanji was eyeballing the archers defiantly, ready to conjure shields in an eye-blink. They would fight the moment Jadyn signalled.

As will I, Soren thought defiantly.

The wolf-woman was still staring at him, undressing him with her eyes. *You're a prize of war*, her gaze said. *My prize*. His sense of unreality deepened.

'Listen,' Jadyn murmured, 'we either fight, or we trust Elindhu to get us out. What do you all think? I need to know before I decide.'

'Fight,' Romara said.

'If it were just us, I'd agree,' Obanji said. 'But we'll take casualties.'

'As will they.'

'And that's something we should also prevent,' Elindhu hissed. 'They're people too.'

They all considered, then Obanji said, 'We trusted Elindhu in coming here.'

'Very well,' Romara sighed. 'But make sure they know it's them getting off lightly, not us.'

While Elindhu spoke to the erling herald, Soren ran through his runes, readying himself for violence, trying to ignore the wolf-woman's gaze.

At last, the mage turned to Jadyn. 'He says we must follow.'

Soren let out a slow breath. He sensed movement on the shelf above and behind them; the wolf-woman leaped down the side of the falls, landed easily and strode towards them, tugging at the furry folds of flesh around her neck – then she peeled her own face off, the wolf head going limp and turning inside out, revealing a human skull covered in wetly pulsing pink tissue.

Soren was not alone in recoiling in horror – then he gasped as skin poured over the pulpy tissue to form a luscious feminine face, framed by a mass of tawny hair. It was the one who had ensorcelled him in the woods. She shot him a savage grin as she strode past, peeling the wolf skin from her body to become the magnificent woman they'd seen earlier, all power and grace.

Soren swallowed. *Holy Elysia*, he thought, shocked to the core and queasy at that ghastly glimpse of what lay beneath the skin – or fur. He was sure the display was mostly for him, but still he couldn't look away. She said something to the herald, then walked into the lake, up to her hips, then her waist.

Elindhu found her voice first and shot a question at the herald, who licked his tusks with a long, snaky tongue, then told them, 'She is Fynarhea, child of the Erlking. She bids us welcome to Semmanath-Tuhr. We're expected to follow her,' Elindhu added.

Fynarhea strode even deeper into the lake, dived, and vanished beneath the surface.

'E Cara,' Aura blurted, backing away. 'Cannot, ney-ney.'

Soren agreed wholeheartedly, and he wasn't the only one. They were all blanching, until Elindhu waddled to the water's edge and scooped up some water, which became a thick vapour running slowly through her fingers and falling back into the lake. She knelt and put her head under the water, then came up with her face and hair wet, but her expression excited. She called to the tusked herald in rapid-fire erling; he replied in kind, and her expression grew ever more incredulous.

'The water is a kind of illusion,' she announced. 'Remember the birds flying beneath the surface of the river, and the fish?' She put her sleeve into the water and it came up wet . . . but not sopping. 'It is both water and not-water,' she called. 'Quite amazing.' She turned and followed the wolf-woman, her robes floating around her, calling, 'Follow me, it's safe.'

'How?' Jadyn called after her. 'I've never heard of a power like this? What is it?'

Elindhu looked back at him intently. 'He says it was made using the *aegis*.'

'Aegis? Akka on high,' Jadyn blurted, looking at Gram, who'd also spoken of the aegis. But the trapper was staring fearfully at the lake, and not listening.

'I can't swim,' Gram mumbled.

Romara gripped his hand, saying, 'We'll do it together.' When he hesitated still, she tugged him after her, saying, 'We'll pull each other through.'

Soren saw Jadyn staring at them, looking a little lost – then he blinked and offered his hand to the petrified Aura. 'Be brave,' the knight urged her. 'You can do this.'

'Aura can't,' the Nepari wailed, 'not magical. Not brave.'

'Yes, you are,' Jadyn replied, while the erlings watched with arrows twitching. 'I know you're not a glyma-wielder and used to being invincible, but that's not bravery. It's those who face the unknown knowing they *aren't* invulnerable who are brave.' He turned to the others. 'We do this together.'

They formed up, facing the water. Soren took Obanji's hand, who took Aura's other hand, saying, 'Let's show these erling putoso, eh?' The Nepari nodded jerkily, squeezing both of their hands so hard her knuckles went white.

They began wading out, breathing heavily. The lake water was very strange: it was definitely wet, but oddly insubstantial, both there and not-there. Nevertheless, their clothing became sodden, dragging at them, and Jadyn looked at Obanji for reassurance.

'Fear kills more people than any war, pestilence or famine,' Obanji said, 'because it clouds judgement and paralyses us. Breathe your fears out of you.'

Soren tried it, and it did seem to help.

They caught up with Elindhu, who'd waited. Only her shoulders and head were above the surface, while they were standing waist-deep, but she looked calm and intrigued. The water was so clear and the moons so bright that Soren could see they were approaching the edge of a shelf of rock. As they reached that lip, the moonlight penetrated the greenish depths, revealing a castle on the lake bottom, with sentries pacing the battlements.

'Oh my,' Elindhu said, in a choked voice, 'it's everything they said—'

She jumped off the shelf, immediately sinking, faster than a body in water should, but more slowly than falling through air. As she fell, her tower of grey braids unknotted, fanning out around her.

She flapped her hands and arrested her fall, then twisted and looked back at them, a wild smile on her face. She shouted something inaudible, then turned and soared like a bird towards the castle below.

'Jagata-mai,' Obanji exclaimed, turning to Soren. 'Lad, the example's set. Are you ready?'

Soren stared at the receding mage, then looked up at the three moons, horribly afraid that if he dived he'd never come back up. But he refused to let Obanji down. 'I'm ready.'

Obanji gave him a proud look, the sort Soren had craved from his father, and together they stepped off the edge and fell into the deep. It felt *exactly* like water, and instinctive dread of drowning locked up Soren's breathing, his limbs going rigid as he clamped his mouth shut . . .

If Elindhu did it, Soren thought, forcing himself to relax, *so can we*.

In an act of will that defied nature he exhaled. Bubbles emerged, streaming out in his wake, and all his senses told him he *must not* inhale . . . But he and Obanji shared a nod and breathed in together, utterly terrified.

But what flowed into his mouth and throat was like wet air, damp but gaseous, and his lungs sucked it in joyously. Immediately the dizziness in his head cleared. He looked at Obanji, whose face was alight with wonder. Their fears evaporated and they laughed, the sound bubbling out of them only slightly distorted.

'Akka on high,' Obanji roared, his voice distorted by the semi-watery air, as he waved back at the surface, where the others still wavered.

They let go hands and on an impulse Soren threw himself into a slow-motion cartwheel, while Obanji held his arms out like wings and allowed himself to float downwards.

What had begun as a descent into terror became something enchanted.

Aura stifled a wail when Obanji and Soren vanished, until the churned-up water cleared and she saw them again, their clothes drifting round them as if in water, trailing bubbles as they dropped towards the impossible castle. Obanji clearly shouted something, for they heard muffled, indistinct sounds, and he was waving and smiling as he and Soren descended into the depths.

Gram was staring after them, as if caught in a nightmare. 'What if they're luring us down so they can change the water again and drown us? What if it's a trick? I can't swim, and—'

'Jag this,' Romara said, jerking Gram off-balance so that they fell together, thrashing at first, then finding some kind of equilibrium between walking, swimming and tumbling. Gram clung to Romara's arm like a child, but she didn't shake him off, instead taking a moment to steady him. They exhaled bubbles, inhaled this strange not-water – and then without looking back, they dropped away.

Aura looked at Jadyn's face and saw naked anguish there.

Because Romara is always with Gram, now . . . Jadyn doesn't know what to do.

It was such a commonplace drama in her world, the dance of hearts and desire, but to him it was clearly all new. In his simple black-and-white world, there was only supposed to be him and Romara. He didn't know how to deal with it.

She resolved to cheer him up, so she squeezed his hand and handed her life over to Akka or Destiny or Chance. 'Sier Jadyn Knight,' she said, curtseying. 'It be our turn. Do we dance?'

Jadyn smiled wanly. By unspoken consent they took a cautious approach, facing each other and dropping their heads under while still standing on the shelf.

She blew out bubbles then sucked in, limbs set to shoot upwards if it all went wrong . . .

. . . but it didn't, and they ended up staring at each other, hair and clothing floating about them, and she felt a manic bubble of exhilaration when she realised that *yes, she could do this.*

She leaped off the ledge, pulling Jadyn with her, and they spun round and round into the depths, before finding a kind of stability and dropping slowly through the liquid sky above the faery castle, hand in hand.

It felt wonderful.

'E Cara mia,' she shouted in Jadyn's face. 'Magnifica – *magica.*'

'Yes,' he exclaimed, his face alight like a child's. 'Yes, it is! It's a magic called the aegis,' he added excitedly, catching her mood. 'The Sanctor Wardens used it and—'

'Aegis? Aegis, I love aegis,' she shouted. 'Y tresa amora, magica!'

She flung her arms round him and hugged, then let go, flipped head over heels and spun away like a top, the water making her clothing ripple round her, wet but not soaked. She was both fish and bird, and wonderfully free.

This is magical, she thought. *The way magic should be: not energy bolts and spying on people, but acts of wonderful impossibility.*

Jadyn was still moving cautiously, his boyish face concentrating hard; it made her laugh to swoop in and grab him, just to gaze into his wide-open eyes, as he smiled broadly, his face lighting up with hope.

She seized his head and kissed him, because such moments deserved kisses.

His eyes bulged, for a moment he kissed back, then he had a panicky moment and pulled his face away . . . then shyly shook his head, mouthing, *No, please don't.*

A shame, but the moment was too wonderful to waste on his precious prudery.

Poor Farm Boy, she thought. *Confused by joy.* She pushed off and spun away into a Nepari aronda, dancing on the air, her skirts and hair floating around her in slow motion as they descended to the bottom of the lake.

Aegis, she thought again. *I want it for myself.*

Wonderfully, a school of fish and birds swarmed around them, chasing minnows and insects disturbed by their passing. She gazed about, then looked up at the rippling silver of the surface to see it exploding into starbursts as the erling warriors followed them.

Jadyn was still experimenting with movement, mock-fencing through a series of drills, then pulsing out energy that crackled wildly, scaring the fish and birds. He tried pushes of force, which made him spin head over heels in recoil, because he wasn't anchored.

On a whim, she shouted, '*Hola, Farm Boy!*' and flung a dagger at him. It spun slowly through the watery air; he caught it by the hilt and tossed it back with a smile of surprise.

She caught it easily and sheathed it, then danced on, revelling in the freedom of movement and the lightness of her body down here. But they were almost at the bottom, and she rejoined Jadyn in time to touch down inside the castle's courtyard. Obanji and Soren were experimentally fencing, while Romara was helping Gram to overcome his fear of the weighty air and the tugging currents shifting hair and clothing, and the claustrophobia of a shimmering lake surface as sky.

As the erling warriors landed all round them, more emerged from the walls and the keep – dozens more, and three of those also had Order flamberges while two others bore crystal-tipped orbs. The glyma was clearly well-known here. She began to count heads, but gave up after sixty, with many still uncounted.

Her fears began to return.

Seeing Aura overcome her fear and dancing was something Jadyn would carry to his grave, though her kiss had panicked him, and he daren't even look at Romara in case she'd seen. But there was so much to take in down here: the world under the lake was wondrous, and the erling castle was truly a thing of beauty, a graceful construction of pointed towers and pale, green-tinged white stone, more confectionary than fortification.

Elindhu was standing on the silty, spongy, rock-pocked lake bottom, looking up at the castle. 'I thought you said there'd be a few dozen erlings at the most?' he asked.

She was gazing round wide-eyed, drinking it all in. 'That's what I was told,' she breathed, the expression on her face of one who'd died and gone to paradise. 'The Halls of Record aren't going to believe this place,' she exclaimed. 'A living example of the aegis, in an erlhaafen—'

'Elindhu!' Jadyn said, before she got lost in scholarly rapture. 'What happens now?'

She jolted, and gave him an apologetic look. 'Sorry, I'm just . . .'

'I understand,' Jadyn told her. 'This is incredible. But we're in danger.'

Me most of all . . .

She swiftly sobered up as the others gathered to listen. 'We'll be taken before their king. In such places, the Erlking's word is law, but there are many traditions and customs that constrain his judgements. Erlings love to bargain, this for that, and they have a strong, almost childlike sense of justice and honour.'

'Really?' Romara joined them, her red hair billowing around her face like a banner. 'How are they on attempted murder?' Her pale face was strained, as if she'd pulled Gram's fears into herself, the inverse of how he dissipated her glyma-rage. But when she glanced at Jadyn, there was no recrimination, so he guessed she hadn't seen Aura's kiss.

Guilt and relief churned in his belly.

'Erlings prize justice and honour,' Elindhu repeated. 'They will keep their word – precisely.' She glanced at the keep doors. 'We should enter, before the Erlking becomes impatient.'

Jadyn led them up the steps, where the tusked herald awaited them. Behind him were large open doors, through which they glimpsed a large hall, dimly lit by some kind of lantern. Fish and birds flitted above the heads of the erlings waiting within: more than a hundred oddly proportioned men, women and children in wafting clothes that varied from gorgeous silks to crude hide and furs. He saw ogres with legs like tree-trunks beside slender sylph-like erlings of unearthly beauty. The only universal trait was their amber eyes.

He went to enter, and the guards – giant trulkas of Vandarai myth – crossed their halberds before him, blocking his path. The herald pointed at Jadyn's flamberge. 'Guests are forbidden to bear weapons in the halls of the Erlking. Leave them against the wall here. They will be safe, you have our word.'

Elindhu nodded and placed her staff against the wall.

Jadyn swallowed nervously, but unbuckled his shoulder harness and placed his own weapon next to the staff, and the others reluctantly followed suit.

The guards uncrossed their halberds and the herald led the way through the parted crowd of erlings to a dais bearing three thrones. The noise in the huge chamber went from a babble to a murmur as they passed, human-like and bestial faces whispering into each other's wildly varied ears. Jadyn felt like he'd stepped into an old fable of talking beasts. Eyes narrowed and many bared teeth as he passed, but no one threatened them.

They reached the space before the throne and faced the erling rulers. The wolf-woman, Fynarhea, was seated in the left-hand throne, one leg draped over an armrest, slouching like a surly youth. She was clad in green silks, but her wolf-pelt was knotted round her shoulders.

On the right-hand throne sat another female erling, but she was ugliness embodied; her sickly olive face was like badly moulded clay, covered in warty lumps the size of coins; her eyes and teeth were the same yellow. She had thin, straggling black hair, but she wore a crown of gold and her fingers glittered with gold rings. Her expression was one of curiosity, mixed with severity and distaste.

The Queen, Jadyn realised. *What a strange creature.*

The Erlking, in contrast, was lordly and stern, with a gold circlet on his silver hair, setting off his deer antlers. His features were typical of the more human-like erlings they'd seen, with big slanted amber eyes, high cheekbones and a gaunt face. His silk robes were lined with ermine.

They were a weirdly mismatched family, but when the squat little toad-queen murmured something, the lordly Erlking responded with what looked to be genuine affection.

Then the herald took a staff from an attendant and thumped it into the stone floor, shouting, 'Welcome to the court of Audebryn, Erlking of Semmanath-Tuhr. Queen Shuenagh and Princess Fynarhea also extend their greetings. Present yourselves, guests.'

Elindhu, who'd wound a ribbon around her swarming braids to tame them, edged to Jadyn's side and murmured, 'Bow, don't kneel. Erlings despise grovelling.'

Together, they performed a shallow bow, while the Queen whispered in the Erlking's ear. It was evident that only a few of the erlings spoke any Talmoni. Jadyn studied the royal trio, seeing hostility and shrewdness.

They're no fools, he decided instantly. *This could go badly wrong.*

'What now?' he asked Elindhu.

'Speak to the herald; he will interpret. I'll make sure he does so honestly. Start with introductions, express regret at the circumstances and express honour at being here.' She tugged his sleeve and added, 'They know who I am, so just talk about the others.'

Jadyn gave her a grateful look, then faced the herald. 'I am Sier

Jadyn Kaen, Vestal knight.' He named his companions, the pentacle members first, then Gram and Aura as being under his protection, in case anyone thought they were fair game.

The hardest thing was giving a plausible excuse for being here at all, as lies didn't sit easily with him. So what he came up with was largely true. 'We are seeking an end to the vyr rebellion, but we are being hunted by evil men. Their pursuit forced us to enter your lands. We meant no harm, but we were assailed and had to defend ourselves. We regret the harm that caused, and we seek honourable reparation, and safe passage onwards.'

Elindhu gave him an approving nod.

The herald translated, while Jadyn studied the trio on the thrones: the stately, timeless king, his squat, ugly queen and the intense, almost feral daughter. He sensed nothing but hostility.

Then the herald addressed him again: 'King Audebryn says that the world is vast, with many other paths, but you entered his lands knowing it was an act of trespass. Queen Shuenagh says that our subject, Ongroth of the Pool, would still be alive had you not. His wife Ungrit would still have a husband and his children a father. Princess Fynarhea notes that they have lost their provider, the centre of their lives, and face a life without his love.'

'Oh, for jagat's sake, he was a feral trulka with the intelligence of a boar,' Romara muttered.

Jadyn gave her a sharp look, but it was Gram's shake of the head that caused her to subside. *She listens to him more than me now*, Jadyn thought wanly.

'We regret the loss,' he stated firmly. 'We had no choice but to come here, and we were attacked at the pool. We sought only to defend ourselves. We did not seek Ongroth's life, and we grieve for his widow and children. We would make reparation, if we are permitted.'

'Careful,' Obanji whispered. 'We surrender nothing.'

'Our blades are outside, and even if they were here, few if any of us would make it out alive,' Elindhu replied. 'There has got to be some give and take. Let's hear what they have to say.'

They watched the erling rulers confer, then the herald addressed them again. 'King Audebryn says that nothing can replace a life, except another life. Princess Fynarhea concurs. Queen Shuenagh says that even such a death gives nothing to dear Ungrit.'

The Queen gestured, and bulbous, obese Ungrit shuffled forward, her goblin children still in her arms. She looked miserably at Jadyn, tears trickling from her eyes and dissolving into the air.

'What would be an appropriate wergild?' Jadyn asked Elindhu. 'What would be acceptable?'

'There are no hard and fast rules,' she replied. 'Let them make the first offer. Remember, they love to bargain, and they won't want to start a vendetta against the Order.'

Heartened, Jadyn faced the thrones again. 'We wish to make recompense,' he said. 'Our mage, Elindhu, tells me that wergild is a concept known to you. It is known also in my land.'

In truth, the concept had died out in Vandarath centuries ago, when the Talmoni Empire swept the old ways aside.

As the herald translated, Jadyn asked Elindhu, 'What can we expect?'

'The things that matter to erlings are land, kinship and honour. They'll want to resolve this so that we're seen to be punished and suffer tangible loss. But they'll also be anxious to be seen as fair. Any contact with the outside world is risky for them. A harsh sentence risks retribution, a feud that escalates into war. So they'll want us to feel that what is decided is fair, too.'

He indicated the widow. 'Her "poor husband" almost killed Gram. Is her sorrow genuine?'

Elindhu gave him a disappointed look. 'Jadyn, these are sentient beings, capable of love. Yes, she's primitive and wild, but her feelings of loss are real.'

'Sorry,' Jadyn muttered apologetically. 'What sort of wergild is likely?'

'Primal things. They love gold, but blood and kinship matter too.'

The herald turned to face them again. 'King Audebryn says that honour and fairness demand that the widow be recompensed, not just in terms of wealth, but in terms of emotional loss. Queen Shuenagh adds that Ongroth gave her children, shelter, food and affection.

Princess Fynarhea notes that his children are now fatherless, and are traumatised at seeing his corpse, coated in blood. Death for death, life for life. The loss of Ongroth must be balanced.'

He means they want me dead. Jadyn licked his suddenly dry lips. *If I'm to die, I'll do it on my own terms.*

Then a thought struck him and he said, 'We too have suffered a death this night.'

The herald blinked. 'How so?'

'Our comrade was drinking at the pool – a man, not some herd creature suitable for prey.' He indicated Gram. 'He was not a meal to be hunted or trapped. And he wore tokens of friendship to erling-kind. Yet he was assailed, pulled under and drowned. His heart stopped. *He died.*' He indicated Romara. 'But this woman brought him back to life.'

The herald threw them an astonished look before turning back to the royal family and hurriedly translating. Elindhu listened intently, throwing in the odd correction. The hall fell silent – then burst into uproar, animal- and human-headed erlings chattering furiously, throwing wide-eyed looks at Romara and Gram.

The Erlking and Queen stared, their composure shaken, before firing anxious questions at the herald. Fynarhea was now staring at Romara, and Jadyn could see the wolf inside her was close to the surface.

The herald faced Jadyn again. Utter silence fell. 'King Audebryn asks by what sorcery this miracle was accomplished. Queen Shuenagh desires proof. Princess Fynarhea asks of the redheaded woman's lineage.'

Jadyn thought, then said, 'Please assure their Majesties that this was no sorcery, but a form of healing that can be taught, and used to save many lives. In terms of proof, we were clearly under observation while at the pool, so ask your own people what they saw. And as to the lineage of Siera Romara, she is a paragon of the Vestal Order whose honour is above reproach, as is her dedication to justice and truth.'

As his response was translated, the hall remained completely silent. The Erlking and his Queen bent their heads together, whispering anxiously, while Princess Fynarhea continued to gaze at Romara with fervent curiosity.

Abruptly, the King called the horned archer who'd tracked Jadyn's party to give account, which he did, regaling the avidly attentive erlings in their tongue. Afterwards, the royal family conferred in whispers, before instructing the herald.

The tusked man turned to Jadyn again. 'King Audebryn accepts that your man died at Ongroth's hands and has been revived. He desires this knowledge. Queen Shuenagh asserts Ongroth's right to protect his pool, and again reminds us all that he is the one who no longer lives. But she accepts that a suitable wergild should be found, especially if the art of reviving the dead can be taught. Princess Fynarhea reminds us that trespassers are not permitted here and that a blood-price remains unpaid.'

'May I offer a wergild for Ungrit, an explanation of the reviving technique and a fee for crossing your borders?' Elindhu asked Jadyn, her voice sharp. At his assent, she spoke to the herald, a stream of erling, then murmured, 'Fingers crossed. A death for a death repairs nothing. Pray they see that.'

Jadyn took a deep breath. *Elysia be with us.*

He had no doubt that his comrades would fight if required, but he was increasingly reluctant to do so. *If we all die, our quest fails. It's more important the quest continues than I live. If they demand my life, or to lock me up, as long as the others can go on, so be it.*

Finally the herald faced him again. 'King Audebryn sets the fee for crossing his border at one elobyne-tipped flamberge. Queen Shuenagh and Princess Fynarhea concur.'

Jadyn flinched. A Vestal knight's sword was his life, and they were sworn to guard them with all their being. He was about to tell Elindhu to contest this, when Romara spoke up.

'Agree to it,' she said flatly. 'I'll surrender my blade.'

Jadyn turned, feeling a stabbing pang in his heart. 'No, Romara, you can't—'

'I have to,' she replied flatly. 'It's killing me slowly anyway. It's for the best.'

'But we need you—'

'Not if I turn into a jagging vorlok, you don't.' Then her face softened. 'Please, I need this. I'm at the point of throwing it away anyway. I need to purge myself of glyma-energy and rebuild my life.'

Trying to imagine surviving this mission without her skill and courage was impossible, but he knew that look. She wouldn't change her mind, despite the agony of the decision.

'Is there a problem?' the herald asked curtly.

'No,' Jadyn muttered, his heart sinking. 'It is agreed.'

The herald bowed and made the next demand. 'King Audebryn sets the wergild for Ungrit in gold – every coin you have; that we might trade with the outside to her benefit.'

Jadyn flinched, but nodded. *Aura said the Eravandar region where Nilis Evandriel is hiding is a wilderness. We may not need coin there anyway.* 'I accept.'

'And to rectify the imbalance, we demand a life, not a death. One of you must submit to Ungrit and let her decide their fate: to wed her and take her husband's place, or to be her slave.'

He blinked. *'What?'*

Elindhu flinched, tried to argue and was cut off by a hand-chopping gesture. 'One life,' the herald snapped. 'The Erlking has spoken.'

Then the ogress Ungrit cooed, eyeing Jadyn thoughtfully and licking her lips.

He felt his stomach churn.

'That's nonsense.' Romara grabbed Elindhu's shoulder. 'I ask again, whose side are you on?'

Gram pried her hand away as Obanji and Soren reached for blades they no longer wore and Aura looked about wildly, seeking an escape route. But the Erlking's guards had closed in, baring teeth and blades.

'We run for the doors, regain our swords, and cut a way out,' Obanji growled softly. 'We have enough residual glyma-energy to make it. On three . . . One—'

Suicidal, was Jadyn's immediate reaction. 'No, I forbid it,' he interrupted. 'Fighting isn't an option. Elindhu, we have to explain our position to them. They may not understand—'

'They understand,' Elindhu replied, gazing stonily at the Erlking, 'but I can resolve this. Just give me a moment.'

Then she faced the thrones and said something peremptory in erling that silenced the whole room. She clearly expected a certain response, but the three royals – all sitting up now and staring – responded with questions. An angry interchange began, then Elindhu pulled a gold medallion from within her bodice, similar to that which the King himself wore.

Jadyn stared, puzzled, as the Erlking, looking outraged, rose to his feet and demanded something else. The warriors around him were clearly dumbfounded now, and even the surly princess was gazing wide-eyed.

'Ha quesa eri monassou?' the Erlking asked slowly.

'Monassou,' the herald repeated forcefully, though even he was wide-eyed. 'Monassou.'

'What does that word mean?' Jadyn asked, but Elindhu ignored him.

The Erlking was shaking his head as the herald said, 'Yava lai.'

It required no explanation: whatever Elindhu had wanted had been refused. She gave Jadyn a sad look. 'I'm sorry. They are still demanding a life, unless I do something for them. "Monassou" means "give us proof": I have made a claim which I must now demonstrate.' She gave him a sad look. 'Jadyn, all of you, I'm sorry. Please believe me, I am on your side and I always will be.'

They all stared at her, mystified.

Elindhu faced the Erlking again, straightened her spine and *grew over a foot*, while her wide, full-cheeked face became narrow and her beaked nose stretched. Her lengthening limbs became spindly, while her robes shifted around her strangely, too short now to cover her legs. Her grey hair came loose and fell down her back, all the way to her calves, now covered in deer fur. And her eyes turned amber.

There was no surge of glyma power, just a shifting of posture and rippling of skin, but to Jadyn it felt like she'd ripped the ground from beneath his feet.

'I am Crysophalae Elindhu Aramanach, Princess of Tyr,' she told the Erlking and his kin, in an imperious voice. 'I demand mercy for my human companions.'

Elysia on high! Jadyn thought in astonishment. *She's an erling too!*

Years of friendship and a mountain of trust built from shared dangers, laughter, meals and songs were ruptured by Elindhu's stunning revelation.

If Romara had had a weapon, she'd have buried it in this damnable *erling's* back. '*YOU MONSTER!*' she shrieked, as rage – all she *ever* felt was *rage* right now – boiled up and out of her. She thrashed in Gram's immense grip, almost breaking free, then reeled as he sucked away all the glyma-strength that was rising to her call.

'*How could you?*' she shrieked at Elindhu. '*HOW COULD YOU?*'

But as the glyma was pulled from her, her anger became betrayal and then sorrow, and she turned and buried her face against Gram's furs, so no one would see her cry.

Elindhu's new face – her true face – might have been austere and calm, but she was utterly furious with these *peasant royalty* who'd forced her to reveal the one secret she'd never wanted known.

She'd come here knowing it was a risk, but she'd been convinced she could resolve it behind closed doors, far from the eyes of her beloved Falcons. For the past ten minutes she'd been demanding that Audebryn Erlking give her a private audience, where she could pull rank over the *jagging upstart* and make him back down.

He'd refused – and now *everything* was in jeopardy – this quest, and these humans she'd come to love.

Her first need was to repair that rift before it became a chasm, and to do that she addressed Obanji, who should have been the commander, if the Order hadn't been so hidebound over class.

'Obanji, I have told you that erlings are physically adaptable. We can alter ourselves to fit our habitat: you've seen that, here and on Avas. The habitat I chose was *humankind* – your kind.'

'To infiltrate our Order and destroy us,' Romara said coldly.

'To protect my people,' Elindhu countered, her eyes on Obanji alone, because of them all, he mattered most to her. 'I'm not a vyr. I'm just one of the few erlings with the Gift. I've served the Order faithfully. No one has suffered from my work.'

'Which was?' Jadyn asked curtly.

She bit her lip, then said, 'To investigate Nilis Evandriel's claims.'

Jadyn winced and looked away. Around them, the erlings were staring, a sea of amber eyes and open mouths. Even the royal family had been stunned into silence.

She focused on Obanji again. 'The person you know, she is still here, standing before you.' Then, on a terrifying whim, she dropped to her knees before him. 'My neck is spindly and weak. Snap it.'

He gaped, then he gave her a helpless look and stepped away.

'Jagat! I'll bloody do it,' Romara snarled, as she rammed her elbow into Gram's kidneys and fought free of him, then she seized Elindhu's head to twist it, her eyes going bloodshot—

Then she let go, panting, 'You *lying* bitch, you *jagging* bitch. I can't do it, damn you—'

Then Jadyn stepped in, shielding Elindhu until Romara had been pulled away, then facing her. He had a pleading look on his face, as if willing her to be the person he thought she was. 'Do what you must,' he said, 'but you must answer to us afterwards. We have that right.'

Romara was glaring at the ground, hands on hips, trying to contain her wrath. Gram was kneeling, clutching his belly, and Aura and Soren looked bewildered. But it was Obanji she knew she'd hurt the most: her oldest friend. 'Falcons Eternal,' she said thickly. 'An erling's vow is forever. So is our friendship.'

The Abuthan stared, folded his arms over his chest . . . and looked away.

She wilted inside, but turned to King Audebryn and his family. 'Do you now accept my claims?' she demanded in erling, knowing she had no authority here except tradition.

But Tyr was the spiritual homeland of the erlings, and her father ruled there. She was pretty sure making an enemy of the High Erlking wasn't something Audebryn would have the nerve to do. She watched the haughty King and his shrewd, ugly Queen cringe, while the predatory princess lowered her eyes respectfully.

'We are honoured to receive you and your companions,' King Audebryn croaked. 'Welcome to Semmanath-Tuhr. We are at your service.'

'We trust you won't rescind the wergild for poor Ungrit?' the Queen squeaked.

Elindhu fixed her with a dire stare. 'Of course not. But Siera Romara keeps her blade, if she wishes. And there will be no slavery, no life for a life. I will have my father pay the widow's price. Meantime, I ask . . . no, I demand guest-right. You will provide us with food and an escort to your southern borders. Then we will leave you in peace.'

'Of course,' Audebryn said, in a hollow voice. 'But won't you stay, and bless our house with your presence?'

He didn't mean it: he wanted them all gone.

It was tempting to stay and rest, but that would risk Borghart bringing destruction to this whole kingdom. Though she was still angry with Audebryn, these were her kind, and they were precious few now.

'Our mission is urgent,' she told him. 'Regretfully, we must press on.'

The Erlking's relief was palpable.

Jadyn sat with his pentacle in a state of shock. They had been shown into a dining hall adjacent to the throne room and shut in, with guards watching over them, but they'd been given fruits, scones, and a honey-mead that was potent but good. Eating in this strange underwater environment was weird, but manageable once they'd got the hang of it.

Elindhu was away negotiating with the Erlking, which was a good thing, as none of them wanted her here right now. Whether or not her secret life among them had been as innocent as she claimed, they all felt betrayed to find such an integral member of their group was someone else entirely.

She'll never be one of us again, he thought miserably. *We've lost her . . . as we lost Ghaneen . . . and soon we'll be losing Romara. One by one, the pillars of my life are falling.*

If he'd been alone, he'd have wept, but he was commander, for now, at least, and he had to stay strong – Obanji and Romara expected it, and poor young Soren should see his role models displaying the virtues of the Order, not breaking down.

Even Gram and Aura need us to show some backbone – though we'll lose them too.

With an effort, he pulled himself out of the shock and misery and paid attention to his surroundings – which were incredible, a storybook come to life. The underwater castle took his breath away, with its flying fish and swimming birds and its uncanny inhabitants bustling about performing banal domestic tasks.

Romara was off teaching the toad-legged Queen and her healers how to resuscitate someone who'd stopped breathing. Obanji and Soren sat eating in silence, like good soldiers, and Aura and Gram were composed, though understandably anxious.

Then the door opened, and Princess Fynarhea entered, an unsettling figure with her wolf pelt draped over her shoulders. 'Sier Jadyn,' she said in her cold, clear voice. 'May we speak?'

Jadyn looked at Obanji, who said, 'Go. I'll keep an eye on things here.'

The princess led him out to the courtyard. Jadyn noticed that their weapons had been taken away, so the decision not to try and reach them earlier was more than vindicated.

'They will be returned once you reach the lakeshore,' Fynarhea told him, seeing the direction of his gaze. 'We keep our word.'

At her invitation, they swam-flew up the battlements, where he gaped at the view: the three moons were shining through the lake surface above, lighting up the large fish and crustaceans sharing the 'air' with diving birds, beavers and other animals, who'd somehow acclimatised to the lake's unique properties. It was, despite his tension, a miraculous sight.

'Elindhu said this was made by the aegis,' Jadyn asked. 'Did your kind do it?'

Fynarhea gave him an appraising look, which gave Jadyn the chance to do the same. The golden-eyed erling was unmistakably nonhuman. Younger than he thought, hard-faced but comely. Her voice had a deep, barely feminine timbre, which was now laced with regret. 'No,' she said, 'it was made for us, a long time ago, by the Sanctor Wardens.'

Jadyn rocked back on his heels. *The Wardens did this?*

'Aye. There is no "erling magic" other than our mutability of form. But some of us, like High Princess Elindhu, have your "Gift", and in bygone times, the Wardens were our friends, so it is said. That was centuries ago. But this lake remains, between two worlds. We don't understand it, but we have grown up with it.'

'But what is it?' Jadyn asked, marvelling that the aegis was real.

Fynarhea shrugged carelessly. 'I've heard the Wardens' power lived in a state of grace that enabled miracles.' Her haughty face took on a regretful look. 'Sadly, few of our kind had the intellect to learn it, and now the Wardens are gone.'

A state of grace, Jadyn thought, in hope and longing. The thought was fascinating, especially as Order theology taught that the Sanctor Wardens had turned to evil. 'Why did the Wardens fall?' he asked, wondering what the erlings knew.

'Fall?' Fynarhea echoed. 'They *fell* to a more numerous enemy. Our bards tell us they were hunted like boars, cornered and slain – by your Order. They were tortured until they confessed to "sin", then executed for those sins. Some sheltered with us, causing the Order to also assail our kind. Thousands of us died in the purge of the Wardens.'

It was as bad as Jadyn had feared. 'But why? What had they done?'

'They defied Jovan Lux, refusing to submit to his authority, in so doing becoming a rallying point to kingdoms that refused to bend the knee to Talmont. Therefore, they had to be broken.'

Jadyn sought reasons not to believe her, but none came. *I've been so proud to wear my tabard and badge. I've always thought it stood for the best instincts of our people.*

'So the Sanctor Wardens really are gone,' he said morosely.

'Long gone, and your Order destroyed every last vestige of them, so they could never rise again,' the erling replied. 'Every sanctuary was burned, every trace of them erased.'

'We were told they turned evil.'

'Those who slew them were evil,' Fynarhea replied.

It was a soul-destroying thought, but he was finding it increasingly hard to deny. 'How do you know all this?' he asked. 'And why are you telling me?'

She gave him a flinty look. 'High Princess Elindhu asked me to. She hoped it might have more credence coming from me than from her, as your trust in her is now broken.'

Aye, that it is, Jadyn thought sadly.

He turned his mind to something else troubling him. 'I've seen the way you look at Soren. You will leave him alone: is that understood?'

The princess gave him a wan look and he realised that for all her arrogant, assured strut, she was young. 'I didn't mean him harm. I've just never seen a boy with a face like his. Fire and ice meet in his body. I just wanted to talk. No one my age ever comes here.'

Jadyn eyed her suspiciously. 'He's an initiate of the Order. You'd do best to stay away.'

'Once, my kind ruled the world and any human would have been glad of our favour. Now we're pushed into the corners and forced to hide away . . .' She bowed her head and deflated, and all at once she was miserable as any young, confused person struggling to understand her world. 'I hate it here,' she blurted. 'We're living out the Erling Twilight like butterflies in cages. In all of Semmanath-Tuhr, there's only a dozen of my kind it's possible to hold an intelligent conversation with. Sometimes life feels *meaningless*.'

Jadyn looked around at the impossible lake and its miraculous inhabitants. 'Life is never meaningless, Princess. If you can't find a meaning for all this, you're not looking properly.'

Fynarhea looked at him, no longer menacing, just wretched. 'I've tried.'

He thought about how it must be to have a life constrained within a few square kylos, with only a tiny number of people to relate to, and felt a measure of sympathy for her. But her problems were her own to solve. 'There's a whole world beyond your borders,' he told her. 'Perhaps there's something out there that will give you what you seek?'

She gave him a quizzical look, then bowed her head. 'I thank you,' she said simply. 'I shall ponder your words.' Then she stepped off the battlements and floated away, leaving him to ponder his own words, because in them lay forgiveness for Elindhu, who'd looked outside her own world and found meaning.

Can I truly condemn that?

The Erlking made good on his promises, not just of supplies, but new packs far easier to manage than the saddlebags they'd been dragging along since losing their horses. King Audebryn also provided grey-green silken leggings and shirts, embroidered with beautiful erling knots and curlicues. Clearly Elindhu's status required him to be generous. Jadyn worried that the cloth was too distinctive, but as their own clothes were worn through and filthy, the erling garb was gratefully received.

Accompanied by the Erlking and his guards, Jadyn's party ascended to the lakeshore. The night had almost passed, the three moons westering, as they waded to the lake's edge, where a glowering Fynarhea waited with the leather packs, crammed with supplies and gear, and their weapons. They all re-armed gratefully, except Romara, and Jadyn saw the pang on her face, even though it was her decision to surrender her flamberge.

If Borghart catches us, she'll be helpless.

It was a terrifying thought.

However, in compensation for giving up her flamberge, Fynarhea unexpectedly presented Romara with a graceful erling sword, a curved tuelawar with an opal set in the pommel. The blade was etched with knot-work; its single cutting edge was sharp as a razor. Distraught though she was, Romara was clearly impressed.

Sunrise was an hour or two away, and Henina-Mons was only a

few kylos from here. The outside world awaited. So Jadyn set his jaw and went to the Erlking, who was conversing with Elindhu. She was in her erling form, taller and straighter than he was used to, a stark reminder of her secret life. But she was still coming with them, at least until they were out of here and could discuss the situation properly.

'Lord King,' he addressed Audebryn, 'we have trespassed and have caused suffering and sorrow. I apologise again for Ungrit's loss. We will not disturb you again, nor will we report your presence to the Order, but those pursuing us are camped on your border. I advise you to hide from them.'

'Our scouts have made me aware of those others,' Audebryn replied. 'A Vestal century, I am told. It makes us wonder why your own people hunt you, Sier Jadyn. Regardless of that, I declare your debt paid. You may leave in peace. Fynarhea will guide you to our eastern border and ensure that our wilder kindred do not hinder your passing.'

With that, the Erlking gestured, his retinue closed in and they all turned, walked into the lake and vanished. In moments the ripples had cleared and the mist-wreathed lake was tranquil, its secrets concealed again.

Jadyn turned to Fynarhea. Her hard, sullen face was inscrutable, and the uncanny wolf-cloak draped over her shoulders was a reminder of the danger she posed. Jadyn guessed that her guide-duty was penance for stalking Soren.

She gestured towards the right-hand side of the lake. 'This way. Follow.'

As they fell in behind her, Jadyn made a point of going to Elindhu's side, as much from curiosity as to shield her from the others. 'So, High Princess,' he asked awkwardly, 'what was that name you gave?'

'Crysophalae Elindhu Aramanach,' she replied. 'Aramanach is my family name. Crysophalae is a ceremonial name. Elindhu is my use-name, the one I chose myself when I came of age. So I will always be her.' With that, she closed her eyes and shrank into the familiar waddling duck body she'd always worn, and her grey braids knotted themselves into her towering bun again. 'Ah,' she sighed. 'That's much more comfortable. My *real* self.' She gave him an appreciative look. 'Thank you for not ignoring me, dear, but I need to talk with our guide.'

With that, she hefted her staff and went after Fynarhea.

Feeling a deep, uneasy sense of unreality, Jadyn fell back to join the others. Obanji looked upset, Romara was still hurling eye-daggers at Elindhu's back and Soren was watching Fynarhea nervously. Gram and Aura remained apart, but were clearly anxious.

Dear Akka, what a night.

'We're still alive, Falcons,' he reminded them, 'and the road lies before us.'

The Forbidden Palace

The Wives of God

The Hierophant is considered by his people to be a living god, and therefore he is above all laws, being the font of all wisdom, truth and justice. Such is the barbarism of these 'superior beings', Great Caliph. Therefore he may (among innumerable other privileges) marry as often as he wishes. Custom limits the number of wives to thirty, one for every day of the month, and ten each from Talmont, Zynochia and Abutha. Degrading though this is, the competition to have one's daughters wed to this despot is nonetheless murderous.

On Talmoni Rule, Inchalus Sekum, Scribe, Mutaza, 1468

Petraxus, Talmont
Summer 1472

Eindil Pandramion III, the Hierophant, God-Emperor of Talmont, sat upon the Throne of Water, an ornate confection of seashells from Erath shaped into a seat, the centrepiece of the barge that departed every night from the Royal Dock in Petraxus Harbour and was rowed half a kylo to the Forbidden Palace, on Toramon Isle, in the middle of the harbour.

It was a freezing, blustery night and not even divinity could shield him from the cold. But the traditions of Talmont were inviolable: his father had insisted that this daily inconvenience was a small price to pay for the privilege of ruling the known world.

But I am a god, his younger self had retorted. *Why should I endure any discomfort at all?*

His father had laughed, then thrown him overboard and made him swim.

And he wondered why I plotted against him ...

Cheered by the recollection, one of the few memories of family he had, Eindil endured the stiff breeze, watching the sun setting over the sea to the west, while the drummer drummed and the guardsmen rowed. Stentor Robias, his only companion, was lost in his own thoughts.

'Which wife is it tonight?' Eindil asked absently. It didn't really matter; he wasn't in the mood for physical congress with some empty-headed bint, anyway. Begetting children felt rather hopeless with the world ending around them.

Robias consulted his notes. 'The newest, Great One ... Countess Carmina Vantrew, she was. I think you renamed her ... ah, yes ... Queen Hippola, after the ancient Aquilani Empress.'

'Hippola ... Hippola ... ?' His memory refused to even give him an image.

'I believe she has planned something special for you.'

Eindil groaned. 'They *all* plan something special, Robias.'

The herald bowed respectfully. 'They do, Great One. Having only one day a month – at most – to impress you does make them somewhat desperate.'

'It's the desperation I despise.' Eindil yawned. 'Especially after a day like today.'

Coursers had arrived with unsettling news from all quarters: fires on the Western Peninsular following the loss of the isles; Kharagh nomads spotted near Denium; Foylish raids into Bravantia; and rumours of vyr enclaves in the Qor-Massif. And a renegade Vestal pentacle still at large. It had been a sour day before the Day Court, and the Night Court had been severe.

All I want is to sleep, not endure some girl's prattling, then damned well have to lie with her ... Surely forty-seven heirs is enough?

But all too soon, the barge docked, and he bade Robias, his only real friend, goodnight. Then he trudged wearily up the marble stairs, through the golden doors that boomed behind him, past the masked guards and myriad servants lined up to greet him, then up the seven flights of stairs that mirrored Jovan Lux's seven-day ascension to godhood.

Couldn't he have done it in three? Eindil groaned.

He finally reached the boudoir and stood, arms outstretched, for his chamber servants to remove first the cripplingly heavy Sunburst Crown, then his layers of silk, leaving him alone in sweaty undergarments, a bony man in his late sixties with thinning grey hair and a limp beard.

For a moment he felt pathetically mortal.

Then the next squad marched in, garbed him in evening robes of gold thread, put another abominable crown on his head, and finally he could move into his bed chamber.

I hope this damnable 'surprise' is that she couldn't be bothered showing up. No such luck.

Instead, he entered to banks of candles and two dozen violinists with conductor, playing Nirodan's 'Overture' – all sweeping arpeggios and overblown drama – while semi-nude dancers swirled silk sheets about in 'artistic' patterns. A drummer began to hammer at a trio of barrel-blasters; the racket from the wine-cask drums instantly redoubled his headache.

Then his latest wife emerged, performing what looked to be a Vandari sword-dance, and he felt his stomach curdle.

She was wearing a costume made of silver plates, a kind of fantasied armour that barely covered her breasts and hips, and she was striking poses with a ridiculously overwrought gold and silver sword, a child's fairy-tale version of a brutal instrument of war.

Worse, she'd had her hair coloured dark and made up her face with bronze, to appear Zynochi. He stared as she pirouetted and minced towards him, waving her fake blade and pulling determined, intrepid faces as she made her way towards him, shouting 'Take that!' and 'By Intropos!' She finished by going down on one knee, thrusting the sword skywards and ripping apart her bodice to display creamy breasts and cherry nipples.

'I am your Exemplar, Vazi Virago, come to serve you in every

319

way!' she declared, as the drummer and violins lurched to a deafening climax.

For a moment he couldn't quite comprehend what he'd just seen – then it struck him like a fist. '*You dare?*' he said into the resounding silence.

The stupid, *stupid* girl looked up at him, her face falling as she realised that she'd made an awful mistake. 'Great One – it's not my fault – my chamberlain—'

'Shut up,' Eindil snarled, suddenly alive with anger. 'You dare ape that which is sacred and holy? A woman who has dedicated her life to our realm – and you dare insinuate that she, holiest of holies, feels carnal desire? You filthy wretch!'

He stepped forward and backhanded the girl across the face, sending her to her knees. '*Who are you again?*' he shouted, spraying spittle in her face.

'Q-Que-Queen Hippola, your—'

'No! Your real name, wretch! Remind me of your family, so that they might share in your dishonour!'

'Uh, uh, Carmina Vantrew, Great One – Vantrew, I'm so sorry, it's not my fault – not my fault – not my—'

'Shut up!' Eindil whirled and faced the staring onlookers. 'Get out, all of you. Out! *Out!*'

The dancers and musicians grabbed their instruments and fled – but when the girl tried to run too, he seized her hair, almost tearing it from the roots, then gripped her throat and squeezed. He enjoyed her blazing panic, bulging eyes and thrashing limbs for a few moments, before loosening his grip on her windpipe, so she could breathe, a little. She wheezed desperately, tears streaming from her eyes and chest heaving.

Vantrew . . . Talmoni high nobility, obviously. Valuable allies, yes, but not indispensable . . .

He lifted her chin and let his eyes bore into hers. 'Carmina, do you understand your error?'

Clutching at her throat, she started babbling her apologies and denials.

He had to hit her to shut her up. 'I said, do you understand your errors?' he asked again.

'I don't,' she wailed. 'Everyone says how much you admire her, so I thought . . .' She broke down, sobbing helplessly.

Killing her would be like murdering a puppy. 'Get out,' he sighed. Then he thought about his options, because he never wanted to see this ridiculous clown of a girl ever again. But to release her from her vows was impossible . . .

Unless . . . He decided her fate. 'Come, I want to show you something.'

It meant another climb, up to the western tower, but without guards: this was a forbidden place, somewhere only the Pandramions, descendants of Jovan Lux Himself, were entitled to see.

At first she was afraid, but he told her he was no longer angry, that he was impressed by her devotion, however misjudged. 'Do this, and all will be forgiven,' he told her.

She was ridiculously grateful, though she didn't stop crying.

They arrived, at the open-topped circular pinnacle of the western tower, where he lit the brazier, then held the girl's hand. She was clad only in a white silk skirt and silver metal hip-mail; her milky skin was goose-bumped, her breasts shrunken with cold.

They didn't have long to wait. Suddenly a pale light blazed above, like a low-circling comet, and then that light came swooping in.

The girl gasped as a golden-skinned man with flickering wings of pure light and blazing eyes swept overhead, then banked and landed before them.

She squealed in awe and fell to her knees.

Eindil's own reaction was less excitable. He knew himself to be face to face with something beyond him, but he'd been promised a place among them, should he discharge his duties as Hierophant to their satisfaction.

'A Serrafim!' Carmina's face was alight with religious ecstasy. Her hands went to her breasts, trying to cover them, as the angelic being gazed down at her, its perfect face intent. 'Oh, *thank you*!' she exclaimed, thinking herself rewarded.

'Eindil,' the Serrafim greeted him, its voice deep, musical.

'Genadius,' Eindil replied, his voice catching.

The Serrafim examined the kneeling girl hungrily. 'Why have you brought her here?'

'She offended me,' Eindil told the divine being. 'I can no longer be married to her, so I surrender her to you.'

If Carmina understood at all, she gave no sign. She was utterly enraptured, captivated by the impossible being gazing down at her with mesmeric eyes, then offering her a hand.

She took it, and he pulled her to her feet. Then in a rush of wings they were both gone; her shriek broke off as she was ripped from the stone platform and borne up into the night sky. For a few seconds they were silhouetted against the stars, then they were gone.

Robias would have to write to her family in the morning, then sound out other noble families for available replacements. Eindil exhaled, and only then did he allow himself to relax. Then he began to shake.

What she did was intolerable, he reminded himself. *She mocked something sacred, and implied carnal desire lies between the Exemplar and me, something that could be used against both of us . . . She had to go.*

But to come so close to these beings was always a terrible thing, because he was never sure that the slightest misstep might not see him taken instead.

'Son, you must always understand,' his father had told him, 'that we, born to be Hierophant and rule the world, the highest of the high, are still subject to powers beyond us. Never forget that. We sit at the apex of a pyramid called Coros, the world we dwell upon, but there are greater pyramids still.'

'How do we deal with those higher powers?' he had asked, as he guessed his father must have asked before him.

'We bargain with them,' his father had replied. 'No matter how lowly we are, we have things they crave, which they can gain only through exchange. Give them what they need and take what they offer. Learn and grow.'

It was the final conversation Eindil had ever had with his father before Genadius Pandramion II died and ascended to join the Serrafim, the last words they'd shared.

Until tonight.

Part Three
ON THE THRESHOLD

14

Santa Cara

The Rise of the Vyr

Almost immediately after the Vestal Order was established, they had to deal with knights who lost control of the glyma and succumbed to violent urges. In 1218, the first true vyr arose: men and women with the Gift who gained the glyma outside of the Order's auspices and ran amok until put down. These incidents gave rise to the office of lictor, Gifted magistrates charged with rooting out heresy in all forms.

THE SHADOW HISTORY (BANNED), 1455

Eravandar, Neparia
Summer 1472

The predawn journey through the lower reaches of Semmanath-Tuhr passed uneventfully as Jadyn's group followed Princess Fynarhea around the lakeshore, then down a steep gully to the ruins of an ancient fortress. Not much remained other than a broken gate and crumbling walls surrounding the collapsed and overgrown inner bailey, a relic of a time when the erlings could openly protect their lands.

Henina-Mons rose stark before them, only ten kylos away now, at the tip of a spur of the Qor-Espina known as the Falagan Ranges. To the right, the plains of Neparia unfolded, a misty, gloomy expanse. The stream they'd followed down the erling valley had become a small river, which now veered into a gorge and emerged below, where it meandered out into the plains.

Elindhu and Fynarhea halted under the broken arch of the old fortress gates. On the flat ground outside, seven stakes had been rammed into the ground; the seven skeletons impaled on them had been picked clean long ago, a reminder of the latent barbarity of erling kind. Fynarhea gazed across the Nepari plains with a lost expression, then turned to Elindhu, exchanged some fluting words, then turned and vanished back into the forest.

One erling gone ... but what of the other? Jadyn thought. 'Elindhu, we have to talk.'

'This is not the place, or the time,' she replied. 'In two or three hours, Borghart's century will probably emerge here – we need to be well gone, without any trace.'

It was a fair point. 'All right, which way is Eravandar?'

'Is that way, behind Henina-Mons,' Aura said. 'Down, round, climb up. Hard way.'

'Borghart will ride us down in no time,' Obanji objected. 'We must hide until he goes past.'

'If he scries and finds us, we'll be trapped,' Romara commented. 'I can't veil now, and you're all low on elobyne energy. We need to find a shard.'

'There'll be none up here,' Jadyn replied. 'In Neparia, the only shards are in Order bastions.'

'If you've a moment to listen?' Elindhu interrupted drily. 'If we take the lowland route, we'll be overtaken, as Obanji says. Fynarhea advised me to stay in the heights, go around Henina-Mons by the northern flank and journey on east into Eravandar.'

It sounded like good advice, but Romara and Obanji gave him doubtful looks, while Aura groaned at the prospect of more mountains to clamber over.

'All right,' Jadyn agreed, 'get us into the heights and away from Borghart, then we'll decide what we're going to do.'

With a martyred sigh, Elindhu took them up a goat-track heading almost due north towards the heights; Gram, at the rear, erased any signs of their passing. They walked in silence, exhausted from continual danger and no sleep. Glyma gave the knights endurance, and Gram had a similar advantage, but Aura was clearly shattered, and finally, Jadyn drew on some glyma-energy himself, then picked her up. 'Hey, Peradura,' he smiled, 'let me help.'

She sank gratefully against his chest and closed her eyes.

As they climbed, the skies lightened to pale crimson until, despite the moons setting, they could see unaided. Each ridge was higher than the last, but Henina-Mons was drawing nearer. Then the sun rose, and Elindhu halted on a slope where they could still see the dark cleft at the southern end of Semmanath-Tuhr, just a few kylos away as the crow flies.

'If we pause here, we might see which road Borghart takes,' she said, planting her staff.

'We're in Neparia now,' Gram noted. 'Can those Solabi men cross the border?'

'They'll come,' Romara told him. 'The laws of close pursuit will be applied.'

Jadyn put Aura down and woke her, then joined the other Falcons in forming a loose half-circle facing Elindhu. He saw the same question on every face: *Who are you, really?*

She looked just as she always had, but now he knew what Elindhu was, he wondered how he'd never sensed her nature before. Surely her beak nose and oddly proportioned face, the hair that had a life of its own, should have told him?

He glanced around to see Obanji looking wistful and sad. Soren looked overwhelmed by what had to have been the most bewildering night of his life. Romara was obviously tense, her inner struggle against the glyma-rage there for all to see. Behind the Falcons, Gram lurked watchfully, anxious that this might undermine their journey. Only Aura, yawning, glassy-eyed and still half-asleep, seemed indifferent.

Jadyn found himself clinging to the hope that this could be resolved – he'd leaned on Elindhu's knowledge and skills too long not to care about her. But if she had other loyalties, she couldn't stay.

He inhaled deeply and took charge. 'Elindhu, please tell us now what you're doing with us. Then we'll tell you how we feel about that. After that, we'll take a decision to either accept your presence or to expel you from our midst. Do you understand?'

The erling faced them, her face regretful, settling her gaze mostly on Obanji. 'As I have told you, I am an erling of the royal family of Tyr. I was born on a reservation, where we struggle to wring a crop from worn-out soil. My people suffer from malnutrition and bury more than are born. The Talmoni garrison – men of the Vestal Order – have always mistreated us, badly. Whatever you have heard of how wonderfully well looked-after my people are is a lie.'

Jadyn saw Romara quiver, clearly wanting to spring to the defence of the Order, but as had become usual, Gram's touch on her arm quietened her.

'But we make do,' Elindhu went on. 'Children are smuggled out to be raised in the wilds, and some fake their deaths to escape. But we can't afford to disappear completely, for that would arouse suspicions. Places like Semmanath-Tuhr are rare, but we have other havens. It's a precarious existence, but we're adaptable in many ways.'

When she paused for breath, everyone was hanging on her words, even Aura.

'So,' Elindhu went on, 'I grew up and became female, the—'

'Sorry . . . what?' Obanji leaned forward. 'You *became* female?'

The erling coloured. 'Oh, yes . . . Erlings are born "rann" – what you'd call neuter – and can choose to be male or female when we reach the end of puberty. It's just the way we are. I found myself to be female, and became so. I can't go back, and I wouldn't want to.'

Jadyn had a thousand questions, but he was too stunned to speak. Judging by the silence, he was not alone. 'Uh, carry on.'

Elindhu looked round the circle apologetically. 'Anyway, my people found that I had the Gift, so I was smuggled out to Elidor, to live with a family of our kind who masquerade as human. Once I had learned how to do so too, my Gift was "officially" discovered and I joined the Order. I was never martial, so I became a mage and scholar. There were many frightening moments when I faced exposure, especially as, like any young person, I had to deal with sexual desire and relationships. I've had to hide behind a persona, repressing emotions and desires – it's lucky for me that the Order is full of people doing much the same.'

That's true, Jadyn thought, *we've all had to find ways to deal with chastity, lust and puberty.* He shot a sidelong glance at Romara, but she didn't notice.

'Eventually, the halls of scholarship became untenable,' Elindhu went on. 'I hit my limits as a scholar, and certain people were becoming far too interested in me. So I elected to become a field-mage and was assigned to the Falcons. The rest you know . . . except that I have come to love you all, in my emotionally stunted way. You're recklessly heroic and you look after each other in the most horrible situations. You fight for your humanity when all around you are losing theirs.' She wiped at her eyes. 'You have become my world.'

Her voice broke and she snorted wetly, wiped her nose and looked skywards, blinking fast.

Jadyn ran his eye around the circle. Obanji was staring at his feet, Soren was staring at the ground, Gram was watching Romara like a worried parent and Aura was wide-eyed.

'I have never betrayed my vows,' Elindhu went on. 'I have never betrayed the Order, or even met a vyr, until Gram. I am proud to be a Falcon. There's no pentacle like us. Most are filled with young people drunk on their own power who break their vows without remorse. But you're all good, decent people. You don't know how rare that is.'

That's because of Obanji, Jadyn thought, shifting his gaze to the older man with greying hair and lined face. *He came from the lowliest of places; it is he who keeps us humble and centred.*

Elindhu clearly agreed, her eyes fixed on her closest friend in the pentacle.

'So now I am revealed,' she said sadly. 'The Code says I must die, but I am not your enemy, and I don't want to die, or to be forced out. I believe in the journey we're on. Imagine, if we can uncover the truth about the elobyne, about the glyma and the vyr – and about the Sanctor Wardens and the aegis!' She spread her hands and said plaintively, 'Please, I want to stay with you. And maybe not having to hide my nature might allow me to contribute more.'

She fell silent and Jadyn found he had no idea what to say. Finally,

Romara raised a hand. 'How many others like you are there in the Order?'

'I've only ever known of two others,' Elindhu answered. 'One was trying to pass as a knight, but he fell to the rage and died. The other was another scholar, but we lost touch, years ago.'

'Has anyone else ever discovered your secret?' Obanji wondered.

'No, I'm good at blending in.'

He looked at her sadly. 'So you are.'

Silence returned.

'Very well,' Jadyn said heavily. 'Now we know. The question is, what do we do now?'

'If I were still in charge – which I'm not – I'd say that she has to go,' Romara said harshly. 'How can we trust her any more? She says our aims align, but do they? Remember, the Code says she should die. Expulsion is mercy, compared to what we should do.'

Jadyn bit his lip. 'Obanji? Soren?'

The young man was staring in fascinated revulsion, his mind clearly not just on Elindhu, but the menacing Fynarhea. 'We can't trust them,' he mumbled. 'They're not even human.'

Obanji lifted his head at that. 'Humanity doesn't equate to virtue, nor does the lack of it. The Triple Empire boasts that there is no war, but there's still cruelty, suffering and oppression, and a thousand other evils. I've known Elindhu for her entire tenure with the Falcons. She's been one of the best of us. If she says she's still with us, I believe her.'

Backing his friend, Jadyn reflected. *As I should back Romara . . .*

'Do I get a say?' Gram asked. 'And Aura?'

'No,' Romara snorted. 'This is pentacle business.'

'Oh, so we can help your quest but have no say in it?' the trapper flared.

'Yeah. Live with it, Vorlok.'

Gram went to argue, then thought better of it.

Aura just shook her head. 'All crazy. Not knowing. But this aegis . . . Floating and breathing water be beautiful.' The Nepari looked at Elindhu. 'You knowing aegis, si? Be it like glyma – only Gifted can do?'

Elindhu shook her head. 'I don't know for sure, but the records suggest that it's an entirely different Gift, another reason the Order turned against the Wardens.'

Aura nodded eagerly. 'Am *wanting* this gift.'

Jadyn looked around, but no one else had any questions. 'Well, Romara's put me in charge, and every day I wish she hadn't, but it falls on me to decide this.'

'It's already two to one that she goes,' Romara observed.

'We've never been a democracy,' he replied. 'Regardless, I agree with Obanji, and mine's the casting vote. Elindhu, you may stay. But you must swear again to uphold your vows. Everything you do, all that you learn, must be placed in our service – the Falcons' service.'

'For jagat's sake!' Romara growled. 'Make a hard decision for once, Jadyn.'

That hurt. 'I'm making one now.'

She stood, her face contorting angrily. 'No, you're bowing to sentimentality.'

'I'm doing what's right—'

'No you're not! You're too soft for that!'

For a moment, Jadyn's own temper flared, until Obanji interposed himself, saying, 'That's enough, both of you!'

For Jadyn, it was, but Romara flung up her arms and stomped away. He started to go after her, but Obanji grabbed his shoulder, muttering, 'Lad, give everyone a chance to cool down.'

That sounded like sage advice, so Jadyn took a deep breath. When Aura tried to approach him, he waved her away angrily. 'The last thing I need is your games,' he snapped.

The Nepari gave him a hurt look, then she too stamped away.

Great work, Farm Boy, Jadyn chided himself sarcastically. *Fine bloody example you are.*

Gram went after Romara – *of course*, Jadyn noted sourly – while Obanji spoke with Soren, his low voice reassuring.

All the while, Elindhu leaned on her staff, tears running down her cheeks.

Jadyn gave them all five minutes to cool down, then he walked back into the middle of the dell, drew his flamberge and planted the blade in the dirt. He knelt, gripping below the hilt, and said loudly, 'Behold this Blade. It is a *flamberge* – the flame-blade of Talmont – forged from Miravian steel by the master-smiths of Hyastar, and entrusted to me by the Hierophant himself. Through the grace of Akka, I am a knight of the Vestments of Elysia Divina, a servant of all. Ar-byan.'

They all looked at him, except Romara.

Then Obanji and Soren joined him, planting their blades as well. Elindhu placed her staff, too, and they made space for her. Gram and Aura watched with curious faces.

'Ar-byan!' his pentacle said together.

Jadyn pulled out his blade and raised his pommel to the sky. 'Behold the Orb, pure elobyne from Nexus, the sacred isle, gifted to humanity by Jovan Lux. Through its holy power, I am more than a man: I am a knight of the Vestments of Elysia Divina, a servant of all. Ar-byan.'

'Ar-byan!'

'I renew my pledge to wield this gift for Akka, for Elysia, for Talmont. May I serve faithfully and do honour to those who have gone before me. I am a Knight of the Vestments of Elysia Divina, a servant of all. Ar-byan.'

'Ar-byan!' the trio before him responded.

Then Romara echoed, in a broken voice, 'Ar-byan. Ar-byan ...' She fell to her knees, head down and wringing out tears. 'Ar-byan.'

This time Jadyn did go to her, knelt and held her shoulders. 'I'm sorry,' he whispered into her hair, inhaling her sorrow, trying to be the rock she needed. 'We'll get through this, I promise.'

'I don't even have a flamberge now,' she sobbed. 'I don't belong any more ...'

'You do,' he insisted. 'We're Falcons Eternal – that means for ever.'

She dissolved into his shoulder.

Then Aura called, 'Am seeing men at erling place.'

Jadyn caught his breath, squeezed Romara's shoulders once more before releasing her and hurrying to the ridge, where Aura was crouching, looking west. They dropped to their bellies to avoid being silhouetted. 'Get in close, all of you,' he snapped. 'Veils, now! Romara, stay close to me.'

The others joined them, even Romara, as they peered towards the distant mouth of the erling valley, four kylos away but still too close. Jadyn found himself beside Gram, who murmured, 'I created a false trail heading downslope before we left. Hopefully, they'll fall for it.'

They watched the distant dots milling about, holding their breath, waiting and praying . . . Then a scrying spell brushed their veils and they braced, knowing that if Borghart used whatever relics he'd used to find Romara and Aura, they'd be revealed. But it failed, and a few minutes later, the whole century of riders formed up and went thundering down the valley road.

'Godspeed you, Lictor,' Obanji chuckled. 'May your next stop be the coast.'

They all grinned in relief and rose to their feet. 'Ah, sorry about before,' Romara said quietly. 'This is hard for me, as I'm sure you can tell. I abide by Jadyn's decision,' she added, turning to Elindhu. 'Don't let us down.'

The mage bowed her head, in acceptance of the apology.

'Then let's move on,' Jadyn said, 'unless anyone else has any more big revelations for us?'

They looked at each other, then Obanji chuckled, 'Well . . . I don't want to shock you all . . . but I'm black.'

'Good grief,' Elindhu exclaimed. 'When did that happen?'

'Heh, it's contagious!' Soren mock-gasped, displaying his arm. 'Someone help me!'

'And I'm a redhead,' Romara offered shyly.

They all laughed hesitantly, as if the act was unfamiliar, but it had a healing effect, a gentle salving of the raw emotional wounds they'd just taken.

Jadyn let out a relieved breath. 'Falcons, let's move. The road lies before us.'

*

Eravandar, where Gram expected to find Nilis Evandriel, was still some fifty kylos east, but the rugged terrain would make it a hard journey of a week or more. In these heights, there were no settlements where they could resupply, just the occasional hunter's cabin. They would be lucky if the food gifted by the erlings would last that long.

The mountain paths Elindhu found were little more than goat tracks, marked by the occasional sigil every few kylos. They maintained veils, but when no more scrying attempts were made, they began to hope that Borghart had used up whatever personal effects he'd used to target Aura and Romara.

He's down to guesswork now, Romara thought. *Akka willing, we've lost him.*

The passing days were enabling her to calm down again, to find balance in the labour of travel, which was a relief. She'd begun to hate herself, especially the way everything that came out of her mouth was laced in vitriol, but as days passed and the residual glyma in her body ran down, she regained some normality.

Until that last fight on Avas, I was the clear-headed one. I was always in control.

One benefit was not having to rely so much on Gram draining the glyma-energy from her. She'd become too dependent on him, and she had seen where that would lead: *I become vyr, like him.* Even though at times he'd been the only one who understood what she was going through, and how to intervene, she had no desire to become such a thing.

The trapper kept hovering near her, which was hard, even though part of her ached for his companionship. She'd never believed a vyr could be a good man, but she respected, even liked him. He had a quiet solidity she admired, and his physical power undeniably stirred her. But he was a vorlok and doomed, so she avoided him.

It's Jadyn I love, she reminded herself. *He's the one I need.*

Even so, pride kept preventing her from apologising properly to him. She'd never known how to back down, so she ended up feeling completely alone, despite having them both so near.

On the fourth day out of Semmanath-Tuhr, they sensed they were nearing Eravandar, and in their haste, began to string out. Gram,

Obanji and Soren were guarding the front and rear, while Jadyn walked mostly with Aura and Elindhu. Romara could have joined them, but she hadn't entirely forgiven the erling's deception, so she mostly kept to herself.

That afternoon, Jadyn was deep in discussion with Elindhu, so Romara was left with Aura or no one. She'd have chosen no one, but the Nepari caught her up.

'E Cara, slowing, grafia,' she panted. 'Want asking . . . personal thing.'

'What? No, I'm not your friend!'

'Am serious.' Aura caught her arm. 'Am worried.'

Romara brushed her hand away, but slowed down. 'Worried about what?'

'Jadyn Knight.'

Romara fixed her with a stern eye. 'Jadyn is none of your business.'

'E Cara,' Aura tsked. 'Aura worry, for Jadyn love you, you no love him.'

'*What?*' Romara exclaimed. 'You've no idea what you're talking about.' She meant to shut up, but her temper led her to blurt, 'You know nothing. We have a lifelong commitment.' She thumped her chest. 'Two hearts, beating in time. Promises and vows kept for eternity.'

'Si, si, nice poem,' Aura snorted. 'But true love, you no having.'

And I wonder why I'm so jagging angry, Romara fumed. 'I know what true love feels like.'

'Si? So Virgin Lady has loved afore?' the Nepari said, peering at her intently.

'No!' Romara felt her cheeks sting with heat. 'Yes—! Uh, I mean . . .'

Aura pulled a face. 'Is not sure, Virgin Lady?'

'It's none of your business,' she said again, before erupting into a furious confession. 'But yes, I was in love; I was sixteen and infatuated with *jagging* Elan Sandreth and I *hurled* myself at him and he gobbled me up and spat me out, so I'm not a damned virgin and I know all about love!' Then she groaned, and buried her face in her hand. *Ah, jagatai . . .*

'Ah, so you think love is angry sexing,' Aura noted drily. 'Who be Elan Sandreth?'

'A piece of scum. You'd probably like him, you illiterate tongue-wag.'

Aura was offended, but not at the bit Romara expected. 'Illiterate? Aura Talmoni no good?'

Romara pounced. 'It's "Do I not speak the Talmoni language properly?"!'

'Too many word. Easier in Nepari . . . or other tongue. Aura speak many. You, just one. So who is stupido?'

'I'm not saying you're stupido – ach, stupid! But Talmoni is *precise*. You speak it like a child.' Romara bit her lip, then decided that having already spilled her guts once, she might as well get something out of it. 'Promise to learn Talmoni properly and I'll tell you about my pathetic past.'

Aura frowned. 'Talmoni slow. Dull.'

'There, you did it again. Say instead, "*The* Talmoni *language is* slow *and* dull."'

'Boring.'

'*It is* boring.'

'E Cara! I learn, promisa mia! You teach, I learn.' She jabbed a finger. 'Now, tell of man.'

'Only if you promise that we practise Talmoni every day. I can't stand the way you butcher it all the damned time.'

'Mmm . . . okay,' Aura muttered. Her eyes narrowed. 'Now, tell about man.'

Romara sighed, sure she would regret this, but she gave the Nepari a shortened, somewhat more chaste version of the tawdry tale of her and Elan. It was a tale of folly, but Aura was delighted by it.

'Essa so!' she exclaimed, clapping her hands. 'Have blood in veins, Knightess.' She cackled and patted her groin. 'Have juice. Is proper woman. Who knew?'

Romara winced. 'Aye. Now, repeat: "*It* is good. *You* have blood in *your* veins *after all*, Siera Romara. *You* have, er, juices, *and are a* proper woman."' She fixed Aura with a stern eye. 'Try again.'

A linguist she knew had told her that once you got one foreign language, others were easier, and the Nepari woman quickly showed a gift for it. They threw words back and forth as they traversed a long high valley, mostly stony ground and tussock, and the hours passed in a blur until finally it was dusk and they were arriving at that evening's camp.

'So,' Aura asked, as they entered the site, 'this Elan still make you juicy?'

'No, not any more,' Romara replied firmly.

'Knightess love Jadyn now?' Aura persisted. 'Is sure?'

'Yes, of course. He's like a brother to me . . .'

'Brother? You want sexing with brother?' Aura wrinkled her nose. 'Have heard such things of Talmoni, but did not believe!'

'Ach! No, you trollop! I'm talking about love, not lust. I wouldn't trade Jadyn for a hundred men like Elan.'

'Mmm, imagine, one hundred men—' Aura giggled. Then she gave Romara a hard look and added, 'Order be stunting emotions, Siera Romara. Forbid this, forbid that; makes strange, unnatural people. Cannot know true love in Order. You find non-knight, find happy.'

'*That's not fair*—' Romara began, but suddenly she was struck by a splitting pain in her skull. She lurched and almost fell. It was over in a moment, but she knew exactly what it was.

'*Jagat*,' she groaned, as the others, seeing her, closed in. 'Borghart just scryed me.'

The last bit of leather and hair bracelet crumbled to ash as Yoryn Borghart marked the direction the seeking spell indicated on his map and pondered the implications. They were on the plains of Neparia, near the coast – and almost at the point of giving up. But now all his usual certainty was returning.

I was right to hold back using that last piece of the bracelet until all other options failed, he reflected with grim satisfaction. *And now the chase begins again.*

Traversing Semmanath-Tuhr in daylight had been unsettling – they'd glimpsed distant silhouettes among the trees, and one man who'd ventured into the trees for a piss had been found with an arrow in his breast. But otherwise it'd been a safe and rapid passage. But now, four days later, they'd explored every road and path on the descent into Neparia and still failed to overtake their quarry.

'Well?' Elan Sandreth snapped. He, like Tevas Nicolini, had been growing grumpier by the day. Sier Rohas Uccello was also anxious to turn back: although the Vestal Order had licence to cross borders, there was no love for Solabi on this side of the Qor-Espina. The local barons had already confronted some of their men, and he suspected there had been complaints made to the local Order about this unwarranted 'invasion'.

'I've found them again,' Borghart told them. 'Northwest of here. They never left the highlands.' He tapped the map. 'They're somewhere in here, in the Falagan Ranges, at the edge of Eravandar.'

Sier Rohas sniffed. 'That's a wilderland.'

'I believe you: there are only three villages marked: Bassata, Santa Cara and Novoluno. We'll go from one to the other and soon unearth their trail.'

'If we can't find them there, I'm calling this off,' Elan muttered. 'We can't chase them for ever, however much we'd like to.'

'We'll catch them,' Borghart insisted. 'Better to say, "They can't hide for ever," Milord.'

'Hopefully, Eravandar is their destination,' Tevas Nicolini put in. 'Vyr thrive in rural backwaters like that.'

'Indeed,' Borghart agreed. 'They aren't simply running: they clearly have a purpose, engendered by whatever they learned in their illegal interrogation of Gram Larch. Eravandar is the key, I'm sure of it. We'll find them there.'

On the fifth morning since leaving the erling valley, Jadyn's group reached Eravandar. They were travelling in rarefied air on paths that snaked above precipitous drops, affording spectacular views of jagged peaks and stark, rugged valleys. They passed a few poverty-blighted farming settlements with thin pastures and straggling crops, with barely a cart track to link them to the wider world. The sense of isolation was pervasive, embodied by the howls of a lone wolf they'd heard calling for the last three nights, plaintive and haunting.

Despite that sense of being alone in the world, they travelled fast, fearing Borghart's men might appear at any moment. Gram scouted, while Jadyn, Obanji and Soren took turns in the rear. The women kept together, and Aura practised her Talmoni on anyone who would listen. She was a fast learner, with surprising persistence.

She can be irritating, Jadyn mused, *but I'll miss her company.*

Around midday, they reached a plateau beneath an old ruined hilltop castle. 'This was an erling fortress,' Elindhu said sadly. 'A clan retreated here, then died out. The song "Falasa Ruung" tells of its fall.'

It felt like the loneliest place in the world, but as they crossed the plateau, they heard a bell chiming. They reached a small ridge and found themselves overlooking a cluster of huts and a tiny whitewashed church to Akka, set in a small gully beside an all-but-dried-up stream.

Aura indicated a clay milestone with a name etched into it. 'Here be Santa Cara.'

'Here *is* Santa Cara,' Romara corrected.

'Si, that,' Aura agreed, her eyes on Jadyn. 'Am learning good, si?'

He grinned warmly. 'Yes, you are learning well.'

For some reason, she blushed. 'Have nice smile. Shame not real man.'

'*It's a* shame *you're* not *a* real man,' Elindhu clarified drily.

Gram, Obanji and Soren barked with laughter, and even Romara snorted under her breath.

Colouring, Jadyn gestured curtly. 'Shall we go on?'

As they headed down the slope, they noticed figures shadowing them through the tangled olive trees and thorny bushes. Jadyn slid his hand over the pommel of his sword, conjuring a ward. All their elobyne crystals were nearly drained, another anxiety with no shards in reach.

We've only got a few days before we'll be unable to veil, then Borghart can track us with impunity. Only thick stone or wide bodies of water could protect them then, and he had no desire to spend the rest of his life hiding in caves and cellars, or seeking a home on the far side of the Southern Seas.

Nudging his horse into the lead, he led them down the slope towards the broken-down huts at the edge of the village, a handful of buildings huddled against the rocky slope. It looked abandoned – but only temporarily, for the ground was scuffed and some chimneys still smoked. Aura called out in Nepari, repeatedly using the word 'paz' – *peace* – but no one responded, and her voice echoed thinly and faded into a watchful silence.

They drew weapons, and entered a dusty square where a tavern and the church confronted each other over a well. Both were weathered old buildings with shut doors and closed shutters. No one appeared as they went to the well.

Obanji tossed the bucket down, then began to haul it back up, filled with water. They refilled their water-bottles warily, facing outwards and alert for trouble.

'Now what?' Jadyn asked Gram.

The trapper looked round, then grunted, 'That way.' The path he indicated ran west out of the square, towards a brush-filled gully, as good an ambush site as Jadyn could have picked.

'How do you know?'

The trapper hesitated, glanced meaningfully at Romara, then pointed out a small cross-hatch pattern etched onto a wall. 'That's a secret vyr mark.'

Jadyn realised that this was a considerable show of trust, primarily in Romara. It was uncomfortable to see Gram's bond with the woman he loved, but he couldn't complain, knowing Romara's unease at Aura's attachment to him.

Outsiders complicate our feelings for each other, he admitted to himself.

Gram took the lead, flitting through the narrow gap between the buildings and along the path, between steep bracken-covered slopes. They were all on high alert, but no one erupted from cover to assail them. They reached an overlook, then descended to a small stream, shadowed by occasional glimpses of people in the bush on either side, though nothing more than silhouettes.

Where the stream emptied into a small pond, they found an open space before a tiny hut with a veranda and a thatched roof. Chickens pecked at the dust and a big dog lay in the shade. It rose when it saw them, standing tall as a pony: a Nepari bear-hound.

'Agynea?' Gram called.

The door of the hut opened and a spindly old woman in a dun smock emerged. Her waist-length silver hair was hanging free. Her face was wrinkled but she moved nimbly, quelling her hound with a word before calling, 'Gram Larch, I prayed you got out.'

There were tears on her cheeks as she came to meet and embrace the trapper, who picked her up and squeezed hard. Then he reverently placed her down and knelt. 'Forgive me, Agynea, but Mother is dead.'

She kissed his crown. 'I know, child. I felt it.' Then she looked up and her gaze pinned Jadyn through. 'I saw you, Jadyn Kaen. I saw you all.' Her Talmoni was flawless, with the softest Nepari accent. Then she inclined her head to Elindhu. 'Magia.'

Jadyn felt a chill, wondering how she knew them. 'We did our duty,' he said throatily.

Her hard face softened. 'Aye, you did as you thought you must. Fritha lost herself, at the end.' She glanced at Aura, frowned, then returned her gaze to Jadyn. 'Why has our disciple Gram brought you here?'

Conscious of listeners in the trees, he answered, 'We come in peace, to listen and learn. Gram has promised that you will enlighten us as to the nature of elobyne, and the crisis we face.'

Agynea pondered that, stroking the kneeling Gram's brow like a mother with a child, then she said, 'Well then, join me for tea. We have much to discuss.'

Agynea's hut was barely big enough for her cooking pit and cot-bed, let alone visitors, so they sat outdoors, cross-legged like pupils around their tutor, except for Soren, who volunteered to stand guard over the horses and watch the path.

The old woman brewed tea, letting the herbs simmer while Gram told her more of the death of his mother, the evacuation of Avas, and most importantly, of the illicit interrogation.

'I heard enough to make me question what I knew,' Jadyn put in. 'I'm not convinced – that will take real proofs, which is why we're here.'

'You've sacrificed much to be here, I'm sure,' Agynea replied. 'The Order doesn't allow renegades to escape if they can do anything at all to stop them. I know that.' She smiled ruefully. 'I've been in your shoes. The bastion that found my Gift – Tar-Borine, near Vantium – had a culture of abuse against women. When I fled, I was hunted like a criminal.'

Jadyn had heard the tale: a thirty-year-old scandal that the Order had clamped down on ten years too late. More than thirty Gifted young women had suffered under a misogynistic grandmaster and his cronies, if you believed the rumours.

'Tar-Borine was an aberration,' he muttered. 'An exception.'

'I doubt there's a single woman in the Order who hasn't faced similar,' Agynea replied.

Romara went to retort, then pulled a sour face and looked away. Beside her, Elindhu nodded sadly. 'Any time a man has power over a woman, the risk is there,' she admitted. 'But I doubt the vyr are different.'

Agynea ducked her head in acknowledgement. 'Of course. Basically, you knights and we vyr are more or less the same: we have a Gift that enables miracles but it can also destroy us. We are tapping into the same source of power and we walk the same ledge between control and madness.'

'We all know that – yet somehow, we're decent human beings and you're all monsters,' Romara retorted.

Agynea faced her. 'Not monsters. *Wild*. The nonhuman aspects we take on when in the grip of the glyma are an unconscious manifestation of what wildness means to us.'

'But your kind embrace the madness,' Obanji replied.

'We do,' Agynea replied evenly.

'Agynea, tell us of the vyr, please?' Jadyn interjected, before this became a circular debate.

She looked around the circle. 'There are, as you know, two kinds of "vyr". There are those who have no Gift, what you might term "ordinary" vyr. They can be anyone, but once they've been initiated into a vorlok's coven, they gain a measure of supernatural strength and ferocity, and some shape-changing ability.'

'What does this initiation entail?' Jadyn asked.

'Drinking a mix of powdered elobyne and the blood of another vorlok,' Agynea replied, confirming what Borghart had said during the hearing, back at Port Gaudien.

'But our leaders are like you: people with a little flame inside them, the so-called "Gift". It's a danger to the untrained, so must be mastered. In your Order, you're trained to use it with discipline, exorcising your emotions lest the power becomes self-destructive. You gain superhuman power – for a time – but when your control finally lapses, you must forsake the elobyne and relinquish the Gift. Some can't cope, and those your Order kills.'

'Veterans of the Order are given land, and our brothers and sisters support us back into the community,' Obanji replied. 'We are honoured for our service. The Fallen are few.'

None of them looked at Romara.

'True enough,' Agynea agreed. 'So, back to the Gifted. To those who manifest it, it feels like a maelstrom – that's still the word you use, yes? In the Order, you're taught to centre yourself, inside the whirlwind and take control of it.'

'We call it the Eye of Silence,' Jadyn put in.

'Yes, that's right – though I never reached that state,' Agynea replied. She leaned forward. 'What your Order doesn't tell you is that your Eye of Silence is *not* the only way to master the maelstrom. In fact it's the most difficult, though it rewards you, if mastered, with the firmest control and greatest mastery, though not the greatest raw power. But many Gifted people aren't capable of such mental discipline, and there is another way.'

'What other method of control can there be?' Obanji asked, for them all. The Order taught that the vyr had no control at all.

'To hurl yourself into the maelstrom, be swept along by it and allow it to take you whither it will,' Agynea replied. 'We ride the

345

Maelstrom, and become ephemeral, without self. It is a far more perilous ride, in which berserk madness threatens to unhinge us, but it rewards those who harness it with more power, because we ride the wind instead of resisting. This is why a vorlok is individually stronger than one of you knights. It is also why we are more plentiful than you: it is an easier path to take, though harder to survive. Most vorloks and draegar never reach true mastery, and even those who do might lose it and burn out in a few years, whereas you aspire to at least a decade in service, and emerging sane.'

'But you seem to have survived a long time,' Jadyn noted. 'How?'

'Through brains and beauty,' she replied drily. 'The mastery I spoke of: those of us who confront the extremes of power can reach what we call *ninneva*, a state of grace, where the madness doesn't affect us any more. I found it, as have many others.'

Jadyn's skin prickled. Just a week ago, Fynarhea had described the aegis as a 'state of grace'.

Is this the same power? he wondered. But he found himself rebelling against her explanation. 'You're saying you're in a state of grace, when your vyr are burning houses, farms, land? According to Gram, the fires are lit to destroy the elobyne shards – but it's costing thousands upon thousands of lives, and incalculable losses to property and wellbeing.'

'Exactly,' Romara added. 'Don't tell us you're some kind of superior being.'

The others, even Elindhu, nodded in agreement.

'If you and others have reached this "ninneva", then why haven't you come forward and ended this war?' Obanji asked. 'Why haven't you stopped this destructive rebellion and found a way to resolve things peacefully?'

Agynea *tsked*. 'Ninneva is a state of mind, not a military rank – you're assuming those of us who have attained it control the vyr movement. We don't.'

'You might not control them, but you're not stopping them,' Romara said.

'How would you know?' Agynea fired back. 'We few who have

attained ninneva are very active in trying to minimise the cost to people and property, but we don't control the vorlokai who haven't attained such a state – in fact, they reject us as pacifists. They have their own leadership, who are as fanatical as your Order.'

'How many are you?' Romara asked. 'You "special" ones,' she clarified sarcastically.

Agynea shrugged. 'I really don't know. We are few, we are secretive and we are mortal.'

'But why not come forward?' Jadyn asked. 'You could guide so many more if you worked *with* the Order.'

'You think we haven't tried? My husband spoke for us all to the Archon himself, twenty years ago. The Archon betrayed him, broke him on the wheel, forced him to confess to monstrous crimes, then burned him.'

'I've not heard of that,' Jadyn told her.

'If it happened,' Romara added.

Agynea gave her a hard look. 'It happened. The Triple Empire wants to maintain total control of the glyma and elobyne, and your Order mandates only one way to use it. Any who fail to find your Eye of Silence are put to death. You kill more of your own than we do.'

Even Romara didn't deny that assertion.

'So, given that you, like us, use elobyne, why are you trying to be rid of it?' Elindhu asked.

'Because without it, there is no empire, and no superior beings crushing the rest of us,' Agynea answered. 'The glyma creates a magical elite, and elites create tyranny. Without elobyne, there would be no Hierophant, no Order, no empire. Every nation would regain self-rule and self-determination, and we'd no longer have the elobyne destroying the ecology. But really, you need to speak to Nilis Evandriel of such things. He is more eloquent than I.'

'What did he say that convinced you of his veracity?' Obanji asked shrewdly.

Agynea considered, then said, 'Two things. One is the claim that the Ages of Fire and Ice form a cycle, revealed by the strata of soil and stone and caused by cyclical movements in the cosmos, giant super-seasons that last for decades or even centuries. He discovered that if this was an Age of Fire, it's come almost a century *too soon*. That should be impossible. Stars and planets don't change their orbits. His conclusion is that today's disruptions are nothing to do with the cycles of Fire and Ice.'

This was well beyond Jadyn's comprehension, but Elindhu was nodding thoughtfully. 'And the second thing?' she enquired.

'Nilis explained that all energy has to come from somewhere. The Order claims that the shards gain energy from orisons, and yes, mass ritual prayers do contribute power – by treating people as fodder. But you also can see, if you observe over time, that the shards take energy from the soil and water and vegetation around them, turning once-lush land into barren wastelands. I've seen this for myself in Bravantia where I grew up. The shards take from everything and everyone, in far greater amounts than is sustainable.'

Jadyn thought about the triple stands of shards he and Aura had seen the Lighters planting in the Solabas forest, and the effect it was already having. Dispiritingly, Agynea's words rang true.

'But if the Order knew it was destructive, they'd seek another way—' he began.

'Oh, they know,' Agynea interrupted. 'But no one surrenders the sort of power they have. And your elites don't care, believing themselves safe even if half the world does become a dustbowl. They all know about it.'

'None of that's true,' Romara protested. 'Our scholars have proven that elobyne is safe.'

'No, they've only *told* you it's safe, and you've *chosen* to believe them. They've proven nothing, because they can't. Nilis Evandriel, the leading scholar on the subject, broke ranks and was vilified, demonised and condemned. Elobyne is propelling us towards global catastrophe, and the stakes are too high for anyone to remain passive. The Hierophant and his conspiracy of Talmoni, Zynochi and Abuthan lords are destroying our world. They must be stopped.'

'If this were so, we would know,' Obanji said.

'Would you? You just do as you're told,' Agynea sniffed. 'Your

Order will never admit the truth, because the shards are the basis of your power. These things *are* linked. They *are* cause and effect. You *have* to see this—'

Her passion was clear, and the evidence Jadyn had seen – especially the triple shards in rural Solabas – had him half-convinced. But he'd also spent years battling the vyr, who'd committed atrocities of their own. Looking round the circle, his impression was that his comrades felt more or less the same, with the exception of Romara, who seemed to be in denial.

'We need proof,' he told Agynea. 'We need to speak with Nilis Evandriel ourselves, find something we can put before the highest courts.'

'He's the most wanted man in the world, and you're a pentacle of the Order,' Agynea replied. 'You're the last people I should send his way.'

'I vouch for these people,' Gram said unexpectedly. 'They listened to me when no one else would. They broke their vows to come here. And I've travelled with them and seen personally how committed they are to finding out the truth.' His eyes went to Romara. 'Yes, they can be headstrong, but they are good people at heart. Words like truth, decency and honour really matter to them. Their desire for understanding is honest.'

Everyone looked at the trapper with varying degree of surprise and gratitude.

'Well,' the old woman said, after a long pause, 'how could I deny my dear Fritha's son? If you are willing, I can send you on to Master Evandriel.'

It was the breakthrough they needed, and Jadyn sagged in relief. 'Is he here?'

'No, but he's not far, either,' she replied. 'He went to seek Vanashta Baanholt.'

Jadyn quivered at the legendary name, which Gram had also referred to recently. 'Aye, we've heard of it: it's where the tales say the Sanctor Wardens received the aegis.'

'E Cara,' Aura exclaimed, 'place for learn of aegis, si?' She looked ready to set out at once.

349

Since Semmanath-Tuhr, she'd been avidly attentive whenever the aegis was mentioned. Jadyn remembered her dancing in the lake and her expression – one he'd seen on the faces of thousands of young people wrongly convinced that they had the Gift. When they failed the tests, they were always devastated, sometimes even suicidal.

I'd spare you that pain, he thought sadly, *for it might break you*. In any case, all the legends suggested the Wardens were even stricter than the Order. *A life like ours isn't for you, Aura*.

Agynea was also reading the Nepari like a book. 'Well, Nilis thought it real, dear, but no one knows how the aegis was attained. He had some hopes that clues he'd uncovered might lead him to Vanashta Baanholt, and if I'd been younger, I'd have gone with him, but alas, I am well past such journeys. The paths he proposed taking are not for the faint-hearted.'

'Please, we must find him,' Jadyn said. 'Wherever he's gone.'

Romara's head dropped and her fists clenched.

Agynea hesitated, then stared Jadyn in the eyes. 'You swear on all you deem holy that you will not assail him?'

'I do so swear,' he said firmly. 'I vow it, on my pentacle's behalf.'

Obanji nodded, then Soren, listening from his vantage, did, and Elindhu followed his lead.

But Romara said, in a cracked voice, 'Jadyn, can we talk? Just you and me?'

The quest was about more than just Romara and him, but he couldn't refuse. He looked at Obanji and Elindhu, and when they indicated approval, he took Romara to the edge of the clearing, where they sat in the shade of an old olive tree as gnarled and tangled as his thoughts.

He sensed people watching – the villagers, who had to be Agynea's coven, hiding on the slopes above. The sun was still high in the sky, illuminating the glimpses of snow-covered peaks above them. The stark grandeur of the landscape reminded him of central Vandarath, his homeland. He missed it, suddenly, and wondered if he'd ever see it again.

'Well?' he asked.

Romara looked worried, but for him, not herself. 'You believe her, don't you?'

'I have an open mind.'

'So do I,' she replied, although she was self-aware enough to pull a face. 'I'm here, aren't I?'

He met her gaze frankly. 'You're here out of loyalty.'

'Aye, and so what? You've been unjustly branded a heretic and that's not fair. But this quest will kill us all. Please, put it aside – even if it is true, put it aside. We get one life, one chance for a few years of happiness – we deserve that. Let someone else untangle this damnable mess.'

Jadyn took her hands. 'I can't – not now I know that the aegis was real. I think Evandriel's like me: a victim of elites who'd rather crush the truth than deal with it. But until I find him, I'll not know, and I can't live with that. So I'm going on.' He swallowed. 'You don't have to come – in fact, you *shouldn't*, not now you've put aside your flamberge.'

'No – no, please . . . we've earned our slice of peace, haven't we?' She gripped his shoulders, stroked his cheek. 'I want us to build a life together . . . maybe even . . .' Her voice trailed off for a moment, then she blurted, 'Maybe we could even have a baby . . . ?'

The enormity of her words was like a physical blow: after ten years of unspoken regard, without so much as a kiss to make their feelings tangible, here it was, an open admission that she wanted *him*, and a family. Her face was yearning, her eyes beseeching, and all he wanted was to hold her for ever, to give her everything she wanted.

While the world burns.

He hugged her tight, whispering, 'Rom, I have to do this. I have no choice.'

'*I love you*,' she said plaintively. 'You know that, don't you? I *love* you.'

'I love you, too, with all my heart. But I still have to do this. It matters too much – not just to me, but to the world. I'm sorry.'

Feeling like he was slamming a door in her face, he released her and returned to Agynea's circle, hoping Romara would follow.

But she gave a choked little cry and walked away.

Agynea's wizened face was inscrutable. He wondered more about her 'ninneva', and whether, despite her state of grace, she'd ever killed for her cause. But he put that aside for now.

'Please, tell us how to find Nilis Evandriel, and we'll be on our way.'

Romara gazed bleakly at Jadyn's back, praying she hadn't placed too much stress on their relationship. *Never use the word 'love'*, she chided herself. *Men can't handle it.*

He'd come around, she was sure, realise his quest was futile and abandon it.

I just have to wait.

In the meantime, everyone was avoiding her like she was an irritable snake trying to shed its skin. *Which is more or less what I am*, she reflected.

Agynea wasn't able to give them any supplies – the village was horribly poor, a hand-to-mouth place where nothing could be spared – but she gave them directions to a circle of standing stones, which Nilis Evandriel believed contained clues about Vanashta Baanholt. Beyond that, she knew nothing.

Romara found herself hoping it was a dead end.

On leaving, Jadyn warned Agynea that they were still being followed by Borghart's men, and urged her and her people to hide. 'They may be only days away.'

'My lungs have gone and I'm too old to go gallivanting about,' she said calmly. 'I'm not going anywhere.'

'Then you'll die here,' Romara told her, meaning to shock her into reconsidering, but the vorlok – or whatever she was now, in her 'state of grace', refused to budge.

'I will pray to Elysia for you, child,' she replied. 'What demon does that?' Then she turned to Elindhu, saying, 'I'm glad that one of your kind has finally broken ranks to seek the truth. You give me hope for us all.'

That was disturbing, given no one had told her what Elindhu was.

They left early, hopeful of reaching the standing stones before dusk, but the paths grew steeper and Agynea's directions became increasingly difficult to follow as low cloud closed in, obscuring the landmarks she'd described. Temperatures dropped, their breath started to steam and their cloaks began to feel inadequate. All they could do was follow the trail.

The knights, being northerners, endured the thinner, colder air easily, as did Gram and the supremely adaptable Elindhu, but Aura was suffering, her lively face the picture of misery. Jadyn, as always, took it on himself to help her.

It's just his usual misguided chivalry, Romara told herself.

But she felt like she was losing him. Perhaps it was just the bleakness of the mountains seeping into her bones, but she felt increasingly doomed. Nilis Evandriel was a madman and Jadyn was crazy to seek him. Her dearest hope, that he'd abandon this foolish quest and finally place their love at the centre of his life, kept being snatched from reach. *I wish we'd never fallen in love*, she admitted to herself. *It's only ever been a torment.*

'Are you all right?' Gram drew alongside, striding like a man born to the wilds.

'What's it to you?' She wouldn't have him thinking he could treat her like a weak, fragile girl. Then she felt ashamed of her temper and added more gently, 'I'm fine. Honestly, not constantly drawing on glyma-energy is good for me.'

'Mmm, I'd noticed how tranquil you are these days,' the trapper said drily.

'Sarky! You're probably pissed off that you won't be able to leech glyma off me any more,' she added, wanting to needle him. 'You'll have to find someone else for that, soon.'

'Who else would be so amenable?' he said, with a crooked smile. 'Seriously though, it doesn't work like that. If Borghart comes, we'll need to stay close and protect each other.'

'I can look after myself. And I'm done with the glyma.'

'If neither of us ever needed that power again, I'll be as happy as you. But in the meantime,' he repeated, 'if something happens, we'll need each other.' He seemed genuine.

'Fine,' she conceded, and her defensiveness deflated. 'Sorry, I'm just on edge. Trying to adjust to life without the glyma isn't easy.'

'Maybe at the end of this we'll find Vanashta Baanholt and all gain the aegis and our worries will be gone.' He actually sounded a little wistful.

She gave a derisive laugh. 'You do know the Wardens all turned evil or went mad, right? There'll be no happy ending that way, I can tell you that for sure.'

'Ah, it's your relentless optimism that keeps me going,' he chuckled.

'You're talking to the wrong person: Jadyn's the optimist, I'm the realist – that was always how we worked.' She glanced at her Farm Boy, a few dozen paces ahead, and found herself saying, 'Aura tried to tell me earlier that growing up in the Order has left us incapable of love.'

Gram's face became unreadable. 'How'd you feel about that?'

'Akka on high, you need to ask? We would die for each other!'

'Aye, you would. You're as closely knotted together as any group of people I've seen. But you all live on the edge of your tempers, you snap and bite, you can barely bring yourselves to apologise, and you all know that eventually you'll fail. It's not easy to endure.'

'It's a crucible – it makes us stronger. That's what the Code tells us.'

'Maybe,' Gram answered. 'But honestly, I think when your service ends, you'll need the help of someone with a more normal upbringing to cope with normal life – maybe not as a husband, but certainly as a friend.'

She stared up at him, confused and then angry, because she knew that he desired her, so his advice was suspect. And Aura had said much the same thing, so his words were double-damned.

'Even if you're right about that, I wouldn't seek out a jagging vyr to help me cope!'

She was spoiling for a fight, but Gram just dropped his head, mumbling something apologetic, and slumped away, leaving her feeling every bit the bitch Aura kept telling her she was.

Jag this, she groaned. *Damn it all.*

Abruptly she wanted to apologise to everyone, but she didn't know how to. Everything she said or did was wrong; she felt like she was caught in quicksand, her every movement sinking her deeper into the mire.

15

To the Stones

Why the Aegis Myth Persists

Some myths fade; others become part of the cultural tapestry. One such is the aegis, the alleged magic of the Sanctor Wardens. Though disproven by imperial scholars, the tale persists. Why? Because we need to believe in a fabled past to soften the misery of the present.

TORMAN GUDURSSON, SCHOLAR, HYSK 1458

Falagan Ranges, Neparia
Summer 1472

The afternoon passed in an exhausting climb above Eravandar Vale into the Falagan Ranges. Each new slope was harder than the last, as the thin soil and vegetation gave way to bare rock and the icy wind, leaving all of them shivering, except Elindhu.

She's adaptable, Obanji thought miserably, *like the chameleon lizards of the Pelas Isles.*

It still hurt, more than he could express, because Elindhu had been his best friend for so many years, but now he no longer knew her. Friendships in the Order were forged of shared lives of shared burdens and danger. He would have trusted her to the end – but now all he could see was the changeling.

But he also couldn't forget that for years she'd not just been the foil to his jokes but the arm round his shoulder and the wise guide he'd trusted so deeply. He'd wanted her to remain in his life after retirement finally claimed him.

How did I not see it? he kept asking himself. *Am I that blind?* He still had no answer to that, so for now, he kept well away from her, and she from him.

Obanji shook his miserable thoughts away as he and Soren topped another rise and stopped to catch their breath. 'How are you doing, lad?' he asked, to distract himself. 'Must be wishing you'd been found by some other pentacle, eh?'

'Not if they were like those *nikka dikka* we saw off in Port Gaudien.'

'Nikka dikka?' Obanji laughed. 'So your ma did teach you some Mbixi, eh?'

'A little,' Soren said, before grimacing. 'Gods, it's been days since I even thought about my family. Do you think my sister's all right?'

'I'm sure of it. Ask Elindhu – she may have some trick she can use to scry her,' Obanji replied, glancing back down the slope to where the erling was soldiering along on her own. *I miss you*, he thought sadly.

'Can you ask her for me?' Soren asked solemnly. 'She scares me.'

'Aye, me too, son,' Obanji admitted. But wounds didn't heal unless you cleaned them, so he clapped Soren's shoulder. 'I'll ask. You push on.'

Soren gave him a grateful look as Obanji sat himself on a handy ledge and waited until Elindhu puffed her way up and planted her staff.

'I'm not getting any younger,' she wheezed.

'Why not turn into a wolf or something?' he grunted, offering her a hand up.

She looked at him anxiously, then with hope, and let him haul her up to the ledge. 'Only a few erlings are like Fynarhea, in having an animal skin. She was born that way – and she will have had a horrible childhood being skinned regularly, so that she could grow up like a normal child. Morphia, it's called. It's not a thing I envy.'

Obanji shuddered. 'Hideous.' Then he looked at her appraisingly. 'She looked young . . . and quite, um, aggressive. I'm a little surprised she chose to be female?'

It was a proxy for a lot of other questions.

'Do you think only men can be aggressive?' Elindhu snorted. 'Don't tell Romara.' Then she flashed him her familiar dry smile. 'Actually, Fynarhea hasn't chosen yet, so she can still be either gender for a few days at a time. Gods, I remember those years: some days I felt feminine, others masculine . . . and some days I was both and neither and horribly, horribly confused.'

'But you're royal?' he prompted. He was still feeling awkward, but her voice soothed him, a comforting reminder that she was, for all her revealed strangeness, familiar.

'That just made me a bigger pain in the backside,' Elindhu chuckled. 'It's a worthless title – my parents' throne hall is a damp cave in Tyr – but the title impresses fools, and it got us out of Semmanath-Tuhr alive.'

'But you're not human,' he blurted, feeling awkward.

She looked up at him, smiling wryly. 'No. Close, though.'

He winced at his poorly chosen words. 'Uh . . . how much did you have to pretend about . . . well, everything, really? To fit in, I mean.'

'It was hard, but worthwhile,' Elindhu answered, her big, bright eyes moist with unshed tears. 'When I joined the Order, I chose to be small and plain, so men would ignore me, and it mostly worked. And the need to control the glyma is as real a matter for me as any of you, so I fought all the same battles of self-control as you. The hard part was keeping my emotional distance, staying aloof so I didn't slip up and reveal myself. I'm not like that, naturally.'

'You never felt aloof to me.'

She smiled tentatively. 'You've always been hard to maintain a distance from, Obanji.'

That ached his heart, unexpectedly. 'Couldn't you have told me?'

'No,' she said simply, flatly.

'I guess not.' He sighed, then asked, 'Soren asked whether you could scry his sister?'

'I've met her, so yes, I could. I'll try once I don't have hundreds of kylos of mountains and the entire Gulf of Foyland between us.'

'Of course. I'll tell him so. Thank you.' Returning to his own concerns, he asked suddenly, 'Um . . . how old are you? I've heard that erlings can live for ever . . .'

'If only,' she scoffed. 'We're as mortal as you, although it's true that we age more slowly. But we have the same needs, to love and be loved, to live in peace, to build a life and raise children.' She looked at the elobyne orb in her staff. 'I've stayed the right side of the glyma-rage by maintaining emotional distance, but I can't hold back time. At some point I'll have to leave the fight to the younger generation, just like you.'

'Will you return to Elidor or Tyr?'

She shuddered. 'Ghastly places, freezing cold and miserable. I'd rather go to – what's that place you're always on about, on the coast of the Mar-Eras? That sounds perfect.'

'Mardium, on the estuary of the Nara River,' he reminded her wistfully. 'There's a cove facing west, where cliff-top houses catch the sunset and the spiced fishcakes are a taste of Paradise. It's truly a blessed place. I'll buy a villa and brew my elixir, and get rich as the Hierophant.'

'It's good to dream,' she sighed. 'I'd love to see it.'

And I'd welcome you, he thought unexpectedly.

Just like that, his mind was made up. She was still Elindhu, still his friend – and when this strange quest was done and they put aside their sword and staff, maybe something more.

'Won't your family require you to return?' he asked. 'To be Crysophalae Elindhu Aramanach, High Princess of Tyr, again?'

'My parents have several children. The crown will pass to my brother and he certainly doesn't want me hanging around, criticising everything he does.' She looked anxious. 'Was my true form unsettling? I don't want to accentuate my differences, so I think it's best if I stay like this, you know . . . ?'

'I didn't recognise that other person,' he replied. 'But you I know.'

'Then we're still friends?' she asked shyly.

'Of course.' He swallowed a lump in his throat, and added, 'Good friends.'

Her answering smile lit up the mountainside.

They rose and walked on, together this time, as the afternoon sun began to break through the thinning banks of clouds to the west, painting the stark mountainous landscape with shifting shafts of light. The lonely wolf call they'd heard since Semmanath-Tuhr was back again, wailing through the peaks, but they never saw the beast. Occasional birds of prey shrieked overhead, trailing them for a while, perhaps in the hope of carrion. A stag wandered out of the mist once, then shot away, leaving them unsure if they'd really seen it.

By late-afternoon they were climbing through swirling cloud, visibility reduced to silhouettes and shadows. Soren led the way, while the older members of the group trudged more wearily. Jadyn was trying to teach Aura how to control her breathing, to battle a hefty dose of mountain sickness.

Then Soren shouted excitedly from the next ridge, and they hurried on as fast they could manage, to find him standing at the crest of a saddle between two peaks. The western sky was suffused in pink and gold, lighting the clouds and glinting on the peaks of the Qor-Espina. Elindhu's angular features were rendered timeless, while Romara's aristocratic face shone like marble; even Jadyn looked ageless. Gram resembled some Old Vandari Thunder God, while Aura reminded Obanji of carvings he'd seen in old Pelasi temples.

Soren pointed due west. 'See? Up there—!'

There was no mistaking it. There, about a thousand paces west of their position, were the outlines of standing stones, dark against the sky.

It was the place Agynea had told them to seek.

'We've held to the right trails!' Elindhu exclaimed. 'And Agynea guided us truly.'

Thank you, Obanji sent to Agynea. *And please, be safe.*

The village of Bassata was virtually abandoned, just a few families clinging on in desperation, for their fields had recently been burned out by wildfires. Novoluno was a rundown den of herders and cutthroats. In neither had anyone seen Jadyn Kaen's party, and Yoryn Borghart made sure they weren't lying.

They arrived in Santa Cara just after midday, At first glance, it looked no more promising; just some thatched hovels around a hut that was supposed to be an Akkanite Church. The place was deserted, but as Borghart peered about him, he could sense watchers, lurking among the broken rocks and bush.

They radiated hate, and he basked in it. 'We've got company,' he warned those nearest, Elan Sandreth and Tevas Nicolini.

'You want the lads to round up a few?' Nicolini asked.

'You think they can?' Sandreth was paying more attention to his nails than the village. 'They'll run like rabbits the moment you move.'

'Be a bastard of a job,' Nicolini admitted, 'but what choice have we got?'

Peering through the darkened doors of the church, Borghart sensed nothing. The priest – probably an illiterate with no more education than his congregation – was likely hiding in the woods as well. With his quarry veiled and nothing to anchor a scrying, magic wasn't going to help them. And tracking was nigh impossible in these stony, barren hills. Only logic could guide them now.

If they didn't stop here but passed by, they could be anywhere, Borghart thought bleakly, his eyes roving. He spotted a wolf on the hillside above and threw it a grave salute. He'd always felt himself to be a predator among the herd of humanity. But this scent was going cold.

Then he saw something that rekindled hope: a small cross-hatch pattern etched on the wall of a building at the mouth of an alley between two houses. 'That way,' he said, intuition and imagination conjuring up their quarry, especially Auranuschka Perafi, and as he remembered her face, he felt sure she'd been here, just hours ago.

He smiled hungrily. 'They were here, this very day.'

'How do you know?' Sandreth sheathed his dagger.

Borghart indicated the cross-hatch mark. 'These are marks the vyr use. We lictors have translated a few of them.'

'How come the Order were never told?' Nicolini complained.

'Because it's our knowledge to impart and sometimes we'd rather let the mice play until they reveal where the rats lurk. You're just a sword-swinger, Nicolini. Leave the thinking to those better equipped to do it.'

Borghart nudged his horse into motion, aware that the

knight-turned-mercenary was simmering at his words. He was untroubled: it never hurt to remind a lesser of his place.

'Follow me,' he said. 'They went this way.'

As the horsemen wound their way down the wooded path, Tevas Nicolini felt the shadowy figures trailing them close in and his mind went back to his time in the Order, fighting vyr in the Miravia, where a forest could be teeming with life one moment, then go deathly silent the next. It was like that now: no bird song, not a breath of wind, and the sense of eyes and nocked arrows being trained on his back.

Sier Rohas Uccello and his pentacle were marshalling their century warily, but Borghart and Sandreth rode out front, as if oblivious to the danger. Perhaps they were, being city men.

If anyone takes an arrow in the back, I hope it's them. Then we can all go home.

Unfortunately, he and his remaining mercenaries were right behind them, far too close if this went badly. They descended unmolested to a clearing near a stream, where an old woman was squatting on a stool in front of a tiny hut, a dog as big as a mule lying beside her.

Shitty place to die, Tevas thought, looking round him, sensing movement everywhere.

At his gesture, his men fanned out. The clearing was too small to hold them all, so the Solabi Vestal Guard behind them were still in single file on the path; they were surrounded by dense brush. If an attack did come, it could be bloody.

Borghart leaned forward on his horse and called, 'Mistress Agynea? What a pleasant bonus.' That he recognised her was a predictable surprise. Lictors and vorloks were like two sides of the same coin.

'Yoryn Borghart,' the old woman replied. 'The pleasure is all yours.'

'There's a tale told of a man who entered a bastion in Vandarath, thirty years ago,' Borghart said loudly, presumably for the benefit of the rest of them. 'He claimed to have transcended the glyma and become something more enlightened than we mere mortals.' He chuckled darkly. 'But I can assure you he was plenty mortal by the time we'd dismembered him and thrown the pieces on the pyre. The grandmaster went looking for his wife – this old hag – but though they chased her for years, she had vanished.'

'My husband was truly enlightened,' the woman said. 'You squandered a rare gift.'

'What about you?' Borghart sneered. 'Are you also some wondrous prophet?'

She looked at him steadily. 'I attained ninneva and have lived in grace, but it is not immortality. In the end, everything that rises must fall.' She cast her eyes skywards. 'It is a good day to die.'

Tevas saw her eyes turn brilliant green as the lictor's went blue. For a moment, the world held its breath.

Anticipating chaos, Tevas' hand flew to his sword-hilt, drawing in enough glyma-energy that his vision flashed scarlet. 'Beware—' he began, a warning to his men.

He was already too late. The vorlok screeched, and from all sides came a cacophony of barely human shrieks and roars.

Tevas instinctively threw up a warding and yanked out his sword, pulsing out energy just in time to slap away three arrows flying straight for him and Sandreth. But those behind were not so lucky; he flinched as he heard some of his men go down. There were many more cries of alarm from men and beasts on the trail above where the Vestal Guard were trapped on the path.

Then dozens of men, women and children erupted from between the rocks and scrub, screaming in hatred. Some of the peasants were armed, but most were storming forward bare-handed, their bodies shifting and changing. A half-naked boy suddenly sprouted tusks and horns; a young woman sported a jackal head and three-inch-long claws, and a big man appeared with a hammer in either hand, and the torso and legs of a bear – and they were all coming for him.

Tevas' horse reared in fright, but he was already leaping from the saddle. Landing before the jackal-girl, he cut her down with one stroke, then parried the giant's hammer before slashing at his other hand and lopping it off. Sandreth had also dismounted; he might not be a glyma-man, but he knew how to move and he swiftly carved a space for himself. Behind them, though, the outermost riders had been caught flailing about on horseback, and were being dragged down, mounts and all, by the howling beast-folk.

But most of them were going for Borghart, and they were led by the vorlok herself.

When Agynea charged, she'd already grown three feet and her face was contorted into a harrowing visage of jagged teeth and horns, with eyes of verdant fire. She and a wall of vyr men and women went at Borghart, who looked shrunken before her towering form.

He blazed flames into her and her minions, roasting those around her, but couldn't penetrate her wards, and an instant later, she was on him, raking talons a foot long at him, while he wielded his energy-limned steel sword, seeking to cleave through her protections. Against his better judgement but propelled by ingrained reflexes, Tevas went towards the lictor's aid – then the witch's giant hound saw him and leaped, jaws wide.

Tevas thrust; the wavy-edged steel plunged between the hound's ribs, the impact almost snapping his wrists. The beast slammed into him, his flying weight smashing Tevas backwards, winding him. The huge hound's jaws snapped closed an inch from his face, spraying hot spittle over him, and Tevas ripped out his sword and thrust again, right through that terrifying mouth and down the beast's gullet, even as he ran out of air and almost stopped breathing.

As the beast fell, Tevas managed a gasping swallow, just as the vorlok turned his way, screeching in fury. Smashing Borghart aside with one hand, her elongated arm raked Tevas' chain-and-leather jerkin, punched through, then gripped him. Before he could even gasp, he was hurled through the air, smacking his head on the hard-packed earth when he landed and rolling to the bank of the stream.

Then he toppled in, face-down and blacked out . . .

Elan saw Nicolini go flying as Borghart planted his feet and hacked at the witch's face, but she managed to block his blow with her forearm, the blade doing no more than opening a gash that cauterised instantly.

He should have run – this wasn't his fight – but he hated looking small before these damned glyma-warriors. He'd never conquered the need to prove himself – so instead, he darted in on the witch's unprotected blindside.

Agynea was moving like time was her slave; she swayed from his blow as if the blow and her evasion were rehearsed. But she was an old woman, and her capacity to fight was waning. Even as she roared out a gout of fire, spewing a glowing torrent of sparks and burning spittle at the lictor, her movements became sluggish, and she gasped painfully. Borghart's wards saved him, though the flames ignited his sleeves and leggings and turned his sword red-hot, making him stagger back in alarm . . .

. . . but the hag lost track of Elan and she too was staggering, wheezing like a punctured bellows as she recoiled from the discharge of such fearsome energy. He flashed in again and planted his blade in her back, right behind the heart. The blade emerged from her chest; she staggered – and a reflexive blow almost took his head off, but he rode her down until the blade was digging into the stony ground, skewering her in place until her death throes subsided.

A few moments later, the vyr coven began to falter, and now the tide turned. Their bestial forms began to fade, and so too their blind ferocity. With fear and the loss of comrades goading them on, the soldiers and mercenaries showed no mercy, cutting them down until they broke and ran, butchering any they could catch like the animals they were – the women too, because no-one sane wanted to screw these animals.

Elan went to Borghart, but the lictor waved him away, his dignity more wounded than his body. 'You got lucky,' he grumbled, fussing over his scorched clothing. 'You wouldn't have lasted an instant without me.'

Thanks for saving me, Elan, Elan thought sourly. *You're welcome, Yoryn.*

Then he saw Tevas, left his sword where it was and ran. 'Here, you fool,' he said, hauling him out of the stream. 'Good thing it's only a trickle.'

Tevas looked up blearily, then gazed around them at the carnage. 'Elysia on high,' he breathed. They'd lost twenty men, maybe more, but the dead vyr numbered at least sixty.

Elan proffered his hipflask. 'Here, suck on this. I thought you were dead.'

'I was lucky, I guess.' Tevas examined the raking wounds beneath his jerkin, then tipped some brandy over them, grimacing. 'Jagat, that hurts!' Then he looked at Elan. 'That your blade in the witch?'

'It is. You know, I've always envied you glyma-men. I was the top fencer in all of Petraxus in my year, but without the glyma, I'm considered a nobody, in terms of martial skill.'

'Aye, but you get to screw whomever and whenever you like, and you're free to leave the worst enemies to the Vestals,' Tevas said. 'Most would call that a blessing.'

'Not me. I'm a Sandreth, bred to lead. But my first concern must now be politics.'

'That's a bloody enough sport. I hope you're good at it.'

'Good enough.' They shared a grim smile, and on a whim, Elan offered his hand. One could always use friends in tough spots and this pursuit was becoming lethal. And men like Tevas Nicolini always needed patrons.

Who knows, it could be a lucrative partnership. Pirates make money, surely?

An hour later, the bodies of the villagers had been piled up and covered with dead branches and oil, ready to be set alight. It was brutal, but Tevas had seen many such deeds. Now he was watching Sier Rohas' men dig graves and reflecting on his own mortality. He'd lost eight of his twenty, and twenty-four of the Solabi Vestal Guard were also dead and as many wounded. It'd been a very bad day.

But not bad enough to deter Borghart, it appeared.

A vengeful Sier Rohas had offered to hunt down more villagers to question, but the lictor told him it was unnecessary. 'I have all I need,' he'd replied, examining Agynea's body.

The lictor took the corpse – now a skeletal old woman with a serene face – and laid it out naked and spread-eagled on the ground.

He carved marks in the dirt with his sword, enclosing the body in circles and lines.

More necromancy, Tevas realised, shuddering at the memory of what the lictor had done to the villager back at Regio Lago. Death-magic was regarded as unclean, but he wasn't about to question its use. So he sat with Elan Sandreth, his new 'friend', to watch the show. It wasn't long after midday, with plenty of daylight left if they could just get a lead on where the Falcon pentacle were. *Borghart said they were here earlier today, so they can't have gone far.*

His preparations complete, the lictor kindled glyma-energy, then stalked to the edge of his markings, faced Agynea's body and started shouting invocations. His markings began to glow purple – then he made a gesture like pulling treacle and a weird pale light rose from the corpse. The watching men recoiled in fear, but Tevas had seen such acts before, and Elan reacted as he always did, with a façade of jaded cool.

A spectral form very like the dead witch now hovered above the body, shrieking at Borghart.

'*Agynea, submit to me,*' the lictor boomed, making a gripping gesture. Inside the wardings, the wraith of Agynea was lifted by the throat, as if held in an unseen fist. '*Where is Jadyn Kaen? Where is Romara Challys?*'

She raked at the air and bloody slashes appeared on Borghart's face, barely an inch from his right eye. Bellowing in rage, the lictor made a slapping motion and the ghost's head cracked sideways. He mimed a plunging and gripping gesture with his left hand and inside the wardings, the wraith went rigid, for a hole had appeared in her chest, above her heart. Borghart wrenched and twisted and she howled. In the lictor's left hand, a ghostly, bloody organ appeared, lifeless and grey, and the putrid stink of rotting meat filled the air.

'*Agynea, where is Jadyn Kaen? Tell me – I command you—*'

Still she fought, her wraith contorting her spirit into something worse, her limbs flailing and more rents and gashes appeared on the lictor's thighs and arms. But he gritted his teeth, and shouted again, '*Agynea, show me Jadyn Kaen!*'

His will prevailed, for it was powered by a still-living body. The wraith wailed and burst apart, becoming a cloud of coloured mist, and for a moment even Tevas saw the fugitive Jadyn Kaen and his party, strung out on a steep hillside. Then the image faded and the light around Agynea's body did too, leaving a desiccated corpse that looked weeks old, the lips and gums pulled back from her teeth, her eyeballs shrunken to prunes and every rib visible. Tevas shuddered as Borghart kindled fire in Agynea's body, and it burned like long-dry twigs.

The Vestal Guard took that as the signal to ignite the pile of villagers, and soon that was a roaring bonfire too.

'Lictor Borghart,' Tevas called, 'where are they?'

The lictor pointed northwest, into the mountains brooding above them. His gaunt face cracked into a hard smile. 'They're only a few hours ahead of us, and travelling on foot. If we ride hard, we can be on them before the sun goes down.'

The pale disc of pink-orange light hung above the western peaks, its glow reflected in the Skull moon, which had risen, pallid and menacing, above the clouds to the east. But Jadyn's eyes were on the standing stones as he and his companions tramped towards them.

The hilltop had clearly been shaped by men, for it was perfectly flat, as if a giant had lopped off the peak, then polished what was left. How such a feat had been accomplished, up here in the rarefied air of the mountains, he could only imagine.

When they reached that flattened peak, they found a new wonder: the ground wasn't just flat but perfectly planed, and like a tree trunk, the rock had contours, lines and seams of many hues, some that glittered in the remaining light. The Falcons all exclaimed softly at the sight.

The standing stones rose like jagged fingers, rough on the outside but carved and polished on the inner side into thrones facing the centre, as if it were the meeting place of a pantheon of forgotten gods. There were eight, equally sized, one for each primary compass point. Each had a hole bored through just below the tip; the setting sun currently shone through the hole in the western throne, projecting an elongated sphere of light into the polished floor, just in front of the easternmost chair. Wind moaned through and frost made the smooth stone treacherous.

Obanji and Elindhu were trying to maintain a scholarly circumspection, but their eyes shone like children. Soren and Aura made no such pretence – they were drinking it in. Gram's craggy face held hope and even Romara's brooding was overcome by the sight.

Jadyn, as excited as any of them, stepped into the circle, wondering if some living power remained here, or if it were just a relic of another time. He could feel the weight of history, the bones of the earth beneath and the eyes of Heaven above – or else he was deluded by hope.

'This is a Sanctor place, surely?' he breathed.

'Perhaps,' Elindhu replied, walking around the stone circle like a gladiator in the arena, balanced and alert, testing her footing. 'There are Warden sigils here, certainly – but look,' she added, pointing out carvings on the armrests of faces formed by leaves, 'Huirne, the Leafman, one of my people's gods.'

'What do you think?' Jadyn asked Obanji, as they joined her in the circle.

'It's a sight to see,' the Abuthan admitted. 'But what's it for?'

'It's wonderful,' Elindhu murmured. 'One could study this for days.'

'One doesn't have days,' Obanji chuckled, putting a big hand on her shoulder. 'We've got about an hour of twilight, and I don't think this is any place for camping.' He scanned the hilltops and grimaced. 'If we need to camp, we'd better find somewhere off the wind line. And there's a storm coming.'

He pointed to the north, from whence the wind was driving a wall of black clouds.

'You're right,' Elindhu sighed. 'We need to find shelter.'

'It'll still be here tomorrow,' Obanji told her.

Jadyn groaned in disappointment. He'd hoped to find Nilis Evandriel here, or some clue of where he'd gone next. There was nothing obvious, but Obanji was right, there was always tomorrow. 'Five minutes,' he said. 'Then we'll look for somewhere to camp.'

Aura hobbled into the stone circle and flopped into the nearest throne, the eastern one. 'Be markings carved in armrest,' she noted wearily. 'Filled with dust, hard to see.'

They crowded round and Elindhu drew a thin-bladed dagger and dug out the grit, revealing a handprint, indented into the stone. The other throne-arm had the same thing, with symbols where the palms would rest.

'Are there hand prints on all of them?' she asked.

The knights spread out and examined the other thrones. 'Aye, this one has the same,' Obanji reported, from the southeast seat.

Romara and Gram had gone to the north side, from where they chorused, 'Aye, here too.'

'So sweet, they sing together,' Aura chirped. 'Like love birds.'

'That's not funny,' Romara snapped.

'How you knowing, with no humour sensing?'

'When you don't have a sense of humour,' Obanji corrected, and Romara flashed him an obscene hand gesture. 'Well, you don't. It's a known fact.'

'Focus,' Jadyn snapped, looking at the fast-setting sun. 'Come on, clear the rest of the hand-markings so we can examine them properly.' He chipped his one clean, and found another indented carving like a square-topped 'A' in the palm.

'I should know that symbol,' Elindhu mused, before starting a complicated debate with herself about the evolution of runic symbols in northern Hytal.

Just then, the wolf they'd been hearing throughout their journey cried fiercely, like a hunter sighting its prey. They all looked up as the howl reverberated through the peaks, and Soren extended his arm, pointing back along the ridgeline.

'Riders!' he shouted in alarm. 'It's Borghart's men – they've found us!'

A large group of mounted men were emerging from the clouds below, the last rays of the sun gleaming on helms and spears; a Vestal century with a man in lictor's black, leading them. That figure raised his blade and elobyne-light bloomed along it. Then with a cry, the horsemen surged up the slope, shouting triumphantly.

Romara reached over her shoulder, then groaned as her hand closed on the erling tuelawar, not her trusty, potent flamberge. *Jagatai*, she groaned inside, *I knew giving up the damn thing would get me killed.*

Beside her, Jadyn and the other knights drew their own weapons, their depleted orbs barely glowing in the dim light. Soren immediately gravitated to Obanji's side, while Elindhu put aside trying to unravel the mystery of the circle of thrones and began to conjure, calling out '*Hajir*,' the rune of air. The clouds around them immediately began to close in, dropping visibility.

Romara felt clear-headed in the absence of the glyma-*jang*; but that only helped her process the fact that while they had the high ground, they were only seven, against far too many.

Gram loomed up beside her, his eyes glimmering with concern. 'Can you do this?' he asked.

She remembered their earlier conversation: without her power to draw on, he was weaker . . . but what would it trigger in her? She was right on the edge now. The next time she'd fall.

Does it matter, if we are going to die anyway?

She nodded and gripped his hand. A frisson of energy shivered into her bones as her residual glyma flared. 'I don't know what's left,' she admitted, as the power was triggered. 'Take it all.'

'Stay calm,' Gram replied, even as the connection between them became a warm, shuddering current of power, dredging at her bone marrow, and the beginnings of his vyr transformation began to grip him. 'Stay with me.'

It occurred to her that he might inadvertently kill her before the enemy even reached them.

So be it, she thought dazedly. *Let it come down.*

Even without Borghart and whichever glyma-knights were among their foes, they would have been in a hopeless position: they were low on elobyne and grossly outnumbered. But Borghart had a full pentacle with him, and Tevas Nicolini too. Then she saw Elan Sandreth, and for a moment she was paralysed. *Dear Akka, do you hate me?* But she straightened her spine and resolved that whatever else happened, he at least would die.

Beside her, Gram's whole frame cracked and strained against the furs that a moment ago had been loose and roomy. His breath gusted hot and his nails spurted blood as they grew an inch, and then another. She could taste the blood in his mouth, feel the heat radiating from him.

She gave herself over to it. *Come on, Elan*, she snarled inside as her defiance stirred. *Let's see what you've got.*

Aura was still on the eastern throne, facing the west, as if pinned in place by the glare of the setting sun. It was partially obscured by the tip of the opposite throne, the hole in it creating a disc of light that was moving towards her across the polished stone ground. She turned and examined the hole above and behind her head and realised that it wasn't really a hole, but a thin wafer of some kind of glass, faceted and gleaming. That seemed important, for some reason.

'Magia,' she called to Elindhu. 'See look, look see!'

No one was listening. The sorceress was caught up in some spell, stirring the air like a cook making broth, while the knights were all drawing on their glyma-magic. Romara's face was set in a death-mask and Gram's body rippled and bulked, as his furs tore.

''lindhu,' Aura shrieked, '*see look! Look at light!*'

Elindhu threw her an impatient glance, her bird-like features lit up by her spells, which faltered as she saw. 'What—?' she exclaimed, then, 'Not a hole – it's glass – or a *lens*—?'

The sun dipped, shining more directly through the back of the western throne opposite Aura, and the disc of light solidified, climbing her skirts and striking her lap, then on up her body. There was a shape etched into the glass lens, painting symbols over her. Aura felt a burst of fear and went to hurl herself aside.

'*Jadyn*,' Elindhu shrieked. '*All of you – stop – look at Aura—*'

Everyone spun her way – then Obanji shouted, 'Aura, get down!'

'*No, no!*' Elindhu screeched, aborting her spell and running for the western throne. '*Aura, stay there – everyone, grab your things and take a throne – now!*'

Despite the urge to leap from the throne and flee, Aura grabbed the armrests and hung on as the beam of light climbed her body, while Elindhu leapt into the opposite, western one, and the others made for their nearest seats. The light reached her chest and for a moment she feared she'd burst into flame, but all it did was warm her goose-bumped skin. Gram snagged his tattered furs on the corner of a rock and left half of them behind as he bounded for the northern throne, Romara, close behind, hurled herself at the neighbouring one. By now the enemy were in archery range, and arrows came flying in, ricocheting wildly as they clattered on the stonework.

'The hands, the hands!' Elindhu called frantically, and they all slammed their hands into the handprints etched into the armrests. An instant later the sunbeam shining through the western throne hit Aura in the face, turning everything in her sight to gold and black silhouettes.

A moment later, it struck the disc behind her head and broke into facets shooting in different directions, and something like fire blazed through her limbs. She saw the others convulse, lighting up as if from within, and she shrieked as her palms, pressed into the handprints on the armrests, were seared. As one, they threw their heads back, howling . . .

Then the world vanished in a blaze of light, and she was pitched forward and fell into blackness . . .

16

Out of Light

The Hierophant

In the kingdoms of the pre-imperial north, secular and religious leaders were rivals, until Jovan Lux formed the Vestal Order and claimed to be anointed to rule by Akka Himself. Those opposing his knight-sorcerers were forced to bend the knee, and Talmont rose to encompass the north. Then he reached out to the lords of Zynochia and Abutha, forging an alliance that transcended nation and creed. Thus, the empire is led by a 'Hierophant' – a priest-king of divine lineage, who unites the secular and spiritual world.

THE BOOK OF FREEDOM, KYRGINIUS (VORLOK SCHOLAR), 1326

What manner of man has the narcissistic egotism to claim divinity, when he was born as mortal and flawed as you or I? A man like Jovan Lux.

NILIS EVANDRIEL, RENEGADE SCHOLAR, 1466

Falagan Ranges, Neparia
Summer 1472

'*What in Devastation?*' Lictor Borghart raged, as he stalked around the outside of the circle of thrones. 'Where are they?' he shouted. '*Where have they gone?*'

Tevas Nicolini had no idea, so he kept his mouth shut. Elan Sandreth was even wiser; he was off with the soldiers retrieving the horses, as the steep slope had forced them to dismount before attacking.

I should have gone with him, Tevas worried, knowing that Borghart's temper usually had him lashing out at the nearest person, guilty or not. Right now, that was him.

Their fighting men had almost reached the summit when the circle of stone chairs had been engulfed by swirling light, as if the Northern Aurora had coalesced in that tiny space. They'd dropped and hidden their faces, fearing some kind of magical storm, but when the light faded, the hilltop stone circle had been empty. Of the fugitives, only a few items of gear had been left behind, strewn outside the stone circle.

We've lost them again . . . But how?

Tevas had no idea, and Borghart looked even more baffled. He'd tried scrying, using the gear left behind by their quarry in their haste to escape, but to no avail. Kaen's party were either veiled or protected by thick stone, and the items Borghart had used weren't personal enough to them.

If this stone circle is some kind of portali gate, then they could be anywhere, Tevas reasoned, though he felt anything but reasonable. In fact, he wanted to scream. *I don't care any more; good on the Falcons for making Borghart look like a fool. I'm done with this.*

A lone wolf was howling – he could see it on the next peak along the ridgeline, yowling at the skies. *I wish I had a jagging bow*, he thought vengefully. *Damned creature.*

It was an hour since their quarry had vanished and the sun had set, leaving this hilltop cold and windswept, and any minute now, they were going to get pissed on by the oncoming storm clouds. Everyone looked thoroughly fed up, even Sier Rohas and Elan Sandreth, who trudged over to join him.

'What happened?' Sandreth asked.

'Jagged if I know,' Tevas shrugged.

'Nor I,' Sier Rohas admitted. 'This is beyond my experience, and my magus is baffled. I'm running out of time before I must take my men home.' He sounded relieved at the prospect.

Borghart stalked towards them, his face like a storm-front. 'This is *impossible*,' he ranted. 'There's no portali here. There's no elobyne – no residual glyma. It's *not* possible.'

'Then perhaps the Falcons were destroyed?' Tevas suggested. 'That ball of energy might have incinerated them. That's my bet. They're dust, and we should go home and proclaim them so.'

'But I've never seen anything like this place, or that spell.'

'Then send scholars back here to investigate,' Elan suggested, taking a swig of brandy. 'But for jag's sake, can we just go? Those rain clouds are going to drown us shortly.'

'No,' the lictor shouted, '*I must know the truth!*'

But then he sagged, and his voice fell. 'I suppose you're right. We'll leave. I'll return here in due course with some scholars and we'll unlock the secrets of this place, for the glory of Talmont and our beloved Hierophant.'

Aye, whatever, Tevas thought, relieved, but at the same time, oddly disappointed. *Jadyn and Romara ran halfway round the known world – for what? To leave us a mystery?* But he'd seen too many lives cut short, too many plans come to naught, to think it unusual. Life was rarely meaningful; it was just random, brutal chance, nothing more.

'Aye,' he muttered. 'Let's go home. They're all dead, and good jagging riddance.'

Fear could kill: the state of extreme terror could cause a heart to stop, or rip itself apart pumping in a blind, instinctive attempt to stave off that which it couldn't comprehend.

Poisons could also kill: foreign substances that bodies weren't made to contain, causing organs to fail, or glands to flood the body with fluids meant only to be used minimally.

Jadyn felt both dread and venom assail his body as he plummeted through forever, flailing as he fell past stars and planets and the faces of dead men and women, through water and earth and shadow and void, howling in terror. He went through one crisis after another, caught up in a delirium that he couldn't grasp. Then the void became a mouth, the maw of the Devourer Herself, *exactly* as portrayed in an illustration of the *Book of Lux* that he had read as a boy.

That's when he realised the fear was in his head. As that thought came, suddenly he wasn't falling at all, but floating. The Queen of

Evil vanished, and so did everything else, leaving him alone in a lightless void.

But the poison was real, and he could name it: elobyne. It was in his flesh, in his veins, and it was burning him up. Even as he focused on it, the burning intensified, his skin charring and his eyeballs beginning to boil . . .

He didn't panic; he'd been controlling elobyne for more than a decade now and he knew how to draw on it, to use it, how to damp it down. So he caught his breath and focused on that, like swallowing acid. It was agony though, the worst pain he'd known, making him howl his lungs out as he writhed in space.

Then it too was gone, and he faded out . . .

. . . and woke to find an impish face inches above his, shrouded by a tangle of black hair, and breath like cinnamon in his nostrils. 'E tresa bueno . . .' Aura trilled. 'Neya, must speak Talmoni . . . Um, is very good seeing you, Sier Jadyn Knight. Si?'

He stared up at her, thinking, *Elysia on high, you're beautiful.*

Evidently he also spoke aloud, because she patted his cheek and said, 'I know.'

'That was the relief speaking,' he mumbled, going red. He rolled and looked around anxiously, counting bodies. Everyone else was there, strewn unconsciously about in the gloom of a circular chamber, the only light coming from runic symbols in the walls, thousands of them, each about an inch tall and glowing pale blue.

'Stay calm,' Jadyn told Aura – and himself. He went to rise, but was struck by a wave of pain, and sagged again. Every muscle in his body felt like it'd been twisted, pummelled and boiled, but he felt whole. 'It'll be all right.'

'Aura esa tranquilla,' she replied, much calmer than him. 'Look at hands, Jadyn Knight.'

'Eh?' He looked down, and saw that the symbols on the armrest of his throne had been burned into his palms, right through his gauntlets, which were now holed. 'What the jagat?'

Aura held up her hands, which were marked identically. 'What is meaning?'

'I have no idea,' Jadyn confessed. 'But we'll work it out.'

He checked his flamberge was still in its scabbard and the orb still maintained some energy – which it did. But he himself had been, he realised, completely drained of all residual glyma, which was unheard-of. And despite being certain he'd fallen a great distance, his pack was still intact, its contents unbroken.

I dreamed it, surely. Where can we be?

He hurriedly checked the wellbeing of the others. Obanji was completely motionless, but breathing, as were Elindhu, Soren, Romara and Gram. They all had marks on their palms: but they were fading like old scars, while his and Aura's were still vivid as a new tattoo.

That's significant, he thought, *but in what way?*

'How long was I unconscious?' he asked.

'Not be knowing. Aura waking ten minute afore.'

Jadyn tried to think it through. *Aura first, then me, and only we have lasting marks?* But he could think of no reason why . . . *No, hang on*, he thought, remembering the second phase of his falling experience – the poisoning that he was sure had been elobyne. *She's the only non-glyma-wielding person among us, so maybe that's why she woke first? But why me second, and not Soren and Gram, the newest to glyma-use?*

'What if no wake?' Aura asked fearfully, gesturing towards the others.

'I'm sure they will,' Jadyn lied. 'What did you experience?'

'Falling, falling,' she replied, breathless with wonder. 'Mare of night, si? But then Aura flies, tresa bella. Wake, all Vestal virgins sleeping.' She indicated a portal in the wall. 'Maybe way out, but Aura stay. Very loyal.'

'Thank you,' he replied, suspecting she'd have been too terrified to leave anyway.

He went to draw from his elobyne orb – then held off; it actually felt nice to not have glyma fizzing through him. The relentless prickling unease it engendered was something he'd got used to, but never enjoyed.

Maybe retirement won't be so bad, if it's peaceful like this?

Aura went to where Elindhu lay, examining her curiously. The erling's beehive of grey braids had come undone, and ropes of hair coiled round her. 'She be erling-kind, Obanji is human, but still love,' she said. 'Is nice.'

Jadyn felt his eyebrows lift. 'Um . . . I don't think . . .'

'How you not know?' Aura exclaimed. 'Is oblivious.'

'You mean obvious? Are you sure?'

'Of course am sure. They not knowing selves, but is clear to Aura.' She smiled, then returned her attention to the marks on the palms of her hands. 'This be sign of aegis?' she asked.

'Is what a sign of the aegis?' Elindhu said, waking abruptly and sitting up, her braids cascading over her face so that she looked like a pile of old ropes, with her beaky nose poking through. 'My, my, wasn't that something!' She took in who was conscious and who not, ensured Obanji was comfortable, patted Soren's cheek fondly, then examined the fading scars on her palms and the vivid marks on Aura and Jadyn's. 'Interesting.'

'I woke to find I had no glyma-energy in me,' Jadyn told her. 'How about you?'

Elindhu clicked a finger and made her fingertip glow. 'No, same as usual.'

They exchanged notes while Elindhu piled her braids back up and re-knotted them, then she lit her staff and walked around the walls. 'Many of these symbols were present at the stone circle,' she commented. 'It's like a portali gate . . . but not the same.'

Jadyn looked around the walls properly. The circular chamber had smooth rock walls lit by an opaque dome of faintly glowing marble. There were unlit torches in racks on the wall, and an arched exit. The air was cold, but not dangerously so, and he could feel a faint breeze. There was also an oppressive sense of weight, as if they were far below ground. There were no spider webs, no smell of animals or damp, either.

'Any ideas?' he asked Elindhu.

'No. Who woke first?'

'Aura, then me.'

'While waiting, we drink wine, dance, have sexing,' Aura snickered. 'Tresa bella.'

Jadyn felt himself colour, just as she'd clearly intended.

'She'll tire of teasing you one day, Jadyn,' Elindhu said, chuckling, 'but not swiftly, if you keep blushing.' Then she returned her thoughts to their current predicament. 'So, we were on a mountain top, and then we fell, yes?'

'Si, si,' Aura agreed. 'Falling is old fear, from childerhood. Many nights of mare. But friend say, "If in dream you fall, grow wings." So Aura grow wings, fly. Is simple.'

'I had no such experience,' Elindhu mused. 'I just fell asleep, then woke.'

'I was falling, and I'd been poisoned,' Jadyn told her. 'But I purged the poison, and woke before striking the ground, in my dream.'

'I'm wondering if it's a test of some sort,' the magia replied, after some consideration. 'Or an *initiation*. You confronted a fear and defeated it, and were rewarded with those marks?'

Aura made a startled noise. 'What is "initiation"? Is aegis thing?'

Elindhu stroked her large nose thoughtfully. 'Maybe? But I can't be sure.'

They broke off their conversation, as the others were beginning to wake. Soren impulsively hugged Obanji, while Gram and Romara looked blearily about, and then their eyes found each other and both sagged in relief.

Feeling a strangely sour taste in his mouth, Jadyn stepped between them and hugged Romara. 'Are you alright?'

She returned his hug, and asked, 'Is this the Devourer's Maw?' – possibly in jest.

'Not if you're here.' He kissed her brow, to remind her of his love.

But she'd seen the fading scars on her palms and his. 'Why are your marks different?' she demanded. 'Why aren't they the same as mine?'

'I don't know.'

Elindhu quietly questioned the newly awakened of their experiences, which revealed that Romara, Soren, Obanji and Gram had just blacked out, without experiencing the ordeals that Jadyn and Aura went through.

'They may mean nothing at all,' Jadyn said hopefully.

'Mmm,' Elindhu agreed absently. By which, Jadyn knew, she meant, *No such luck.*

Aura sat, examining her newly marked palms. On each there was a different symbol, bluish-green and etched so deep she was surprised they weren't visible on the backs of her hands as well.

E Cara, I'm going to have to wear gloves for the rest of my life.

Her body ached as if she'd raced up the hill, then dived off a cliff into the sea. But far from being terrified, she was tingling with excitement. Yes, she was now entangled in arcane and terrifying dangers, with glyma and elobyne, swords and magic, mountain tops and old myths; but these markings gave her hope.

Maybe, just maybe, she belonged in this world of magic and power, too.

Elindhu and Jadyn had taken torches from the wall and left to explore while the rest recovered. Gram, Obanji, Soren and Romara were huddled together, the Order veterans reassuring the young man. None of them had experienced what she had.

They have their Gift, the Devourer purred in her left ear. *Maybe you have something better?*

Better? Akka jeered. *My Gift is what enabled the Order to wipe out the Wardens.*

Which of you created the aegis? Aura demanded.

Both divinities looked embarrassed. *Uh . . . not us . . .*

Typical, she thought, banishing them with a sharp, 'Begone!'

The knights heard and threw her puzzled looks. 'What happened to you, Aura?' Obanji asked.

Feeling a little shy, she showed them her hands: the symbols were still dark and solid, while theirs continued to fade. 'You've been marked by Fate,' Obanji suggested. 'Elindhu thinks it's an old Hytali runic script, from the time of the Sanctor Wardens. Maybe Agynea was right about them being involved.'

'I don't care what they are,' Romara grumbled. 'And I don't see why Jadyn and Aura, of all people, are the ones marked. There has to be another explanation.'

'Maybe Aura be special,' Aura suggested, to annoy her. 'More special than knightess.'

'I wonder where we are?' Obanji interjected. 'And can Borghart get here? If all it took was to sit down on those thrones at dusk, we can expect him and his mates to arrive here at sunset tomorrow. Or maybe even dawn?'

'Perhaps he tried immediately after us, and failed?' Soren suggested.

'I hope so,' Romara replied. 'I hope it killed them all.'

'We've never been that lucky,' Obanji chuckled.

'True,' Romara admitted. She looked around the circle. 'Can I just say something? I've been a jagging bitch this last month. I know it, and I'm sorry. You've got no idea what it is like when your control breaks and the rage takes you. It permeates every thought you have. But right now, after drawing on it in the circle, I've got very little residual power left. I feel myself lightening up. So thanks for putting up with me.'

The men made awkward forgiving sounds, looking everywhere but at her.

Obanji pulled out his large hipflask. 'Well then, this calls for my famous elixir of life. You know, I don't know if I've ever mentioned it, but when I retire, I'm going to head for the Mar-Eras and brew this stuff. It's going to make me richer than the Hierophant.'

Jadyn and Elindhu left the chamber to find a long hall, hundreds of paces in length, with rows of thick pillars supporting a vaulted ceiling. The mosaics on the ceiling had mostly collapsed, but some traces of the original decoration remained. Elindhu held her torch up to illuminate the best preserved ceiling mosaic.

'Surely that's Sanctor Warden art?' Jadyn asked.

The mosaic depicted two helmed and armoured warriors, a man and a woman, in green tabards, with bronze torcs around their necks. They were holding up a shield bearing a simple triangular Foylish knot pattern that seemed familiar.

'I'm sure you're right,' Elindhu replied. 'It's good to see they included both men and women. See the Foylish knot pattern? You'll find it on the keystone of every portali gate - on the shadowland side. The Wardens originated in Foyland.'

'That's not far from here,' Jadyn noted, before amending his words. 'Not far from that stone circle, at any rate. I've no idea where we are now.'

'I'm thinking we're in much the same place,' Elindhu replied. 'It's most likely to me that we're inside that same peak. I'm guessing it was a little like the lake in Semmanath-Tuhr – not as solid as it felt. Either way, we need to find a way out.'

Jadyn indicated the passage beyond. 'The blocked stairs we found at the far end are the best bet. The air's clean and moving, and the aegis wouldn't bring us here for nothing.'

Elindhu grinned toothily. 'Well, look who's a believer now.'

'I guess I am. The aegis is real, the Sanctor Wardens were real, and we, the Order, exterminated them.' He held up his hand, showing her the marking on his palm. 'Any theories on what this means?'

'Yes, but you're not going to like it.'

'Try me.'

She gave him a sympathetic look. 'You and Aura have been marked for the aegis. The rest of us haven't.'

His heart sank, because that had been his thought too. 'I pray that's not so. I had this hope that it would be something anyone could attain, if their heart was true.'

'A power that only nice people can use? Ha! You're an incurable romantic, Jadyn. But let's not presuppose anything. And keep your chin up. Leaders need to stay positive.'

'I'm trying. But the responsibility is crushing, at times.'

'You're doing fine. Romara was right about this being primarily your journey. You envisaged it and you'll see it through. I'm confident of that.'

'Is that a foretelling?'

'It's a gut feeling,' she said warmly, patting her belly.

He grinned. She was still Elindhu, their funny-faced mother hen of a mage, and the cleverest person he knew. 'Um,' he began, as a thought struck him, 'you don't have to hide your true form, you know. Not if you don't want.'

'I'm not so sure,' she said hesitantly. 'Sometimes familiarity is reassuring.'

'Do whatever makes you comfortable,' he urged. 'You can trust us to accept it, either way.' He patted her shoulder affectionately. 'Let's gather the others and get out of here.'

They took stock, finding that when they'd rushed to the thrones, they'd left behind much of their food, though at least they had their water flasks. And their orbs were very low.

'Once above ground, we'll need to veil again,' Jadyn noted, 'so save your glyma until then.'

They lit the wall torches and followed Elindhu back to the chamber with three stairs, all leading up and hopefully out. Gram, who'd donned an erling tunic, his furs having finally fallen apart, waved the others away. 'Let me look.'

He examined the three passage entrances, sniffing his way a few paces up each before declaring that two had no airflow, but the third smelled fresh.

'Then let's try it,' Jadyn decided, taking the lead, torch held high.

They climbed up cautiously, noting ventilation slits that made their torches flicker. The stair was long, and ended in a closed door which opened into a dusty, mouldy hall. Once they were all through, they closed the door and found it was all but invisible, inset into the carved stone wall.

'Whoever was last here probably never found the chamber below,' Elindhu guessed.

'But was this place abandoned or sacked?' Obanji wondered.

That question was soon answered. The hall led to more complex dwellings, with many intersecting corridors and dozens of large rooms, but there was a deathly, decayed feel to it all. Old bones, human and animal, littered the dirty halls, and rusted weapons were strewn across the floors. Doors had been smashed and furniture broken or burned: clearly this place had been fought over, a long, long time ago.

'Sacked, then,' Gram rumbled. 'Your Vestal Order did this.'

'It's not the only explanation,' Romara objected, half-heartedly.

They completed a desultory poke through the stores and armouries, finding nothing of worth. A tight spiral stairway choked with debris led upwards, so once Gram had used his bulk to force a way through the main blockage, he led them up to an entrance hall with more shattered doors opening out onto a barren ledge. At the edge was the shattered stump of an old bridge, and rushing water could be heard below. The wind moaned and far above a vulture cried out. The sun was up, telling them that at least one night had passed.

They were at the base of a mountain, on a ledge above a gorge, with a river rushing below, and the peak above lost in clouds.

I think Elindhu's right: we fell into the mountain, Jadyn thought. *If so, Borghart could be up there still, just a few kylos away.*

Gram joined him at the lip of the chasm, pointing out a stair carved into the rock that ran all the way down to the river. 'There may be fish down there.' He scanned the slopes and pointed to some bushland a kylo away. 'And there's bound to be something edible in there, and maybe something I can trap.'

'If you can do that, the rest of us will stay underground,' Jadyn agreed. 'You'll be fine, I'm sure: they don't seem to be targeting you for scrying. Just make sure you're not seen, if anyone does come down here.'

'Maybe all they saw was us vanishing in a ball of fire,' Gram replied. 'Hopefully, they think we're dead.'

'It's something to pray for. If we can stay hidden for a few days and give them no reason to change their minds, we may yet throw them off our scent. We'll rest here and move on once we have enough stores to permit.'

With that, Gram headed down to the river, and Jadyn went back into the underground Sanctor complex, to try and better understand it.

*

None of Borghart's party were used to defeat, so the slow descent from the alpine peaks was as depressing a march as Tevas remembered. The lictor had been scrying their quarry, but getting nothing, while Tevas' surviving dozen mercenaries muttered resentfully, giving Borghart filthy looks behind his back.

They'll be no happier with me, Tevas reflected. *I'll need to watch my back.*

Right now, all he had to look forward to was hundreds of kylos on the road, the need to kill someone to regain control of his operation, and somehow making up the losses of men and money from this futile pursuit. If he ever could.

His wrecked future played on his mind all the way back to the now-desolate Santa Cara, where jackals chewed on the charred bones of the villagers. Sier Rohas took the remains of his Vestal century west towards the high passes, while Elan, Borghart, Tevas and his remaining mercenaries headed for the Blood Sea ports. The journey passed in gloom and bitterness. When they thought he couldn't hear, his men spoke of deserting, and sure enough, at the first major town they came to, four did just that, leaving just eight still hanging on. They took a room in a ghastly tavern, needing rest, food and drink, before hitting the road again.

His prospects dismal, Tevas swallowed his pride and bought Elan Sandreth the most expensive brandy the inn stocked. 'Milord, I'm sick of piracy. Do you have need of a glyma-man in your service?'

Elan gave him a sideways look. 'Harbouring a discharged Vestal knight who's violated his vows and continued using the glyma is illegal,' he noted. 'That's none of my business if you're operating with Borghart's protection outside the empire, but inside it, it puts me in an awkward position. I'm sure you understand.'

His hopes fell. 'Of course, Milord.'

'On the other hand, a glyma-wielding warrior is always useful, if he's loyal and reliable. But haven't you all but burned out, if you're no longer in the Order?'

'I got out before losing control,' he replied. 'If I use it sparingly, I'm fine.' *For now, at least.*

The young nobleman considered. 'The Sandreth family demands unquestioning loyalty.'

'I'd expect no less.'

'Even if that meant harming someone you cared for?'

He means Jadyn and Romara.

'I learned to put personal feelings aside long ago. I do what must be done. If you take my pledge, you gain my unstinting and willing obedience.'

Elan considered, then slapped his shoulder. 'Consider it done. I'll formalise it once we're back in civilisation. House Sandreth is known for generosity, but that largesse must be earned.'

They clasped hands, lifted their tankards and toasted in silence.

Thank Elysia, Tevas sighed. *I can actually go back to Vandarath. I guess my heart never really left the north.*

But his thoughts were interrupted by Borghart, who'd been upstairs burning through the last fragments of the gear they'd scavenged from outside the standing stones, trying to scry their prey. He thundered down the wooden stairs and strode up, slamming down a smouldering fragment of what looked like animal fur and shouting triumphantly, 'By the Blood, that Avas man wore these rat-hides! The vyr prick is still alive!'

Damn, Tevas thought, *Damn you all the way to the Devourer's Maw.*

Aloud, he said, 'Great news, Milord.'

17

Across the Lake

An Immutable Law of Nature

It's said the erlings once ruled northern Hytal, before the coming of humankind. Certainly, their ruins dot the landscape. But as mankind expanded, the erlings retreated. When conflict arose, humanity was victorious, and the erlings, slow to breed and unable to unite in strength, faded away. This is how life is: the superior species supplants the weaker one. It is an immutable law of Nature.

THE CHRONICLES OF HYTAL, 1469

Falagan Ranges
Summer 1472

Gram spent several days fishing in the ravine, with considerable success, while Obanji and Soren saw to gutting, smoking and drying the catch for travel. There were snow hares too, and other game to trap. Jadyn and Romara concentrated on foraging berries and roots for travel, while Elindhu studied the abandoned Sanctor complex, looking for arcane knowledge.

Aura was tasked with lugging up water from the river, even though the Vestal knights were all muscular and better suited to such menial tasks. *I'm a lady – I shouldn't have to work at all*, she thought grumpily, but when she pointed this out, she received no sympathy, just the additional task of preparing the meals.

Then Gram made a discovery: going downstream along the treacherous ravine, he found a shelter where someone had stowed a pair of wooden-framed boats of cured hide, canvas covers to keep them dry, and two paddles in each. They looked old, but certainly more recent than the wreckage inside the old caves, which suggested that hunters and trappers came here at times, a warning that they might not be alone for long.

Their plans to move took shape. They'd replenished their supplies and scouted the river, going far enough downstream to learn that it flowed into an area of wilderness between the Falagan Ranges and the Qor-Espina, where towers of rock and flooded valleys created an inland maze of rivers, lakes and precipices that even Elindhu knew nothing about.

'An ideal place for a secret monastery,' Jadyn said, with infectious enthusiasm.

Aura was captivated with the idea that perhaps she might one day be his equal. Naturally, Akka kept whispering in her right ear that she shouldn't get her hopes up; while the Devourer kept telling her that it would never happen, that she was nobody and never would be.

She ignored them. *I want to touch the aegis again. I need that in my life.*

It wasn't the first time something shiny had captivated her and turned her life upside down. In her desire for escape and a life that wasn't drudgery she had fled her pious village in Neparia. She'd ended up in some horrible places and situations – then Sergio swept her up and for a time they'd lived a mad dream, stealing and pretending, thieving and playing tricks, living in the moment – and in the end, losing it all. She knew she was staking stupid amounts of faith on this glimpse of wonder, but she couldn't help dreaming.

Three days after emerging from the mountain, having ensured the boats were water-worthy, they were ready to move. They were given a boost before they left when Elindhu found recently etched symbols on the walls of the circular underground chamber, the letters 'N.E.' and some sigils that only she understood.

'Nilis Evandriel was here,' she announced. 'He's seeking Vanashta Baanholt downstream.'

They were all cheered by that, and even Romara's mood lifted, despite her inner struggles. After so long on the run, a goal they hadn't even known they were seeking might be in reach.

They left the safety of the cave system on the fourth morning.

The two boats sank low in the water but remained buoyant as they allowed the swift current to sweep them along. Gram took control of the first boat, having spent time on fishing boats in Avas, and, somewhat to everyone's surprise, Elindhu also had some experience, so she took control of the second boat.

Aura, sensing Jadyn wanted to be near Romara, rode with Gram, Obanji and Soren, while Elindhu took Jadyn and Romara, who was in a light-hearted mood as the glyma slowly left her system; she was almost a different person.

I can almost see what he sees in her, Aura thought, oddly jealous. *Not that I care.* Though she saw little in the way of passion between them; they were, as both had indirectly admitted, more like brother and sister who'd somehow mistaken filial affection for love.

The river journey gave her time with the other three men, but her usual routine – to charm at least one, in case she needed protection – felt pointless. Soren was bashful and too young, Obanji was wily and only cared about Elindhu anyway, and Gram was clearly infatuated with Romara, however much he might try to hide it.

She wasn't too concerned about that: for the first time in her life, she knew that if danger appeared, every one of these people would come to her defence anyway, because that was the way they were. *Good people.* She'd met so few of those that she forgot about trying to manipulate them and just enjoyed their company, as they teased and bantered with each other.

I like them, she realised. *They are like friends.*

She'd not really had many of those in her life. Many people she'd laughed with, drunk with, danced with, slept with; but there were few she'd have entrusted with her purse, let alone her life. It felt good to be with them, and the hope she'd felt since Semmanath-Tuhr remained.

Then they hit rapids and were swept along beneath spectacular cliffs, bursting from between rocks and even plunging over low water-falls, the icy water filling the bottom of the boat as they shouted in alarm.

'Bail!' Gram shouted, tossing Aura and Soren pots from the old caves, and they set to work, frantically scooping water from the bottom of the boat and tossing it overboard, barely staying ahead as more and more slopped in. Obanji and Gram paddled furiously as they were tossed about, but it felt like a game, and soon they were all laughing uproariously.

The other boat surged past, Romara and Jadyn paddling purposefully – and the race was on.

Everyone threw themselves into the chase, speeding down a gorge where the water raged fiercely. Aura whooped and hollered along with them all as they exchanged the lead several times – and burst out into a small lake, startling a large stag on the shore, which stared, then bounded away.

Gram rose and mimed shooting a bow – his weapon was stowed, unstrung. 'Got him!'

Soren winked at Aura, rose behind Gram, planted his hands – and shoved. The big Avas man was thrown off-balance, flailed desperately as he went in, raising an immense splash. The boat rocked, Soren flailed for balance himself . . . then Aura lifted her right foot and shoved it into his buttocks, sending him face-first into the water, as well.

'Ha ha! Got you!' Aura shrieked, then she jabbed a finger at the grinning Obanji, who was reaching for her. 'Ney, ney, don't you—'

He picked her up, thrashing and kicking, and hurled her into the air – she splashed down, squealing, going under in a cascade of bubbles, shocked by the freezing water and terrified she'd drown. But her feet hit the bottom and found it was only four feet deep. She staggered to the boat, drenched and cold, as Soren and Gram did the same, all with the same look on their face.

'No, no, we'll lose the stores!' Obanji laughed, steadying the boat.

E Cara, he's right, she fumed, as the two men threw up their hands, making laughing threats of what they'd do to the Abuthan once they were ashore.

In the other boat, Jadyn and Romara were wrestling, while Elindhu – who was clearly above such childishness – held it steady – until the erling smacked her staff into the backs of Jadyn's knees and he went over, dragging Romara with him. They came up spitting and coughing.

'I think we have our champions,' Elindhu declared drolly, beaming at Obanji.

Jadyn hooted with laughter, the child he'd once been clear on his face, and the others were just as merry, as they pulled the boats towards the tree-lined shore, joking and boasting.

'Stupido,' Aura told them, soaked and shivering. 'You be infantos. All wet, all die of cold.'

But it had been fun, like being young again.

'You're right, it was idiotic,' Obanji chuckled. 'We should dry off.' He glanced up. 'It's almost dusk anyway – let's make camp.'

As they disembarked, they roped the boats to a tree at the water's edge, ready to be launched at a moment's notice, and removed only what they needed for that evening. For the next few minutes they were all business, setting up camp for the night while taking turns to go into the woods to strip, dry off and change into the soft grey-green embroidered garb the erlings had gifted them. When they returned, Elindhu and Obanji had a fire to warm them all. Clothes were wrung out and hung to dry on a wooden frame Jadyn had made. After that, they sat around the blaze, laughing and chatting as they prepared a fish stew with some of the fish Gram had smoked.

After the stress and almost permanent anger of the past few weeks, Aura found seeing them all so light-hearted almost disconcerting, as if they'd all changed shape and species, not just Elindhu. Strangest of all, she felt like she belonged, a feeling she'd not had since losing Sergio.

Where are you, Sailor Sergio? she asked the setting sun. The ache of his betrayal still hurt, but increasingly, it was becoming an abstract question. One day, she would look him in the eye and find out why he'd abandoned her, but she was in no hurry. *He'll keep.*

'So, let's talk about Vanashta Baanholt,' Elindhu said, once they were all eating. 'According to my calculations, based on the symbols in the Sanctor ruins, it should be close.'

'What do you know of it?' Obanji asked.

'What do I know?' Elindhu said, peering out from under her grey pile of hair like a nesting moorhen. 'Well, "vanashta" is a word from the erling tongue, meaning "enlightenment", but "baanholt" is derived from an old Hytali word for "hermitage", which says something about the inclusivity of the Wardens. It was said to be a monastery where Sanctor acolytes gained the aegis. But when the Wardens were overthrown, no one could find Vanashta Baanholt, which is why some misname it "the Vanishing Bastion". Even captured Wardens didn't know where it lay, and it's never since been found.'

'Surely nothing can be hidden from the glyma?' Romara said doubtfully.

'You'd think so, given our Order spent two centuries looking for it . . . while denying it ever existed,' Elindhu agreed drily. 'I imagine access was strictly controlled, and maybe even those who went there didn't know exactly where it was. And maybe it doesn't look like a monastery?'

'Makes sense,' Jadyn said thoughtfully. 'But in that case, how will we know it?'

'The markings Nilis Evandriel left told me how to find it,' she said, clearly pleased with herself. 'They formed a riddle that requires a scholar's knowledge to solve.' She then launched into a lecture on ancient Hytali runes and how they were associated to particular stars in the night sky: by using this almanac, or star map, she could find the lost Warden place.

It got too technical and lost Aura's attention. All she really wanted to know right now was that it was close. She had a feeling that her life's thread, so twisted and knotted, was about to become even more tangled.

I don't care about saving the world – I just want to feel what I felt turning cartwheels under the lake in Semmanath-Tuhr. I want to make wishes that come true, and make everyone say, 'Look, it's her, the Magic Girl! What will she do next?'

She'll get herself killed, Akka grumbled in her right ear.

Or end up back on the street, the Devourer hissed into her left.

Neither were happy with her at the moment – jealous, she was sure, because the aegis wasn't their magic. But she had a head full of hope and didn't care what the High Powers thought.

*

Sleep wouldn't come and Gram woke with his head hurting, as it was constantly these days, or so it seemed. His was the next watch anyway, so he rose, pulled on his erling clothes, which were the best he'd ever worn, and went looking for Romara, who was on first watch. He found her on a boulder atop a jagged outcropping, with a full view of the little inlet and the moonlit lake – a gorgeous but cold sight, much like her.

'Hey,' he called softly. 'I'll take over.'

She made no attempt to move as he clambered up and joined her. She was wrapped in a blanket against the cold, and her face was lit by moonlight, her frown lines softened and her mouth relaxed, the serenity of her expression enhancing her beauty.

'I'll stay a while – I'm not sleepy anyway,' she replied. 'And I've got a lot to think about.'

'Do you want me to go?'

'No,' she answered quickly, then she dropped her gaze. 'Do you agree with what Aura said before: that all we Vestals are emotional wrecks?'

Those words really got under her skin, Gram realised. *Probably because they're true.*

'I'm the wrong person to ask,' he replied, diplomatically. 'I've got the same problems as you.'

'But you're so much better at handling it,' she said, with a hint of bitterness. 'It doesn't feel fair. I've had a decade or more of training, yet here I am, teetering on the edge of the Fall. And there's you, barely a month into being a vorlok and you're this jagging oasis of calm and strength. You put me to shame.'

'But there you have it: I'm just a month in.' He thought about that, feeling it might be important. 'I've had years to grow, I've been married, I've worked and laboured and suffered without touching that power because it scared me. I have that maturity. You Vestals are thrown into it during your teens. You never learn how to be normal.'

'So you agree with her?' Romara accused.

'Maybe I do,' he admitted.

She gave him a hollow-eyed look and sighed. 'I hate it when that minx is right.' Then she gave him a solemn look. 'You'd make a fine knight. Just like Obanji, and that's a high compliment. If you seek the Eye of Silence, you'll reach it, despite your age.'

Instinctively, he rejected the suggestion. 'I appreciate the thought, but it's too late: once I let the glyma trigger, I see red, just like you. And I wouldn't want to be in your Order. I know from the inside it looks different, but to us outsiders, it's the enemy.'

Romara sagged into herself. 'When I think about knights I've known who left the Order, not many seem able to cope. They can't let the glyma go, like opium addicts. Even Exemplars have fallen. And I'll probably be one of them, unless someone helps me through.'

'Jadyn will do that.'

'He's still got years in the Order, and he's got this damned quest . . . And he's been marked for the aegis – along with that damned Nepari – whereas here I am, about to be washed up and irrelevant.'

Her hand was twitching as if she wanted to grip a weapon, so he covered it with his own. 'You'll never be irrelevant. You're a strong, driven woman. One of the best I know. Whatever you do next, you'll do well.'

She didn't seem to hear. 'I'm questioning everything I know, now. The Order and what we do. What I've achieved. What life is for. The people I'm with.' Her voice began to crack. 'If I'm in love with Jadyn and he's in love with me, why is it that when my life is breaking down, he's too caught up in quests and riddles to notice? Why when I'm having a crisis is he always off taking care of blasted Aura?'

Because old relationships can go stale, and new ones are fascinating, Gram wanted to answer, but he sensed that was the wrong thing to say. He also felt a queasy sense of jealous satisfaction, because whether it was the forced rapport he and Romara had, or the time they'd spent together, he couldn't deny that he wanted to be with her. And with her glyma fading, she was so much more relaxed, which only magnified that attraction.

I want her happy, of course I do . . . but I'd rather it was happiness with me.

But there were layers to Romara and Jadyn he had no conception of. Trying to step into that arena would probably see him cut down.

So he swallowed his longing and resigned himself to the role of supportive friend.

'Jadyn's just being chivalrous to someone he pities,' he told her, releasing her hand.

'Is he?' she blurted. 'He'd better be.'

'Tell him how you feel,' he advised.

'You don't understand,' she replied. 'We *can't* talk about these things – we're Vestal knights. Self-control is what defines us. Emotions and needs and desires can't just be bandied about! They have to be internalised and broken down. Ordinary people might be able to talk about such things, but we can't.'

Which is precisely why you should, he thought. But he knew better than to challenge her on it. 'You two have a bond,' he reminded her. 'Ten years of shared service. You love each other. Surely you can talk?'

'Aye,' she said raggedly. 'About anything *except* feelings. Anyway, he wants to go on with this damned quest, while I want to retire and finally live. But I can't make him see sense.'

He rocked back on his perch, thinking, *Elysia, what a mess.* 'You'll work it out.'

'It just hurts when that Nepari bint makes him laugh. No one thinks I'm funny.'

'I do,' Gram countered. 'It's just really *subtle* humour.'

'Jag off.' But she gave him a shy smile before looking away.

They fell into an amiable silence, and Gram felt the glow of knowing that he'd eased her tension a little, dissipating some of her fatal anger. So he just enjoyed being near her, and the taste of cold clean mountain air, and the majesty of night sky.

'Can I ask you about your marriage?' she said, eventually.

He hung his head. 'I'm not proud of it. There was a woman I wanted, when I was young, eighteen or so. I courted her, proposed – via her father, as is the custom on Avas. It turned out she was in love with someone else.'

She wrinkled her nose. 'Bad luck.'

'No, arrogance,' he confessed. 'I saw her, I desired her and more or less bought her, while barely getting to know her. To be fair, she pretended she liked me. I later found she'd been seeing another, who couldn't then afford to court her. So I got her, only to be cuckolded.'

'What happened?'

'I broke his jaw, then cast her out,' Gram admitted. 'She's with him now. He's a candlemaker and they're happy together. It was a scandal, but people forgive and forget. I guess they're refugees now.'

She frowned. 'You've said vyr are constrained in physical relations, like we knights? So how could your marriage function?'

'It was over years before I got involved with the vyr. I suspected I had the Gift but I avoided being tested, being equally nervous of both the Order and the vyr. So it wasn't an issue. It was only after it fell apart that my mother drew me into her coven and I was given elobyne powder. It was a small amount, so I could hold the power at bay, but now, through you, my system is becoming flooded with glyma. I'm being sucked into the maelstrom and I'll either become a monster or, if it's in me to do so, I'll break through and find ninneva.' Gram shuddered. 'I'm not ready for that trial. I may never be.'

He'd thought she might pull away, but instead she met his gaze. 'You're a strong man, with the wisdom of the trees and mountains in you. If anyone can reach this ninneva, it's you.'

'Thank you,' he murmured. It was perhaps the best thing anyone had ever said to him.

Dear Elysia, I want her so badly.

To distract himself, he flailed for something else to talk about. 'Um, what's an Exemplar?' he asked. 'You mentioned them earlier.'

She gave him a sideways look, clearly knowing he was changing the subject. 'There's only one Exemplar at a time. They're the champion knight of the Order: the best at magic and fighting, chosen at a biannual tournament of the regional champions, the best of the best, from all over the Triple Empire. The current Exemplar is Vazi Virago. She's just a strip of a girl, a Zynochi dervish – but she moves like time and space don't exist. Her blade is everywhere when she defends and a blur when she attacks, while her mastery of the glyma is terrifying. I saw her defend her title in Hyastar and she ruled the field – no one else stood a chance. It was inspiring, though it made me feel utterly inadequate, too.'

'How so?' Gram asked, more comfortable now that they weren't talking about him.

'Well, it's easier to accept being second best when the other people are just bigger or stronger or whatever. But she's just *better*. You can't define why, she just *is* – she's a force of nature.'

To Gram, such driven people sounded like fanatics. 'Then I pray we never meet her.'

'Ar-byan,' she agreed fervently. 'Although I have, actually. I was like a swooning girl, even though I'm six years older than her. Anyway, Elysia willing, I'll leave this life behind, and be grateful to do so. I just pray this quest doesn't kill us all.'

He tried to reassure her. 'You and Jadyn will be fine. Once you put the glyma aside, you'll be free. And you're not even thirty yet, so you've got your best years before you.'

'Akka willing.' Yawning, she moved away. 'Well, I think I can sleep now. Thank you for talking. I do believe you're honest, even if it turns out you're wrong about everything.' She tilted her head absently. 'Sometimes it's easier to talk to someone who doesn't matter than someone who does.'

His face froze, and she suddenly realised what she'd said.

'Oh jagat, I didn't mean you don't matter,' she blurted. 'You do, absolutely, you've saved my damned life, you big lummox.' She seized his shoulder. '*You matter.*'

He looked at her, somehow keeping his whole body rigid, when all of a sudden glyma kindled inside him and he wanted to seize her and show her exactly how much she mattered to him . . .

But he managed somehow to swallow it all.

'Get some sleep, Siera,' he growled. 'Give your mouth a rest.'

She grimaced, then sighed, 'Sorry! I'm a jagging idiot, aren't I?'

She didn't wait for an answer, just stamped away, while he exhaled, letting the accumulated tension and glyma-rage seep out of him into the soil.

In seconds, every bush within ten paces of him had curled up its leaves and died.

Next morning they set out with an air of purpose rather than the laughter and singing of the previous day, as if they sensed that today was *the* day. Increasingly, too, they were captivated by the journey through beautiful wilderness, a fractured landscape in which the river flowed past giant pillars of stone hundreds of paces tall, festooned with scrubs and trees, homes to nesting eagles and colonies of other birds. The current was steady, but the river was so winding that they covered many kylos on the ground, but probably few as the crow flew.

Nevertheless, Jadyn felt a mounting sense of progress. They were getting closer, according to Elindhu, who'd taken readings from the stars before dawn.

'But remember, it may not be what we expect,' she reminded them, 'so keep your eyes open.'

All day, every bend promised fulfilment, but it was near dusk that the moment came. A deep ravine spat them out onto a long narrow lake, a beautiful, tranquil place with deep green waters and mist-shrouded forests on the slopes around them, standing amid grey-green peaks that all but blocked out the sky. The cloud had thinned and the sun broke through, glimmering on the rippling water in hues of pink and gold.

Jadyn lifted his eyes and blinked in awed hope.

On the headland of the first bend in the lake, that sunlight gleamed on the walls of a multi-level building, and on the red-clay tiles of sloped roofs. A lot were damaged, and much had been swallowed up by climbing plants, but the entirety was mostly whole.

He shipped his paddle and stared, unable to quite believe it was real. The other boat drew alongside, and they all had bright eyes and enthralled faces.

'Elindhu,' he called, 'is that it? Is *that* Vanashta Baanholt?'

She peered, then frowned. 'The design is Rudanite – they were a monastic sect prominent in the region two centuries ago, who were later deemed heretical and expunged. They thought the world to be flat,' she added, with a chuckle.

Soren looked at her in astonishment. 'Is it not?'

'You and I clearly need to talk,' she told the initiate. Then she turned back to the view. 'It's too soon to say, but it does feel like we're in the right place. The Rudanites may simply have found this building and taken it over. They were a rich order at one point, despite being crackpots, and they went everywhere.' Then she lifted a finger to heaven. 'Akka willing, it might well be our destination.'

Everyone cheered wearily, then put aside weariness and worked their paddles, ploughing across the water.

The Sanctor Wardens' lost monastery, Jadyn thought, in a daze. *The place where the aegis was once taught.*

He glanced towards Aura, who had the look of a hopeful child on her face. They shared a smile and she held up her hand, showing the dark rune carved there. He did the same: it was their bond, whatever it meant.

As they closed in on the headland, Gram spotted an old stone jetty below the promontory holding the building. It was damaged, but looked usable, so they took the boats in, disembarked and hauled them up onto a partially submerged stone wharf, and tethered them to some broken wooden staves protruding from the water. In the thick surrounding bushes, birds shrilled and chattered, peering down at them with bright eyes. An overgrown stairway could be seen winding up towards the ancient ruins.

Jadyn felt like he could fly up on wings of hope, and noticed he wasn't the only one. Elindhu was bright-eyed and chirpy, Obanji's weathered face had years smoothed away, and Soren was eager as a puppy. Gram looked quietly hopeful, his eyes cast upwards, his back straight.

He noticed Aura hanging back, though. That puzzled him, until he realised what she must be going through. *She's built this up in her mind and now she's scared of disappointment.* As the others began making their way up the stairs, he went over to her. 'Come on, Peradura, let's go and see. We'll never find out, down here.'

She gave him an apprehensive look, then set her jaw, looking up with fear and hope in her eyes. 'Am coming.'

'Bravo . . . hey, I used a Nepari word!'

They shared a smile and went to the stairs. The stonework was reasonably intact, despite places where thick tree roots had broken through, and others where tree branches blocked the way. Gram and Obanji led the way, forcing a path up to an ancient courtyard overlooking the lake, with a gatehouse through which a well could be seen. The ruins rising above them were much more solid and imposing when seen up close.

Jadyn joined Romara, blowing a little from the climb. 'Whoever lived here must've been fit.'

'You're getting soft,' she answered lightly.

'Or just old,' Obanji added, as Soren and Elindhu arrived.

But as Gram approached the gatehouse, a harsh voice rang out and soldiers rose from behind the low wall surrounding them, helmed and armed with crossbows.

'Halt!' one man shouted. 'Don't anyone move.'

18

The Pinnacle of Knighthood

Exemplar

It's natural in the exacting world of the Vestal Order for those who excel in martial and magical skills to be exalted. The title of 'Exemplar' is the most highly sought after honour in the Order. It is won on the tourney field against the other regional champions, every two years. The victor, who is acclaimed as the Hierophant's Champion, is expected to embody all the highest ideals of the Order. Only two women have ever gained the title, including the current Exemplar, Siera Vaziella 'Vazi' al'Nuqheel, of Vintab in Zynochia, who took the name 'Virago' or 'Warrior Maid' to mark the feat.

CHRONICLES OF TALMONT, 1471

Falagan Ranges
Summer 1472

Jadyn froze, his eyes flashing to Romara's as the uniforms of the men surrounding them were revealed: the black-and-white quartered tabards of the Vestal Guard. He and his pentacle drew on their elobyne orbs, though they were all but drained, and glyma-energy came streaming back into his body, setting his nerves jangling.

His eyes searched the courtyard, assessing his options – and noting that Aura hadn't emerged from the overgrown path behind them. *Stay there*, he silently urged. *Go back.*

Romara flicked her cloak over her sheath to conceal her lack of a flamberge. Obanji, Soren and Elindhu stepped in front of her, while Gram moved beside her protectively. None of them were wearing tabards, but the forest green erling tunics, so they looked more like mercenaries than knights of the Order.

Boots clattered in the gatehouse and Jadyn expected to see Lictor Borghart appear, gloating at the ease of their capture. But the figure was someone else entirely: a woman, tall and slender in form-fitting armour, with gold engravings adorning the breastplate and a plumed helm under her arm. Her vivid blue eyes contrasted with the deep bronze of her skin; her narrow, delicate face framed by ebony hair tied in a no-nonsense pony-tail. She looked more like a doll than a living woman, but she moved with grace and poise.

Jadyn knew exactly who she was: Vaziella al'Nuqheel, better known as Vazi Virago, the youngest-ever Exemplar in the history of the Order. He, Romara and Obanji dropped to one knee, as mere knights must, Obanji pulling Soren down into a genuflection, and Elindhu gestured urgently for Gram to do the same.

'Exemplar,' Jadyn blurted. 'We are honoured.'

'Siera Vazi, we don't know these people,' the voice that had given the orders called.

'But we do; at least one,' Vazi Virago replied in crisp tones, her Zynochi accent barely discernible. 'This is our sister-knight, Siera Romara Challys.'

Jadyn held his breath, waiting for the axe of condemnation to fall, but instead, the Exemplar offered Romara her hand. 'Sister, welcome. It's an unexpected pleasure to see you.'

'Exemplar, I'm surprised you remember me,' Romara blurted, her relief barely hidden.

'Women are a minority in the Order, and few have your longevity of service, let alone become a century commander,' she replied. 'Your career has inspired many women. Please, rise, all of you.' She looked at Jadyn. 'You must be Sier Jadyn Kaen – Romara spoke of you. And all know of Obanji Vost,' she added, without warmth. Then she looked at Elindhu, Soren and Gram. 'My apologies; you I know not.'

Jadyn, seeing Romara hesitate, struggling to justify Gram's presence, covered for her by saying, 'This is Gram, our guide. Elindhu is our magia, and this is Soren var'Dael, an initiate.'

They all rose, trying to look relieved, not petrified. *How in Perdition is the jagging Exemplar here?* Jadyn wondered. *This is supposed to be a lost monastery, for Elysia's sake.*

Clearly the Exemplar was just as taken aback, saying to Romara, 'Siera, I must ask: How is it that you are here?'

Jadyn's mind raced: *If Borghart's here, or she already knows we're renegades, then she's toying with us. But I don't sense that, which means this is a coincidence, and that she's been out of circulation for at least a month, if she hasn't had word of the Falcons going renegade.*

Romara had clearly reached the same conclusion. She stepped forward, as if she was still commanding the pentacle. 'We were sent here by Lord Walter Sandreth,' she said, and Jadyn mentally applauded. Sandreth had Order connections, but he was Vandari, so unlikely to be patron of the Exemplar's own mission, which was likely to be at the Archon's behest, or even at the wish of the Hierophant himself.

'Walter Sandreth?' Siera Vazi said, with a frown. Though she looked young, Jadyn sensed a complex mind at work. 'Why would he send you here, Siera?'

'Lord Sandreth asked for secrecy,' Romara said, 'but as Exemplar, your wishes obviously overrule his. We were most recently on Avas and got wind of a vyr nest in the mountains here. The trail led to this place ... whatever it is ...'

Rom, you're a goddess, Jadyn thought, full of admiration.

The Exemplar looked thoughtful. After a moment, she said, 'Let's discuss this in private; even my men don't know the full story of why we're here.' She waved her centurion forward. 'Prade, assign some men to assist with our guests' luggage and ensure their boats are secured. Where's your century, Siera Romara?'

Clearly the men had spotted their boats as they crossed the lake. Jadyn wondered if they'd counted heads. *If we don't confess to Aura's presence and she's found, trust is broken. But she hasn't appeared ...*

They gambled on silence.

'This mission required speed and secrecy, according to Lord Sandreth,' Romara replied. 'We left our men in furlough and travelled light ... and anonymously,' Romara added, gesturing at her non-uniform tunic.

The Exemplar looked satisfied, and Jadyn dared to hope she'd been taken in.

'Gram,' Romara said to the trapper, 'please help these men with the boats.'

The trapper accepted the role of servant, and raising his voice, he directed the soldiers to follow him back to the boats, so that Aura had ample warning to hide. Centurion Prade followed with half a dozen men – but the rest remained in position, their crossbows lowered but still in hand.

Another Vestal knight appeared, a heavyset man with a sculpted beard. Vazi Virago introduced him as Sier Tylkor Kervassien, her seneschal. Jadyn knew the name: he was reputedly one of the deadliest swordsmen in the Order. 'An honour, Sier,' he said carefully.

'Your names are known to me,' Tylkor replied, shaking Jadyn and Romara's hands. Soren as an initiate and Elindhu as a mage weren't deemed his equals, so he only nodded to them. 'And Obanji Vost,' he added, turning to the Abuthan. 'It's good to see you again. I still remember my beating in the Denium tourney.'

'I was a seasoned warrior and you a debutant,' Obanji said, taking his hand. 'Your rise to be the Exemplar's seneschal surprised no one. I heard you fought the Kharagh in '68?'

As the two men fell to reminiscing, the Exemplar turned back to Romara. 'Please, walk with me and we'll discuss our missions away from flapping ears,' she said, with a hint of warmth. 'Woman to woman.'

Jadyn swallowed, but he could do nothing but let them go, and pray Romara retained the poise to deal with the maze of treachery that was Petraxus and Order politics.

The doll-like Zynochi girl looked nothing like a champion warrior, but Romara had seen her fight and harboured no illusions. The glyma wasn't just a leveller – at the elite levels of the Order, it was *everything* – and she'd seen Vazi Virago batter men twice her size on the tourney fields. So it was with real respect – and no little fear – that she followed the young woman up mossy, worn stone steps, trying to get a grip on the story she must now spin.

Having to step in and get Jadyn out of this mess had come naturally, and it had been necessary, for Jadyn was a political innocent. But she was out of touch with such matters herself these days, and also burningly aware that the blade in her shoulder harness wasn't a flamberge but an erling tuelawar whose provenance she may well be obliged to explain. And they were all wearing erling cloth.

Why, oh why, did you send the Exemplar here? she berated Akka. *Do you want us to fail?*

Given that she and her Falcons were now heretics and rebels, the answer was probably a resounding *Yes*.

Vazi Virago led her up into the main part of the abandoned monastery, where more of her soldiers were chopping away the woody vines to clear the walkways. A few torches were already alight in the darker spots, guttering in the breeze gusting through the broken windows. The balconies they traversed stank of bird droppings and vermin, and vines had penetrated most of the upper windows, spreading out like giant exploring tentacles.

They reached a balcony overlooking the lake; the sun was behind the mountains and the stars were coming out over a scene of spectacular tranquillity. But Romara barely saw it, her mind too focused on what to say.

'It looks like our missions overlap,' Vazi commented, staring at the lake. 'The Archon sent us here, after a scholar uncovered a cache of old Warden documents pointing to this place. It was deemed to be of the highest priority. Do you know what this place is?'

'We think so,' Romara replied. *Any credible mission sent here would have to have some inkling*, she reasoned. 'We believe it's an old Sanctor base, possibly Vanashta Baanholt itself.'

'Indeed it is.'

The confirmation sent a thrill through her, but Romara contained her reaction to a terse nod.

'Tell me, why would Lord Sandreth send a mission here, instead of deferring to the Order?' Vazi asked.

'I don't know,' Romara bluffed. 'It makes me wonder what games are being played over our heads.'

Everyone in the Order hated being used as playing pieces by the Day and Night Courts in Petraxus. The Exemplar proved no exception. 'Let's discuss this more fully over dinner – bring your seneschal and we'll work out what we're going to do. I do warn you though that Lord Sandreth's wasted his money.'

Romara shrugged. 'I don't care about his lordship's coin, but it's disappointing to waste my pentacle's time and effort. I'll want to know why this mess happened when we get back.'

'I'd appreciate you getting to the heart of it,' Vazi replied approvingly. 'It's good to meet you properly, Siera Romara. We women knights should work more together.' She indicated the lower courtyards, where the men waited. 'Let's rejoin our pentacles and get them all acquainted.'

The rest of Vazi's men had now arrived in the inner courtyard, and for Romara's part, no introductions were necessary. Exemplars could hand-pick their pentacle, and Romara knew the faces and names, if only from a distance: Sier Faidal Unbaro, an Abuthan; a Vandari, Sier Runa Branstak; and Siera Mildra de Arum of Talmont, renowned fighters, all. They were too elegant for arrogance, but their air of superiority was clear, and subtly grating.

After introductions and some stilted conversation, Centurion Prade arrived with Gram, followed by a few men carrying their baggage.

'You're travelling light, Siera Romara,' Tylkor Kervassien commented. 'You'll need more than this if the weather turns.'

'There were mishaps,' she replied, feigning embarrassment. 'The terrain here is treacherous and we lost most of our gear. In truth, it's a relief to meet you.'

Tylkor grunted, more amused than sympathetic. 'I suppose we can share a little. Prade, show them to the northern wing: there are free rooms up there.' He indicated the building above. 'It's safe to roam anywhere above ground, but for now, it's best you stay out of the mines.'

'Mines?' Jadyn asked.

'We've found old tunnels beneath the monastery,' Vazi told them. 'My magus is studying them as we speak. Perhaps we can show you them tomorrow, if he deems it safe?'

'Safe' – in other words, once they've claimed anything of value, Romara interpreted.

Prade led the Falcon pentacle to their assigned rooms, but Vazi Virago and Tylkor Kervassien took Romara and Jadyn along a walkway to a look-out perched on a precipice over a waterfall. It was a beautiful evening and an impressive view of the lake and the giant pillars of rock rising from below. Birds swooped and shrilled in the twilit landscape.

'An incredible place, and so unspoiled,' Vazi commented. 'But a long way from everywhere.'

'A fine place for a monastery,' Romara commented, feeling remarkably calm and clearheaded, perhaps due to the low levels of glyma inside her. 'Perhaps I'll found an abbey here when I retire? We can be the first order of nuns to permit marriage and drinking.'

Unexpectedly, the Exemplar laughed, a brittle sound, which broke some of the tension. 'I might even join it, if only to escape those Day Court lords who stalk me all the damned time,' she remarked. 'Whenever I'm at court I feel like the prize in some kind of game.'

She went on to give them a sparse account of her century's journey here, following a river upstream from its delta on the Mar-Ortas, the Blood Sea. 'I'm commanded to recover what we deem of value before destroying this place,' she concluded.

'*Destroy?*' Jadyn blurted. 'But this is Vanashta Baanholt—'

'A place of unholy power,' Tylkor said. 'It must be understood, then rendered harmless.'

'It is innately heretical,' Vazi agreed. 'Tainted thoughts are not for the weak-minded.'

'Of course,' Romara said quickly, before Jadyn could give them away. 'I'm sure if Lord Sandreth had known fully of this place's history, he would have commanded the same.'

'Then what did he think he was sending you into?' Vazi asked flatly.

'A vorlok coven,' Romara replied.

'I didn't know the Sandreth family had such interests?'

Romara met the Exemplar's subtly chilling gaze, realising that her almost girlish looks masked a reptilian coldness. She was a classic angular Zynochian beauty, but she had an untouchable quality that made that beauty forbidding, not enticing. She was, Romara decided, quietly terrifying.

'House Sandreth are loyal imperialists,' Romara told her. 'Although I'm coming to believe that Lord Walter may not have briefed us completely,' she mock-confessed; her pentacle must be seen as victims, not instigators.

'The regional lords always have their own agendas,' the Exemplar grumbled. 'Nothing they do is pure. It angers me when they draw us into their scheming.' She half-turned, and Romara relaxed a fraction, until she swung back and asked suddenly, 'Siera Romara, the outline of your blade hilt is unusual. May I see it?'

Jadyn stiffened a fraction, but Romara managed to conceal her unease, flipping her leather hilt-cover aside and drawing the tuela-war. She offered it hilt-first to the Exemplar.

'My flamberge broke in the body of a vorlok on Avas. It was wielding this, so I took it. At need, I replace the pommel with an elobyne orb.'

'But you don't intend to use it permanently, surely?' Vazi frowned, examining the weight and balance of the erling weapon curiously. 'An Order flamberge is made from the finest steel in Hytal, and by the best craftsmen.'

Fortunately, Romara had anticipated this moment. 'The truth is,' she said, hanging her head, 'I can feel my time coming . . . Avas was hard, seeing all those innocents cast from their homes. It took me to the edge. So I'm trying to manage my glyma-use. When we return to the north, my intention is to retire.' She lifted her head, seeing sympathy clouding the faces of the Exemplar and her seneschal. 'Jadyn knows, but not the others – although they're not blind.'

Vazi and Tylkor exchanged glances, then she said, 'I'm sorry to hear that, Siera Romara. You've been an inspiration to women of the Order throughout your decade of service. And I appreciate your candour.'

She examined the beautifully etched blade again, and handed it back. 'It's a beautiful weapon. I pray it will serve you well in retirement – although not with an orb in the pommel, of course.'

Romara forced a taut smile. 'I'll not go that way, Exemplar. A convent full of babies and wine, remember?'

Vazi and Tylkor chuckled softly and once again the tension was alleviated. 'Please, settle in,' the Exemplar said, ending her subtle probing. 'You'll join Tylkor and me for the evening meal in an hour. You will excuse me – it is the hour after dusk, and I must perform the khutbah.'

The khutbah was a Zynochi religious ceremony in honour of Akka, one of many such rites carried over from pre-Akkanite times in both Zynochia and Abutha. 'Sali'mah,' Romara said, to show she understood.

Vazi Virago smiled tightly and turned to leave, Tylkor trailing her.

'Exemplar,' Romara called after her, 'my magia, Elindhu, would welcome meeting your magus and comparing notes on scholastic matters, if he's available?'

And maybe she can discover what's in the mines beneath here . . .

Vazi hesitated, then said, 'We'll consider. See you at dinner, Siera. Excuse us.' She turned and strode away, a lioness in woman's guise. Tylkor followed her like a shadow, all the darker for her light.

'They say the Hierophant himself is fascinated by her,' Jadyn commented. 'I've heard that he wants her for his concubine.' He leaned in and whispered, 'Rom, what are we going to do?'

'I have no idea,' she admitted. 'Let's join the others, and try to work something out.'

Jadyn was a bag of nerves, but he was heartened to see the old Romara was back, poised and clever, with a deft grip on the intricacies of Order politics. It gave him hope to cling to, even in this worrying predicament.

No one mentioned Nilis Evandriel, he noted. *Did he beat them here and go on somewhere else? Or is he lurking nearby?*

They found their comrades in their assigned rooms on the third level of the complex, side-by-side cells sharing a balcony-walkway overlooking the lake. Each room was large enough for two bedrolls, but there was no usable furniture. They gathered in Romara's room. Everyone was edgy, even the usually phlegmatic Obanji and Elindhu.

'Where's Aura?' Jadyn asked, once they were sure they were alone.

Gram shook his head. 'By the time I got back to the boats, she was gone. There was no sign of her, but there's a lot of trees down there and she's smart enough to hide.'

It sounded reasonable, though if she was caught, he had no idea how they'd explain her. But on a long shot, Jadyn draped his green scarf over the balcony, to mark his position in case Aura was watching.

'What now?' Obanji asked.

'We've got to learn what we can, then get out alive,' Romara answered.

'That's not a plan,' Elindhu commented, 'That's a prayer.'

'I know. But what choice have we got?'

She looked away. 'None, I suppose.'

Jadyn rubbed his brow wearily, seeing no clear path through this. 'For now, we play along, and if it feels like we're in danger, we'll make our excuses and leave. Meantime, we'll try to mingle, see what we can learn. And remember, act like Romara's in charge.'

'Was she ever not?' Obanji chuckled.

'Jadyn's just my puppet,' Romara winked at him.

'String or glove?' Elindhu asked slyly.

'Careful,' Romara warned her, laughing. 'Come on, puppet, we'd better clean up if we're to dine with the greatest knight in the Order.'

'I can't believe that girl's really the Exemplar,' Soren marvelled. 'She looks so young.'

'Don't be fooled. She's won the last three Exemplar Tourneys,' Obanji told him. 'She's never been beaten.'

'I'd love to take her on,' Soren replied. When they all looked sceptical, he added, 'My father made me go to every sword-fighting competition on Avas. I've beaten boys much older than me. Practically grown men.'

'I don't think that's quite the same standard as the twelve regional

Exemplars of the Order of Vestal knights,' Romara said drily. 'Let's get you trained up first, eh?'

'I'm going to be the best,' Soren maintained, deadly serious.

Maybe he will, Jadyn mused, *or he'll end up dead before we do.*

But Obanji clapped the young man on the shoulder. 'You can do it, if you put the work in. You have the potential, believe me. Champions and Exemplars are getting younger every year. But Vazi Virago was nineteen when she won her first Exemplar Tourney. You've got two years of learning before you match that.'

While the others threw in their coppers' worth, Jadyn went to the balcony and gazed out, wondering where Aura was. *We're teetering on a precipice and if they catch her, that could push us over the edge.*

Aura ran her eyes over the parapet above, waited for the patrolling sentry to move off, then ghosted into the lee of the wall, dropped under a fallen tree and slithered into the undergrowth. From there she worked her way to the right, creeping under an overhang and stepping over a stream trickling from above, making for the western flank of the old monastery. It was largely intact, but heavily overgrown.

How many Talmoni are here? she wondered. Clearly these soldiers didn't know what Jadyn's people had done or they'd have come to blows already, but she doubted someone as transparent as Jadyn could hide anything for long. *They'll be discovered any moment*, she worried, knowing that would leave her in a hopeless situation.

She'd been trailing the others upwards, but hanging back a little, trying to deal with her hopes and anxieties over this place. When she realised they'd been spotted, she fled back to the boats, only to realise that the ambushers must have seen them coming across the lake, so she couldn't steal one without triggering pursuit.

More than that, she didn't want to lose the Falcons, because they were now her friends. What little she'd seen suggested they'd managed to bluff these other Vestal Order people, which was good, and no one had come looking for her, but she was at a loss as to what to do.

They are of the Order, like Jadyn, Akka said, in her ear. *You can trust them. Just surrender yourself into their care.*

Remember the lictor, the Devourer retorted. *These will be just as bad.*

Aura instinctively agreed with her, Queen of Evil or no.

She was famished, though, and the cooking smells that rose as the sun set were a torment. With the lake below, water wouldn't be a problem, but she needed food.

I'll have to steal it, she thought, making Akka sigh and the Devourer smirk.

What else she should do wasn't clear. She didn't want to abandon her travelling companions, not now that she felt that this quest was for her, too. If this was a place where the aegis could be found, she wanted to explore – but the hazards were clear.

As she gazed out over the lake, she saw something gliding by with just a nose above the water – perhaps a river crocodile, a known hazard in Neparia and Solabas. It added to the subtle air of menace here, sapping her courage.

But she steeled herself as she paused to let the sentries march past just a few paces above her head. Most guardsmen settled into a predictable rhythm, she'd learned from experience. So she counted their steps, then flitted onwards until she could see the north-facing wing above. Thick vines covered the walls, and she began to calculate how she'd scale them ... then she saw a piece of fabric fluttering from one of the empty window holes: a distinctive green scarf.

Farm Boy is not completely stupid, she allowed. She ran her eye over the route again, measuring distances and angles. *There to there to there ... I could do that.*

But it was too light still, so she edged back into the base of the rock wall, where she spotted an old fracture, with a pool before it. She clambered down and quenched her thirst, then noticed that the water was coming from a rivulet emerging from underground, through a crack large enough to crawl into.

No time like now. She wriggled in, trying hard not to flinch at the cobwebs and the dank mud that stained her new garb, but that couldn't be helped.

She expected it to become narrower, but instead it widened.

E Cara, I wonder where this goes . . .

Having been encouraged to mingle with the exemplar's men, Soren followed the sound of steel on steel and the barking voice of a sergeant to the main courtyard below, where a cohort of Vestal Guard were drilling. The sound reminded him of his father's carping voice, the clatter of swords and the smell of adolescent aggression. The local military bases ran competitions, trying to suck in local youths to aid recruitment, and the prizes were often substantial enough for his father to let him compete.

Sometimes those purses kept us alive . . .

The courtyard was high on the cliff, overlooking the water. Thirty men were being taken through a basic drill, hounded by a loud sergeant. The three junior knights of the Exemplar's pentacle were watching them. Soren saluted them, then drew his sword and joined the soldiers.

In minutes, he was lost in the drills, not really noticing anything except the way his body and his blade moved, making the little corrections he knew his father would have bawled him out for, then finishing with a flourishing combination that he'd been trained to throw into this particular sequence.

Everyone else had already finished the drill and stopped to watch, leaving him the only one moving. He finished, blade across his body in mid-guard, perfectly balanced. When he looked around, the men-at-arms were glaring, for trying to show them up, and the sergeant was bristling, thinking Soren was trying to belittle them all.

Inevitably, one of the knights sitting on the edge emerged from the shade; Sier Faidal Unbaro was a burly Abuthan with tightly curled black hair and a face that totally lacked Obanji's warmth. He flexed his arms and drew his flamberge. 'Chinjama wi Mbixi, umfana?' he asked.

Soren shook his head. 'Sorry. I grew up in the north.'

Sier Faidal studied him briefly. 'You move well, for an initiate, boy. But let's see what you've really got.'

'I've only just gained the glyma,' Soren told him.

The other man shrugged. 'No glyma, then.' He rolled his shoulders and presented his blade. 'Are you familiar with Kenendos rules? No head shots, no limb shots – body only, where we're armoured.'

Soren knew those and many other rules. He extended his blade. 'I'm Soren var'Dael.'

'Well met, umfana.' The knight touched his blade to Soren's, then stepped away—

And immediately crashed back in, seeking to dominate from the outset, smashing a blow at Soren's chest hard enough to break ribs – but Soren stepped out and dashed Sier Faidal's blade sideways, knocking it askew and riposting, deftly stalling the other man's onslaught.

They circled, each assessing how the other moved.

Faidal grunted in appreciation, then waded in again, a flurry of blows that grew faster as they came, trying to force Soren backwards and right to expose his left side. Soren let him come, noting his favoured blows, then countered, launching a combination that forced the older man into a desperate parry, then flashed jabs and slashes at his shoulders, forcing him to back up, and then he lunged . . .

. . . too soon. Sier Faidal wasn't unbalanced enough for the blow to land, and he dashed Soren's blade away, then battered into Soren's left shoulder-blade, a painful hit that made him wince and gasp.

'Touch!' the knight grunted in satisfaction, backing out.

The soldiers burst into cheers, while Soren pulled a rueful face.

'Some promise, umfana,' Faidal remarked, pretending he wasn't blowing. 'Not bad.'

Soren beamed as if this were the highest praise. Then he bowed to the nearest of the remaining pair of knights. 'How about you, Sier Runa? May I have the honour?'

Runa Branstak, a balding Vandari with straggling dark hair and a full beard, stood and stretched. 'You sure, boy?' His accent marked him out as from the Toras Coast, a wild place from whence raiders once terrorised the coastal north. With his horned helm and chest-length beard, Sier Runa looked like a remnant of that age.

They touched blades, then he hurtled at Soren with a volley of blows, battering him backwards, then sweeping aside an attempted riposte as he lashed out with his left foot, sweeping Soren's feet from under him.

Soren crashed down, but twisted away as the next blow clanged off the mossy stones. He rolled and came up, then countered, unleashing his own series of blows, left-high, right-high, right-low and left-mid, fully testing the startled Vandari's defence. Then he unleashed exactly the lunge that lost him the bout against Sier Faidal.

Sier Runa roared and hammered his blade at the off-balance Soren's back, and despite his mail shirt he got another bruising and went down, bellowing in pain.

'I yield,' Soren shouted, as the Vandarai, looking as if he'd forgotten this was a friendly duel, swung again. Soren batted it away from his prone position, then dropped his blade. 'You win!'

The Vandarai, panting hard from having to defend himself so unexpectedly, punched the air while his soldiers crowed again, and this time Soren couldn't miss the vindictiveness.

'Not so jagging flash now, are ye?' was the general sentiment.

Runa loomed over him, offering a hand up. 'Style, but no substance,' he rumbled, as he hauled Soren up with the semblance of chivalry, then swaggered away.

Soren picked up his sword, and turned to the remaining knight. The Talmoni woman had a close-cropped scalp and blunt, battered features. 'Siera? May I also test your skill?'

The soldiers murmured gleefully, enjoying this interruption to their own drill. 'Sucker for punishment, this twerp, ain't he?' someone remarked.

The woman strode to meet him, her expression disdainful, as if she shouldn't have to dirty herself with runts like him. No one but Soren had noticed that Obanji had appeared, sitting on the stone wall, but he didn't acknowledge him, instead watching the way the woman walked, and noting that she was left-handed.

'Siera Mildra de Arum,' she introduced herself curtly. 'Ready?'

She came at Soren in an impatient rush, but her technique was flawless and fast, meeting every riposte with another blinding attack, twice almost taking him in the throat, then slashing at his belly – but he darted away and began counterattacking, raining in blows of speed but little substance, searching for a weakness.

Then he tried a variant on his hitherto losing lunge ... She recognised it instantly, stepped aside and flat-bladed him in the ribs, breaking the skin somewhere beneath his mail.

'You've got a tell, boy. Can see that blow comin' a mile off.' She leaned in and murmured, 'So you can kiss my arse, you little shit-smear.' Then she too sauntered off, rolling her hips contemptuously, while the soldiers punched the air and Soren sagged to the ground, out of breath bruised and bleeding.

'We're the Golden Dragon century, kid,' the sergeant said. 'You don't strut into our arena like you own it.' Then he turned to his men. 'Show's over, you lazy bastards! Back to work.'

Soren pulled a rueful face and slouched away, calling, 'Thanks!' to the three knights as he passed them. They ignored him smugly.

Obanji caught him up on the stairs, leading back to their rooms. 'You all right?'

'Aye,' Soren mumbled, head down, thinking hard.

'That's the worst I've ever seen you fight.'

'Sorry.'

Obanji caught his shoulder – his bruised left one. 'What did you think you were doing?'

Soren glanced back to make sure they were alone, then said, 'I learned that Sier Faidal has technique but no footspeed. Sier Runa is very strong but impatient, and muddled when defending. Siera Mildra is the best fighter, but she's over-cautious, and obvious in attack.'

Obanji snorted softly. 'Aye ... But—'

'But they learned nothing about me,' Soren said shyly. 'Because I don't fight that way.'

Obanji's face crinkled into a grin. 'You've got balls, "kid",' he chuckled. 'But don't forget: they used no glyma. Until you've nailed your shielding and tightened up on using glyma to attack, they'll still take you apart. How's that shoulder?'

Soren's face sobered, but he shrugged. 'It'll be fine.'

Obanji pulled back his collar, then shook his head. 'It'll be bruised for days, lad. And it's bleeding. Let's see Elindhu.' He ruffled Soren's hair. 'I hope you think it was worth it.'

Soren grinned. 'I reckon it was. But I really wanted to face the Exemplar and Sier Tylkor. They're legends. From them, I might have learned something.'

Obanji put an arm round his shoulder. 'Well, lad, as it happens, I've actually fought against Tylkor. I can tell you all about that prick.'

The Exemplar had told Jadyn and Romara they shouldn't venture into the mines, but Elindhu decided to go anyway. This was Vanashta Baanholt, and she was burning with curiosity.

The worst they can do is tell me to piss off, she decided.

She waddled down to the lower levels, where she found a dark corridor that ended in a guarded cave mouth framed by ancient timbers. She drifted into a rough-hewn recess out of sight, conjured a veil of shadows around herself to get close, then slowly and carefully reached out and grasped the minds of the two sentries.

Her best work was impossible in a fight, but given time, she could do things her sword-swinging comrades could only dream of. *I'm allowed to be here,* she whispered into their minds, taking all the time such spells needed to work. *I'm not worthy of notice or recall,* she instructed their subconscious. *You'll forget I was ever here.*

As a consequence, the two guards didn't even look at her as she emerged and walked between them, entering a rough-walled cave with a hard-packed gravel floor rutted by cart wheels. It became a ramp that opened into a large chamber supported by wooden pillars.

There was a man standing in the middle of the floor, robed in velvets and wearing a silver rune-etched Foylish torc. His staff was planted in the ground, the orb in the tip glowing red; it was making runes carved into the wall facing him shimmer. He had an air of barbarous wisdom, an heir of the Foylish drui, the shamans of old.

He detected her instantly. 'Who's dat?' he rumbled, in a heavy Foyle accent.

Elindhu recognised his face, which was singularly ugly, with oddly bulging eyes and bad acne scars. His eyebrows were tufted like a fox-owl's feathery horns and his bald pate was fringed with greasy hair. She dispelled her veil at once – he'd rip it apart in seconds anyway – and stepped into the light.

'Magister Arghyl Goraghan? It is but I, Elindhu Morspeth of the Falcon century.'

Goraghan was on the Order's Mage Council and known for caution, tenacity and skill. He was very much her superior. He leaned on his staff and peered down at her. 'Ye name be known'a me. How come ye t'be here?'

She bowed her head, keeping her staff inert. 'My pentacle was sent here, not realising you were also here. I expect we'll be sent home, but I thought I might as well have a look around.'

'Down 'ere's f'bidden. The guards—'

'Were there guards?' She risked a wink. 'I didn't notice them.'

The mages of the Vestal Order were generally made to feel second-best by Vestal knights, because in a straight fight, they were, even though they were the ones who opened the locks, deciphered the clues and patched up the fighting men and women. This permeated down to ordinary men-at-arms, who were inclined to both fear and despise them, because a mage was both frightening and vulnerable. It was something mages bonded over, and often led to them sharing subtle ways to assert themselves.

For a moment she thought Goraghan's lugubrious face would turn hostile, but instead he made a gobbling sound she realised was laughter, and said, 'Good on ye, Elindhu Morspeth. Come, see this.' He gestured to encompass the symbols glowing on the wall around the entrance to a deeper cavern. 'Ye be Elidorian, I'm pickin' from yer voice an' yer nose!' He chuckled. 'Yer ney beauty, but perky. I'd lay ye.' Then he roared with laughter. 'If'n I weren't ugly as shit an' a sworn virgin.'

Oh, you're one of those, she thought, disappointed.

Men dealt with enforced celibacy worse than women, she'd noticed. The knights of the Order were often a mess of repressed lust and dangerous to be alone with, despite their vows; there were sometimes horrible results. Although male mages were often characterised as sexless wimples, many were as awkwardly aggressive as any knight.

But she wanted something from him, so she pulled an appraising, speculative face, as if this were a game and she was a player. 'From the right angle, you're a handsome man, Magister.'

'Aye? What angle's that?' he guffawed.

'A hundred paces away, looking in the other direction.'

'Ha!' he bellowed. 'I like 'e! An' say, en't ye a specialist on erlings?'

'That's me,' she answered brightly. 'You want erling lore, I'm your girl.' She batted her eyes a little, because some men were fools for that, even from a plain thing like her.

Visibly encouraged, Goraghan waved grandly at the etched walls. 'Erling script, but da style's odd, wouldn' 'e say?'

It was a test, but an easy one. 'The writing isn't erling but early Tyrsian, adapted into a cursive form,' she told him. 'It's characteristic of the Sanctor Wardens and their writings.'

'Aye, I thought so,' he said, belching. 'I like yer 'air, by da way. Braids like silken ropes – ye can tie me up wit'em later.'

She tittered dutifully, then addressed the glowing symbols. '"*Let the aegis shield your soul*",' she recited – he'd know it already, if his reputation was to be believed. 'The aegis?' she added quizzically, feigning surprise. 'I've always thought it a myth.'

'Ach, no. As real as you or me.'

'Are you here to unravel its mysteries?' she asked.

The big magus grunted like a boar. 'Nae, sadly. I'm curiosity itself, I tell 'e, but our Vazi says I've got a week to learn what I can, then we'll destroy it all.'

'Why?' Elindhu blurted.

'It's no use to us. It en't stronger than da glyma, so what's da point?'

'But it doesn't need elobyne—'

'True, but Talmont has a monopoly on elobyne, lass. So da only folk who'd benefit from d'aegis are our enemies, like the vyr. So that's why we'll be destroyin' it.' He ambled closer, smiling. 'But I'm mighty pleased to have ye 'ere. I can catalogue it faster wit' your help.'

Damn, she thought, hoping she hadn't roused his suspicions. 'Can you show me the rest?'

He looked down at her, chuckling. 'Oh, aye, but only after ye've shared table with me.' He patted his big belly. 'Me stomach's tellin' me it's long past meal time.'

She'd bad experiences with men who lured her to some apparently innocent tryst – her powers weren't martial, and even someone without glyma could disarm her easily enough. A few had, horrible experiences she'd learned from. But Arghyl Goraghan sounded more lonely than lustful, for all his ribald words. And there was a lot more to learn, that was clear.

'Of course,' she said, giving him a coy smile.

'Well, then,' the gross mage beamed. 'I've not had good scholarly company in months, thanks to this damned journey.' He gestured towards the surface. 'Let's go back up, an' I'll put on me Sacrejour best. Then we'll crack a vino an' get prop'ly lammy, eh?'

Exactly an hour after the Exemplar's invitation, a squire knocked. 'Siera Romara,' he called. 'The Exemplar is ready to receive you and your seneschal for dinner.'

'What's your name?' Jadyn asked the squire, who looked barely eighteen. As part of the Exemplar's century, he was probably a prodigy, and thus a name worth knowing.

'Bern Myko, Sier,' the lad replied politely, looking pleased to be asked. 'Please, follow me.'

It suited them that only he and Romara were invited. Obanji would remain here with Soren, and Gram, as a guide, was beneath notice. He was uneasy about Elindhu dining with the Exemplar's magus, but on her advice, they'd decided it was worth the risk.

But be careful, for Elysia's sake, he'd begged.

He and Romara left their weapons behind, as disarming for a meal was expected in the Order, a tradition born of the need to prevent alcohol-fuelled glyma-rage from turning arguments into murder. They followed the puppy-eager Bern Myko through the overgrown, partly ruined complex, descending three levels and crossing to the main

421

building. In the dining room, wine had been poured and interesting cooking smells permeated from a neighbouring refectory.

Vazi Virago and Tylkor Kervassien were awaiting them, both in tabards but having shed their mail-shirts and armour. The garb accentuated the Exemplar's doll-like beauty, her flawless Zynochi looks and disconcerting symmetry, as if every human flaw had passed her by.

She greeted them with polite coolness, and they stood admiring the emerging belt of stars from a south-facing window, then she took them to the east window and showed them the land-gates. There was a bridge over a ravine, and a road winding off into the snow-topped mountains – the route her century had taken to get here.

'How long have you been here?' Romara asked, sighing in pleasure at her first sip of wine.

'Two weeks, after a month hunting for this place,' Tylkor said. 'Enough time to open up the mines and delve a little.' He wrinkled his nose. 'That Foylish windbag Goraghan is taking an age to catalogue it. Most of us just want to torch the damned place and go.'

He gave Vazi a meaningful look; clearly this was a point of contention.

'Goraghan says it was abandoned only a century ago, long after the fall of the Sanctor Wardens,' Vazi said. 'He believes the Rudanites used it until they fell off the edge of the world. It was then looted by brigands, but the mines were sealed when we found them.'

'What's down there?' Romara asked. 'Er, if you're permitted to tell us, of course.'

'Unfortunately, we're not,' Vazi said, her voice becoming distant. She focused suddenly on Romara's grey-green erling tunic. 'This is beautiful. Where did you get it?'

'In Foyland, on the way here,' Romara answered promptly, having anticipated the question. 'They gave us their best, in exchange for aiding them against a vorlok in their territory. We'd never have found this place without their help.'

Vazi and Tylkor exchanged a look, then the grizzled knight said, 'With all due respect, you shouldn't be here at all. The Hierophant's mission outranks yours, and that's that. I know you've come a long way, but as far as I'm concerned, you can turn straight around and go home.'

He was within his rights to say so, Jadyn knew, but it wouldn't do. He glanced at Romara and decided to take a risk. 'We'd agree, but for these.' He raised his hands, his palms showing.

Tylkor stared. *'Perdito!'*

'What are they?' Vazi asked, suddenly animated. She stepped in front of Jadyn and took his hand in her cold grip. 'Akka on High, it's the same . . .' She seized his left, looking at Tylkor with widening eyes. 'And so is this. *The same marks.*'

Jadyn felt the thrill of vindication. If she'd seen them before, it had to be in the mines.

We have to get down there – provided she doesn't decide I'm a vorlok and lop my head off.

'Where, and how, did you get those marks?' Tylkor demanded.

'In Avas,' Romara put in, to protect Jadyn from having to lie. 'There was a pagan shrine – a stone there burned these marks onto Jadyn's hands and we don't understand them. But our mage found clues that led us here.'

The Exemplar looked intrigued, but not hostile. Up close, she was terribly young, and he wondered at the wisdom of placing such authority in the hands of a relative innocent. 'Burned in,' she breathed, examining his hand again. 'But it doesn't feel scarred or seared,' she marvelled. 'I've never heard of such a thing. Do you have the same markings, Siera Romara?'

Romara showed her hands – the scars had already peeled away and were indiscernible. 'These are from picking up a burning torch by the wrong end during a fight,' she said, feigning a rueful smile. 'Our magia thinks Jadyn's marks are something to do with Sanctor Warden magic – the aegis – but we've been sceptical – everyone knows that's a myth.'

The Exemplar dropped her voice, even though there were just the four of them present. 'The aegis was real, Siera Romara. Surely you realise that by now? The Order teaches otherwise to dissuade the foolish from seeking it. Sier Tylkor and I are here expressly to ensure no one who found this place can revive its use and threaten the Triple Empire.'

Jadyn stiffened, wondering if he'd made a dreadful mistake after all. *If they're here to destroy the aegis, what will they do with those marked by it?*

'But to destroy it, we have to understand it,' she went on. 'There's a door in the deepest chamber that we can't open, marked with these symbols. It might even be the reason Vanashta Baanholt exists. Perhaps you are now the key to that door, Sier Jadyn?'

Jadyn's pulse quickened, his throat dry. 'I have no idea,' he mumbled.

'I wonder that we've never heard of such a thing before.' Her eyes bored into him. 'Although our Order has destroyed so many Sanctor relics, so perhaps we'll never understand them.'

For a moment, Jadyn wished he could truly confide in her. If *she* was convinced by his tale, then the entire Vestal Order would listen. But it was too great a risk: Exemplars were like lictors, thoroughly indoctrinated.

'You'd be wise to keep those markings secret, Sier Jadyn,' Vazi remarked. 'I can't imagine a lictor would be so understanding as I about a knight with pagan sigils on his palms. And the scholars would want to dissect you.'

'Jadyn's as uncomfortable about them as anyone,' Romara replied. 'We're being careful about who knows.'

Vazi Virago mused, then came to a decision. 'Your arrival here may be fortuitous. Your magia has made a favourable impression on Magister Goraghan, as he's asked me to sanction her helping him in the mines. It would speed the process hugely, to all our benefits.'

'Elindhu will be in heaven,' Romara said.

They all smiled at the strangeness of mages and their predilection for poking their noses into dusty, forgotten places, and relaxed a little.

Vazi called for the meal, and a pair of squires brought in platters of steaming stew and leafy vegetables, and more wine. After they withdrew, the conversation turned to neutral matters: the rigours of the road, the summer weather, the bizarre customs of foreigners.

'We'll show you the mines tomorrow,' Vazi decided, once the meal was done. 'And the portal marked with the symbols imprinted on your hands. I am fascinated by this revelation.'

A portal – if I can open it, maybe we can leave her and her people behind? Jadyn wondered.

Most of all, he was just relieved she didn't want to do it now.

But once they're all asleep, we may have to try it ourselves, without an audience.

'We look forward to seeing it all,' Romara answered, clearly tuned into his thoughts. 'And thank you for letting us help your mission.' She leaned in and added, 'I do mean *your mission*, Exemplar. We are entirely at your disposal, regardless of Lord Sandreth's involvement in sending us here. Anything we can do to aid you, just ask.'

Vazi and Tylkor nodded approvingly, and the conversation turned to gossip, though Jadyn never lost the sense that he and Romara were deer supping with wolves.

They had finished the wine and were about to make their excuses when the squire, Bern Myko, returned. He bowed to Vazi Virago and announced, 'There are horsemen approaching the eastern gates, Exemplar. We've seen torches on the road, a kylo or more away.'

Tylkor blinked in surprise and bumped his wine cup as they all rose – reflex took over and Jadyn's hand flashed in and caught it before it spilled, his fingers brushing the Exemplar's as she also reached in. Their eyes met, her pupils dilating fractionally as if in recognition.

'You're ahead of me, Sier Jadyn,' she said, an assessing look on her face. 'Bravo.'

He sensed that didn't happen often.

They all went to the east-facing window, overlooking the mountain road leading to this place. A distant line of orange dots could be seen in the darkness. 'These ranges are like Tinker's Way in Petraxus,' Tylkor grunted. 'You can't move for bumping into someone.'

'Who else knows of your mission?' Vazi asked Romara, in a vexed voice. 'Is the whole of the Day Court mounting expeditions?'

'I know of no others,' Romara replied, as Jadyn's heart thudded painfully.

Ten to one it's Borghart . . .

'Jadyn and I will fetch weapons and join you,' Romara offered.

'Good thinking,' Vazi agreed. 'We'll arm, and reconvene at the gates. Myko will guide you.'

'We can find—' Jadyn began, but Romara spoke over him.

'We'd appreciate that,' she said quickly, and it was her Vazi listened to.

Tylkor and Vazi evidently had rooms above, because they went up the nearest stairs, while Myko led Jadyn and Romara back to the north wing, passing soldiers hurriedly arming themselves, and heading for the gates.

Romara touched the lad's arm and asked, 'Where's the mine entrance from here?'

The young squire indicated a corridor leading into the bowels of the hillside. 'Down there, then left to the main shaft,' he told them. 'But no one's allowed down there, on the Exemplar's orders. It's guarded.'

'I only wanted to orientate myself,' Romara replied smoothly. She looked round, then said, 'Ah, we know the way from here. You should arm as well, in case these strangers aren't friends.'

Myko gave her a grateful look and dashed off.

Jadyn turned to Romara. 'We've got to get out of here.'

'I know,' she hissed, as more soldiers stormed past. 'We need to find the others.'

They took the stairs at a run and burst into Romara's room, where they'd left Obanji, Soren and Gram. 'Trouble?' Gram asked, looking up in alarm. 'What's happening?'

'There's a column of riders approaching,' Jadyn replied. 'It could be Borghart.'

'Oh no,' Soren groaned, but Obanji just *tsked*, as if the universe was meeting his low expectations.

Jadyn darted along the hall to Elindhu's room, but it was empty. *Damn, she's still with the Exemplar's mage.* Trying to work out how to deal with that, he hurried to his own room to grab his sword – and stiffened as steel pressed to his throat and a sultry voice spoke in his ear.

'Be still or I slip your throat ... Ach, merda! I *slit* your—'

426

'Aura!' he gasped.

'He-he, si, is Aura! Got you!' She stepped back and posed like a dancer. 'Am back! So brave, so loyal—'

'Hush!' he interrupted, 'we're in trouble. We've got to leave – right now.'

Her eyes widened – then they both sucked in sharp breaths, as boots hammered on the stonework below and the night came alive.

19

Vanashta Baanholt

The Fall of the Sanctor Wardens

*Some say the Wardens fell into evil, others that the Triple Empire persecuted
them. But a third rumour persists: that the aegis they wielded was weak, and
that using it against the Vestal knights was akin to riding a donkey in the jousts.*

BELLASYN FRAY, SCHOLAR, PETRAXUS, 1462

*Falagan Ranges, Neparia
Summer 1472*

Tevas Nicolini scanned the dark bulk of rock and tangled undergrowth looming over them, silhouetted against a star-strewn sky.
The three moons were newly risen, casting an aura of wonder over
this majestic place, where granite pillars rose from the lakes like
accusing fingers. But all he wanted to know was whether the gates
would be opened; or a hail of crossbow bolts and glyma spells would
rain down on their heads.

The latter, knowing my bloody luck.

He glanced at the suave nobleman beside him; Elan Sandreth was
watching with no apparent concern as Lictor Borghart conferred with
whoever was inside. Behind them, Tevas' remaining mercenaries
clustered nervously.

'You look worried, Tevas,' Elan commented.

'We're pursuing renegade knights and lo and behold, we've just
run into men from the Order in a place that reeks of heresy,' Tevas
muttered. 'Ten to one, everyone here's a traitor.'

Elan frowned. 'This could indeed be a nest of vipers,' he mused anxiously. 'Stay close.'

For four exhausting days the lictor had been slowly burning through the mangy furs they'd found at the stone circle, scrying the Avas trapper through these mountains. 'Borghart's convinced Gram Larch is here,' Tevas grumbled. 'We should have camped at dusk and approached by daylight, like I suggested, but jagging Borghart won't bloody listen to reason.'

Only eight of his mercenaries remained, but they'd found a local hunter willing to guide them through this spectacular landscape of pillared stone, giant cliffs and ravines and a maze of waterways, until they found an ancient road that, remarkably, led right here. Right now they were all exhausted, every muscle protesting and the horses blown. Sleep had been minimal and meals scanty, but Borghart's blood was up.

And now he's walked us into the jaws of the unknown.

He and Sandreth exchanged worried glances as Borghart, looking perplexed, returned from the gates, where he'd been negotiating with the Vestal watch captain. He kept his voice low as he pulled Tevas and Sandreth aside, excluding the guide and mercenaries.

'It's the Golden Dragon century,' he said, his voice incredulous. 'The Exemplar's own century! Vazi Virago herself is here, at the Hierophant's behest.'

Holy Elysia, Tevas groaned inside. *I'm dead.* Exemplars were famously intolerant of men like him, who continued to wield the glyma after retiring. And the Zynochi bitch was reputedly an utter stickler for the Order's laws.

'Vazi Virago?' Elan gave a low whistle. 'Is she as *delicosa* as they say?'

'You'll treat her like a living saint or she'll have your head,' Borghart warned. 'The guards have sent for her, so for now we're denied entrance.' He gazed up at the darkened walls, silhouetted against the moons. 'It's some kind of ruined keep or monastery.'

'Did you tell the captain about Challys and Kaen?' Tevas asked.

'No. That's for the Exemplar's ears only.'

'Could she be in league with them?' Elan asked.

'Impossible,' Borghart replied, though his eyes told Tevas that he was considering that possibility. Lictors were prone to see heresy everywhere and paranoia was part of the job.

Tevas left Borghart and Sandreth to talk, returning to his remaining Pelasians. 'Relax, lads, it looks like they're legitimate Order,' he told them.

'*Relax?*' one man spat incredulously. 'Now I'm bloody terrified.'

Just then, the main doors swung open, and a shining figure stepped through the gates, followed by a more darksome silhouette. Borghart dropped to one knee and Tevas, confirming that his blade's orb was still covered, followed suit. Elan Sandreth remained standing: the noble classes had a longstanding aversion to kneeling to the Order's hierarchy, despite relying on them to uphold their status.

'Lictor Borghart, welcome,' Vazi Virago greeted Borghart coolly. 'You may rise.'

Tevas was struck by the otherworldliness of the Exemplar: in her gleaming armour, long black hair tied back severely and her perfect Zynochi face, she looked like a young girl's fantasy of a heroine. Yet to attain her rank, she'd outperformed famed champions, passing tests both martial and magical that were well beyond his own capacities.

A Killer Angel.

It didn't surprise Tevas that Tylkor Kervassien was her second. He knew the man's war-ravaged visage and hulking, brutal demeanour, as they'd graduated from the same bastion, but though Tylkor clearly recognised Tevas, he gave no acknowledgement.

'Exemplar, it's an honour,' Yoryn Borghart said, rising. 'I'm pursuing renegades, on a matter of absolute urgency,' he added quietly. 'They were traced here.'

'Renegades?' Vazi Virago replied, in a neutral voice.

'Siera Romara Challys, Sier Jadyn Kaen and the pentacle of the Falcon century,' Borghart said. 'They have with them two vyr; a big Avas man and a Nepari whore. All have been condemned for heresy – they escaped custody in Port Gaudien. We've trailed them across half the continent.'

Tylkor Kervassien made a growling noise in his throat, then asked, 'Do you have proofs?'

Borghart pulled out his arrest warrants and handed them to the Exemplar. 'This is from my own hand, countersigned by Lord Sandreth, Governor of Vandarath.'

Vazi Virago blinked. 'Sandreth? But . . .' She glanced at Tylkor, then back at Borghart. 'They're here. They claim Lord Sandreth sent them.'

Elan snorted. 'I am Lord Sandreth's son, Elan, and I can assure you my father is nothing to do with them.'

They watched the Exemplar's burnished face go from astounded to coldly furious. '*Skamach!*' she swore. 'We've been lied to. But there's no Nepari woman with them.'

'A thief and a fraud,' Borghart replied, with a scowl of disappointment. 'She may be in the shadows, or have left them. I want her alive, but right now, the renegades are the priority.'

'A moment,' Vazi said. She pulled Sier Tylkor aside and conversed with him in a low voice, while Borghart fumed, Elan shuffled and Tevas steeled himself for violence to come. Three more knights joined them: he recognised them all.

Faidal Unbaro, Runa Branstak and Mildra de Arum . . . Jag me, she's got some of the best blades in the Triple Empire right here.

It didn't make him feel any safer; at some point they could turn on him.

Vazi Virago addressed Borghart again. 'Come. Let us confront our "guests". I will take the lead in this – it is my jurisdiction, Lictor, not yours.'

'Of course,' Borghart replied stonily.

He hates being outranked, Tevas noted, hoping he could remain outside. He was dreading the moment the Exemplar or Tylkor realised that he still had a flamberge.

'Bring your men.' Siera Vazi said, killing his hopes. She turned to her centurion. 'Prade, reinforce the guard on the mines with another dozen men. The rest of you, follow me.' As her forces split, she drew her own glittering flamberge. 'Lictor, let's get to the truth of all this. A lie is a wound in the side of Elysia.'

Her eyes gleamed blue in the half-light as protective spells coalesced about her.

She led them down a big, pillar-lined hall. The interior of the fortress was larger than the exterior hinted, but it was falling down in many places.

I wouldn't want to be here in an earthquake . . .

Tylkor Kervassien finally deigned to address Tevas. 'What are you doing with an Order flamberge, Nicolini?' he growled. 'You were discharged.'

'My old commander gifted it to me,' Tevas drawled. 'And Lictor Borghart's sanctioned me using it. You really want to have that talk right now? We're on the same side.'

Tylkor gave him a disdainful look. 'We'll see about that later.'

Their boots echoed through the huge structure as they traversed a tunnel and found a central courtyard, where soldiers of the Golden Lion century were formed up, awaiting their captains. Siera Vazi gazed up at the next wing, the northern one, so Tevas inferred that the Falcons were up there. Then a squire came hurrying towards them, calling, 'Exemplar, what's happening?'

'Myko,' Vazi Virago replied. 'Where are our guests?'

'They're coming . . . .' He glanced backwards and up. 'Erm, they must be delayed . . . Shall I—?' Then he read the mood of his commander and drew some conclusions. 'They're still up there, Exemplar. Level three, far end of the north wing.'

'Good, well done.' Vazi was radiating calm. 'Go to Magister Goraghan and discreetly inform him that his guest is to be detained – take two guards, and stay well clear.' Then she turned to Tylkor. 'You take these stairs, and I'll take the far end. Let's capture them alive, if we can.'

'I sometimes t'ink we mages are the loneliest o' beings,' Magister Goraghan mused, his lugubrious face drooping. 'Travellin' wit' a bunch o' uppity sword-swingers, an' isolated from our peers. It's a sadness as da years turn and I lose touch wit' old friends.'

'It is,' Elindhu agreed neutrally. 'But we do have the fellowship of our peers.'

Her wariness was always pricked by any man's professions of loneliness, for conversations often turned awkward at such a point. But so far she hadn't regretted this invitation. Despite his appearance and lack of attention to personal hygiene, Goraghan was engaging company. He'd lived in many places and had a raconteur's ear for a story.

He'd put in a lot of effort to charm her, too. He'd recovered an ancient wooden table and chairs from the building and set them in a rock garden below the training yard, where a stream pooled, then trickled down the slope to the lake below. He'd produced a bottle of fine red wine, which he'd brought all the way from Talmont. It might be served in battered clay cups, but to her parched palate it tasted divine.

'I tell ye, da mages o' Petraxus are a rum lot,' Goraghan chuckled. 'Ney humanity, lass. A life's not worth spit there, an' friendship less. Like serpents bitin' each other's tails, they are. I tell ye, I've ney friends there.'

'Do you think there are other Sanctor relics like this place, hidden from our eyes?' she asked, keen to pull the conversation away from his complaints.

'Undoubtedly. The Wardens dominated Hytal afore we Vestals, an' when they saw their end comin' they tried to hide.' He leaned forward. 'There's runes etched into t' deepest parts o' da mines that name it an *Elysium*, an innermost sanctum, named for Elysia, who was a Hytali goddess afore the Akkanites co-opted her.'

'An Elysium? I've not heard of those,' Elindhu said encouragingly, although she had.

'I'll show ye tomorrow,' Goraghan declared floridly. 'It's a pleasure to meet as intelligent and beauteous a woman as 'e,' he told her, before ruining his words by farting. 'T'is an irony of our role that as knights come and go, burnin' out or bein' cut down, we mages go on, our active lives prolonged, and thus our loneliness.' He wiped at his sweaty face. 'I think increasingly o' retiring, I tell ye.'

'Surely you're too young?' she replied politely.

'Ach, I'm older than I look – fat plumps out wrinkles.' He laughed, eyeing her openly. 'I'm glad yer Knight-Commander Challys has agreed to us workin' together below. It's goin' to be a rare old pleasure, I know it.'

'I'm grateful too,' she agreed, honestly. 'It's a wonderful opportunity.'

He beamed at that. 'Ye're a strange bird, but I like yer feathers, Elindhu Morspeth. I warrant you've been a temptation to many a fellow, eh?'

He's going to make some drunken proposition soon, Elindhu sighed inwardly, and gathered her hands into her lap, readying her excuses. *What a shame . . .*

Just then, a squire entered and whispering urgently in Goraghan's ear. The magister listened initially with a frown, then he grimaced sourly. 'Oh dear, t'is sad, indeed,' he said. 'I'll handle it. Back me up.'

The squire nodded, and glanced sharply at Elindhu as two men-at-arms stepped into the light, blocking the stairs. They had weapons already drawn.

We've been unmasked, she realised as the squire, his face pale, also drew steel.

Goraghan rose and gripped his staff. 'Regretfully, lass, ye must yield. Don't make me hurt 'e.'

The sounds of shouting, thudding boots and smashing wood began to reverberate through the complex above. Elindhu snatched up her staff and backed away, desperately kindling glyma-energy as the four men closed in.

As the Exemplar's men ran towards the two staircases, aiming to pincer and trap the Falcons on the floor above, Tevas found himself directly behind Sier Tylkor. *Fine, he can do the fighting.* He readied shielding wards as they pounded up to the next level, where a long balcony overlooked a sharp drop into bush and then the lake. A dozen or more open doorways opened onto it; the doors must have all rotted away long ago.

The Exemplar appeared at the far end, her face and hair lit by the moonlight. Tylkor signalled to her and they moved towards each other, checking the rooms one by one, blades ready and their wards glimmering, with their men behind them.

But the rooms were empty, and only the scuffed grit on the floor betrayed that anyone had ever been here. 'They've gone,' said Tylkor. 'But they can't be far away.'

Tevas found himself beside the Exemplar, who turned abruptly and faced him. 'I'm told you know these people?' she said. 'Where would they go?'

'To the place where they can hurt us the most,' he answered, with a strange burst of pride.

She hissed, and for a moment Tevas caught a glimpse of the serpent behind her Serrafim face. 'The mines,' she exclaimed. 'They're making for the mines.'

The sounds of fighting broke out in the courtyard below, where the men-at-arms had been training earlier; the mages were dining there, right now.

'Go!' Tylkor shouted. 'Down – down! *Find them*—'

About thirty seconds before the Exemplar's men reached their balcony, Jadyn and his comrades had climbed down the vines, retracing Aura's route to the balcony, though they weren't sure they'd take the weight of armoured men. It took nerve to trust their strength and clamber down as the men-at-arms came pounding to their abandoned rooms only a few paces away. But the clatter of the Exemplar's men and the dense foliage masked them, enabling them to reach the ground levels even as the guards reached their rooms.

'Is this way,' Aura murmured, pointing to the bushy slopes at the steps that led to the docks and their boats. 'Virgins follow. Escaping, simplicia.'

Jadyn hesitated, hearing a burst of cursing above: their absence had been discovered. 'Go!' they heard Tylkor Kervassien roar. 'Down – down! *Find them*—'

Jadyn flattened himself against the wall as several faces peered out and down, but no one shouted in discovery, thanks to the darkness and untamed vegetation. The moment they vanished, he peered out again, the three Coros moons providing just enough light to measure the drop below. He took a breath, then leaped, followed by the others. Aura and Soren were the most agile, landing like cats, but everyone reached the ground safely.

Aura gestured to the path leading down to the boats. 'This way now.'

Jadyn stopped her. 'Elindhu's with the magister – we can't leave her behind.'

'I'll fetch her,' Obanji said. 'She's in the rock garden.'

He went to go but Jadyn grabbed his shoulder. 'Find her, then make for the mines – but if you can't get in, take the boats and get out. Don't throw your life away. Soren, go with Obanji.'

The initiate was looking overwhelmed, but Obanji clapped him on the shoulder. 'We'll handle this, lad. Jadyn, Rom, see you soon.' Then they slipped sideways round the base of the rock wall and vanished silently into the shadows.

Aura turned, fretting visibly. 'Mines? What is mines?'

'We think there's a Sanctor place underground,' Jadyn told her. 'Right below us.'

'It's too late for that,' Romara countered. 'We should just take the boats and get out.'

'No, not if we go now.' Jadyn faced Aura. 'Stay with us or not, it's up to you.'

'E Cara mia! Vestal be insanitary!' Then she clutched his sleeve and said, 'Follow Aura. She know better way.'

She ran away through the foliage to a stream, just as another squad of guards clanked past a few paces away, heading down the steps to the lake.

'Come,' Aura whispered, once they were gone. 'Follow.'

Then she dropped to her knees and crawled into the rock. Jadyn stared, then realised the stream must flow from a small cave. He shared a look with Romara and Gram, then took a deep breath, dropped to the ground and followed her through the little tunnel. In moments he was in pitch-dark.

'Feel way, dark be not long,' Aura whispered, from just ahead.

She was right; after about a dozen paces of groping their way along a snaking passage, they turned a sharp bend and emerged into a tunnel of rough-hewn rock, lit by distant torchlight on the right, where a major passage intersected. Jadyn claimed an unlit torch, but didn't light it yet.

Romara and Gram emerged behind them, their boots as soaked as his, and stood, looking round and blinking. 'This way, I guess,' he muttered, indicating the junction. They hurried to it, and peered left and right.

'That way's out.' Romara pointed left, up a gentle slope.

'We're not looking for a way out,' Jadyn reminded her. 'We need to get further in.'

He turned right, facing a gentle downwards ramp, cut square and smooth. The Exemplar had called this a mine, but these tunnels didn't look to have been hewn to extract ore. As they descended they passed rooms with the remnants of old mosaics, suggesting this was an underground complex, like the one they'd found beneath the stone circle.

Another Sanctor Warden site, Elysia willing.

They emerged into a chamber, where several lit torches were flickering on the walls. They took one each before entering the space, looking round. It was similar to the chamber they'd found themselves in after being transported at the standing stones, circular with arcane symbols etched into every surface, and an exit opposite.

Then they heard distant boots and more shouting, which sounded dangerously close.

We have to go on and hope we're on the right path.

'Come on,' he said, pointing to a doorway on the far wall, and raising his torch, he hurried on recklessly, careless of ambush or pitfalls, into another tunnel, which then split in two.

Gram dropped to one knee and sniffed at the dirt. 'This one,' he said definitely, pointing to the left.

They plunged down a spiralling stair and spilled into a hall, a chamber like the inside of an Akkanite cathedral, with partially intact statues of armed men and women in Foylish war-gear lining the walls. Jadyn paused in awe – but there was no time.

'This way!' he called, spotting another door at the far end, and they hurried past pillars, alcoves and sarcophagi, round an altar with an inlaid Foylish knot, which was repeated on the doors at the far end and again, embossed on a giant shield carved in stone above a door-frame standing some twelve feet tall. The twin doors were closed – and there were two large symbols etched on them, identical to those on his and Aura's hands.

'That's it . . . the way we must go.' He looked at his palms. 'We can open it, I'm certain.'

Romara flinched and Gram looked anxious, but Aura was staring wide-eyed, all her hopes and fears scrawled across her face. 'E Cara, is place, si!' she babbled. 'Am scaring. Needing to pee.'

Then they heard more shouting, the sound of pursuit getting closer.

'We've got no choice.' Jadyn headed for the doors, but then spun as a group of figures burst through the doors at the far end of the hall.

Elindhu backed up against the low pool wall, her heart thumping. The orb on her staff was alight, Magister Goraghan's was brighter, and the squire and the two men-at-arms were closing in, blades glinting.

'I'm sorry, m'dear,' Goraghan grumbled. 'I truly am. What a feckin' waste. Please just yield.'

Her mind raced as she prepared, but this was combat – not her forte, but her worst nightmare.

'Why'd a nice lass like yerself go rogue, eh?' Goraghan waved a hand at Vanashta Baanholt towering over them. 'Cause o' this place? Ye're a fool, if so. The Sanctors were weak – that's why we wiped 'em out. They were feckin' stargazers, but they couldnae fight.'

She blanked his words, seeking a way out. A mage could do much, but she had neither the speed, the strength nor the spells to deal with the brutality of combat.

Behind her, the lip of the garden overhung a drop onto the rocks far below. *Maybe it's better to die like that than be taken alive?* she thought wildly, and in that moment she decided. Shrieking defiance, she unleashed a brilliant burst of light into their faces to dazzle them, then lunged towards the drop.

But the squire, Myko, had wards in place and he darted to block her escape, while Goraghan's staff ate up her light – then he shouted something, and darkness rolled in to engulf her.

'*Lumis*,' she cried, to counter his spell, then she added, '*Pulso-isar!*' for good measure, wrapping unseen cords of force round the throats of the squire and the two men-at-arms, impeding their windpipes. They all dropped to their knees, clawing at their throats.

If it was just them, she might have kept it up long enough to throttle them, but Goraghan bellowed, '*Negatio!*' and her bindings fell apart. The soldiers were still winded and gasping through bruised throats, though, so for now it was one on one . . .

But the big Foylish magus didn't need help, gesturing dramatically and unleashing a burst of force that battered her backwards. Her heels caught on the lip of the pool and she tripped over and in, trying to inhale as the water closed round her. She came up dizzy and spluttering, her beehive collapsing as the immense mage clambered in above her.

'I be so sorry,' he apologised again, 'as I do like 'e.'

She tried to ensorcell him, to freeze his thoughts and somehow get clear, but his staff whipped round and smacked hers away, then he simply dropped on top of her, his bulk bearing her down and under again. Her spells unravelled as he gripped her throat and squeezed.

She thrashed about, but he was like a boulder with a grip of iron. Her vision flashed as she flailed, spewing a stream of bubbles, a silver cascade that drifted towards the churning surface. Sparks burst and died inside her skull as she fought, but to no avail.

Her remaining strength dissipated until she lost the ability to move, to think, to go on. With nothing left, she succumbed limply to the liquid darkness, and her vision went black.

Arghyl Goraghan rose from the pond, his clothes sopping and his breath coming in gusts, and stared down at the woman lying spread-eagled on her back on the bottom of the pond, her strangely attractive bird-face going slack and empty. The gentle current caught her and dragged her down into the deepest part of the pool behind the lip and the falls, where her corpse fetched up against a rock and wedged, out of his reach. Her lifeless eyes bulged, her open mouth gaped and her cloud of braids rippled out like water weed.

Why'd 'e 'ave to go an' be a heretic, lass? He'd had hopes of her: she'd been intelligent and knowledgeable, with a touch of the spunk he liked. Most women made it no secret that they found him repulsive, but sometimes he met one who didn't care, who looked past his looks and liked a laugh: someone not too proud to let an ugly man touch her. You could work round the vows of chastity and the dangers of pleasure if you were careful.

It could've been fun. What a waste.

'Sir,' the young squire, Myko, gasped weakly, 'is she . . . ?'

The other men were still massaging their damaged throats.

'Aye, she's dead,' he grunted. 'Fish her out afore she fouls our drinkin' water. I'll report to Exemplar Virago.'

Obanji and Soren only got as far as the training yard, when a dozen soldiers burst in, with Faidal Unbaro and Runa Branstak leading the pack.

'We'll handle this,' Sier Faidal drawled, and the soldiers shrank to the rear.

Obanji took the left, drawing in what would effectively be the last big flow of glyma-energy he could muster until they reached a shard – if they ever did. The Vandari, Sier Runa, came at him, while Sier Faidal went straight for Soren, whose orb barely flickered at all.

Runa roared out a guttural Vandari war-cry and charged like a raging bull. Their blades hammered together, while invisible forces ripped at each other. The Exemplar's men had more power summoned and quickly displayed the greater mastery; because in seconds Obanji felt his protections shred and only hard-earned experience kept him alive as repeated blows forced him back and back, away from Soren's side . . .

Sier Faidal Unbaro was a forest fire, sending waves of force and flame, almost overwhelming Soren's fledgling shields. The Abuthan knight's face was merciless, and Soren felt momentarily out of his depth, reminded of his father's last moments, overmatched by the draegar that dismembered him.

But somehow, he read the older man's next blow and danced aside, at the price of being separated further from Obanji. Realising that defending would only prolong his defeat, he unleashed a blinding riposte that tore Faidal's shields and slashed his tabard, forcing the knight backwards – and suddenly he had a foothold in the fight.

'*Kuenbasa!*' Faidal followed the foul curse by lashing out with his left hand and sending a ball of force into Soren's midriff that could have broken his spine – but he sidestepped deftly, then flashed into the same combination he'd used in the practise bout . . .

Obanji was parrying desperately, but Runa Branstak was an Order champion; younger and faster and stronger and too damned good. Every blow Obanji blocked jarred through him, igniting pain and numbness in his ageing body, and he began to falter, seeing the end coming . . .

Faidal smashed Soren's leading thrust aside, but let him flow into the next blow, the lunge that had got him 'killed' thrice in the practise bouts. Soren did it again, gambling everything . . .

. . . and Faidal, recognising the combination, took the bait, sidestepping and lining up the counter that would plunge his steel into the back of Soren's neck – but this time the lunge was a feint that became a flashing spin, as Soren whipped his whole body round and crunched his glowing blade into the older man's side, straight through leather and chain, sending blood spraying as the Abuthan staggered . . .

Seeing his comrade struck shocked Sier Runa, who lost his flow – just for an eye-blink, just a momentary lapse – but enough for Obanji to drive in, forcing the Vandarai knight to focus solely on him, which allowed Soren – spinning away from the stricken Faidal – to ram his blade without ceremony or mercy into Runa's back, so that the tip punched through and emerged from the middle of his chest, and the shaggy giant crashed to the ground.

A moment later, Faidal swayed and collapsed beside him.

The soldiers baulked, their faces filling with fear, and they backed up, none willing to be the next to die. Obanji swept up Runa's blade in his left hand and pointed both glowing swords at the frightened men. 'Back off,' he called, 'or you'll all go the same way.'

The men-at-arms gave ground as Soren joined him, with Faidal's blade now in his left hand, its orb glowing strongly. 'The rock garden's down the steps behind us,' the boy panted. 'Elindhu's supposed to be there, but I can't hear anything.'

'No one gets left behind,' Obanji replied.

But just then, a bulky shape dripping water heaved himself up the steps behind them, blocking their retreat. Obanji didn't need to be told the newcomer's identity; it could only be Magister Arghyl Goraghan, the exemplar's mage.

He was carrying two staves.

Ah, jagat, Obanji breathed, looking at Elindhu's staff. *I'll miss you, old girl, erling or not.* He set his jaw and prepared himself to avenge her, or die trying.

'Look, one of you needs to actually get wet,' Bern Myko snapped, losing patience with Jeras and Henasson, who were prone to slacking. 'It's only water.'

The squire had been directing the two guardsmen in retrieving the drowned mage's corpse, but she was wedged too deep for them to reach in and pull her out without getting soaked themselves.

'We know that,' Jeras grumbled. 'Can't ye do it – ye're the initiate, after all.'

'Yeah, give it some . . .' Henasson waggled his fingers in a magical way.

Myko frowned. He was just starting and he found spell-work arduous and draining. One day he'd be like the knights he served, but right now it would be embarrassing to struggle in front of cretins like this pair. 'Wade in and get her, for jagat's sake,' he snapped. 'That's an order.'

The two men faced him, clearly longing to punch him for pulling rank, but knowing there'd be dire consequences if they did. 'Aye, aye, no need to get sweary,' Jeras grumbled, looking at Henasson. 'Toss ye for it, Hen?'

Henasson won, so Jeras clambered into the pond, waded to the edge of the deep part, took a deep breath and went under. A few moments later, he hauled the lifeless woman to the surface, her limp body sagging in his grip, her face hidden by the rope-like grey braids.

'Funny-lookin' bitch she were,' Henasson grunted. 'All beak and hair.'

'But still humpable,' Jenas allowed.

'Oh, all women are that.'

Then they all froze as they heard swords clashing somewhere above, and shared a 'rather us than them' look.

'Ignore that,' Myko snapped. 'Our job's to bring the magia up, so just do it.'

The two men huffed in exasperation as Myko gazed up towards the sounds of belling steel and fierce shouting. He hurried to the foot of the stairs, where he saw the silhouette of that fat slug Goraghan reach the top, just as the clash of steel petered out.

I hope that means these traitors are all dead. A bright career had been predicted for him and he didn't want to die before it properly started. 'Hurry up,' he called over his shoulder to the two men grasping arms and legs and tugging ineffectually at the dead woman. 'Haul her out.'

He faced the stairs again, straining his ears ... until a sound behind him made his hair stand on end: a strangled cry was cut off instantly, followed by the sound of flesh and bone crunching into stone, and a wet hiss.

He turned, his heart in his mouth.

Jeras' boots and shins were hanging over the lip of the pool. The rest of him was out of sight under the surface, which was rippling but going still. A dark shape crouched on the lip of the pond, gripping Henasson's throat with something like tentacles. His head was bleeding heavily, a red smear on the rocks hinting at the cause. Amid those ropey cords was a dark copper-hued face with amber eyes leering from above a beak-like mouth. The tentacles jerked, Henasson's neck snapped and the creature clambered wetly from the pool and made for Myko.

Myko backed up, rote lessons in wardings rising to his lips as he pulled in glyma-energy . . .

But before he could fully control those forces, the gangrel creature launched itself towards him and more of the ropey threads lashed out, gripping his sword arm and encircling his neck. He tried to wrench his blade free, but the creature was too strong. Its tentacles, formed from thick cords of wet hair, moved with hideous speed and strength – then the creature's amber eyes filled his sight, something like lightning crackled through him, his legs became jelly and he collapsed, the creature's pungent wet aroma filling his nose.

'*Isar gebir*,' it rasped.

The mental binding impaled him and his body and mind went numb.

Obanji and Soren, caught between the soldiers and the sorcerer, stood back to back, filling their lungs and readying themselves to utilise the energy from their newly acquired swords.

'We take the mage,' Obanji breathed, 'on three . . .'

But as they tensed muscles, a fresh voice cut through the courtyard. 'Hold here, you men,' Siera Mildra de Arum snapped at the milling soldiers, appearing at the door behind the line of men-at-arms. She glared at Obanji and Soren over the corpses of her pentacle comrades. 'See how deep the murderous heretics strike at our sacred Order,' she said dramatically, as if reciting lines of a play. 'The Devourer take their souls.'

Her presence – for she was a glyma-knight of genuine prowess – rallied the frightened men-at-arms, and the two dozen men locked shields to protect her, forming a line blocking the way to the interior of Vanashta Baanholt. Behind them, Magister Goraghan had planted Elindhu's staff in the ground and kindled his own. Light was shimmering between the two elobyne orbs, a cord of crackling energy.

Is he the deadlier, or she? Obanji wondered. Usually a mage was useless in combat, but given time to prepare, they could be deadly.

'Sier?' Soren muttered. 'To the lake?'

Obanji decided: Elindhu was down there and they might just have taken her prisoner. But before he could open his mouth, the obese man in the velvet robes turned the glimmering cord between the two staves into a swirling vortex of light that flashed towards them, enmeshing them in a net of force which lifted them off their feet and held them there, flailing and helpless, as Siera Mildra's men closed in.

Obanji locked eyes with the magister; his jowly face was filled with strain, eyes bulging and lungs gusting at the effort of maintaining the spell.

He can't hold this for long, he realised, *but he doesn't have to* ...

Siera Mildra's men poured towards them, blades raised. 'Break ... free ...' Obanji gasped. 'Fight—!'

He and Soren strove for purchase, but nothing gave—

—until something darksome appeared behind Magister Goraghan, vine-like limbs wrapped round his head and throat and amber eyes blazed. The man-sized creature latched onto the mage's back and crunched its mouth into the back of his neck.

Goraghan went rigid, then collapsed – and so did his binding spell.

Obanji and Soren fell to the ground and somehow rose before the men-at-arms could react. They charged, unleashing power from their stolen flamberges; the gleaming blades crunched through mail, dashed aside weapons and for a moment there was a space.

Then light blazed from the creature that had bitten the mage, now a spindly erling woman with coppery skin and serpentine hair. Obanji's heart thudded.

Elindhu – thank Akka.

She flashed blinding radiance into the faces of the men facing Obanji and Soren, who went on the attack, going straight for the dazzled front rank.

In seconds, they'd carved through and were into the second rank, Soren a blur and Obanji a bludgeon: the artiste and the artisan, moving as one. Behind them, Elindhu had reared up and was sending bursts of energy at anyone trying to flank them. They broke through as Siera

Mildra attempted to rally the wilting defenders with a show of power, smashing a blast of force into Obanji and rocking him backwards.

Obanji staggered, which gave a trio of soldiers enough time to come at him, forcing him away, leaving Soren to face a foe vastly more experienced and powerful than he ...

Seeing Siera Mildra's next spell being hurled from behind two guards, Soren began to evade, but he realised in time that he couldn't, because he'd leave either Obanji or Elindhu exposed. So he threw all he had into shielding, with what limited skill he'd managed to hone in the short time he and Obanji'd had together. He reeled as the energy crashed into him, the concussion making his hearing throb and senses reel, then sprang forward again, desperate to reach her before Siera Mildra did it again and flattened him.

It meant leaving Obanji alone, but he went anyway, stabbing one guard in the shoulder and disarming him, then kicking him away and opening the throat of the other with a spinning slash that took him right up to the woman now towering over him, flowing into the sequence he'd used to deadly effect on her fellow knights.

She parried grimly, shouting, 'For Akka and Elysia!' and broke his combination with a riposte he hadn't seen coming. He barely managed to stop her, and when he tried to trick her with the lunge-feint that had done for Faidal, she wasn't having it, staying well clear of the surprise blow.

'You don't fool me, traitor,' she snarled, swinging into another attack.

He nearly lost his sword, ducked under a blow meant to behead him, tried to counter and almost lost his hand.

For the first time in his life, he'd truly met his match ...

Desperate blocks weren't enough – had Obanji not been a glyma-knight, he'd have been impaled or chopped down in moments as blows rained in from all sides – but he was, and his glowing blade took its toll, breaking weapons and bones, sending his foes reeling back.

Then a man he hadn't seen materialised from his left and before he could adjust, a flanged mace-head smashed up under his arm into his ribcage, almost knocking him off his feet. Bones fractured and stabbed inwards, his breath burst from his lungs as he staggered . . .

. . . as Elindhu flashed in, driving the shod butt of her staff into the mace-wielder's temple, poleaxing him. '*Hang on*,' she called to Obanji, who was floundering, gasping for air.

But the remaining half a dozen soldiers had them cornered now, and Soren was being driven backwards before Siera Mildra's fearsome onslaught . . .

Soren gave ground. Sensing that time had run out, he did the insane . . .

He feigned an error, dropping his guard too far for it to be mistaken for a feint, and let Mildra's next thrust through. The blade, searing with glyma-energy, would have skewered his chest, had he not twisted just enough . . . but it still punched through his left shoulder and out of the other side. The blade he'd stolen spun away and clattered to the ground.

But even as he took that agonising blow, he was swinging, having sacrificed any defence for one chance at an unopposed blow. His knees gave way, but his blade was already whistling round and up in a treacherous blow modelled on what Gram had done to him a few weeks earlier with his fist.

The sword speared Siera Mildra's belly from below, lanced up and impaled her heart.

She emitted the faintest gasp, her eyes rolled back and her legs crumpled, shorn of control. She folded over his sword as he flipped it sideways, sending her crashing down alongside him.

Pain was flooding his shoulder and his mind, but he channelled it into one last effort, kicking her off his blade as he rose to his knees and hacked at the back of the man attacking Obanji, severing his spine. The soldier collapsed, and Soren wobbled at the edge of passing out.

But Obanji grabbed and held him up. Both of them were wheezing in pain, but the few remaining soldiers, seeing their champions down, turned and ran.

For a long moment Soren stared sightlessly over the Obanji's shoulder. Elindhu joined them, her dress soaked and torn, her ropy coils of hair writhing about. With a lit staff in either hand, she looked like some kind of erling goddess.

Elysia, Soren thought wildly, *I love these people.*

Elindhu pressed her hand to his shoulder and warm, wet bliss flooded the wound, numbing the pain. The sheer relief took his breath away. When she removed her bloodied hand, the wound was sealed – until he tried to flex it, which felt like someone was sticking another knife in it. Then she turned to Obanji, who was struggling to breathe, and did something that gave him some ease. 'Broken ribs,' she cautioned. 'I've aligned them again, but the fusing will take time, so you will need to have a care.'

They surveyed the carnage: wounded men were trying to crawl away, while the dead lay strewn about in bloody pools, sightless eyes accusing them. Magister Goraghan was twitching on the ground, his visible skin pasty, veins bulging. 'What did . . . you do . . . to me . . . ?' he panted, looking up at Elindhu, then he went limp and fell on his face.

'Poor man,' Elindhu said. 'I didn't want to kill him, but he'll be paralysed for some time. Where are the others?'

'Jadyn and Romara took them to the mines,' Obanji told her.

'Then let's follow,' the erling replied. 'Falcons Eternal.' She lit the way with her staff, while Soren and Obanji lurched along in her wake, holding each other up.

We could escape, Soren realised, *but it's never even crossed their minds. Falcons Eternal.*

'Well fought,' Obanji panted. 'Three of the finest knights in Talmont, all downed by you.'

Soren went to thank him, then thought about that. 'Three good knights who died thinking we were evil,' he replied. 'I can't take pride in that.'

The Abuthan gave him a sharp look, then replied gravely, 'Well said. Sorry we dragged you into this, lad. If I don't get the chance to tell you later, hear this: you've got it in you to be Exemplar one day. Don't let them tell you that you can't, the way they told me.'

More likely I'll die on the Exemplar's own blade, Soren thought.

They had just found the entrance chamber of the mine when they heard rushing footsteps and a first wave of Vestal soldiers appeared a little way behind them.

Exemplar Vazi Virago and Seneschal Tylkor Kervassien were among them, together with Lictor Yoryn Borghart.

'We're just ahead of them,' Obanji gasped, 'so *run!*'

Fighting through the pain of their wounds and the exhaustion of having already fought for their lives, they pelted towards the far end of the chamber, and the stairs leading down to the mines.

Jadyn, Romara, Aura and Gram stared as the dark shapes at the far end of the chamber coalesced into Obanji, Soren and Elindhu, running as hard as they could. The mage was in erling form, eerily alien but uncanny and menacing, and the two knights were blowing and bloodied.

They escaped – but they came back for us: Falcons Eternal!

'Come on!' Jadyn shouted to them, even as light flared and armoured figures pounded into the hall behind them. Vazi Virago was at their head, glittering and imperious, flanked by Tevas Nicolini and Tylkor Kervassien. Behind them came Lictor Borghart, Elan Sandreth and at least two score of Vestal Guard.

Jadyn felt his hopes buckle, while Romara swayed as if about to faint. His orb was now all but inert and Romara didn't even have a flamberge. Gram bared his teeth defiantly while Aura drew a dagger, but he was struck by a wave of hopelessness, for any fighting would end in defeat.

These doors are our only chance—

He ran to the big double doors, placed his left hand in the print on the left door, but when he reached across, he realised he couldn't stretch far enough to touch the right-hand rune. He cursed Akka, despairing—

—until Aura slapped her right hand on the other sigil and the runes instantly burst into vivid glowing white life and with a rumble, the doors began to slide apart – just too slowly.

'*Yes!*' he shouted, and, '*Come on!*'

Obanji, Soren and Elindhu reached them, turned to face the enemy and present weapons, as Vazi Virago's force formed up, the ranks bristling with crossbows and spears. The Exemplar, Sier Tylkor, Borghart, Nicolini and Sandreth were now lurking behind the shield wall.

'Where are the rest of her pentacle?' Romara asked.

'Slightly too dead to make it', Obanji panted.

The Exemplar's soldiers stopped just forty paces away and the archers took aim – but instead of immediately commanding them to fire, Vazi Virago and Sier Tylkor stepped forth, their faces filled with cold anger.

'Halt, you Falcons: traitors and heretics all,' the Exemplar called. 'Yield or die.'

'Please don't yield,' Tylkor added grimly. 'I want to gut you all.'

The doors behind them were sliding open, too damned slowly. Realising she could do nothing there, Romara left Jadyn and Aura to deal with them and went to Gram's side, the erling tuelawar in her hand. Without glyma she felt naked, but she could sense the other's spells locking in front of her, giving her a little protection.

She gripped Gram's hand. 'It doesn't matter now,' she told the vyr. 'Let's do our worst.'

If the rage takes me, let the Devourer swallow me whole . . .

The trapper looked at her grimly and she felt his reluctance, but he complied, drawing on her residual glyma energies, the little sparks that remained like burrs beneath her skin, and awakening them. Her heart began to pound, her eyes to bleed, but she felt the power flow from her to him, allowing her to still think and feel. Through a scarlet haze she sensed him reach out with his other hand to grasp Elindhu's staff, feeding his potency with remarkable control, even as the power gripped him. His face altered, jagged teeth emerging as he struggled into his other shape. She could taste all of him, feeling him boring into her soul, and when he gazed at her, she felt a flood of bloody glyma-rage and desire flow between them.

The maelstrom spun her senses, her flesh and bones rippled and

bunched in strange ways, and she felt the urge to howl – then someone shouted, 'Loose!' and a torrent of crossbow bolts and arrows
came hammering at them, striking the wards Obanji, Soren and
Elindhu had woven, cracking against the web of unseen power. Most
snapped, many more were deflected, a few hung in the air, stuck as
if halfway through a pane of glass – but one of them did hammer
through, a bolt from a heavy crossbow powerful enough to punch
through plate-mail, and it slammed into Gram's right shoulder. The
vyr staggered, howling in shock, and Romara shrieked because it felt
like she'd been hit too. The blazing energy that had been flowing into
her wavered, and then ebbed away as Gram swayed drunkenly . . .

'No!' she shrieked, clutching at him – but Vazi Virago was shouting in frustration, perhaps at the ineffectual volley. She didn't call
for another, instead shouting, '*Attack!*'

The wall of Vestal men-at-arms surged forwards . . .

'Hurry!' Aura shouted at the slowly moving doors. '*Apurate, te jago
caga! Apurate!*'

Jadyn knew how she felt; they'd tried to drag the sliding panels
open faster, but their efforts made no difference. A quick look over
his shoulder told him that the first volley of bolts and arrows had
broken on their shields, but now the enemy were advancing, a rank
of soldiers protecting the glowing figure of the Exemplar and her
seneschal, Tylkor Kervassien.

'Jadyn,' Aura shouted, as finally the opening was wide enough for
her slim figure, 'can do—' She slid between the panels and vanished,
calling, 'Need light—'

Jadyn wavered, knowing that even if they all got through the
doors in time, someone would have to hold the portal until they
got it closed again.

'Back up, Falcons,' he called. 'Rearguard!'

His comrades reacted instantly, with Obanji and Soren anchoring
the line, backed by Elindhu, while Romara put her shoulder under
Gram, and hobbled them both towards the opening portal. The vyr
was clearly out of this, and without the glyma, so was she.

We're jagged.

Muttering a prayer, Jadyn went after Aura, finding her a few paces beyond the portal. His orb-light lit up the space, revealing a bridge over a precipice, an arch of stone that extended a dozen paces into the air before ending in a rough break. It looked as if it had been destroyed a very long time ago.

'No, no,' he protested, 'there must be a way. It can't just end here.'

He ran to the edge of the precipice, but below was nothing but a dark void. The sky above was like night on a peak, distant carpets of stars glittering, but there was no sound, no wind, nothing but a biting cold. *Is this really it? A ledge at the edge of nothing – a dead end?*

Aura was shrieking at the bridge, beseeching it in Nepari to be other than broken, but nothing changed. Perhaps the old Rudanite monks had been right and the world was flat, with an edge – maybe this very place was what had inspired the whole cult.

Then Romara hauled Gram through; the trapper was clutching at the bolt buried in his shoulder joint. Romara looked deathly, weeping tears of blood, and Jadyn shuddered at the sight, fearing that no matter the outcome now, something vital was already lost.

Elindhu, Obanji and Soren, fast on their heels, were forming up in the now-gaping door – and the first wave of soldiers were upon them, blades beginning to hammer down on them. The portal had at least forced the enemy to fight on a narrower front, but Vazi Virago and Tylkor Kervassien were shouting to clear the way.

'Hold them,' Jadyn shouted, *'buy us time to close these jagging doors!'*

He ran back to the doorway, casting about for a way to close it again. The surface of the wall was etched with symbols, but none matched those on his hands. *'Akka, Father, help me!'*

Romara, her face wraith-white and gaunt, lowered the groggy Gram to the ground. In the doorway, Obanji and Soren, with Elindhu shielding, were facing the Golden Dragon century, but their dogged defence couldn't last, not when they were already wounded and their glyma almost spent.

Aura was at the broken edge of the stone bridge, pleading to Elysia to help.

We're going to die right on the very edge of discovery, Jadyn realised. *Just a few minutes longer*, he begged Heaven; *Elysia, have mercy—*

But the weight of numbers was taking its toll on Obanji and Soren, forcing them back, step by step, though some of the soldiers were down and more were wounded and trying to crawl back through the forest of men behind them.

Jadyn shouted, 'Elindhu, what do we do—?'

Without a sideways glance, she shouted, 'Seek *Yagna*, the Rune of Ending. *Hurry!*'

He leaped to the task as the soldiers drew aside to allow Vazi Virago and Tylkor Kervassien to emerge through the press to take on the beleaguered Obanji and Soren. Jadyn glimpsed the Exemplar's face, a golden goddess wielding the sword of justice, her face set as if she intended to rip apart the fabric of the world.

The Rune of Ending? This is the end of us all!

Vazi Virago knew that many in the Order hated her. Until the advent of the glyma, war had been the domain of men and their brutal strength, while women were regarded as mere chattels, prizes for the victors. Those attitudes were still deeply rooted in the Vestal Order, even though the Order's strength was the glyma, which was found as much in women as men. But the glyma was an equaliser, which allowed a slender lightweight like her to go toe-to-toe with men of much greater height and bulk.

Her training years as an initiate had been a nightmare: she'd felt under siege every minute of every hour, belittled, scorned, jeered, groped and even assaulted – when they weren't trying to seduce or coerce her into betraying her vows. On one occasion her male cohorts had even attempted gang-rape as a means to get her thrown out, so she couldn't continue to humiliate them on the training field.

She'd survived, body intact, and in her wake, a trail of broken trainees with shattered limbs and egos. No one had destroyed so many careers as her, because she never left a jibe unavenged. Even though she instigated none of these incidents, the bastion's grandmaster tried to have her cast from the Order to protect the other initiates.

He failed.

That she was now Exemplar could be traced to her single-minded determination, but she'd had other advantages, including an ability to draw more heavily on the glyma without losing control than anyone she'd ever met. She was a furnace of power wielded with icy precision.

Second, she had complete emotional detachment – she couldn't begin to picture what love, hate, friendship, loyalty or resentment might feel like; all the myriad illogical but overriding moods and motivations that others let guide their actions meant nothing to her. She didn't even feel their absence. Even in childhood she'd been utterly alone, every interaction a transaction towards an immediate or future gain, nothing more.

And third, she was able to analyse and intuit the actions of those around her to an extraordinary degree, enabling her to envisage the immediate future so precisely that it was as if she could hear the words and see the movements before they happened – especially in combat, where the vagaries of human nature could be boiled down to movement of feet and hands and steel. Little surprised her, and very few people could blindside her.

But Romara Challys and Jadyn Kaen had. *How?* she wondered, as she joined the fray. *Why them?*

It wasn't Romara – she was old money, well-connected, a political animal, clearly dissembling about the precise reasons she and her pentacle were here: able enough, but brittle. But Jadyn Kaen's easily overlooked presence had fooled her; his guileless transparency and pro-Order utterances had caused her to put aside suspicion and see their arrival as mere coincidence.

It's him, not her . . . She remembered the wine cup he'd caught, and the moment of recognition it had engendered. *He's the real danger here.*

At some point she'd come to see her ability to vividly imagine the future as a gift, although not linked to the glyma, the sacred Gift of Jovan. At first she'd thought herself the only one, but others had shown flashes at times. *He's like me . . . but lesser, because all others are.*

And right now, it was he, not Romara, directing the defence here, she realised, as she stepped through the men she'd thrown ahead to weaken and soften the defenders. Before her, the Abuthan, Obanji Vost, and the initiate, Soren var'Dael, were at bay, already wounded, but fighting with grit and skill.

Wounded animals are at their most dangerous – but I am perfection, she reminded herself. *No one betters me.*

So she advanced with confidence, Tylkor's dark rage beside her, as ever. She chose to assail Obanji Vost. She'd been told he had once been regarded as a possible Exemplar, but he'd never fulfilled that promise. Now he was almost forty and on the downwards slope.

While Tylkor went for the initiate, she drove at Vost, her blade a blur as she whipped through a combination before ramming the point at his right thigh, seeking to end this fast. But he parried and for a few seconds he actually matched her blade speed, despite his clear exhaustion and existing wounds. But he couldn't sustain it and lost track of her movements. Caught trying to block a feint, his defence opened up and she drove a blade at his throat—

But the Abuthan found an unexpected burst of energy, sufficient to shift his feet with the grace of a younger man, crash her blade aside, and make her give ground. It gave her a moment to glimpse the fight beside her, to see Tylkor dashing the initiate's blade aside, roaring, '*Pulso!*' and driving raw force at the initiate's chest at close range.

But with remarkable grace, the boy arched his whole body backwards and the energy-blast smashed past him, straight into the shielded Elindhu Morspeth, who staggered, but flashed a blinding burst of light back into Tylkor's face—

As she did so, the initiate re-aligned his blade and thrust with sufficient power to penetrate the momentarily dazzled Tylkor's wards. The flamberge, alight with energy, flashed through her seneschal's guard – and his chainmail and boiled leather belly armour, lighting his chest from within.

Tylkor staggered – her trusted iron fist, her right hand for the past two years – then crashed over backwards, and Vazi felt a burst of irritation that she'd need to find someone else as reliable and durable. The young part-Abuthan whipped out his blade and flashed it back to high guard, wide-eyed but eerily calm, as if all this were nothing to him. She saw herself in his eyes, a potential future Exemplar.

Over my dead body!

'Back up,' she snapped at her men. 'They're mine!'

Then she threw all her awareness into the kill, going for the boy with an advanced combination he'd surely have never seen before—

—except, miraculously, the youth read her intent, blocked the killing thrust and even dared to counter, a clever riposte that forced her to stop and *deal* with him – but Obanji Vost was there again, despite his wounds, and for a few moments the three of them exchanged blows like a dozen blacksmiths at their anvils, the hammering blades forcing her men to stay well away so they didn't impede her.

Beyond them, she glimpsed a ledge and a stone bridge arching out over a void . . . but only for a dozen paces before it ended abruptly. Jadyn Kaen was standing on the ledge with a black-haired woman, surely the Nepari they'd been warned of.

There'll be no escape this time. I have questions I want answered.

She renewed her one-woman assault, drawing on more and more glyma, feeding her speed and strength, until the two men had no choice but to give ground, their skill and endurance beginning to break . . .

She foresaw the killing moves and flowed into them, glorying in the victory to come . . .

The Exemplar was a true force of nature, her glowing blade a lethal blur, and though they were two to her one, she couldn't be contained. But Obanji's body and spirit were willing and he rolled back the years, forcing away the pain of his wounds and matching her speed and precision, smashing her thrusts aside. For a moment he sensed opportunity – and vindication.

I could have been Exemplar, the thought intruded.

But that had been a decade ago, a lifetime for a knight. The wave of energy that sustained him was ebbing, while she was getting stronger and faster. Flurries of blows constantly crashed into his guard, forcing him to adjust his footing or be smashed off his feet, and incredibly, she was putting Soren under exactly the same pressure, matching both of them blow for blow, despite being smaller and slighter of build.

Then he glimpsed Lictor Borghart edging in behind her to even up the numbers. He battered away another attack as Borghart shouted at the Exemplar to give him space – and still the portal they guarded was gaping open.

'Jadyn,' he cried, 'shut this jagging door!'

'Hold on!' Jadyn shouted back, then, 'There! Elindhu, it's on the outside of the lintel!'

'Got it,' Elindhu shrilled. *'Aiee!'*

The exclamations of triumph were followed by the sound of the stone panels beginning to slide closed again . . .

A fearsome swipe of the Exemplar's sword almost ripped Soren's flamberge from his hand; he reeled back, trying to counter as the silver-clad woman drove herself into the narrowing gap, reducing her room for error to nothing – but there were no errors. With a flawless, sight-defying spin, she slashed at Obanji's face, making him stagger, even as she flashed out a dagger and turned Soren's flamberge – and then it was she between the closing door panels, forcing the two men back into the open space behind.

Too fast, too smooth, too good. Soren had never seen anyone like her; it was as if she moved to different laws of space and time, and every action was flawless: every foot she planted, every parry and blow and riposte, every movement, whether arching her back from a swing, then stabbing, or lashing out with fist or feet . . .

She'll kill us all.

But freed from trying to shut the door, Jadyn appeared on one flank and Elindhu on the other, still in erling form, blasting energy from her staff directly into the Exemplar's shields, until even she was reeling at the onslaught, not even her sight-defying moves enough. She went rigid momentarily, quivering as shock after shock ran through her, and Soren, seeing an opening, drove his flamberge tip at her side.

She survived only by dashing the blow aside with her mailed fore-arm, yowling in pain as blood sprayed everywhere.

Then Borghart lunged through, one hand gripping the left-hand door, pushing against it to stop it closing, while with the other he flung glyma-force into Soren's chest, sending him flying. He hit the stone floor shoulders-first, the impact winding him as he slid towards the precipice. He was on the edge, about to fall – but Jadyn had seen and was twisting from the fray and pulling with the glyma, arrest-ing Soren's terrifying slide just as his feet went over the edge. He scrabbled away, trying to rise—

—and in that second, Obanji and Elindhu were facing Vazi Virago alone . . .

When Soren went flying, Jadyn just managed to stop him from flying off into the void, but the Exemplar was through the portal and among them, and Borghart was pushing through the slowly closing doors.

'Wedge them!' the lictor bellowed to those behind him.

'*Stop them!*' Obanji cried, putting himself between Elindhu and the Exemplar – who promptly turned all her cold precision on him, and struck like a tempest. But he responded with an Abuthan ululation and met her blow for blow, using his bulk to stand firm. Seeing a chance, he locked her blade with his, then as their bodies collided, hammered his armoured forehead into the bridge of her nose. He struck shields, his eyes inches from hers, teeth bared with ferocity.

Then her left hand blurred and punched into his throat and he staggered, hit by a crippling weakness and an inexplicable taste of blood flooding his windpipe . . .

. . . and he saw that she'd slipped an unseen dagger into her hand, and realised . . .

His knees went and the ground lurched beneath his suddenly leaden feet . . .

Jadyn parried, knocking Borghart's blade aside and lunged, scouring his chest, but unable to make the killing strike because another blade had intruded. He glimpsed Nicolini's bald pate and cursed. Then he saw Obanji reeling back, clutching at his throat, and gasped in shock . . .

Everything changed.

Obanji reeled and Elindhu was caught mid-spell and suddenly exposed. The Exemplar was a blur, scything her gleaming flamberge through the mage's staff; and the power in it erupted, a wave of energy that concussed through both women and sent them staggering backwards, the Exemplar slamming into her men, who caught her – but Elindhu had nowhere to go. She flew toward the void . . .

Soren lunged for her, but he was off-balance as they collided. They teetered at the edge, then Borghart swatted at them with a force-spell and sent them into the void.

Time slowed as Obanji's dazed vision focused on Elindhu, caught in the frontline where she had no chance; he had a moment to appreciate the beauty of her tall, lissom erling frame and to drink in the glorious elegance of her true visage and honey-gold eyes.

Then her staff was snapped in two and she was flung backwards, howling wordlessly as she flew out toward the edge of the stone platform, Soren lunging for her desperately. He had a moment to capture that sight, of she who he loved and the boy who was his younger self: then a blast of force sent them both into the darkness, even as his body betrayed him. The flow of blood from his throat was a raw flood of weakness, stealing what little control he had left of his failing limbs.

Obanji tried to cry out one last warning to Jadyn, the last Falcon standing, but there was no air in him. He crashed down as the emptiness rushed in, and swallowed him whole.

Jayden felt his heart rip in two as deadly blows felled Obanji. Soren and Elindhu were blasted over the edge of the ledge and vanished, and suddenly there was no-one left fighting but him. Gram and Romara were engulfed by the Exemplar's soldiers, and Aura was behind him, still frantically seeking an answer to the mystery of the bridge. He backed toward her, thinking, *It's all over now.*

His enemies had clearly come to the same conclusion, for they unhurriedly renewed wards and fanned out, intending to take the rest alive. Vazi Virago, Yoryn Borghart and Tevas Nicolini advanced on him, while behind them Elan Sandreth smirked at the sight of his stricken "wife". Romara tried to rise, but he levelled her with a blow to the temple and Gram, his mind linked to hers, fainted away. Jadyn's world shrank to this stone ledge, the broken bridge and the void.

Vazi Virago levelled her blade at him.

'Yield,' she said in a clear, cold voice. 'I have questions you must answer.'

Aura had kept herself alive while shielded by the Falcons, but these last few minutes had shown her just how out of her depth she was, surrounded by men and women who could manipulate nature itself. Any one of these foes could break her in half with a gesture.

She felt terrified and useless.

Reaching this place had given her hope that she too might somehow belong in this world, but the last few seconds had utterly destroyed that notion. There was no way forward and no way back. Seeing people she'd come to care about being cut down had taught her that all hope was in vain, anyway. The powerful were anointed by the universe itself, and little people like her didn't matter in the slightest.

This is Life, she thought. *Unless you're one of the Gifted, you're no one.*

There are many gifts, Akka told her. *I gave you what you need.*

Reach out and take it, the Devourer urged. *Come on, Peradura! Show them all.*

Perched on this broken bridge at the edge of creation, with nowhere left to run, she had no idea what the Queen of Evil meant. This was a trap and she'd run right into it. Borghart was here and this time, lopping off her hands was the least he'd do to her. She could see it in his gaze, which was now locked on her.

Better to die than be taken alive by him.

She backed to the very edge, wishing she could sprout wings and fly, but knowing that no such miracle would occur . . .

Why shouldn't it? Akka demanded. *Make it real.*

Aye, you can do it, Aura, the Devourer added. *Look around you.*

Aura's eyes flashed about – and she saw a sigil carved into the stone pillars of the bridge, something like an eye – *and it was blinking at her.*

She felt as if her blood and marrow were evaporating and swayed, on the edge of fainting – until she felt a moment of *connection*, and light burst from beneath her, revealing that there *was* a bridge after all, stabbing out into the void in a glorious, resplendent arch. Glowing specks of light, the dust of the cosmos, were suddenly illuminating a path that normal light couldn't find: a bridge of stardust, extending into infinity.

'*JADYN KNIGHT!*' she hollered, placing both feet onto the bridge. '*RUN!*'

At her shout, Jadyn saw the impossible bridge and Aura on it, shouting his name like a bell sounding in his soul. The paralysis of seeing his beloved comrades down broke; he'd been so stricken any kind of spell could have felled him, but his enemies, even the mighty Vazi Virago now froze as well, to gape at the bridge.

Aura's cry reminded him that dying wasn't the only option here, not with the path to the aegis open. Survival instinct took over, and he darted onto the span, trusting to fate as he placed his weight fully onto the path of light, which took his weight unwaveringly.

We were marked for this, he thought, renewing his shields as Vazi Virago came after him, appearing between the bridge pillars and staring up at him. Borghart was with her, a vision of cold fury.

Behind them were Tevas Nicolini, who he'd once loved but who'd betrayed all they'd shared; and Elan Sandreth, who lusted for Romara and now had her. His enemies, still standing while his friends lay captured or dead.

Obanji, he wailed inside, *Elindhu . . . Soren! Romara! Gram . . .* How he'd ever deal with this, he had no idea.

The gods conspire against us. The world hates us.

Then cold anger responded: a resolve to go on, to give meaning to their sacrifice.

He reached back and grabbed Aura's hand, because she was all he had left, and defied these *hateful scum* to come and get them.

Aura stood her ground, though she was trembling with fear, gripping Jadyn's hand like an anchor as she watched the viper Lictor Yoryn Borghart and the resplendent Exemplar Vazi Virago stalk to the end of the bridge – and realised in a flash of intuition or foresight as vivid as any she'd experienced that these two could also walk the bridge.

Vazi Virago reached the point where stone met solid light, planted her feet, then probed with her right foot, warily testing the glowing, sorcerous part of the arch, and as she did, Borghart joined her, his eyes locked on Aura.

'I knew it.' He pointed at her. 'We're the same, you and I. Come back and serve me and I will let you live.'

She remembered the lictor's cruel games, the way he licked his lips when he cut her, and all his chilling promises of what he'd do to her when he had no further use for her.

He'll destroy you, Akka warned.

Then he'll devour you, the Queen of Evil added.

She watched as the lictor and the Exemplar unconsciously gripped each other's arms and planted front feet tentatively on the shimmering path of light . . .

. . . and it held . . .

Light flickered beneath their feet and the bridge took on more substance . . . Vazi Virago's eyes lit up and a cold smile creased her flawless face. Borghart grunted in triumph. Looking again at Aura, he said, 'No one escapes me, witch.'

Beside her, Jadyn raised his blade – but Aura was inexplicably sure that this wasn't a problem for swords. *I opened the way – so I'll decide who walks it.*

'Neya, bastidos,' she shouted, and as she did, the span of light from the ground before her feet to the stump of the bridge shuddered, rippled and then came apart in a burst of luminous dust. She saw the Exemplar and the lictor stagger, almost going over the edge; but they threw themselves backwards in time, landing on their rumps and roaring in shocked indignity.

'*Besad mi, perdedores!*' Aura shouted, punching the air. *Kiss my arse, losers!*

She was pleased to see them take her exhortation in the spirit it was intended.

Vazi Virago and Yoryn Borghart came to their feet, spluttering in thwarted rage, but Jadyn, whose mind had been set on fighting to the death, turned to the *miraculous* woman at his side, wondering how he would ever repay her for her genius. But his joy was tempered by the terrifying realisation that their enemy had the potential for the aegis, too. Somehow – stupidly – he'd thought it might be a power only the virtuous could wield. But he thrust despair aside, because the bridge ended at his feet and for now, at least, they couldn't reach him.

Best we leave, before they work it out . . .

'I told you I'd find this path,' he called to Borghart, before he left.

'This isn't the end between us,' Borghart retorted. 'We'll meet again.'

If that was precognition, perhaps he was right: a chilling thought.

'You have the Devourer's own luck, heretic,' Vazi called, 'but you won't escape us.'

Jadyn didn't feel lucky at all. Shorn of his pentacle, the anchors of his life, and especially the loss of Romara, he felt hollowed-out, brittle and frightened – but at the same time, weirdly exhilarated and full of hope. He'd made it this far, and he wasn't alone. He looked at Aura, who was calm now, her eyes brimming with fear and hope, and took strength from her.

'This is not vyr magic,' he called out, for everyone to hear. 'This is the aegis.'

'Vyr – aegis – heresy,' Borghart replied. 'It's all the same thing and you'll burn for it.'

Jadyn looked past him to where Obanji Vost lay dead, an Exemplar in all but name to those who knew him. Romara and Gram in the hands of his enemies; the love of his life and the man she'd turned to instead of him, on this doomed journey. Elindhu and Soren, lost in a void from which there was surely no returning, their bodies lost for ever.

He glanced down into the darkness, wondering if he fell, would he ever land? But his path felt solid, blazed across the sky.

I must follow it, he resolved bleakly. *I have to salvage something from all this loss.*

There was one last thing he had to do before leaving. He looked at Vazi Virago. 'Exemplar, we are not traitors. Elobyne is killing our world. If you are truly the pinnacle of knighthood, renounce the glyma and follow us.'

In response, Vazi shouted, 'Come back, or we kill Siera Romara.'

It was a clear bluff, that made no sense on any level. 'No you won't,' he told her. 'You need her alive.'

She glared, then snarled. 'Crossbowmen, bring them down!'

Jadyn was already standing in front of Aura, wards up, and at his motion, they started moving backwards, fast. His shields held, deflecting the lethal bolts, and in moments the shifting darkness was swallowing up their enemies, sight and sound. Another shaft flashed harmlessly by, then another, shot blind ... then there was nothing.

Jadyn and Aura slowed to a walk, treading the span of pale light beneath a canopy of stars. As he walked, the grief came crashing down. He could barely see for the tears flooding his eyes, and had he fallen, he'd have welcomed the end. Without Romara, without his pentacle, the future felt meaningless.

But Aura's hand held his, and that human contact kept him going, until he finally wiped his eyes and faced her. 'Thank you,' he said, his voice choked. 'I'm glad you're here.'

'I make bridge come,' she exulted. 'I wish for it – it come! Then I wish it go and gone. Am magica, hechicera, bruja! Am Magic Girl.' She had tears in her eyes, and rapture on her face.

'You're amazing,' he told her honestly. 'You saved me.'

But only me, he mourned. *If only we could have protected the others.*

'What is place?' she asked, calming down enough to look around 'Where be we going?'

'I don't know,' he admitted. It was like the world beyond the portali gates, but different, and he'd never seen it before. 'But it looks like we're going all the way.'

20

To Those Who Follow

The Kharagh Invasion

The Kharagh were not an invading army but a migrating nation driven west by famine. Once they were defeated, the Wardens persuaded the King of Hytal to grant the surviving Kharagh mercy and permit them to settle. Kharagh communities now dot eastern Hytal.

This act of clemency was divisive, and was cited by Jovan Lux, when he decreed that the Sanctor Wardens had fallen into evil and must disband. 'No good can come of mercy to enemies,' he wrote.

CHRONICLES OF THE NORTH, 1346

Vanashta Baanholt
Summer 1472

Soren var'Dael woke from a strange dream, to find not darkness but light.

He dreamt of an underground river, the water boiling round him and sweeping him under, then up again, but in his stupor it wasn't frightening. Someone kept forcing air into his mouth, kisses of life that kept his candle flickering, drinking sustenance from another's lips, as they tumbled on and on through wet darkness, luminous bubbles streaming around them, strung out like stars in the night sky . . .

And then the stars were fishes, their eyes peering at him, little mouths opening and closing. He smiled at them and closed his eyes.

Sometime later, sound returned, a roaring churn of water and an urgent voice that drew him back up to life. He found himself on a stony beach at the edge of a lake, near a place where an underground river gushed from a cave.

Huh?

He realised that he was naked, though wrapped in a blanket, and beside him was a woman, with a strangely angular face, and a mane of wet silver hair that was constantly shifting like river weed in a current, even though she was unconscious and they were well above the water line. She too was cocooned in woollen blankets and she slept.

Elindhu, in her erling form, he realised, startled and then sagging with relief. *The void was an illusion – there was an underground river below us, he realised. We fell together . . . and I think she must've kept me alive . . .*

Then he remembered Obanji, and despair clouded his senses.

Just then a canoe, paddled by a lean man with a hard face, dark hair and a wolf-pelt around his shoulders, glided into view among the willow at the lake's edge. He was clad in an erling tunic of deep green with knot-work embroidery in the seams, and had a bow and a tuelawar.

Fynarhea, he realised, with a gulp. *Fynarhea in male form.*

'You're awake!' the erling exclaimed, pulling the canoe up the beach then hurrying toward them. 'Soren, there are patrols coming. Help me get the Crysophalae in.'

That's Elindhu's ceremonial name, Soren remembered. 'Is she alright?'

'She is exhausted,' Fynarhea told him. 'She has drained herself and her body must recover now. But she will wake, I am hopeful.'

Hopeful? The word just made Soren more anxious. It imparted urgency, making him sit up and look about more closely. His and the magia's clothes were laid out on a rock to dry, so he hurriedly dressed, under Fynarhea's gaze. 'How is it you're here?' he asked the young erling.

'Your Jadyn Kaen told me I must find meaning in life,' Fynarhea replied. 'He said the world is burning and he was fighting to save it. This moved me. Seeing this, Elindhu, tasked me with following you all, for a time, in case I was needed. I lost you in the mountains, but found you again here. But where are the others?'

Soren swallowed around a lump of harrowing sadness. 'Obanji's dead . . . maybe all the others . . . Dead or captured, which is worse.'

Fynarhea grimaced. 'I am sorry for your losses. Elindhu clearly felt for your Obanji.'

'We all loved him,' Soren blurted. 'He was my hero.'

Fynarhea's face hardened. 'Then he must be avenged. Who slew him?'

'Vazi Virago . . . She's mine. I'm going to take her apart,' Soren vowed.

Fynarhea smiled grimly. 'A life for a life. Honour demands this.'

Soren met the erling's gaze, remembering his delirious dreams before he woke. 'Did you pull us out of the water?' he asked. 'Someone kept me alive, or I would have drowned.'

'Not I,' Fynarhea admitted. 'I found you both asleep, wrapped in blankets. So I left you here and went back for the canoe. It must have been the Crysophalae.'

'It must've been,' Soren agreed, in awe. 'She must have spent the last of her glyma on keeping me alive, to be so spent herself.'

'Then you owe her a life-debt, and must serve her, until you have saved her in turn.'

There was a romanticism to the notion that Soren, raised on tales of knightly chivalry, found appealing. And it was a purpose, something he badly needed right now.

I have no idea what to do now, he realised. *But she will.*

'Then that's what I'll do,' he vowed.

A few minutes later, the stony beach was empty, and they were paddling along the shore, away from the monastery, as evening fell and mist rose to conceal them.

After all we did to get here, we failed, Romara thought, in her mind facing a void of despair that no bridge of light could span.

She was locked in a cell in Vanashta Baanholt, her wrists bound in manacles that lictors liked to travel with, that were forged to deaden the ability to use the glyma. The cuffs were joined by a chain that was looped over a cast-iron ring, set into the wall of the cell.

For some reason, she and Gram had been locked here together: but too far apart to make physical contact. Perhaps they wished to observe what transpired between them when they woke. But right now Gram was deeply comatose, barely breathing. He was similarly chained up, and hadn't moved since they locked him there.

She took no comfort from having woken. Death would have been preferable, she knew. They were prizes: a draegar and vorlok, bonded in a way she doubted even the Exemplar would have seen before. *They'll dissect us like scholars examining the entrails of strange beasts . . .*

She bowed her head, closed her eyes and wished for death. But instead, she slipped into a dream, in which she was staring into a mirror, that reflected a hideous hag, her mouth a bloody slash filled with crystalline teeth, with corpse-pale skin stretched over a deformed skull and tangled hair the colour of blood.

This is what you are, a voice whispered. *A monster.*

But then she felt strong arms close around her from behind, and saw Gram in the mirror, an immense form with an intoxicating male scent that filled her nostrils and rekindled her desire to live. He was in beast form, huge and shaggy with a wolf head and a bear's form, but beautiful to her eyes. She turned and buried her face in his neck, feeling his heart pounding against hers.

This is just a dream, she realised. *I'm going to wake soon and find he's died while I slept.* But it felt good and right, lending her an inner peace that enabled her to turn away from the void of despair, and cling to the light.

Her heartbeat, she noticed, fell into step with his, two drums hammering in time with each other, and the sound resonated through her, and drove her onwards, back towards hope.

The plight of the pallid, barely breathing woman opposite Gram melted away his vyr-rage. He was drained anyway. The wounds that should have killed him had been cauterised by the last of her glyma, thanks to the depth of sharing they'd gone through in the moments prior to capture. She'd kept him going, and somehow, he'd done the same for her.

He felt guilt, of course: he'd become the thing he'd fought all his life to avoid, and he'd dragged her into it too. But it didn't feel the way he'd thought it would. Instead of wild chaos, rages and fury, he felt only a floating kind of peace and tranquillity.

And now, gazing on Romara's face, he fell deeper and deeper in love, body and soul, heart and mind. And when he closed his eyes, he slipped inside a dream of her in her terrifying yet striking draegar form, pressed against his chest, sharing a transcendent sense of peace and harmony.

Maybe this is ninneva? he wondered.

If that was so, perhaps this wasn't a defeat at all, but a kind of victory.

This bridge is like a portali gate, Jadyn realised as he and Aura walked. As they passed along it, the cord of gossamer light faded behind them, so they dared not stop. The void below filled with mist and glimpses of a barren landscape, telling him they were now in the shadowlands. He'd used such paths before, but was still relieved when an oval-shaped shimmering disc like the surface of a perpendicular pool appeared ahead, marking the end of their journey. It was framed by a giant Foylish triple knot in the shape of a triangle.

Just like that mosaic Elindhu and I found, he thought.

He realised that he and Aura were still holding hands, but he found no reason to let go as he led her through the shimmering archway – and they stumbled into a small room built of red-clay bricks. There was an unmade bed and a desk strewn with papers, some pots and crockery on a bench beside the wall, and a metal wood-burner opposite.

Jadyn turned to examine the portal, and saw its opaque haze fade, so that it looked like a mirror, and when he touched it, it was solid. The path was closed.

No one can follow, friend or foe . . . for now. And we can't go back.

He went to the window and peered out, to see it was dawn already. They were in a dilapidated tower on a cliff overlooking a narrow strait, and a landscape of rugged brown hills, wreathed in black smoke. It was just enough light to see a little harbour opposite them.

'Where are we?' he wondered.

'Am knowing!' Aura exclaimed, her face lighting up. 'Is Cap San Yarido, Neparia west-south. Have sailed by with Sergio.'

Southwest Neparia? Jadyn thought. *We've come hundreds of kylos!*

He stared numbly as his sense of loss returned. Obanji was surely dead, and Romara and Gram were prisoners, which chilled him to the core. Elindhu and Soren were probably dead too. The world was on fire, and their beloved Order had lit the pyre. Everything he'd anchored his life to was gone and all he had in this world was the accursed Order blade he wore.

But I'm still alive, and we're on a journey towards something that could make things right.

For a long while he gazed blankly at the rising sun, glowing like an elobyne orb. There was smoke haze in the air, making the sea and sky glow, but here the air was salty and cool.

There was no question in his mind: if any of the sacrifices of the past month were to be worthwhile, he had to go on. *I've been marked out for the aegis. I have no choice.* Why him, he had no idea, any more than he knew why he'd been born to the Gift.

No Romara, no Obanji, no Soren, no Elindhu or Gram. It's just me – and Aura.

It felt unfair, cruel and capricious, as if Akka and the Devourer were rolling dice for their souls, but he felt compelled to see this through. He would learn of the aegis, then use it to try and end the abuse of elobyne.

But he wasn't sure that Aura would feel the same.

He went to her, took her hand and held it palm-up. 'Thank you for being with me,' he said, raising his marked right palm. 'I'm sorry, but it looks like we've been claimed for the aegis.'

'Sorry? Ney, am *not* sorry.' She met his gaze firmly. 'All life, Aura is bullied and used. No more. Now, Aura fight back. Make bad men pay. Make lictor pay. Is good. Tresa buena.'

He smiled, enjoying her determination, but at the same time

troubled. 'Agynea called the aegis a state of grace. I doubt that revenge is in the rules.'

Her chin lifted pugnaciously. 'Aura be making own rules now.'

He bit his lip; feeling pretty sure that this wasn't a path they could control. But for now, he was just grateful that she was with him.

He looked around the room, then down at the desk – where he spotted a handwritten note left on top of a pile of papers. He read it with widening eyes.

To those who follow.

If you are a fellow seeker of truth and enlightenment, marked by destiny, as I have been, then you are my soul-kindred, a pilgrim on the road towards revelation. Journey on, my friend, knowing that I have gone before. We are treading a path laid down long ago by wiser men than me. Perchance, we shall meet along the way.

Seek the Shield of Heaven, where earth kisses sky at the centre of the world.

Nilis Evandriel

Jadyn swallowed, then waved the note at Aura. 'Nilis Evandriel was here, and he exhorts us to go on.' He took a deep breath and emptied himself of grief and anger. 'I've lost everything, so all I have left is to do so. I want to fight back, and the aegis may give us the means to do so. So I shall go on ... But you don't have to. I want you to stay with me, but you can still walk away.'

Aura looked at the man with the battered face and unruly blond hair, with ideals she'd never had. A good man, not so dull as she'd thought, and bound for an early grave, probably. But the marks etched on their hands bound them together.

So be it.

It wasn't just the shared sigils that made her decision. Somehow, Jadyn had become irrevocably important to her. He'd thrown himself between her and danger, he'd held her when she'd needed holding, and if he wasn't so damned prudish – not to mention fatal to touch – she'd have slipped beneath his blanket weeks ago, because she knew he'd be earnest and gentle and eager to please, which was never bad.

Those who are with you in the moments that matter are the people who matter, her mother had once told her. Where was Sergio now, and all the others she'd once prostrated herself before? *They are nowhere, but Jadyn is right here, offering me a place in his world.*

Then she thought about the horrifying power and implacable hatred of those hunting them, the way they'd almost broken her, and what they'd do if they caught her. But somehow, that didn't scare her as once it would have.

How would it feel to have the power to fight back? *Damned good.* She'd never been a fighter, more a runner, so it was time to be more than that.

But she would never manage it without Jadyn, and she doubted such a naïve man could succeed without someone as clear-eyed as her helping him, to see through the veils of deceit the world wove.

'Jadyn will fail,' she told him bluntly, 'unless Aura lights your way. This I will do, for you and for us. I be with you, Jadyn Knight. Together, we do this.'

Borghart gazed into the void from the broken edge of the eerie bridge. The lighted path was gone and he couldn't make it return, but he could sense the echo of it, and how it had felt that moment when it took his weight. He'd been staring out at the darkness for hours now, pondering all that had passed, and what it meant.

He knew Vazi Virago was on her way before he heard her.

'I saw what you did,' she said, appearing behind him. 'The bridge held you, until the Nepari forbade it. You have this aegis, too.'

'It upheld you too, Exemplar,' Borghart retorted sharply, even though she was the most terrifying fighter he'd ever seen. 'Don't you want to walk it too?'

'It's heresy,' she said, but he could hear the doubt in her voice.

'Yes, it is. But I remain that which I am, a sworn lictor, the champion of imperial justice. I will hunt down these renegades and eliminate them, by any means possible. If that means walking in their shoes, I will do so. Are you going to try and stop me?'

He turned to face her, studying her eerily perfect coppery-hued face, her sculpted brows and tightly bound black hair, her athletic silhouette and fiercely burning eyes. She was both the most beautiful and least desirable woman he'd ever seen, more reptile than human: a calculating killing machine . . . and therefore a kindred spirit.

And right now, she was vulnerable, having lost her entire pentacle, many soldiers – and her quarry. He suspected she'd never failed before, and was struggling to deal with it.

'We need each other to unravel this,' he told her. *Despite her prowess, she needs an older head to guide her. She had Tylkor Kervassien for that, but he's dead. I'll take his place.*

As he knew she would, she wilted before his certainty. 'I suppose we do. But tell me, how did four people with this "gift" arrive here at the same time?'

That she said *four* was her admission that he was right about her own potential for this heresy.

'Perhaps the aegis is calling to those with the talent for it?' he suggested. 'Or maybe the talent itself led us here? Think about it: this ability we share – Kaen and Perafi, too – shows us the consequences of paths of action: a kind of precognition. I knew I had to follow them, without knowing precisely what made it imperative. Now I do.' He met her gaze steadily. 'Imagine such a gift, fully harnessed.'

You could rule the world with it, he mused. *Surely you see that, Exemplar?*

She did see, that was writ clear on her face as she considered his words, her expression one of pure self-interest. He wondered if she'd been born without emotion, or had had them all cauterised. Either way, she was as ruthlessly unsentimental as he.

I can work with that.

'They have escaped us using that power,' Vazi conceded. 'To pursue them, we need it too.'

He was encouraged by the word 'we', a subconscious admission that she needed him. This alliance felt fated, so he acted like it was. 'Jadyn Kaen and Auranuschka Perafi are the most dangerous threat the Triple Empire currently faces,' he told her, his certainty of this crystallising as he said it. 'If we hunt them down, we will win the undying gratitude of the Hierophant.'

And then we'll take his throne.

ACKNOWLEDGEMENTS

I'd like to thank JFB/Arcadia/Quercus for their continued faith and support in this new series, our fourth together. Special thanks to Jo Fletcher and to Anne Perry, and to Nicola Howell Hawley for the lovely map. Much appreciation also to my agent Jon Wood for getting this across the line; and my usual team of Kerry, Paul and Heather for their critiquing and always valuable feedback. And as always, for the support of friends and family, and especially my wonderful wife Kerry, without whom none of this could happen. I am eternally grateful.

Tinkety-tonk and down with the Nazis!

David Hair
Wellington, New Zealand, 2024

Read on for an exclusive sneak peek of Book 2
in The Talmont Trilogy, *The Drowning Sea*

Petraxus

Talmont, Autumn 1472

Eindil Pandramion III, the Hierophant, God-Emperor of Talmont, Zynochia and Abutha, shifted uncomfortably on the Throne of Pearl, his thoughts trapped in a spiral of despondency despite the circling priests with their swinging censers sending plumes of holy incense to the gilded ceiling, their sonorous voices begging Akka to cleanse His humble servant – Eindil himself – of all sin.

It was vaguely amusing, given it was theologically impossible for Eindil to sin. Scripture proclaimed him faultless, his every deed sanctioned by Heaven: a Living God, with dominion over Earth and Sky. Paradise awaited him, no matter what he did.

'In Paradise, we are cleansed of desire, cleansed of all hunger,' the priests chanted.

But I don't wish to be cleansed of desire and hunger, Eindil thought. *I wish to be desirous and hungry, so long as my desires and hungers can be sated. As they are, right here.*

His life contained everything he wanted – or *almost* everything. He had gigantic palaces filled with every luxury imaginable, and thirty beautiful wives to choose from. He had myriad children and grandchildren to dote upon. Every man alive was subservient to him. These were things all wished for. But it was that which he didn't have that consumed him.

Where is she? My Vazi Virago – where is she?

According to reports, the Exemplar was hunting heretics in the south. Her perfect face swam before his eyes, a divine visage wrought in burnished copper, framed by glorious ebony hair and the most lustrous golden-brown eyes. A child of the Zynochian caliphates, so young and delicate-looking, and yet she was the greatest sorcerer-knight alive.

I am sixty years old, but when she is in my presence I feel like a stammering boy.

The day he finally possessed her would be the day he truly attained Akka's Paradise.

A gong roused him from his reverie, signalling the end of the morning's blessing, and he gazed blinking upon this many-pillared hall in his Holy Palace in mighty Petraxus. Hierophants had ruled Coros from here for two centuries now, ever since Jovan Lux revealed the sacred elobyne and united the three great powers, Talmont, Zynochia and Abutha, into the Triple Empire. Jovan's holy blood ran in Eindil's veins.

He was the twenty-first Hierophant, but still he was afraid. *Will I be the last? Have we come to the End of All Things?*

As the priests shuffled away, Eindil signed to Robias, his stentor, both herald and major-domo, to approach. Robias was a typical Aquini, a race prone to baldness; his pate gleamed in the lamplight as he knelt to kiss the footprint of Jovan on the lowest step, then sat back on his heels and unfurled a scroll.

'Good morning, Great One,' he said. 'Greetings on this Holy Day. May Heaven shine its light upon you. Let Elysia wash away all your pain and discomfort and Akka bless you with insight and wisdom.'

It might be a Holy Day, Eindil's weekly break from court duties and advisors, but with his empire afflicted by disasters and rebellion, he had to stay abreast of current events.

'Ar-byan, Robias,' Eindil replied. *May it be.* 'What tidings?'

Robias consulted his scroll. 'Seven coursers arrived overnight, Great One. One came from the Caliph of Bedum-Mutaza, with greetings and love, extending his formal invitation for his city to be your quadrennial residence. He assures you that all is prepared.'

One of the traditions established by Jovan Lux was for the reigning Hierophant to spend every second year in Petraxus, while the alternate years he would alternate between Dagoz, the capital of Abutha, and Bedum-Mutaza, the centre of the old Zynochian Empire. The palaces there were magnificent, but Eindil was a child of the north; he loathed the heat and simmering resentment in the south.

Tradition was tradition, however. 'That is well,' he responded, for the court scribes to record. 'I eagerly await my return to my beloved Bedum-Mutaza, and the joy of seeing his Highness, my cousin, again.'

The next six missives were all bad. The island of Shyll, last of the empire's possessions in the northwestern archipelago, had fallen to vyr rebels, with twelve elobyne shards destroyed. Grain riots in Mardium, Lerzia and Bespar, on the coast of the Inner Seas. An earthquake in Viromund, with hundreds dead and thousands displaced. And vyr attacks in southern Bravantia had burned out swathes of grain fields. The armies were already overstretched and the Vestal Order couldn't be everywhere.

It was a struggle not to let his head hang.

'Any word from Dagoz and Bedum-Mutaza of rebellions there?' Eindil asked.

'Nothing official, Great One.' Which told him, unofficially, that the news was bad and he'd learn more in a less public setting.

The foundation of the Triple Empire had ended open war on Coros. Talmont had elobyne, the sorcerous crystal that empowered the Vestal Order to rule any battlefield, but the north lacked manpower, unlike their heavily populated southern rivals, Abutha and Zynochia. Jovan Lux's genius had been not to overthrow but to unite the powerful southern rulers under his ambit. As well as taking ten northern brides, he'd married ten Zynochi and ten Abuthan women, creating a multi-racial elite who owned *everything*. Inside two generations, every throne on Coros was ruled by one of his descendants, and Abutha and Zynochia were as invested in the success of the Triple Empire as Talmont – and they were all yoked together by their dependence upon elobyne.

Open warfare might have ceased, but internecine vendettas,

rivalries and resentment remained as toxic as ever. Empire politics were a perennial bloodbath, even for hierophants; four had been murdered in the south by kin, hushed up as untimely illnesses so as not to alarm the populace. His reluctance to travel there wasn't just based on comfort.

'Is there no good news, Robias?' Eindil asked tiredly.

'Happiness comes from bird song, Great One, not coursers,' the herald quipped.

No, then.

Eindil tried to appreciate the vivid morning sunlight streaming through the massive stained-glass windows, creating shifting shafts of glorious red and green and blue light that penetrated the smoke of the censers, a magical display of Heaven's Light.

All is not lost, that Light proclaimed. He wasn't convinced.

But the day awaited. He rose and went to his Mentus Sanctorum to await this morning's Confessor. It might be yet another pointless piece of ritual but at least this one came with coffee. He trailed Robias through the maze of corridors behind the throne hall, out of the shadowy halls into the light, barely noticing the grovelling servants, their faces pressed to the floors.

The gardens were awash with roses, the scents dispersed by the playing fountains. Statues of nymeths and huirnes cavorted lasciviously along the path to the meditation chamber, a wonder of marble lattice-work. A coffee pot steamed on a stool beside the low but ornate throne and Robias was already pouring as Eindil sat.

He had just taken a first sip when a white-robed and hooded figure emerged from the garden – and Eindil realised it wasn't a Confessor.

Assassin, was his first thought – and Robias, blanching, was about to signal the nearby guards. But the hooded man raised his head, showing just enough of his face for Eindil to recognise him. His fears of untimely death vanished – but not his fears of worse.

'Leave us,' he told Robias. 'Take the guards out of earshot. All is well.'

If Robias heard the fear in his voice, he didn't react, signalling the soldiers to withdraw, then sitting on a stone seat within calling range.

Eindil took a shaky breath. 'Father,' he said hoarsely. 'How do you fare?'

The newcomer sat opposite him and lowered his hood, revealing a man in his prime – no, *beyond* his prime, for Genadius Pandramion II had never been so flawlessly perfect. His skin was smooth and unblemished, without even a hint of stubble; his thick hair was perfectly styled, blond again, as it had been in his youth. His frame was muscular, lithe. Only his eyes, grey and unwavering, gave any hint of his true age.

He'd died thirty years ago, aged seventy.

'I am well, my son,' he replied, his voice free of the rheumy tones Eindil remembered. 'And you?' Their conversations had always been stilted and formal.

'I grow old,' Eindil said wistfully. 'The Sunburst Crown is heavy.'

Genadius nodded. 'I remember it well, the weight of the world crushing my skull. I was grateful to pass it on.'

The Church taught that hierophants did not die as mortals did. So beloved of Akka were they that they were taken bodily to Paradise. There were no tombs of past hierophants, only memorials. Eindil's father had been dying in his bed one night, his body gone by morning.

And now this.

Eindil had thought it religious nonsense, before he ascended the throne and met such 'Alephi' – the Undying – on previous visits to Nexus Isle, where it was said all the dead Hierophants now dwelt in harmony, serving Jovan Lux.

But he'd never been visited by an Alephi – or Serrafim, as the Church named them, here in the palace in daylight. 'Why are you here, Father?'

Dear Akka, does he know it was I who poisoned him?

'I come to tell you that the time is nigh,' Genadius replied. 'The End of All Things approaches.'

Eindil knew full well that Coros was destroying itself. An Age of Fire was already upon them, bringing death, plague, war, fire and flood. The soil was drying, the snows melting and the seas rising, while the pitiless sun burned the land black.

Nothing can be done, the priests said. *This is fated.*

'What must I do?' Eindil asked fearfully.

'To quote Scripture: "The Serrafim shall mark the Faithful for Elysium, the sanctuary of the faithful",' Genadius replied. 'One man in a thousand shall live, and the rest shall burn. So you must decide whom you wish to save.'

Eindil reeled. *Is it so far advanced?* 'How shall I know whom to save?'

Genadius smiled coldly. 'That's up to you. My advice: if you like them, trust them or desire them, preserve them. If you like their singing or their art, or their cooking, save them. But remember: *One man in a thousand*. And though I say "man", I include women, for what is forever without them?'

It was a crushing responsibility – and who knew that Paradise would be so venal? But Scripture also said, *In Heaven as it is on Coros*.

'Where is Elysium?' he asked. 'Will we be taken up into the skies?'

'No, my son. Paradise will be revealed to you. We are building it right now, a holy place the unwashed and blighted can't reach. Within it, we will dwell in eternal bliss, while outside the walls, the wretched sinners will wail and gnash their teeth. That is how life is: the deserving are rewarded, while the undeserving perish.'

Eindil shuddered. 'One man in a thousand?'

'Aye.' Genadius rose. 'Be strong, my son. Protect the elobyne at all costs, for on it our salvation rests. Even if the whole of the world rises against us, hold firm. It is sad, but not all can be saved. Harvests will fail and disasters multiply, but hold the course and know that all is according to Akka's will.'

'His will be done,' Eindil echoed, his mind churning. 'Father, what's it like – ?'

Genadius smiled his reptilian smile. 'I have no discomfort, no pain. No illness nor imperfection. Food and drink are optional – glyma-energy provides me with all I need. I am perfected, as you will be.'

'Was Mother also saved? I would love to see her!' Memories of her kindly face, her long, soft grey hair scented with camellias, washed over Eindil. She had been a giver of life and love when his father was distant and cold. All these years later, he still felt her absence – none of the grasping whore-brides he'd wed could fill her place in his heart.

Genadius shook his head. 'She was not worthy.'

'But you said, "choose who you will",' Eindil started.

'And I did,' Genadius said dismissively. 'She is gone forever, my son. Even I cannot restore her. But mourn her not. Think only of the Paradise of Elysium that awaits us.'

With that, he rose and swiftly vanished into the depths of the lush garden.

He could have saved Mother . . . Why wasn't she 'worthy'?, Eindil wondered.

Scripture might say she was with Elysia, but clearly she was just dirt now, and the Elysium the Alephi were creating would never welcome her.

She is gone forever. He would never sink into her arms and find true peace again.

But he could make his father pay.

Eindil bade Robias bring him a blank scroll, ink and a quill. On the parchment he wrote the first name of those he would save: Vaziella al'Nuqheel, known to the world as Vazi Virago, Exemplar of the Vestal Knights, the greatest knight alive, and his only dream. She would be his avenging angel.

Let the world burn, so long as in the end there is just she and me . . . standing over my father's corpse. Ar-byan.

THE DROWNING SEA

Book Two of The Talmont Trilogy

Coming 2025